"Shhh," she whispered, massaging his thickly muscled shoulders with her hands. "It's all right."

He groaned. Again and again Garrett murmured, "Welcome to sunny Beirut . . . sunny Beirut . . . the gateway . . ." He tossed and twisted, seemingly in agony.

". . . the gateway to hell."

She knew he had to be remembering something, but what she didn't know.

". . . . the gateway to hell . . ."

Stella looked down. His eyes were open; he stared at her with unnerving focus.

"Are you awake finally?" she whispered, her words anxious, her voice gentle.

He lifted his hand. Slowly, painfully, he touched her cheek, caressing her jawline with his thumb.

"Rare angel . . . saved me," he murmured as if the words calmed his very core. He lowered his hand, but his feverish gaze stayed trained on her face.

"I—I think you'll be okay," she stammered, trying to think of things to comfort him. "You're—you're not in Beirut, by the way."

"I know . . . I've found my way to heaven," he whispered before his eyes closed once more, and he fell into a deep, near-comatose sleep.

<u>BOOK YOUR PLACE ON OUR WEBSITE AND MAKE THE READING CONNECTION!</u>

We've created a customized website just for our very special readers, where you can get the inside scoop on everything that's going on with Zebra, Pinnacle and Kensington books.

When you come online, you'll have the exciting opportunity to:

- View covers of upcoming books
- Read sample chapters
- Learn about our future publishing schedule (listed by publication month *and author*)
- Find out when your favorite authors will be visiting a city near you
- Search for and order backlist books from our online catalog
- Check out author bios and background information
- Send e-mail to your favorite authors
- Meet the Kensington staff online
- Join us in weekly chats with authors, readers and other guests
- Get writing guidelines
- AND MUCH MORE!

**Visit our website at
http://www.kensingtonbooks.com**

MEAGAN McKINNEY

STILL OF THE NIGHT

ZEBRA BOOKS
KENSINGTON PUBLISHING CORP.
http://www.zebrabooks.com

Prologue

If you are born without wings, do nothing to keep them from growing.

—COCO CHANEL

It was not an auspicious place; Cane Town never had been. The little town had formed out of utilitarian necessity at the end of the plantation system, when freed slaves needed a place to take their crops to be sold. Shacks quickly sprang up along the crossroads of Old Highway 13 and the Great Bayou Road. Enterprise followed. Now a convenience store had muscled between the old bargeboard shanties. Slick glossy signs promised lotto millions and a case of lung cancer. The silver gray and rusted buildings faded from the garishness of the all-night convenience store like snow against a flame.

The way into Cane Town was always dusty with pollen. Beneath the steaming Louisiana sun, the road out shimmered like a hallucination. On one side of town was the Lafourche levee, on the other were fields thick with spikes of sugar cane.

Cane Town was the only benchmark between the

Gerring Oil Company refinery and the NorAg Grain Elevator. For miles outside of town, along the Great Bayou Road, magnificent sprawling live oak trees dotted the landscape, vestigial ghosts of the plantation houses that had long since fallen down or been pulled down by advancing industry. But Cane Town itself had no trees at its crossroads. The heat beat, unrelenting, onto the black tar roof of the All-Day–All-Nite. Cars pulled up and pulled away without the need for shade because no one took a stroll.

There was nothing to see and nowhere to go.

But if Cane Town merited a mention in *Fodor's*— which it did not—it would have two items of note.

The first was a run-down turn-of-the-century feed store that marked the dead center of Cane Town. It fronted the Great Bayou Road and the lonely intersection of Old Highway 13. From the balcony of the building, the view of the Bayou Lafourche was surpassed only by the precious breeze that in August barely tiptoed through the second story.

The building had its heyday in the twenties, when it had been turned into a private club that catered to high-stakes poker players and a select number of hoodlums needing to cool their heels outside of New Orleans. It was rumored that during Prohibition, the Kingfish, Huey P. Long, bought his whiskey—and probably his women—upstairs in the club's most private rooms. There had been more than one stabbing at the club, more than one gangster taken out and deposited in the swamps to the west of town, where he went unmissed to this very day.

In order to make a circa 1902 grain store into a modern 1920s nightclub, the building's original display windows on the first floor had been replaced with opaque black glass. Nobody could look out, but more importantly, during the age of Eliot Ness, nobody could look in either. The clunky Victorian door had gone to the junk pile; in its place was a chic rounded-top Deco model with a sliding panel placed at eye level so the poker-faced bouncer could see who waited outside for admittance.

The high-tech, industrial baked-enamel door had given the club its name. Decades later, the infamous door was still there, but the fierce Louisiana heat had alligatored the enamel and made it chalky. The crisp Deco edges were now chipped, revealing the black undercoat and rusty steel. The door had become a faded, worn-out testament to the words on the original neon sign that still hung from the arches of the upstairs balcony. During the day the sign proclaimed the club's name in black Deco-gothic letters: The Scarlet Door.

During the night, when what remained of the original old orange-red neon tubes were lit, the sign said instead The Scar.

Not too many patrons visited the club any longer. At five, a few of the shift workers from the grain elevator would enter the bar and pony up a tip for a stripper to perform a lap dance, but those were the single men. The married ones bought their Dixie beer at the All-Nite and took it home. It was cheaper that way. Didn't make the wife so mad.

Fodor's would have to mention the second attraction in Cane Town with a note of irony. Directly in front of The Scarlet Door, on a twelve-inch strip of parish property, stood two pristine white crosses. They were cemented into the corner of Old Highway 13 and the Bayou Road, right in view of The Scarlet Door's broken neon sign.

Tourists eager to see a plantation house not created by Disney drove by the crosses daily. Most believed they'd been erected there by Bible thumpers objecting to a nudie bar. But if one looked closer, there was more to the story than that. In distinct block carving, the name St. Vallier was placed on both of the horizontal pieces, along with the date—almost a year before to the day.

The new owner of The Scarlet Door had objected to

them. He'd first complained to the town council, but when he was tired of the intractable locals, he took it upon himself to eradicate them. He cut them down with all the ferocity of a slash-and-burn farmer in the rain forest.

But to his dismay, new crosses returned. They reappeared the next day like insidious jungle vines. Or insidious heartaches.

The Scar.

The final set of crosses were steel reinforced and set in concrete. The grief was not gone; neither, it would seem, were the white crosses. And no mortal club owner was going to see them mowed down. And no passing tourists on a package tour merited an explanation.

Because the crosses had not been erected to further the agenda of the religious right. They were placed to remember the two who had died on the spot in a spectacular car crash one fateful summer night.

The crosses had been tenderly set in the public ground by the loved one left behind. The fact that the neon spelled out what was obvious made the crosses all the more noteworthy.

For like a scar, the crosses gave silent testimony of past violence. They served as a memorial to the two lives that had been extinguished in that exact spot upon the soil, and to the raging soul who was now alone.

And like any other scar . . .

They served as a warning.

PART ONE

No Cold and Timid Soul

CHAPTER

1

You who never arrived
in my arms. Beloved, who were lost
from the start,
I don't even know what songs
would please you. I have given up trying
to recognize you in the surging wave of the next
moment. All the immense
images in me—the far-off, deeply felt landscape,
cities, towers, and bridges, and un-
suspected turns in the path,
and those powerful lands that were once
pulsing with the life of the gods—
all rise within me to mean
you, who forever elude me.

You, beloved, who are all
the gardens I have ever gazed at,
longing. An open window
in a country house,—and you almost
stepped out, pensive, to meet me. Streets that I chanced
upon,—
you had just walked down them and vanished.
And sometimes, in a shop, the mirrors

*were still dizzy with your presence, and, startled, gave back
my too-sudden image. Who knows? perhaps the same
bird echoed through both of us
yesterday, separate, in the evening . . .*
—RAINER MARIA RILKE

From the very first, the faces of the Bellocq whores had drawn Stella St. Vallier in like a looking glass. She had yet to be able to look away. They haunted with a worn-out, mundane beauty that had endured through the decades. The old sepia photographs showed women looking much like her, at times tired and worried, yet, incongruously, at times still wanting to play. Their lonely expressions and the occasional bright, childlike smile followed like a question mark.

And though she'd done her Ph.D. on them, they still followed her. Speaking questions that continued to go unanswered.

"I hear today's the day. Still seems a shame."

Stella looked up from the boxes of photographs she was packing. Dr. Glen, the head of the Newcomb women's studies department, stood just inside her office door. The woman, as usual, looked bohemian and polished at the same time, with her short-cropped silver hair and Donna Karan suit.

"Have a seat," Stella offered.

"Can't. I've got a budgeting meeting. I just wanted to remind you that we'll have you back in one year—that's a promise, isn't it?" The lines on the woman's face deepened. "We don't want to lose our most forward thinker."

Stella pointed to the old sepia photographs for which her thesis had been known. "I think I'm more retroactive than forward."

Dr. Glen smiled. "Whatever. You've brought a lot to the department. A year's sabbatical is too long to go without."

"I've got to save Tara," Stella said, the playfulness—just like in Bellocq's women—somehow still intact.

"Yes. Well, when you do, we'll welcome you back like Rhett Butler with open arms." Dr. Glen put out her hand.

Stella straightened and took it.

"Go take care of the past, Stella, but know there's always a future here for you." The woman departed with a smile and a sage nod of her head.

Once alone, Stella returned to her packing. She came to her favorite Bellocq and reflected on it a moment.

It was said the camera never lied, that the beauty of a photograph was in its utter completeness.

But whoever had said those things never saw Bellocq's work. Stella was quick to point it out in her thesis. A photograph of a prostitute was by its very subject a lie. A prostitute's world wasn't about truth and beauty, it was about money and addiction and the necessary eroticism to complete the vicious circle. A 1912 photograph of a whore also had to exude a certain naughty coyness and a temporary beauty.

But Bellocq's beauties endured.

Which was why she liked most of all the "all dressed-up lady," as she called her. The prostitute had on her very best hat, shirtwaist, cameo, and dress. She was sitting primly in front of a black tarp background that the photographer must have provided.

But Bellocq didn't take the woman's picture as she clearly thought he would. He tricked her. And not into taking her clothes off, but into something even more naked. Something soul revealing.

The woman sat, her legs crossed—a prostitutelike demeanor for those times—and while her face was placid and her hands comfortably clasped in front of her, the whole of the picture was taken, not just the subject's face and bosom for which she was obviously posing. Behind the black tarp, tattered laundry hung in limp sentinel. The hiked-up skirt, the crossed legs, the impoverished background, were all truths despite the locket and cameo, despite the pale ostrich-feather hat and starched shirtwaist.

Bellocq was brilliant because of the very conundrum that his camera didn't lie when it was supposed to. The

women he photographed in their ill-fitting Sunday best
or their nude poses had been tricked somehow into revealing the truth. The women laughed, relaxed, played
with their little dogs—in short, were displayed to the
viewer's discomfort as very human, very female, almost
childlike.

You couldn't fool Bellocq. The truth came out.

But Bellocq had managed to fool everybody. He was
an obscure hydrocephalic Frenchman who hovered
around the brothels of Storyville, clearly making friends
with his subjects as the comfort of his sitters' expressions showed. But the reasons behind his work still remained a mystery. As a professional photographer, he
couldn't sell the realism of his subjects, certainly not in
those times. And he shot thousands of pictures of his
girls. Yet the few that remained with him at the time of
his death were mostly defaced. Many of the faces of the
nudes had been scratched off the negative as if in a fit
of pique. The will to obliterate was now on many of the
photographs. A nude girl in black stockings, her face
relegated as if to the masked masses at a Mardi Gras.

One theory was that the women in the photographs
had become "respectable" and they wanted their faces
off the negative.

Stella didn't buy it. Not in the age before penicillin
and halfway houses, when very few of the women in the
photographs probably lived to forty. Besides, the negatives were glass plates. It would take less time to smash
the plate than to retrieve it and deface it.

Bellocq himself had defaced them. It was he who
kept them, even in their defacement. The vicious black
scratches across the face of the nude were a disturbing
cry of anguish.

An echoing wail of rejection. To you who never arrived.

Stella put away her last Bellocq. The scratched faces
still left her uneasy. She tried many times to examine
her own obsession for Bellocq. She wondered what he

would see if he photographed her; if she would be in her nicest dress and her nicest pose, or if she would be nude and blindfolded, undone by her past and her loneliness.

She taped up the box and hauled it to her car. The die was cast. Her homeplace burdened her, and the need for its survival weighed on her like survival weighed on the Bellocq woman. Like a stinking horny drunk.

It was time to go home again. To face the truths that waited there for her. Even though she wanted to be like the all dressed-up lady. She wanted to be humored and be told lies.

"I hate to tell you this, love, but survival is, and always has been, a decision between the unpalatable and the disastrous."

Stella, lost deep in a weighty tome titled *Land Husbandry and the Sugar Cane Planter,* was slow to realize that Rose had just said something to her. She looked up from her book as if startled from a daydream.

"I'm sorry, Aunt Rose. What did you say?"

Her great-aunt Rose, surrounded by embroidery hoops and half-crocheted antimacassars, occupied a wicker chaise in front of one of the parlor's bay windows. Well into her nineties now, she was frail but fundamentally healthy. Her emotional Mediterranean eyes peered at Stella from a small, sharp face that had always been more striking than beautiful.

"Pouf! Does it matter what I said? The question is, why did I bother? Stella, when you disappear inside that mind of yours, I fear we'll never get you back. You're not even thirty years old, and yet you daydream like some of my own familiars."

A frown line appeared on the bridge of Stella's nose. Distractedly, she said, "I'm sorry. I know I'm no company. I should have stayed upstairs. It's just—I feel so antsy today. God, I'm so sick of looking at this stuff, I could scream."

"Then don't look at it! Go find yourself an intrigue. That's the trouble with you. You're always conquering the world from your own front yard. It's a beautiful Saturday afternoon. The sure cure for melancholy is romance."

That fantastical suggestion evoked a little fluming snort from Stella. As always, Rose's solution for every problem was a handsome, charming man. To Great-Aunt Rose, who was an unmarried woman of her generation, a man loomed large as the cure-all—or the poison—of the spinster's life. Stella had the deep suspicion he was just snake oil.

Overdosed, Stella left her book on a turkey-work footstool and crossed the huge double parlor. She loved these rooms at this time of day. They had so many windows and French doors, it seemed one giant view of moss-draped live oaks and emerald grass. The old window draperies were the crowning touch with each long valence goblet-pleated at every other repeat of the faded 1930s era floral chintz.

"With whom shall I 'intrigue'?" Stella mused indulgently, having heard all the options and all the lectures a thousand times before. "One of the roustabouts who pays for a peekaboo at the strip club in town? Or perhaps good ol' farm boy Billy Ed, who could treat me to a romantic night at the dog races before we make out in his TransAm?"

"What, I shudder to ask, is a TransAm?"

Stella smiled inwardly. "My point is that Cane Town is hardly a mecca of intrigue, Rose. You have to leave to get any of that, and I came back, remember?"

"Yes, my point exactly. You shouldn't be here trying to save the family fortunes. You should have never come back. Shadow Oaks probably can't be turned around. So enough. Go see the world. Go find your destiny."

Unmoved by the advice, Stella seated herself on the

bench of the family's piano, a brass inlaid rosewood classic of six octaves made in 1820 by Thomas Hoskison. She tapped a few notes. It needed tuning. "I had to come back to help. You know it. I couldn't stand by and let you and Maman handle this place. It's too much."

"The St. Valliers have been here a long time, maybe too long," Rose said a little darkly. "I myself can attest to over ninety years here in this house. . . ." She looked around the room, at the draperies, at the fine old furniture that would have brought a fortune at Sotheby's if it didn't bear the markings of every St. Vallier child who'd ever run through the house on a rainy day. The old woman's thoughts seemed to trail away into depression.

Stella took a deep, invigorating breath. "We're the last St. Valliers left, Rose. I had to come back," she reassured her aunt, her own voice layered with yearning. "I just wish I were better at cane growing. I just wish everything were easier."

"You need help. And I'm too old to help you."

Stella lowered her eyes for a moment. Then she said with forced gaiety, "We've got one more shot before we throw in the towel. Let's not give up yet. You know I'm going to fight to the end. I always have."

"But at the expense of your life? At the risk of ending up a lonely old woman like me?" Rose jutted out her chin. "I can't let you do that, Stella."

"It was my choice to come back, Rose. My choice. As you said, we're the last two left. I can't just walk away and forget about this place."

"You could be making more St. Valliers. . . ."

"Aunt Rose, listen to you! And you're one to talk. You stayed here at Shadow Oaks. New Orleans isn't even a thirty-minute drive from here, and yet I bet you've not ventured there more than a dozen times in all your life."

"I'm not the great adventuress you are, my dear. Never have been. But I do have experience with the natural tendency to coquette. Of *that* I know."

"To coquette?" Stella repeated, amused. She flipped through the sheet music in search of something cheerful to dissipate her mood.

"To coquette, yes. To flirt, to seduce, to *enjoy* the masculine sex rather than constantly compete with them to see who can belch loudest."

No Rose without a thorn, Stella reminded herself, her inward smile deepening. The old dame belonged to the magnolia South. Rose St. Vallier grew up in those dusty, indolent days when the draperies that lined the parlor were new and cheerful, not sun-faded and torn. When women of her social class still hid blushing smiles behind palmetto fans. When they harbored no greater ambition than to own the loveliest skin in the parish.

It was another world—with no mortgages, no spreadsheets, no undergraduate degrees in business that now seemed utterly useless in the face of the mountain she had to move to make Shadow Oaks profitable again. Indeed, Great-Aunt Rose's world was so far away from what Stella knew, it could have existed on another planet in another time/space continuum that only Carl Sagan could have imagined.

Fingering the yellowed ivory keys, she played a few chords but could find no music that suited her odd, jangled mood. After a few impatient glissandos that went nowhere, she gave up and closed the piano cover.

Rose watched her wander aimlessly through the spacious, sunny, high-ceilinged parlor with its detailed plaster and woodwork. The old woman's eyes went liquid with emotion. "Go put on that beautiful lavender silk dress, Stella, the one with the sheer irises on it. Whenever I see you in it, I think of me when I was your age, and all the hope and beauty that I was back then."

Stella went to her and hugged her. "You're still all hope and beauty, Rose."

"Don't let yours wash away, Stella. Don't."

It seemed to Stella that they had had the same kind of conversation every day since she'd graduated from

Newcomb, but somehow this one seemed different. A bit more desperate perhaps. They were, after all, running out of time. Now Aunt Rose's resounding and urgent plea to actually *live* her life, not just use it up like time in a bottle, seemed to echo with infinite reverberations.

Rose must have seen the shadow that crossed her face. The older woman tried to make amends for causing the gloomy mood.

"Leora said to tell you dinner will be served at six. She's making us that crabmeat-and-spinach casserole you loved so much last time, remember? And just for you, Leora's famous brandied peaches for dessert."

"Wonderful. In the meantime, I'm taking a walk," Stella announced abruptly.

"But you just took a walk to see the fields," Rose shot back. "They aren't any higher yet, of that I can assure you."

"Call me morbid, but I guess I want to see Atlanta as much as possible before Sherman comes and burns it down."

Aunt Rose couldn't resist a parting shot.

"Once we mate with despair, dear," she lectured Stella's departing back, "we are worthless."

Her aunt's pious bromides sometimes stepped on Stella's nerves. A spat with her was like trying to debate with *Bartlett's Familiar Quotations*.

"Well, once I truly mate with despair—at least I'd be having sex," she mumbled to herself before she headed toward the center hall and the massive carved-mahogany front door.

Late October in southern Louisiana usually ushered in the most pleasant weather of the year for the sugar cane parishes. But for a moment, as Stella left the air-conditioning and stepped outside onto the wisteria-knotted veranda, the air felt warm and moist like a dog's breath.

Then a susurrant breeze cooled her skin and sent mimosa leaves scuffing and sliding across the foot-wide cypress porch boards. She gazed up into a seamless blue sky whose afternoon sun had heft as well as heat. Chinaberry trees and pink-blooming azalea bushes dotting the lawn seemed to shimmer under the golden weight. For a few moments, at least, she sloughed off her former mood. In that instant the world reminded her of a newly emerged butterfly, quivering and fragile and beautiful in the burnished sunlight.

Lately, however, she was too wrapped up in apprehension to notice the beauty around her. The plantation had been in the red for seven years running. Her father had thought this would be the magic year, but it hadn't proved itself. If a profit didn't show, the bank had written to warn they would call in the farm loan January first.

As she descended the wide steps, the festering worry insinuated itself again. Was *she* marked out by fate to fail where others before her had not? Not only fail herself, but fail her family and Shadow Oaks too?

She knew these weren't questions she could simply finesse her way around like a clever plot twist. Just mental brick walls against which she kept repeatedly colliding.

Plenty of headaches; no illumination.

That thought reminded her she had work to do. She decided to check for mail, then take a walk through the garden while she mulled the germ of an idea inspired by her recent research into the sugar cane business.

She walked down a long drive paved with large Belgian pink-slate blocks. It curved through a lawn of lush winter rye grass that needed trimming. Two stately fieldstone gateposts marked the turnoff from Parish Road.

The walk was nearly a quarter mile. Yet, not one vehicle passed by out on the road to disturb the steady crackle of insects. Since the interstate had been completed a decade before, the remote pocket of Lafourche Parish had attracted nothing but cobwebs.

She flipped open the wrought iron letterbox and saw that Mr. Kelleher hadn't been by yet. Halfway back down the drive, she paused to gaze at the house with its peeling paint and flower beds choked with crabgrass. The days when Shadow Oaks could employ a bevy of maids in coifs and aprons, not to mention a full-time groundskeeper, were long gone. The family home now reminded her of a beautiful flower one day after it was picked, still essentially lovely but wilting in a vase.

The house was a fine example of the Greek Revival in cane country: large in scale, simple in design, admirably proportioned, and surrounded by exquisite gardens. Atop white columns that no longer gleamed, magnificently carved Corinthian capitals boasted images of Mercury, god of commerce, and Luna, goddess of the moon. The entire mansion was still surrounded by a short iron fence from the last century. It once restrained the rooting pigs that used to roam freely through the area, the South's first garbage disposal system.

Death, Stella mused, was only one of the Four Horsemen of the Apocalypse. His three equally fearsome companions were Conquest, Slaughter, and Famine. All four riders had ravaged Shadow Oaks at one time or another. Yet, there she stood, her pillared facades a bit dingy but still proud, her spirit as strong as her iron balconies.

Proud and strong. Solid. Like so many generations of St. Valliers who had lived there.

In contrast, Stella's main hope for saving Shadow Oaks seemed as insubstantial as a promise written on water. Yet, more and more lately, that hope had taken hold of her as Shadow Oaks teetered on the edge of financial ruin.

Thinking such things naturally guided her onto the crushed-shell walk that circled past the great front veranda of the house. Small gardens, bright with azaleas and bougainvillea, flanked each side of the house. These in turn joined a larger rear garden by way of rose-covered trellises. This large garden had a floor of crushed limestone, the effect softened by clumps of maiden grass. Pale peach-colored ballerina roses and white wax-myrtle trees lined the walks, and a three-tiered stone fountain formed its centerpiece. It also included her favorite shady retreat, a wisteria arbor with a cool stone bench.

Today, however, she didn't linger in the garden. Instead, she aimed for a narrow lane that started just behind it. The lane ended at nearby Bayou Lafourche. It separated the grounds from the outbuildings and the vast cane fields beyond. Lined with dogwood and pecan trees, it also passed the large wrought iron gate of the St. Vallier family cemetery.

Her thoughts shattered at the approaching drone of a small aircraft. She stepped clear of the tree cover and glanced west, toward Senator Myron Leblanc's adjacent property.

Sunshine gold-leafed the surface of the bayou. A little blue-and-white Piper Cub was skimming in over the treetops just behind the bayou. Leblanc had a private airstrip behind the line of cypress trees, out of sight. Once in a while she spotted Leblanc's sleek Lear jet arriving in a regal swoop from Washington or some other important place. Usually, though, it was smaller prop-driven planes.

Thinking of Leblanc made her pause to survey her own property. Again she was reminded how everything lately turned on a very thin dime. Straight north from where she stood, she saw a lone figure out in the fields driving a huge John Deere with an air-conditioned cab. That was Autry Duplantier, one of the few original workers who stayed on after Stella's father mechanized the operation at Shadow Oaks. Now Autry was overseer of "the grinding," as cane growing and processing were still called in Louisiana. He was drawing a wide cultivator through the rows of sugar cane.

On a chance, she waved to him. Autry surprised her by waving back, despite the distance and his failing eyes.

The older man had taken to working long weekends now. She knew Autry did it for her father—or, rather, his memory—and also because there was no choice. Despite the efforts of the locally organized cooperative, most of the independent cane planters had ceased to run their own sugarhouses, as Shadow Oaks still did. Now Leblanc and others simply sold their cane by the ton directly to the big sugar mill in Thibodaux. The new method drove the price down and destroyed the economy of the old sugarhouses.

Which was why she came more often to visit her dead.

She pushed open the iron gate to the cemetery. Plump marble cherubs grinned at her in the streaming sunlight, hardly setting a somber tone. At one time the headstones and markers had been kept meticulously edged; fresh strips of sod had been laid down every year. Now the place had the sad, neglected feel of a Cape Cod lighthouse.

A red granite memorial just inside the gate caught the eye by its relative newness. She paused. She had a brief image of the police car parked out front of the big house, and then of marble-white gloves and shiny new coffins. Of a weathered old preacher with caving cheeks reading from a clasped Bible. And herself, staring through a blur of tears as her parents were lowered into the dewy earth.

She followed a flagstone path to the very first row of graves. Then she stopped at the cracked-marble vault in the far corner of the cemetery.

Ornately chiseled eighteenth-century letters identified it as the burial chamber of Jules de St. Vallier and his wife, Genevieve. Stella had heard her ancestor described as a roguish pirate by some, a criminal scoundrel by others. But she suspected she would have admired him greatly. At least, judging from the stories her mother and Rose used to tell her.

Jules, around whose famed beauty of a bride rumors had sprung up like toadstools after a hard rain; Jules, who built the original eighteenth-century house that had later been expanded to its present size; Jules, whose fabulous riches were often sought but to date never discovered.

"Jules," she whispered out loud, as if trying to wake him up. The man who built Shadow Oaks. And now, she prayed from the core of her being, the one who would also save it. If only she could find—

"Shit! Watch it, wouldja? Damn near threw that one in the water!"

The unexpected words sliced rudely into her thoughts. She went back out to the lane and looked toward Bayou Lafourche again. From there she couldn't see anyone, but she spotted heliographs of light reflecting off the windshield of a vehicle. It was parked in the narrow tractor lane between the cane field and the bayou.

Parked on her property.

Like most of the old families in the parish, she wasn't outrageously anal about property rights. Locals often parked along the bayou to fish, and that was fine by her as long as they didn't trash the area. But this felt all wrong. That wasn't the tone of a fisherman.

Staying close to the trees for cover, she walked farther along the lane, approaching the bayou. As she drew near, stretches of swampy backwater appeared to the north, visible beyond the cane. Pure white egrets dotted the swamp like randomly tossed flags of surrender.

But she focused her attention on the parked vehicle.

She was close enough now to identify it as a fairly new Jeep Cherokee. She thought she recognized it from town but couldn't link it to a face.

Abruptly, a man appeared behind the Jeep wagon, and she had her face.

A thin, sharp-nosed face. And permanent pouches like bruises under his eyes. She knew him all right, although she'd yet to meet him face-to-face. He was her nemesis, P. G. Toutant. Present owner and manager of The Scarlet Door, Cane Town's one and only strip club.

She paused and stepped out of the lane. Before he spotted her, she wanted to see what he was putting in the back of his vehicle. Whatever it was, he got it inside before she could see it.

Her pulse quickening, she moved in closer when Toutant disappeared again on the bayou side of his Cherokee.

From her new spot, she gained a larger perspective. A second man was present, this one on the west bank of the bayou, Senator Leblanc's side. He was younger than Toutant, built more solid. She had seen him around somewhere but couldn't quite place him.

She glimpsed the small plane behind him, its gleaming blue and white paint flashing through the cypress brake. The man was tossing something across the bayou to Toutant. Something white; tightly wrapped bundles as absent of color as the egrets.

She felt the blood of anger rush into her face when she realized what those packets must be. Toutant fastidiously pinched the creases of his chinos and hitched them up a bit so he could squat to pick up one of the bundles. She watched him like a jackal.

They were loading illegal drugs on her property. The thought slammed into her with all the power of a locomotive. Reflexively, she stepped forward to confront them.

Then she spotted it, and she pulled up short. Her

knees went watery. She tasted the corroded coin flavor of fear.

The man she recognized but couldn't name dangled a shotgun from his left hand. Both blued barrels were sawed off to ten inches.

For a long while, as the seriousness of the situation sank in, she felt a paralyzing stupefaction. Then reality pressed in on her. Prudently, she faded back behind a pecan tree and tried to impose order on the panicked riot of her thoughts.

Toutant loaded a few more packets, then she heard the Cherokee's tailgate chunk shut. She watched him lift a hand to the other man, then get in behind the wheel. Toutant made a quick U-turn, crushing a few rows of cane, and headed back out toward Parish Road.

Despite the leaden fear in her stomach, her entire body quivered with anger. She waited until both men were out of sight, then she hurried back toward the house, determined to report what she had just seen to the police.

It would take the law to put those two behind bars. And that's exactly where she meant to put them.

CHAPTER

2

He always behaved nice. You know, polite.
—ADELE, the only known prostitute
to have posed for Bellocq

"I still don't understand, Chief Archer. I reported this on Saturday afternoon. Yet it's almost noon Monday before anyone responds?"

Jervis Archer shrugged one muscular shoulder. He stood beside Stella on the grassy bank of Bayou Lafourche, where the body of water wound from the front of the great house to the side behind the old cemetery. He stared at her, his thumbs hooked into his leather gunbelt.

"It wasn't a nine-one-one call, Stella. No life in danger."

She felt a tight bubble of resentment rising inside her. Jervis Archer was the one reason to give up the farm and move out of town. She'd developed an aversion to him as a teenager when they'd both attended Benjamin Harrison High School. Back then he and some of his football-playing cronies had been accused of gang banging Sophie Parsons. Sophie was a dropout, a known cokehead, heading for her third abortion, but when her bruises and accusations were met with general dismissal on the public's part, and derision on Jervis's part, she took a full bottle of Valium. They'd found her dead in the middle of the dew-laden football field, a note to Jervis clutched in her hand. *Jervis I loved you* was all it said.

After that Jervis started asking Stella out on dates. He told her it was time he was seen with a better class of girl.

Perhaps Sophie Parsons was trash, but the betrayal in the note had haunted Stella. *Jervis I loved you.* She had always refused Jervis's invitations, and now, though it was a hundred thousand years ago, she could see in his gaze that he still resented it.

"One of the men had a weapon," she said evenly. "It was a drug deal. Not some high school kids smoking pot, this was a big amount of cocaine or heroin or—or something."

"Something," he agreed, goading her with her own vague word.

He flashed that odd and disjointed half smile that had always made her nervous, even when they were teenagers. She'd never been attracted to him; she didn't like his big, hairy hands with spatulate fingers, or his flat voice that seldom varied in pitch or tone. He watched her now from cool, clear blue eyes like glittering chips of ice. In his crisp butternut khakis and felt Smokey the Bear hat, he had the jut-jawed good looks of so many vain backwater bullies. But nothing inside her stirred. And nothing ever would where he was concerned, no matter how hard he tried.

"The law doesn't care what we *might* have seen," he added as if educating her. "I need something I can hang an evidence tag on. Something besides tire marks and a little crushed cane. What proof have you got?"

"Proof?"

"You got video? They leave any of this alleged dope behind?"

"Of course not. But—"

"I figured as much."

Anger made her pulse throb. "Look, I suppose that white powder was flour for the starving kids in Central America. One of Leblanc's charity projects, right?"

"Lotsa white powders in the world," he reminded her.

She stared at him with exasperated disgust. "Oh, that's right. How dare I rush to judgment? The glove didn't fit, did it?"

The half smile reappeared. "You said one of the men was Toutant. How 'bout the other one? The one you think flew the plane. Recognize him?"

"I know I've seen him somewhere, but I can't place him. You're going to question Toutant, aren't you?"

He nodded. "Sure, I'll talk to him. Seein' how much he likes you, I guess we'll get this straightened up right away."

She wilted a bit inside. Toutant hated her for the crosses. She was going to have an uphill battle there.

"I'll do it for you though."

Stella raised her gaze to him. She got the impression that he was only speaking pro forma, but there was something in his eyes that demanded gratitude. She had never quite been able to shrug off his pursuit of her. Even at Newcomb he'd arrive in the city and looked her up. Now she wondered why she had called the police at all. He seemed much more interested in studying her than the supposed crime scene.

The day was humid and warm, and she wore a matching white shirt and shorts with strappy sandals. She had always taken pride in her legs. But just then she wished they were covered up.

"I'd like you to speak with Senator Leblanc also," she added. "That plane landed on his property. He may not know what's going on, and he ought to at least be informed."

By then the two of them were walking back down the lane toward Shadow Oaks. She could see the former slave quarters behind the main house, narrow shanties with batten shutters and carpenters' chisel roofs, now used for storage. Beyond, rising out of a green-waving sea of sugar cane, was the big sugarhouse. The clinker-built structure needed paint and repairs. In a couple of months, when Autry would begin the pressing and boiling, its twin chimneys would belch smoke night and day.

"I don't know 'bout talkin' to Leblanc," Jervis snorted. "Now, just hold on, Stella. You know that old saying? 'It's rude to visit Rome and insult the Pope.'"

"The Pope? Leblanc? Bit of a stretch, isn't it?"

"I wouldn't be so sure of that. Senator Leblanc is a pretty big nabob around here. He's brought in plenty of jobs."

"Like the big sugar mill in Thibodaux?"

He nodded. "Sure. Some of you growers may not like it. But I got kin working there."

She stopped walking to stare at him, her eyes filled with indignation. "I don't believe this. If you aren't going to contact him, I will. And I can tell you have no real intention of investigating Toutant, so I'm going to confront *him* myself too. Maybe I can't stop the drug trade, but I can at least boot it off my property."

"Look, you riled Toutant enough with replacing those crosses after he cut them down. I'd appreciate it if you just let me do my job. You'll stir up the shit, and then the parish board will be howling."

By then she was walking fast, wanting to get back to the house and rid of this bog-trotting Deputy Dawg.

"Apparently, you have a very restricted idea of just what your job entails, Chief Archer."

"This is exactly how well-intended citizens get themselves into trouble. They poke into something that's none of their mix."

"None of my—but it's *my* property!"

"Fine. Then you'll need to post signs against trespassing."

"You just don't get it, do you? It's not trespassing I'm worried about. It's the drugs."

"We all worry about drugs."

By then, however, she suspected his words ran only lip deep. His next remark reinforced that impression.

"Be careful, Stella."

For a few moments, Stella felt an icy finger move down the bumps of her spine. She recalled something Autry had told her about Jervis—how his name would surface now and then when locals discussed the murder of Albert Fontainbleau. Jervis Archer was apparently the last person to see the man alive, and he was also the one to head the investigation into his disappearance.

It had all been a little too sketchy and incestuous. Finally late last summer the New Orleans councilman's body—or parts of it anyway—had been found scattered all over a cane field in the south parish. He had been fed, part by part, into a cane cutter. It took a DNA lab to finally identify the victim as Fontainbleau.

"Careful?" she repeated, an edge to her voice.

"Sure. Careful what you say and who you say it to. You know how people are. They'll take a pimple and build it into a peak. Now, Senator Leblanc? A man's good name is nothing to fool with, that's all I'm saying."

"Neither," she informed him coldly, "is a woman's. Must I remind you, Chief Archer, that the St. Vallier family settled in this area before anyone else now living here, Leblanc included?"

He grinned. "I always liked it when you get all huffy, Stella. I've never known a woman who looks so pretty when she's pissed off. Makes me want to keep you riled."

His presumption made her ill. "Did you come out here on police business or to hit on me?"

He cocked his hat forward a little, openly staring at

her bare legs, a hostile gleam in his eye. The one she knew so well when she refused to go out with him. "One don't get in the way of the other."

"Ah, yes," she riposted, scorn poison-tipping each word. "The favorite activity of you southern machos. You're the bird dog and I'm the quail, right?"

Her insulting tone made his face shut tight as a fist.

"I guess some of that comes from deep-rooted families," he told her, "think it makes them important. But you know? Any family's got deep roots if you trouble to trace them."

They had passed the family cemetery and entered the main garden behind the house. The rear loggia came into view as they rounded the path, and she wanted only to get rid of the jerk.

"I'm sure you're right," she answered in parting. "But I couldn't tell you. I've never had to trouble to look."

He hated her for that remark—she could see it in the way his jaw muscles bunched. Snobbery was not her usual tact. But this presumptuous, vulgar boor inspired her to slash where he was vulnerable. And one clear Achilles' heel for Jervis was his hangup about uppity bitches.

But now that he was angry, it didn't take long for the iron hand to come out of the glove.

"Look, Stella, why'n't you just get real? I've got no time to traipse all over hell in search of God knows what. As for Leblanc—I'm damned if I'm going to bother such a busy man on your say-so. He's rolling in it. All you've got is a name and your stiff-necked pride."

As angry as his words made her, her best friend, Mattie, had once told her essentially the same thing: Up north, a family lost its status when it lost its buying power. But in the south, status clung to a name based on past glory. It hadn't pissed her off, however, coming from Mattie.

"Just let me get this clear," she said, ice in her words.

"Basically, you're not going to do a damn thing about what I told you, right? You're not even going to pick up Toutant for questioning?"

"Sorry, Stella. Not unless you got hard evidence of a crime. I got other weenies to roast. Take care 'yourself."

He headed around the corner of the house to his car parked out front.

"Fine!" she shouted behind him. "If you won't do your job, *I* will!"

Jervis called back. "It's your funeral."

Infuriated from her encounter with Archer, Stella stormed into the kitchen through the rear entrance, slamming the paned-glass door shut with reckless force.

"That crude, stupid *creep,*" she fumed. "And we pay him to protect us? 'We *all* worry about drugs, Stella.' I wish someone would roast *his* weenie!"

Aunt Rose sat at an English oak gateleg table, playing mah-jongg with an elderly black woman. Leora La-coutre was "Leora" only to Rose, "Maman" to everyone else. She had been employed as the cook at Shadow Oaks since way before Stella was born. By now Maman was family and Aunt Rose's inseparable companion.

Maman's long, aristocratic face looked up from the tiles to study Stella's grim demeanor.

"Sweet heart of Jesus, Stell! That tongue of yours been salted in a pickling jar?"

Stella could never get used to such a young and vibrant voice emerging from Maman's serene old face.

"You should have heard Jervis, Maman. The man is an absolute pig! I believe utterly everything that's ever been said about him."

"Mmm-hmm, there it is. That Jervis got him a mean-looking mouth. That's where meanness always shows in a man, y'unnerstan'. Right 'round the mouth."

Maman's placating tone and manner worked a calming effect on Stella. So did the cheery kitchen. Though fully modernized, it was faithful to tradition with its copper hood, glass-front cabinets, and plantation table. Fresh anemones in hand-painted vases adorned a rosewood sideboard.

It was Aunt Rose's instinct to eradicate anger by way of the taste buds.

"Dear, won't you have a dragee?" she asked, offering her a crystal plate of glazed candies.

"Never mind that pogey bait," Maman censured Rose. "Stell needs some meat on her bones. La, that girl gettin' skinny on us! Hon, you try some of that shrimp-and-mushroom soup Maman just made this morning."

"I'll have some later. I'm too ticked off to eat right now. That . . . *asshole* Jervis!"

Stella narrated the gist of her encounter with Chief Archer. The moment she finished, Rose clucked her tongue.

"Mmm-hmm," Maman said to the world at large, laying a tile in place.

"Stella," Rose said gently, "getting yourself all worked up against Senator Leblanc is going to be trouble. And for what? Mince pie, that's what."

Rose had a good point, and Stella was caught upon it.

"Myron Leblanc," Rose informed Maman in the face of Stella's stubborn silence, "is a true southern gentleman. One of the last guardians of the code duello."

"That's a crock," Stella interjected sullenly.

"He *is*. Every year at Christmas? He personally visits all of his neighbors and gives each of them a ham."

"Big old picnic ham," Maman chimed in. "That's right."

"Every woman has her price," Stella scoffed. "You know he gets the hams from lobbyists."

However, Rose was not daunted. "Well then, just think how much his charity organization has done for children. He's a busy, important man who always finds time for others. Why, do you know I saw an editorial in the *Times-Picayune*. He's actually been chastized by his colleagues in Washington for spending *too much* time in his home state."

"If he's such a home boy," Stella interposed, "then why didn't he join the sugar cooperative with the rest of us? The volume growers like him sell their cane directly to the big mills. We can't even compete, he's driven the price so low."

"I never pretended to understand commerce." Rose's tone made the word "commerce" seem more like "pornography." "But Myron Leblanc would do no such thing. He cannot be blamed for the vagaries of the marketplace."

"That's not how Autry sees it," Stella insisted. "And he's been in the sugar business for fifty years. He says Leblanc gives a short measure and a long price. And you know father never could stand Leblanc."

"Your father," Rose said, and Maman made the sign of the cross, "was a wonderful man, may he rest in peace. But like his prideful daughter, he could sometimes form judgments about people too quickly. Autry is loyal to your father, so he's biased."

"That's it," Maman affirmed.

Stella's combative edge, sharpened by her encounter with Jervis, now began to dull. At times she felt Aunt Rose and her singular notions were enough to vex a saint. But she dearly loved her aunt and fiercely admired the old girl's cheerful readiness to face the future. A trait Stella often resolved, but seldom managed, to emulate.

"Oh, you're right, Aunt Rose."

Stella finally pulled out one of the chairs covered with needlepoint and sat down with the older women.

"Whatever it was I saw on Saturday, there's absolutely no reason to assume Senator Leblanc knows about it.

But I am *not* just blowing this thing off. I'm going to make a few phone calls. Maybe write the senator a note. And Toutant has to at least know that *I* know."

She lapsed into silence while Aunt Rose and Maman played their game. This business with Toutant was just one more problem she didn't need. Thanks to her harried accountant, she knew the grim fiscal realities of their situation. If the season's grinding at Shadow Oaks failed to return six or seven percent over cost, 170 years of tradition would go the way of fringed surries and mule-drawn trolley cars.

"You worry too much, Stella," Rose announced suddenly with eerie conviction.

Stella looked up, and wondered if she'd been thinking out loud. Softly, she said, "If I don't worry, who will?"

The question went unanswered, as it should have been. It wasn't up to ninety-year-old ladies to save the family farm, and Stella knew it.

"Jules's money is here somewhere," Rose said lightly. "That ought to put us right."

Stella wanted to throw up her hands and roll her eyes. When Rose harped on that old fairy tale, she knew the art of rational thinking was lost. "Okay, okay. It will save us. So just tell me where it is, and I'll haul it to the bank."

"Mother told me so many stories she swore were true," Rose chanted. "And there's Colette's diary. *She* didn't consider the treasure a mere rumor either."

"So where is it? Was it secreted out of these walls in the last century? If it existed at all, it's sure as hell gone by now." Stella knew she was being more caustic than necessary, but the conversations were getting old. No new information was ever provided.

Rose's lined lips held a ghostly smile. "The St. Vallier treasure is real. Like God in the universe, it is everywhere felt but nowhere seen."

Rose had made other such enigmatic pronouncements of late concerning the St. Vallier treasure. Although tantalizing, they were frustratingly useless. "Senile" was too harsh a word for Rose, but Stella feared her great-aunt's quirks were increasing with age.

"If it's real," Maman pressed, "then why can't it be seen?"

"One has to know what to look for, Leora. It's like reading a cozy. The answer to the question 'who done it' does not turn up at the end a big surprise. It has been there all along but overlooked."

"Overlooked?" Stella protested. "Shadow Oaks was practically dismantled by vandals searching for the treasure, and according to Colette's diary, they never found anything."

"Those wicked thieves who tore our place apart after the war when we were downtrodden were not St. Valliers, I tell you, and I curse them to this day, as my mama did and her mama before her. But you, child"— Rose turned to Stella—"you're a St. Vallier. You could find it if you knew where to look."

"Fine. Then you tell me, where do I look?" Stella asked, already knowing the answer from the same repeated pathos-filled conversations.

"Start with the lovers of the past."

Stella could have mouthed the words right along with Rose.

"Look to their lives. Genevieve St. Vallier never stopped drinking life to the lees. Never grew 'old' either, though she lived to be ninety-one. She just waltzed herself tired, then went to sleep."

Waltzed herself tired, Stella repeated. God, she still loved that phrase. But of course, waltzing required a partner. So did most things in life that seemed to matter.

Exhausted, she pushed her chair back. "Well, back to the salt mines. I'd better get on the phone. Get that letter over to the senator."

She was halfway to the dining room when Rose's voice drew her up short. "Stella?"

She turned around. "Yes?"

Rose's emotional eyes held Stella motionless for a moment. "Start with the lovers of the past," she finally repeated, her words low and sharp with meaning. Useless, enigmatic meaning.

CHAPTER

<u>3</u>

"Yes, I would like to speak with an agent in the Drug Enforcement Agency." Stella held the line while she was transferred.

"Browning," said the male voice at the other end of the line.

"My name is Stella St. Vallier, and I'm calling from Cane Town, Lafourche Parish. Are you an agent?"

"Yes," came the curt reply.

Stella dove right in with the details of what she'd seen on the bayou and of Jervis Archer's lack of interest in her report. Finally, she ended with, "I just really wanted to tell someone in an official capacity. I know I don't have much evidence, but it certainly seems suspicious and—"

"You said this was in Cane Town? And it was on your and Senator Myron Leblanc's property?"

"Yes," she answered.

"Give me your name and number, and I'll get back to you."

She gave him the information and swore he'd hung up on her before she had given him the last digit to her phone number.

"Myron Leblanc's property, eh?" Browning's supervisor punched something into his computer. He read the screen, then slid away from his desk and stood. "We can't get involved. The U.S. marshals have an operation running down there. They want no interference, not even to go after traffickers. I guess they've got something bigger on the burner down there. We can't get involved."

Browning shrugged. "So what do you want me to do?"

The supervisor nodded. "Call the woman back. Tell her you looked into it and there's nothing for her to worry about."

"You mean shut her out." Browning met his supervisor's gaze.

"Exactly. It's no longer our jurisdiction whatever goes down in Cane Town now."

"Once more all around, Dabs."

Garrett Shaw plunked a cork-lined tray down on the bar.

"That's Scotch straight up for the old man," said Dabney "Dabs" Boudreaux. "And an Abita Amber for Steele. I forget what those other two had."

"A bourbon sour and a martini," Shaw reminded him.

Dabs snorted. The bartender at The Scarlet Door was a big, soft-bellied man with a face so fat, it folded onto itself.

"A martini," he repeated above the thumping of the jukebox. His tone mocked the word.

Shaw grinned and lowered himself onto a Naugahyde barstool. "Show some respect for your betters, bar dog. 'Least nobody ordered a Perrier."

He cast a quick glance around the lounge while Dabs made the drinks. The Scarlet Door wasn't usually this busy so early on a weekday afternoon. But several offshore oil rigs had been evacuated in Terrebonne Bay, just southwest of Cane Town, because of a tropical storm alert in the Gulf. Many riggers chose to travel the extra distance inland to party full-bore in New Orleans. Others, however, preferred nearby Cane Town. Especially since P. G. Toutant had arrived and made the town more amenable to oil patch roughnecks.

Garrett had been hired three weeks earlier as the new bouncer. The job was working out well. Already he was one of the crew, fitting in like a cockroach in the projects. But he was still edgy whenever he thought of the badge that sat on his desk back in Texas. He'd lasted three weeks at The Scarlet Door, and common sense told him he wouldn't last three minutes if they found out who he really was.

Normally, he'd be manning his usual observation post, a spring-back chair just inside the main entrance. But today there was a special meeting in the "conference room." That was Toutant's name for a windowless room at the rear of the building, usually kept padlocked.

The room, Garrett had noticed, included a convenient door that opened onto a narrow alley behind the club. A door sheathed with a quarter-inch steel plate— pretty heavy-duty for a tits-and-ass bar. A door through which passed a few faces who wouldn't like to be spotted around there, Shaw had realized by then. Faces so important that Toutant wouldn't even let his usual cocktail waitresses carry drinks back to them.

"All set, Cowboy," Dabs told him, setting the last drink on the tray. "Don't let any of 'em pinch your ass."

Garrett took the tray and started across the lounge toward a little hallway at the rear, behind the pay phone and the bathrooms. By then he had learned to breathe through his mouth around there. The dump featured a distinctive bouquet of stale cigarette smoke and permeated sweat. Sheetrock walls had been plastered over with paper patterned in gold fleurs-de-lis. A small platform bathed in colored lights rose from the center of the room. It was currently occupied by a tired, tattooed peroxide blonde with bad teeth. She was bumping and grinding to a jukebox rendition of "She Works Hard for the Money."

Toutant sat hunched in one of the booths along the banquette, checking the previous night's register tapes. As Garrett passed, he signaled to him.

Shaw swerved over to his boss's table.

"What you need, Chief?"

"The two dudes at the table right behind me are lighting up shots. Macho rigger shit. Last summer some redneck burned the hell out of his face doing that, almost got me shut down. Tell them to nix that frat-boy crap or hit the bricks."

Shaw nodded.

"These boys are trouble," Toutant added, never once looking up from the tape spinning through his hands. "Watch yourself. And go easy on the furniture."

When Garrett reached their table, a roughneck in Levis and a muscle shirt was lighting up his friend's shot of tequila with a Zippo. A blue ring of flame popped to life as fumes ignited just over the glass. The rigger sucked the shot down quick, fire and all.

Both men cheered and high-fived.

"Sorry, gents," Garrett called out amiably. "No more flames in this club. Fire code and all that."

The barracks-room bad boys looked up at him

through a drunken fog of conjecture, sizing up the risk. There were two of them, and each had a size advantage. This guy's in shape, their eyes seemed to tell each other. But those are just show muscles.

"Hey, where the fuck is Mickey?" demanded the one who had just finished drinking.

Mickey was the hulking Slav weightlifter who used to be the bouncer before Garrett.

Shaw shook his head. "Couldn't tell you," he lied. "Quit, I guess. Maybe the stress got to him."

The rigger wore a Marlboro T-shirt that strained around his pectorals and biceps. He stared at the tray in Shaw's hand. Then he took in the jeans and the faded black shirt Garrett wore.

"I don't listen to no dumb fucks like you, boy," the rigger said, flicking his Zippo and making his partner laugh.

Garrett reached out with his free hand and inserted his index finger at a spot between the roughneck's collarbone and neck. A few pounds' pressure precisely on the nerve point, and the big roughneck collapsed back into the booth, yelping like a kicked dog. His face twisted in pain.

Garrett literally held him pinned motionless with one finger.

"A big fellow like you," he informed his hapless victim, still speaking in his unruffled, amiable tone, "should have more brains."

The subdued rigger's partner threw back his head and laughed. He watched the bouncer from newly respectful eyes. "You don't take no prisoners, do you?"

"Rape the horses and shoot the women." Garrett withdrew his finger, waiting to see what Muscle Boy would do. But the fight had gone out of him.

"No more fires, *capisce?*"

"Roger that," replied the troublemaker's buddy. "Hey, man, where'd you learn to do that thing? Was that, whatchacallit, *tai chi?*"

"Miles to go and promises to keep." Garrett excused himself, heading toward the rear hallway again.

Stella truly did go to her bedroom armed with good intentions to read and take notes. But her earlier clash with Jervis chafed at her. So did the call-back from Agent Browning.

"Nothing's going on," he'd told her, a dismissive tone to his voice. "The public's always allowing their imagination to get the best of them. But you can forget about what you saw. Senator Myron Leblanc's not letting any illegal activity happen on his place, I assure you." Then the man abruptly hung up.

For perhaps half an hour she tried to enter into the plodding reality of *Land Husbandry and the Sugar Cane Planter.* Finally, she gave it up as a bad job and closed the book.

The sunny little alcove in the master bedroom was actually a small cabinet room off the rear loggia. Originally, it had been a room for storage and use of the chamberpot. The matching room on the opposite side of the loggia was used for another purpose altogether.

Restless, she studied her bedroom, the one once shared by her parents not so long ago. Framed Audubon prints of Louisiana shorebirds flanked a lovely Kentucky cherry plantation desk; the Victorian inkwell was shaped like a nautilus shell. Fabric in a sun-bleached palette slip-covered the Signouret chair. On the desk, boxes with ormolu edges that once held tea now held paper clips and rubber bands. She considered these boxes symbols of what she wanted her own life to be: the past, still real and solid, imposing order and form on the chaotic present.

The same thing, she mused, that Aunt Rose was urging her to discover. But how? *How* does one bridge that awful chasm between imagination and reality?

Inexorably, that perplexing thought drew her out of the reading nook and back into the spacious, sun-drenched bedroom.

There they all were. They stared at her, each one a different symbol, a different strength: ten generations of the St. Vallier clan. The west wall of her room show-cased oil portraits or photos of every woman who had reigned as mistress at Shadow Oaks. From the fabled beauty Genevieve—her likeness cut in black-velvet sil-houette beside her husband, Jules, a fad of eighteenth-century portraiture—to Stella in her college graduation photo, her eager smile bright with the thought of her promising career, bright with the idea of finding true love.

But true love had eluded the last St. Vallier. Stella had dated, of course. She'd even been engaged once. But her love hadn't had the tragic end that Rose's had. Instead, true love had died, bit by bit, with the cold re-alization that shallow and narcissistic Matthew was not the one she had waited for.

Her mother's lapis lazuli eyes gazed demurely from a photo taken only months before the auto accident. In them was a plea for patience, shadowed in wisdom. And there was her great-grandmother Jacqueline, Rose's oldest sister, who drowned with husband, Edward, in the tragic maiden voyage of the *Titanic*. That was a key trait of the St. Vallier line: Even their tragedies were steeped in romance. But Stella feared that legacy had ended with her. Her love life had ended with all the flat dispassion of a high school crush. Now life at Shadow Oaks loomed before her, a dull, prosaic, uneventful damnation.

All the eyes staring at her seemed accusing now. She wanted to either look away and dismiss them or stare diligently back until their secrets were revealed. But none of the silent women could tell her what she needed to know about romance *or* finances. They were in their way like the Bellocq women. Mistresses of their own silence. Giving questions but few answers.

Her eyes paused on an early tintype. It showed a beauty wearing side-lacing silk boots and a crinolined dress with pagoda sleeves. Her dark hair was formally capped in tulle and crepe. In the fashion of the 1860s, her waist was cinched by stays laced tight as turnbuckles.

Colette de St. Vallier. Her husband, Henry, had been killed leading a charge at Antietam Creek. According to her diary, corroborated by other plantation records, she had single-handedly saved Shadow Oaks during the tumultuous days of southern Reconstruction. No mean feat, especially for a cane grower. Cotton could simply be planted and picked. But the cane growers had to rebuild expensive sugarhouses, including heavy steam presses melted for munitions in the war.

Somehow, against all odds, Colette did it. One important clue to her strength had been handed down through the female generations. It was preserved under glass beside her photo, by her own request: a yellowed clipping from the May 1854 *Harper's Magazine*. Colette had taken it through life with her, from girlhood to death. It was a short verse by Sarah Bolton.

> *Voyage upon life's sea,*
> *To yourself be true,*
> *And whatever your lot may be,*
> *Paddle your own canoe.*

She called it Colette's anthem. Childishly simple from today's perspective. But among the women of Colette's day, those inspiring words must have resonated like the bugle notes of "Boots and Saddles" to a cavalryman.

And the irony in them still. Those naive words mocked Stella. Colette saved Shadow Oaks during the greatest disaster in America's history. As her candid diary revealed, the young widow also enjoyed a heady love life once she'd put her mourning veil aside. Yet Stella felt overwhelmed by a few pressing banknotes. Felt, too, that love had somehow given her the go-by.

She turned away from the haunting, intimidating gallery of accomplished women. Her Ph.D. seemed paltry compared to what they'd managed to do.

Through brand-new eyes she saw her Venetian four-poster with its privacy curtains, eight-foot-high canopy, and bedcover in corded *broderie de Marseille*. Colette's bed. A mirrored satinwood armoire reflected the elegant ambience of the bedroom with the window-to-window swag treatment and faded pastels of the eighteenth-century Aubusson rug.

She suddenly realized that she had not inherited Shadow Oaks from her ancestors. Rather, like generations before her, she was merely holding it in trust for the St. Valliers to come. *If* they came.

But it was all worth fighting for. Fighting hard if need be. That meant, among other things, that she must make a renewed effort on her research. Much more immediately, it meant she must confront Toutant. She didn't care what the DEA and Jervis told her. Something fishy had been going on on the bayou the other night. Nobody was going to use St. Vallier land to make his drug deals. Nobody.

To say she dreaded going to The Scarlet Door was an understatement. The rat's nest was the only serious blight on Cane Town's civic image. But she had to go there. Not only because Toutant could be breaking serious laws on her property, but also there was the completely unacceptable way that Jervis Archer had bullied her earlier that day.

She recalled his remark about well-intended citizens who get themselves in trouble. Was that comment just cracker-South machismo? After all, men like Jervis didn't like "pushy" women with a take-charge manner. Maybe she should have been more passive and helpless. Should have appealed instead to his male ego. Would the Big Strong Man please help scared Little Ol' Me?

But no. Male ego was part of it, of course. But there was more to Archer's remark. The threat seemed more in what he'd left unsaid.

She glanced at an antique enameled clock on the fireplace mantel. Three-thirty, and obviously, she wasn't going to get any work done. If she left soon, she might catch Toutant before The Scarlet Door got too busy.

She resolved to change clothes right away and drive into town.

The moment she'd committed to that resolution, a cool little frisson moved up her spine. She had long wondered if she possessed some sixth sense attuned to disaster. Even at age twelve she'd felt it, just before Hurricane Nan wiped out the entire cane harvest: a heavy sense of dread that left her with a loss-of-gravity tickle in her stomach. She'd felt it again before the police cruiser had arrived that night with the deputy to tell her her parents had been killed in a freak auto accident in town.

And she felt it now. Danger was as real as a man beside her.

CHAPTER

4

I do not believe that women are better than men.
We have not wrecked railroads, nor corrupted
legislatures, nor done many unholy things that
men have done; but then, we must remember
that we have not had the chance.

—JANE ADDAMS

"Gentlemen, events are truly working to our benefit. Fortune favors the bold. And lately, so does the weather."

Senator Myron Leblanc spoke with a deep, authoritative voice that nearly shook the wall studs. He was in his early fifties, a strong man growing soft. Blunt and bullnecked, he had a leonine head topped by a graying crew cut.

There were three men with him, seated at a Formica-topped table pitted with burn scars: Clifford D'Antoni, Lafourche Parish district attorney; Hiram Steele, the area's representative in the state legislature; and Barry Woodyard, a New Orleans city councilman.

Leblanc's bodyguard, who had just admitted Garrett, sat on a folding chair near the hallway door. He was a young African American with a shaved head and thick scar tissue around his eyes. Garrett assumed the lump under his left arm wasn't a tumor.

"Actually," Leblanc was saying as Garrett moved around the table, serving drinks, "Hurricane Mitch was simply kismet. For our purposes, it's perfect timing. They've got this new, reform-minded president in Honduras, Carlos Flores Facusse. Nice guy. And guess what? Not only is his wife a knockout, she's also a Louisiana gal. An LSU grad who really knows how to milk a smile. She's on the tube here all the time, and, boys, donations from all over the Deep South are at record levels."

"Thank you, son," he added in a lower voice when Garrett set his Scotch down and cleared away the used glass.

This was the first time Garrett had the chance to observe Senator Leblanc up close. He had that aggressive, controlling manner of those who obviously consider themselves the central figure in any gathering. Maybe, thought Garrett, he really believes what he told a news anchor in Baton Rouge: That he was appointed by God Almighty to direct the collective purpose of the people.

The bodyguard had noticed that Garrett was moving around the table with sacerdotal slowness. Shaw set the martini down at Barry Woodyard's place and took the empty glass. Woodyard, he had finally decided, was being eased into Albert Fontainbleau's violently vacated spot.

"I mean, I saw Mary Flores Facusse on TV the other night," Leblanc resumed after sipping from his drink. "She had me crying, my hand to God. Her descriptions of what it's like for the little *niños* down there, it's touching. Poor little bastards."

D'Antoni chuckled. The D.A. wore a white linen suit with wide suspenders. "Simon Peter's got diddly on you, Myron. Didn't I read that you majored in marketing at Vanderbilt?"

Leblanc smiled. "Actually, that was my minor. My major was theater."

Everyone at the table laughed. Garrett could feel the bodyguard's eyes on him. He set the bottle of Abita down near Hiram Steele.

"If the situation down there is really so bad," Woodyard chimed in, "it's good to know the kids really do get a healthy chunk of the money. Hell, you think about it, we take only a small percentage of the gate."

Woodyard seemed to understand immediately that he had misspoken. The room went still and quiet, and Leblanc turned to smile at Garrett. "That'll be all, son. Thank you."

The bodyguard wasn't so diplomatic. He stood up and held the door open for Garrett.

"Next time, just give me the tray," he told Shaw on his way out.

As Garrett crossed the lounge, Toutant again waved him over. He pointed to the opposite seat, and his subordinate sat down on the banquette.

Toutant had to lean close to be heard above the music. "I heard you handle those assholes at the next table, Cowboy. You got a good head on you. You know how to control a situation without busting up my furniture."

Toutant had finished with the register tapes. Now he was drinking black coffee. Garrett had never seen him touch booze or any other kind of drug. The man was all business.

"Where'd you say you worked before here?" Toutant asked.

"Dockyards in Galveston. But all the ports have switched to these damn piggyback containers. Roll 'em on, roll 'em off, all you need is a crane operator. It's put a lot of longshoremen like me out of work."

"You sure that's the only reason you left Galveston?"

Garrett spread both hands in a sincere gesture. "Ah, you know . . . let's just say, I'm glad you agreed to pay me under the table. This is not a good time for me to establish a paper trail."

Toutant grinned, though with his tight-to-the-bone skin, it put Shaw in mind of a skull's rictus. "Sure, I know. You're all right, Cowboy. Listen, there's plenty of room for advancement around here, you take my drift? Mickey was a strong right arm to me. I had him broke in just right. And wham! Right out of the friggin' blue, the feds pop him for income tax evasion."

"Shit happens," Garrett sympathized.

"Don't it though? Anyway, keep in mind what I said, okay? I need a good man. The thing with you, Cowboy—you're not too full of yourself, but you're not a kiss-ass either. That's the kind of guy I can trust. Think about it, huh?"

Garrett recalled that mausoleum stillness, moments ago, following Woodyard's indiscreet comment about "a small percentage of the gate."

"You can count on that," Garrett assured his boss.

Stella turned the ignition switch on and patiently waited fifteen seconds for the old Peugeot's glow plugs to warm up before she started the diesel engine.

Maman always joked that Stella drove "one of them old French tanks." But Stella had fallen in love with the slow yet comfortable little sedan in college and kept it ever since. Although her friend Mattie, a historian by training, had a different theory about why she kept the car.

"For you," Mattie had once suggested in a burst of candor assisted by a few glasses of rosé, "the past isn't just a fascination—it's a refuge."

Stella backed out of the porte cochere and followed the meanders of the long drive. She turned east on Parish Road, fighting hard to quell a stirring of nervous nausea in the pit of her stomach.

With Jervis Archer's crude stag-in-rut stares in mind,

she had changed from her shorts into a modest wrap-skirt of tussah. An ivory crepe blouse and pale moon-stone earrings completed her simple outfit. She had brushed her hair back behind her ears and clipped it into place with tortoiseshell barrettes.

The three-mile drive into town passed through the old but still-beating heart of the sugar cane country. A swamp lay behind each plantation, though nowadays they no longer provided fuel for making sugar. The steam-powered presses were electric.

Twice she spotted workers driving the huge mechanical cane cutters that had eliminated most field labor. She slowed down to watch, fascinated despite the familiarity of the sight. The giant vehicles straddled several rows at once and left the cut cane lying neatly alongside.

If this were January and harvest time, she knew the next step would be to defoliate the cane with tractor-mounted flame throwers—an amazing spectacle eerily like a scene from a war movie. But it was too early for harvest. The immature cane being cut now was the "seed" for the next crop. The stalks would be laid flat in shallow furrows. If all went well, a new plant would spring up from each joint in the cane.

Love that well which thou must leave ere long.

Again, as she negotiated the final curve before town, she felt it: the ache of desperation and fear at the prospect of losing all she had, all she was. God, yes, she was willing to fight. But it was tough to find the stamina when fate and circumstance seemed continuously against her.

The outskirts of town were mostly modest bungalows and narrow shotgun duplexes. A boat of some type was visible in most of the yards, there being more water than land in the parish.

She turned onto Highway 13, the only route through Cane Town's abandoned business district. The usual commercial melange of fried chicken joints, liquor stores, fleabag motels, and pawnshops rolled past, then a subdivision, a tacky blur of middle-class America. Then she spotted the water-stained boards of The Scarlet Door, and a cold hand squeezed her heart.

The emotion she felt now was not just fear at the prospect of entering that filthy club. Nor of confronting Toutant. Instead, the feeling was raw and consuming like a festering wound.

The intersection where The Scarlet Door was located—Highway 13 and Bayou Road—was the very spot where her parents had been killed. No one knew to this day the exact circumstances of their death. The driver of an eighteen-wheeler had plowed over them. He had died instantly too. The drug tests had proved inconclusive. But she'd been continuously haunted by the thought of her parents' last moments; that her father's last view of the world had been the outside of a cheesy strip club, her mother's last glimpse of this world the round-top peeling fluorescent red door that ushered like the gate to a run-down hell.

Stella's remedy had been to plant the crosses. She'd done it with the blessing of the town council—hell, nobody went downtown anyway—and she had tried to regain her false sense of security when Toutant took over The Scarlet Door and mowed her crosses down.

Forcing herself now to shake off the mood, she angled into a slag parking lot beside the club. Immediately, her heart sank—though it was only late afternoon, the crowded parking lot already looked like a pickup truck dealership. She managed to shoehorn her car between a Harley-Davidson and a pickup with Yosemite Sam mud flaps.

A bright bumper sticker on one motorcycle caught her eye, and she had a premonition of what she was about to endure: IF YOU CAN READ THIS SIGN THE BITCH FELL OFF. The misogynistic message made her almost lose her courage. But the image of Toutant loading those white packets steadied her resolve.

"I don't think we're in Kansas anymore," she muttered sarcastically as she slid out from behind the wheel and locked her car.

Rock music pulsated through the walls, sounding like a tinny radio. She smoothed her skirt with both hands. Then, on an impulse, she walked behind the dingy frame building with its peeling paint. A black Jeep Cherokee sat in the narrow rear alley, hugging the building. Toutant's vehicle. The same one she saw him driving on Saturday.

At least he was here.

She went around to the front. Slatted jalousies flanked the "scarlet door," which was grimy with the hands of a thousand drunks. As she placed her hand on the doorknob, she again almost backed out. Dread was so heavy in her limbs, she feared she couldn't even move.

But Colette's trite poem egged her on: *Paddle your own canoe.*

She opened the door and immediately winced at the combined blast of blaring music and acrid air. It was so dim at first, she had to pause inside the door a few moments while her eyes adjusted to the dark.

The first thing she saw clearly was the spotlighted "dancer" on the platform. The flat-chested, listless performer possessed the élan of a sleepwalker. Stella wondered if she knew the girl, but she didn't recognize her as a local.

Probably stoned out of her mind, she thought. *I'd* want to be if I were up there.

Then Stella realized with a start that a man sat on a tall, spring-back chair only a few feet to her right. He was gazing pointedly at her.

He possessed a distinctly handsome face, no doubt about it. But the scornful twist of his mouth was hard to interpret. She remembered what Maman had said, how meanness in a man always shows around the mouth. Mean or not, she got an immediate impression of a man who stood outside the pale of normal human events. He was a spectator, never a participant. The life-and-death struggle of civilization was merely one more sporting event placed in front of him for his amusement. He was neither Christian or lion. He was emperor.

He watched her from penetrating, no, *invasive* eyes as gray as morning frost.

Involuntarily, she took a step backward.

"You lost, princess?" he demanded, eyes taking her full measure. "We don't serve cappuccino here."

He spoke with a dusty twang that made her think of West Texas and the chaparral country.

"I wouldn't drink bottled water in this place," she informed him, her enunciation cold and precise. "I came to see Mr. Toutant."

He slid off the chair and stood up. Taller than she'd thought, he towered over her by a foot.

"C'mon, I'll take you to your boyfriend."

She followed him into the main lounge, feeling as lost as a duck in the desert. From the back wall, plaster had cracked and fallen, exposing the lathing beneath. A long back-bar mirror multiplied the squalor of the place. Multiplied, too, the number of customers. To her discomfort, she spotted a few locals she knew, but she refused to meet their eyes. It was neither the place nor time for greeting.

Just her luck, the music suddenly ended and the dancer went on her break. In the interval of silence, the bouncer called out, "Hey, Dabs? We got a visitor for Mr. Toutant!"

Too late she realized he'd done it deliberately to get the entire club's attention. She suddenly understood with a panic that *she* was the object of all eyes in the room.

The enormously fat bartender grabbed the waistband of his drooping slacks and tugged them up.

"God*damn!*" he said, staring at her as if she were a rare artifact. His lipless grin unnerved her.

She shuddered as the fat man fondled her with his eyes. As were several dozen other horny males, thanks to the smartass bouncer in the cowboy boots. Everyone was watching her from sly, slanted, expectant glances.

"Maybe P.G. is gonna prick the vent!" somebody yelled out, and the place erupted in bawdy cheers and whistles. Heat flooded into her face.

A rough-looking biker type dressed in jungle camouflage stepped over from the bar, trailing a reek of whiskey. He thrust a felt-tip pen out toward her.

"Sugar, would you draw a happy face on my dick? I promise never to wash it off."

If she could have moved right then, she would have bolted from the place. At least the bouncer had enough sense of decency to step between her and the drunken Rambo, fending him off.

"Follow me, Miss Princess," he ordered her, grinning slyly.

The bouncer led her behind the bar to a door marked MANAGER. It meant that she had to squeeze within inches of the overweight, smelly bartender. She shuddered at the stench of body odor coming from him.

"Smells nice, doesn't she?" the bouncer said to the bartender, his mocking eyes watching her while he said it.

The fat man worked his rubbery face into a leer. "You ain't just birding, Cowboy. God*damn!*"

The bouncer grinned. He knocked on the door and threw it open. "You got a visitor, boss," he announced.

The bouncer stepped aside. She spotted Toutant sitting at a battered kneehole desk, working an adding machine. He glanced up at her, the pouches under his eyes even more pronounced in the glare of a Tensor lamp.

"Yes?" he said, politely standing. "You want to see me, Miss . . . ?"

She turned to look behind her. With henchmanlike

deference, the bouncer had left and shut the door behind them. She was completely alone with Toutant.

She had never met the son of a bitch who had cut down her parents' memorial crosses. P. G. Toutant. She'd just heard of him. So far as she knew, no one around Cane Town knew much about him. He had shown up in town a while earlier with a chunk of venture capital he used to buy The Scarlet Door. The bachelor lived in the apartment over the club and kept pretty much to himself.

"I'm Stella de St. Vallier," she informed him, though she suspected he knew full well who she was. She was the notorious lady with the crosses, not to mention the land across the bayou from Leblanc.

"Of course," he said, ushering her farther inside the cramped office. "One of the first families in the parish. Please have a seat, Miss St. Vallier."

His unguent, self-satisfied voice irritated her. He motioned for her to take a seat. There was a chrome-and-leather chair in front of the desk, ridiculously pompous in this dump, but she remained standing. Suddenly she felt butterflies stirring in her belly.

"How may I help you?" he asked, his gaze flickering over her like a vagrant eyeing an unfinished bottle of Thunderbird.

"I'll be quick and blunt, Mr. Toutant. I saw you on Saturday. On my property," she added when he feigned confusion.

"Saw me on your property? I don't understand."

"I believe you do. You and another man transferred a shipment of what looked like drugs from his airplane into your Jeep. I saw the whole thing."

He made only a token effort to look surprised. Again she had the impression there were no revelations here. She recalled Jervis Archer's remark from last Saturday: *Be careful, Stella.*

"Drugs?" The faint shadow of a smile touched his lips. "There must be some mistake, Miss St. Vallier. Ask anyone, they'll tell you: I'm so law-abiding, I'm pathological about it."

She stared at him, the vision of him mowing down her parents' memorials running again and again in her mind. For a moment, anger gripped her so tightly, it left her jaw aching.

"Mr. Toutant, I am not given to hallucinations. I don't have proof positive it was drugs you were moving, but I know full well what I saw. You and another man conducted some kind of illicit transfer on my property. And I've come to tell you I won't tolerate it."

He pulled on the end of his chin, unable to hold eye contact with her for more than a few seconds.

"You are way off the beam here, miss. I'm just a hardworking, honest businessman. You've mistaken someone else for me. I'm a good citizen."

She found his calm equanimity even more enraging than fake outrage.

"Perhaps you're just a good liar," she said.

His phony smile melted like an iceberg in the Caribbean. He dropped the pretense of polite respect.

"I don't know what's biting at you, lady, but you got a lot of mouth."

"That's right," she agreed. "And that mouth will go to the law too. Law outside of Cane Town. And that's precisely what I mean to do if I ever see you on my land again."

"Law?" Now that he had dropped the acting, Toutant had no trouble meeting her accusing stare. "Just remember, babe. The oldest legal code in existence is an eye for an eye." He nodded to emphasize his meaning. "Screw me, screw you. Now, get the hell out of here."

Despite his order and menacing tone, she stood poker rigid, refusing to leave. She was indeed frightened, in deep and going deeper, but she was damned if she'd let this two-bit bottom feeder push her around and use her hallowed property for his crimes.

"Don't threaten me," she said, so angry each word seemed bitten off.

"Like I said, you flap your mouth too much."

Toutant did a quick about-face. He pressed a dingy white button at the top of his desk. The bouncer opened the door, ready and waiting.

"Show Miss St. Vallier out, Cowboy."

"Just a moment here," she objected, but her arm was grabbed in a walnut-cracking grip.

"You bolted to the floor?" the bouncer demanded. "Mr. Toutant just requested that you vacate his place of business."

She heard Toutant laugh behind her as her captor dragged her out behind the bar, then through the lounge floor.

The club erupted in laughter. "Hey, Cowboy!" one of the patrons hollered. "Strip 'er buck, we'll see if that rack on her is real! I say it's all in the bra!"

"Oh, she's for real," Cowboy fired back, that smirking grin back on his face.

Then, mercifully, she was outside again, breathing fresh air.

Her arm was released.

"It's not often I'm told to escort a beautiful woman away from this place." The bouncer's expression was hard and distant. Wiped clean of even curiosity.

Stunned for the moment, she merely leaned against the building and rubbed her arm where he'd gripped it.

Then it dawned on her she'd been manhandled and ejected from a club she wouldn't have sent Jervis Archer to patronize. Fury got the better of her.

"Hey, *thug*," she spat out, so angry, the words exploded from her mouth, "you tell your boss he'll get more than a visit from me the next time I see him on my property."

"Here's a safety tip, lady," the bouncer said, dominating her with his intense chilly gray eyes. "Toutant looks like a skinny little wuss. But most people who muck with him end up playing the cobra to his mongoose. Whatever your gripe is with him, just forget it."

"Do you know anything about my gripe with him? Are you involved with him? Did you deliver any packages for him lately too?" she demanded.

"Lady, your car's out here. I suggest you start the engine and scat."

"Are you afraid of him? So yellow that you'd push around a woman half your size just to show shallow loyalty?" Her mouth twisted in derision. "Sure you would, because you stand for nothing. You possess nothing. You are nothing—just some minimum-wage loser like the rest of the patrons in this scum-bucket club."

"Princess, you've got thick, shiny strawberry-blond hair, a rack most women get at the doctor's, and the most beautiful sea-green eyes I think I've ever seen. If you want to hang around here, I'm sure P.G. would hire you to strip. Hell, he'd pay you double what he pays that emaciated coke fiend in there." He leaned closer to her, putting a shadow on her face. "But if you're just nosing around, let me help you find your way home. Your kind does not belong here."

"I don't want him on my property," she said, her voice suddenly showing fear at the edges. The bouncer unnerved her more than did Toutant. His gaze was deep, violating. His hands and body looked strong enough to rope a steer. She would be no physical match for him. None whatsoever.

"You really are something, girlie. Sweet to look upon, prickly to deal with."

"Tell him," she said.

"Forget it," he shot back.

"Just tell him what I said. I never want to see him on my property again." Her words held firm, but she backed against the jalousies flanking the door. They rattled just like her nerves.

"You're out of your element, princess. Go home."

"I won't—"

He pressed her against the slats. His muscular chest met with her "rack." She was trapped by the enormity of his frame.

With a hard finger he tapped her fragile shoulder. "Do what's good for you, baby doll. I don't want to see a delicious piece of ass like you be rubbed all over the highway."

She stared up at him, suddenly believing she was frightened enough to find religion.

His face was wiped of all expression; his eyes were the temperature of absolute zero. "I'll tell you one last time, princess, whatever your gripe is, *just forget it.*"

CHAPTER

5

*I asked a man in prison once how he happened
to be there and he said he had stolen a pair of
shoes. I told him if he had stolen a railroad, he
would be a United States senator.*
— "MOTHER" MARY JONES

U.S. Marshal Garrett Shaw could usually seal himself off from the past. But sometimes, despite all his careful control, memory became a rudderless ship in dark waters.

Alone in his rented room at the Delta Manor boardinghouse, five minutes' drive from The Scarlet Door, the thoughts sometimes would rush him. Then he would see that fateful October night all over again, the images still stark and raw even after sixteen years.

He could still hear the speeding truck as it crashed through the security barricade, tires screaming like banshees; still hear the stuttering racket when sentries opened up too late on the intruder with M60 machine guns; still hear his own useless cry of protest just before that god-awful explosion.

The floors of the tall concrete barracks pancaked

downward, one atop the other, and there was a collective scream from those not fortunate enough to die in their sleep. And always—always that scalding comber of fire and wind lifted him into oblivion.

But the present always intervened to save him.

Now only bird chatter and the screeching sound of water coursing through pipes disturbed the early morning stillness. It was October '99, not October '83. But for a few moments, even after he woke up in the here and now, the old anger came back, and his thoughts became rough and ugly.

His bare feet slapped the floor. Garrett stood there beside the narrow iron bedstead, shivering in his boxer shorts, while he stretched out the night kinks. Then he knocked off two sets of twenty-five push-ups followed by two sets of sit-ups.

The exertion dulled his anger. But he could not quite shake off the thoughts. The memories clung like cobwebs in his psyche.

He took a cold shower, stepped into clean khaki trousers, and pulled on a blue knit shirt. Then, instead of getting right to work, he slid open the drawer of a battered nightstand beside the bed.

He took a photo album out of the drawer and flipped it open to an eight-by-ten black and white photo. A forty-eight-man Marine Corps "Zappo" platoon stared at him—four dozen young grunts in helmets and flak jackets, M16 rifles at sling-arms.

An almost baby-faced Lieutenant Garrett Shaw stood down front holding a sign that read WELCOME TO SUNNY BEIRUT, GATEWAY TO THE MEDITERRANEAN! Like salty marines, every one of his men was growling and making his best war face for the camera.

My men, Garrett thought. Half of them killed that night. For a moment, his throat felt like he was trying to swallow a nail.

Each of their names had been indelibly burned into his memory by that explosion. How goddamn many times, he wondered now, had he sent scathing memos to battalion HQ, protesting those chicken-shit billeting arrangements for his men? Why in God's name would marines in a combat zone be housed in one compact high-rise building? "Cluster-fucking," as Garrett learned to call it early during his training at Quantico. Those men should have been scattered all around the airfield at Beirut, widely dispersed in small, reinforced bunkers.

But politicians had been in charge, not warriors. And just as the pols botched it in Vietnam, they botched it in Beirut.

In truth, it wasn't just terrorists on a holy jihad who killed his men—it was also those spineless, mealy-mouthed, self-serving politicians. A tribe of back-scratching cousins who swore to seek justice but instead sacrificed those marines on the altar of political expediency. At least, that's how it looked to Garrett from ground zero.

Such thinking, however, only evoked more angry tension. He slammed the photo back into the darkness of the drawer. But yet, if not for the anger, he would not be the creature he was. It was the anger that had eventually determined Shaw's civilian career, that drove him to join the U.S. marshals' elite federal task force specializing in the investigation and prosecution of corrupt politicians.

The burning need was personal, not moral. He had no illusions about saving the world—but every low-life, on-the-take pol that he sent to the slam gave him the same visceral satisfaction as landing a hard right cross to the man's jaw.

A sudden uncharacteristic grin hit him. Sure, he wanted to clean up his little corner of the world. But when he'd received his assignment this time, he didn't know the job description would involve manhandling defenseless little princesses who'd stumbled from their tower.

With amusement he recalled the doe-eyed woman

who'd blustered into The Scarlet Door last night, all huffy and pretty and proud. Christ, did *she* get the shock of her life, or what?

He didn't know her first name or the reason for her talk with Toutant, but he sure as hell'd love to see her do a pole dance and flip that red-gold hair at him. She was a real class act too, with wide blue-green eyes and opalescent skin. Definitely his type. If he wasn't working, he'd be begging her to have dinner with him. She'd probably accept too. Not many women turned down a fed. But, he thought with a wry little smile, she sure as shit wasn't going to have anything to do with a bouncer who worked at a shithole. That she'd made perfectly clear.

His room included a tiny kitchenette behind a folding screen. He put some water on for coffee, then glanced at the cheap electric clock beside the bed. A little after eight A.M. That meant it was past nine in Washington. He picked up the phone and punched in a long distance number.

"Warrants Division. Falcone speaking."

"Morning, Stevie. Holding down the fort?"

"Hey, Garrett! How's the sex life down in Cane Town, *paisano*?"

"I'm holding my own," Shaw replied, and both men laughed despite the fact that it was an old joke between them.

"Seriously. How's it going?" Falcone asked.

"Seriously, it sucks. Right now, buddy, we're neither up the well nor down. I'm getting all kinds of convictions except the kind that will stick in court. I'm convinced now that it *was* Leblanc who put the contract on Fontainbleau."

"Any hunches on the button man?"

"Zilch. Leblanc gave the order, but I don't know who fed him into the cane cutter. The why is easy enough to figure."

"Hell yes. It doesn't take a rocket scientist to answer

that. Not when a man is about to spill his guts to a grand jury."

"The way you say," Garrett agreed. "That's why I called. I want you to check out Leblanc's charity organization, this United whatever."

"United Southern Children's Charities. I did check it out. So has IRS. Many, many times. Nobody could find flies on it."

"Keep digging," Garrett insisted.

"Why? You psychic now?"

"All is not copacetic there, I assure you. It came up in conversation in front of me, right? Suddenly the room goes tense, like somebody farted in church."

"All right, I'll see what I can nose up. But just remember—we are dealing with people who have plenty of contacts in high places. We poke around too much, they might find out we're trying to salt their tails. Then we are fucking crisped. What about this Toutant character? Still think we can turn him state's evidence?"

"Maybe yes, maybe no. He's a guy who figures percentages and angles."

"Sure," Falcone said. "But he'll foul the nest before too long. They always do."

"Toutant," Garrett pointed out, "is tougher than he looks. But he's also a one-man outfit, loyal to nobody but himself. If we can put some heat on him, I think we can turn him."

"But go easy. Fish drop to the bottom in hot weather. And you make sure to cover your butt, buddy. You blow your cover with this bunch, you'll be wearing one of those suits with no back in it. I oughta know, I'm Sicilian."

"Yeah, so for your sake I'll be buried in my Italian shoes. Wherever I go, dago."

"Ark. The mob wanna-be makes another funny."

"Lots of *amore* to you," Garrett said, making kissing noises before he hung up the phone.

The water was boiling by now. He made a cup of instant coffee and sipped it black while he turned the Fontainbleau case back and forth in his mind, examining all of its facets.

Getting rid of Mickey, the old bouncer, was easier than rolling off a log. Especially since the loser hadn't filed an income tax return in six years. But how in hell did this St. Vallier woman factor into the equation? He knew it had to be her family commemorated by the white crosses in front of the Door, but she hadn't come because of them. Toutant was finally leaving the crosses alone; she had won that battle. But even so, obviously, Toutant had pissed her off royally. How? Garrett would have liked to question her, but that was risky. For an undercover cop, nothing was more imperative than protecting his cover.

But he might have to talk to her if that stubborn, bullheaded little fool kept nosing in. She had no idea what a hornet's nest she was about to step on.

He finished his coffee, rinsed out the cup, and decided to drive to New Orleans. He still had eight hours before he had to report for work at The Scarlet Door. He wanted to find out a little more about Barry Woodyard, the New Orleans city councilman who had been at that secret meeting yesterday of what Garrett called the "Louisiana Ring."

As Shaw had learned the hard and bloody way in '83—the rat race was over, and the rats had won. But that grim fact couldn't take the joy out of being a rat catcher.

"The actual nuts-and-bolts part about making sugar ain't all that complicated," Autry Duplantier exclaimed. "But *bon Dieu!* It keeps you busy. I mean busy like a moth in a mitten."

Stella studied the old Cajun face she'd grown to love. It was weathered to the color of red clay, and the eyes crinkled deep at the corners like the spine of an old paperback. He pointed at two huge iron cylinders that rolled against each other. Her eyes followed to the cane press that filled one corner of the big sugarhouse.

"You just feed the cut cane into the rollers and squeeze alla juice out the stalks. The juice runs into them vats over there. You boil it and you boil it and you boil it. The more you boil it, the more sugar you get in the syrup it leaves at the bottom of the vats. Then you crystallize it with plenty o' heat. Stink? *Ciel!* Smells like hair on fire."

Stella nodded. She knew the process, of course. Smelled it too. But now she wanted to truly understand it, step by step, taught by a man who was a master at it. Autry wasn't going to be around forever.

"You get you a residue drained off from the boiling," Autry went on. "Lots of it is molasses, so it's salable by-product. Best to get it all done by middle of January on account you have to get the next crop laid by. Next crop should be in no later than July."

She knew the crop was "laid by" when it had grown strong and tall enough to survive on its own, without requiring hoeing to destroy competing weeds and grass. But she was more interested in another phrase Autry had just used: salable by-product. She had discovered some interesting articles recently about a possible new source of revenue from the grinding. At least, she hoped it might be possible.

She studied the two big iron rollers again, her face preoccupied.

"After the cane is squeezed dry," she said, "what do we do with the waste?"

"Do with it?" Autry repeated. "What, you mean the bagasse?"

She nodded.

He shrugged. "Use to was, some of it was dried out and used as fuel for the mill when wood was scarce or wet. Now, with 'lectricity, it's just waste. I pay a couple high school kids to haul it out."

"I'm reading a book by an agronomist at LSU." She walked closer to the cane rollers. "He says that bagasse could have some promising new applications in things like the animal feed industry."

"Shoo," Autry scoffed mildly. "A professor says so? It's just bagasse."

"I suppose you're right. Still . . . my accountant says if we don't figure out some way to increase profits quick, there's a good chance we're going to tank. And soon."

For a few moments, misery filled her as if she were a bucket under a pump. Autry seemed to see how worry suddenly molded her pretty face. He pushed his pillow-tick cap up higher on his forehead.

"We're in a dirty corner, all right, *chère*. But you know? That look in your eyes right now? That's just how your papa looked, too, when he made up his mind to change this operation. He mechanized it, and he saved it. Could be I spoke out too quick just now, hon. Things got to change, even a old coot like me knows that. Could be this professor fella got him a good idea about the bagasse. You keep reading them books, see what you can do. Ol' Autry be right behind you."

She cracked a smile. "Old coot, huh? This place would have been a golf course long ago if it wasn't for you."

"Sorry I held us back," he quipped, and they both laughed.

Although the operation at Shadow Oaks was fully mechanized now, one wall of the sugarhouse was still covered with dozens of traditional cane knives hanging from nails. These specialized tools looked somewhat like machetes with hooks on the ends.

Good thing they'd been saved. Twice, in Stella's memory, violent storms had tangled the sugar cane stalks so completely that machines couldn't be used. Experienced migrant workers from Mexico had been called in to harvest by hand, a procedure that demanded great skill. The workers had to strip the stalks of all blades, lop away the tops, then slice the stalks free of their roots. There was absolutely no wasted motion, and the rhythm of the workers was almost hypnotic to watch.

Autry saw Stella gazing at the knives.

"You know, since 1828, the only harvests missed at Shadow Oaks was them last two years of the Civil War and then in 1867 when Bronze John visited."

She nodded. Bronze John was the yellow fever. In '67 it killed half the laborers and two of Colette St. Vallier's children. She could never read Colette's last diary entry for that year without crying: *Dear God, how much more?* But even in despair, Colette endured.

"Autry? Do you believe the story about Jules St. Vallier's treasure?"

"I'm thinking maybe it's true. But, *chère,* you know plenty of people looked for them jewels. Could be, somebody found them and never told. Or maybe he hid it too good, eh? I tell you this. I think our Stella has a better chance with selling bagasse than she got for finding a treasure."

Good old Autry. He had never been one to gild the lily, a trait she appreciated.

By then she had drifted to the big double doors. Looking out over a sea of waving cane toward the bayou, she watched the spot where she had seen Toutant parked last Saturday.

"Autry?"

"Hmm?"

She turned to look at him. "By any chance, have you noticed anything . . . unusual going on along our property line with Leblanc?"

The Cajun had never been good at dissembling. His eyes suddenly fled from hers. "What you mean, unusual?"

"Trespassers loading something into a vehicle. Loading it from airplanes on Leblanc's property?"

The old-timer shrugged. "Aww...maybe I seen something like that once or twice."

"Why didn't you mention it to me?"

He shrugged again, offering no explanation. But something veiled in his face suddenly made her skin grain with an unknown fear.

"You were protecting me, weren't you?"

"Well, you got that St. Vallier temper, *mais non*?"

She was irritated at Autry for a moment. But it passed quickly. His loyalty and hard work had earned him the benefit of several doubts.

"Your intention was sweet," she told him. "But please. If you see anything again, will you tell me?"

He nodded reluctantly.

Autry's discomfort made her recall that disastrous visit to The Scarlet Door. Since then, she had spent too much time reliving the moments she'd spent outside with the bouncer. The guy had sparked terror within her. For several seconds as she'd looked up at him, she wondered if he was going to hurt her. He was such a big man, even Jervis Archer would think twice about provoking him. But at that precise moment of her fear and captivity, her emotions had worked against her somehow. Instead of struggling and screaming out her demand to be released, she had suddenly become still and silent. She'd looked up at him; he'd stared hard at her. It shocked her to think of it, but she'd dwelled on it now like the mind pictures of a fatal accident. There was no other explanation. He was a crudely attractive male; she a lonely female. Her unexpected passivity had been bred in her genes from caveman days, and it had been sparked by her own sudden, fierce—and definitely unwanted—sexual arousal.

Even now she hated to think of it, hated to ponder its meaning. In the end she attributed her reaction to the simple fact that she hadn't had any in so long, her affections could be cast anywhere, like a net upon the sea, haphazardly trapping whatever swam by.

But in the deep recesses of her mind, she feared it might be something else. It was her dark fascination for Bellocq's work rising up within her. When he finally stepped away from her, she'd ran to the Peugeot, feeling naked and tricked.

Overshadowing it all, however, was something far more ominous. His warning her off Toutant had been vicious and complete. So, was Toutant the greater threat, or his steel-muscled henchman?

She didn't know, and she realized she was smart enough to leave the question forever unanswered. The next time she had a problem with any of them, she was going to let the DEA handle it.

She said good-bye to Autry and headed through the fields toward the house. Blackberry brambles and honeysuckle crowded the narrow lane. She reached the carved gate of the cemetery and pushed it open. The marble cherubs watched her from blank eyes as she paused at the granite memorial of Michael and Patricia de St. Vallier.

"I wore it yesterday, to keep me safe," she told her parents in a quiet voice. "Just for you."

She reached under the collar of her blouse and pulled out a beautiful star sapphire pendant on a heavy platinum chain. It had been the last gift she'd ever received from her parents before they were killed.

Turning the pendant over, she read the inscription even though she knew it as well as her name. In the streaming sunlight, the words that had been her parents' play on her name Stella still warmed her. *Let this be your lucky star,* it said.

Luck. The word resonated with irony.

It had no place in the relentless, coldly practical struggle to survive in a bottom-line world. Jules had his Genevieve, Edward his Jacqueline, Michael his Patricia. In a world where even Jack had his Jill, she had no one. Just Jervis Archer skulking around as he had skulked for years, looking for the chink in the touch-me-not armor. And the trial of yesterday at The Scarlet Door—where even handsome men like the bouncer were soulless brutes who licked the boots of criminals.

Her eyes quivered as if she'd gotten shampoo in them. The day went blurry through her tears. She looked up toward the front of the graveyard where Jules's cracked-marble vault rose above the other graves.

Rose's enigmatic advice for finding his treasure whispered in her ears, indistinguishable from the wind soughing through the nearby cane: *Look to the lovers of the past.*

She stared at the tomb for a long time, her thoughts yearning and dark, her empathy for the Bellocq women running high.

CHAPTER

6

"If brains were horseshit, you two would have a clean corral, you know that?"

Senator Myron Leblanc's voice was clear, strong, and resonant in the small conference room. Only two men shared the Formica-topped table with him, P. G. Toutant and Jervis Archer. They had been summoned to the emergency meeting at The Scarlet Door less than an hour after Leblanc received Stella de St. Vallier's note.

"If you wander near a point, Senator," Archer said, his voice flattened of emotion, "feel free to make it. You ain't the only one's got a job to do."

Leblanc frowned. He was used to looking to the sycophantic faces surrounding him for support. But he got none of that from these two. Especially not from Archer.

"A point? Christ, it's the same point I've been making all along, Chief. The quickest way to ruin a good thing is with drugs."

"We've plowed this ground before," Archer replied.

"Like I already told you. I'm damned if I'll help another man get rich unless there's something in it for me."

Leblanc's neck swelled and his face got red. But he clamped his teeth rather than retort. When he had calmed somewhat, he turned to look at Toutant. With the exception of the haggard pockets under his eyes, the club manager's lean, hard face seemed carved out of bone. His stringy build left a seersucker shirt drooping off his shoulders.

"Couldn't you two at least have given this woman some cock-and-bull story?" the senator demanded. "Something besides just calling her a damned liar? Now you've got her Irish up. If she sent me a note, then who else might she contact? I'll have to call her now, do some damage control."

"She *is* a firebrand," Toutant conceded, looking at Jervis. "The senator's got a point."

"Christ yes. I knew her father," Leblanc blustered on. "These St. Valliers are not afraid of a fight."

Jervis shrugged. "Fine. The nail that sticks up gets hammered down. Even Fontainbleau found that out."

" 'Hammering nails' should always be a last resort. Far better to use wit and wile."

"Opinions vary," Jervis replied, obviously bored by the conversation. He clearly had a visceral dislike for men who talked too much.

"I'm telling you," Leblanc repeated, his voice again yielding to his anger, "that this drug operation of yours could sink *all* of us. When I told you, Chief, that I owed you a favor, I didn't mean I was willing to jeopardize everything I've worked for years to build up! I want you to deep-six this drug running."

Jervis flashed his disjointed smile. "Take the pine cone outta your ass. I ain't about to crawfish to you or anybody else, big man."

Leblanc was on the verge of exploding again. But Toutant, more conciliatory than his partner, cut Leblanc off with a no-big-deal gesture.

"Senator, Stella St. Vallier is a nuisance, that's all. Jervis and I can handle this without scrapping our operation or risking yours."

Percival Toutant's reasonable tone calmed Leblanc somewhat. The senator had always prided himself on his special knack for finding a person's weakness and then using it to his own gain. But so far, trying to find a vulnerable spot on these two was like trying to find that one soft place behind an alligator's eye. Diplomacy was all he had left.

"Gentlemen," Leblanc said evenly, "at the very least, *please* alter your operation so this woman won't have to know about it."

"We have," Jervis assured him. "I told Harley, no more daytime deliveries—"

"I told you I don't want any details," Leblanc hastened to cut him off. "When this dope operation of yours goes tits up, I'm damned if I'm going down with it."

Archer looked at Toutant, and both men grinned.

"If us two *do* go down," the chief assured Leblanc, "it could become a mass burial. You remember that when your buddies in the DEA are planning busts."

Choleric blood rushed into Leblanc's big, square face. But he let the remark lie. Again he looked at Toutant.

"I see you hired a new bouncer. The hell happened to Mickey? I liked him."

Toutant explained about Mickey's bust. Suspicion immediately glinted in Leblanc's eye. He frowned so deeply that his salt-and-pepper eyebrows touched.

"Income tax evasion?" he repeated skeptically. "The feds bothered to pop a loser who probably never cleared twenty K a year in his life? You check this new guy out?"

"Cowboy's all right," Toutant assured him. "I can whiff the cop stink from a mile off."

Leblanc looked disgusted. "Jesus Christ Almighty! I

thought I was working with professionals here. At least pre*tend* you've got more brains than a rabbit."

Leblanc pulled a pen and a flip-back notepad out from the inside breast pocket of his jacket. He jotted a hasty note, still scowling. His bored bodyguard, meantime, sat by the hallway door, ignoring all of them while he wiggled a loose tooth.

"How much longer," Leblanc added, putting the notepad away and looking at Toutant again, "will you two be heading your little cartel?"

Toutant shook his head. "How long is a piece of string? Why do you ask?"

"Why do you *think* I ask? For one thing, that's my property you're landing on. Also, my organization cannot continue indefinitely to launder the money. Just because it's nonprofit doesn't mean we aren't monitored. It's exactly the opposite."

"The thing is," Jervis cut in, "you never bitched so much before the hurricane hit. You and your pals were happy to take your cut then. Now you got church donations coming out your wazoo, all of a sudden drug money is too dirty to touch."

Leblanc did a slow boil, his mud-colored eyes drilling into Jervis. Neither man gave quarter.

Once again Toutant poured oil on the waters.

"Don't go poking into the senator's business," he chided his partner. "We run our gig, he runs his."

"Fine by me," Archer said. "I ain't the one who's whining."

Leblanc sighed and shook his head. With an effort, he kept his tone reasonable. "Chief, they don't call it dope for nothing. You only see what's happening at your end. But I also see what's stirring in Washington and Baton Rouge. And Cliff D'Antoni gets another view of events from the parish D.A.'s office. Right now it doesn't look too good. Apparently, Fontainbleau's death may have sent up a bright red flag to the wrong people."

"Meaning what?" Toutant demanded. "An undercover sting?"

Leblanc nodded his crew-cut head. "I'm not sure of that yet. But quite possibly."

"So that's why you're so worried about Cowboy?"

"Hell yes. And that's why *you* should be worried."

"Your concern is logical," Toutant agreed placatingly. "But believe me, I've been making judgment calls like this for years. Cowboy's way too original to be a cop. If you could see how he handles the roughnecks around here, you'd know what I mean. Cops all have authority hang-ups. But Cowboy can control men without busting them in the chops or getting macho."

"Let's hope you're right that's he's legit. But don't assume a damn thing. Keep him completely in the dark about the drugs."

Leblanc stood up, signaling that the meeting was over. "Meantime, I'm going to call Stella St. Vallier and smooth her feathers. For Christ sakes, boys, don't queer this deal by letting her see anything else. I shit you not, that woman could put all of us in a world of hurt."

Stella began reading and taking notes right after lunch. By late afternoon her eyes were blurry and she had a headache from so much close concentration on the technical aspects of sugar processing. But at least she felt she might be making some headway: The bare nubbin of a Shadow Oaks survival plan had begun to form in her mind. A practical plan, not some fantasy of lost treasure. The first step involved sending a letter of inquiry to Professor Perkins, the LSU agronomist who wrote the book she was studying.

When the phone on her desk chirred, she welcomed the interruption.

"Hello?"

"Good afternoon," a strong, mellifluous male voice

greeted her. "This is Myron Leblanc calling for Stella, please."

"This is she, Senator."

"Stella, how *are* you? I confess, I'm mortally embarrassed—you are my closest Louisiana neighbor, yet when is the last time we visited?"

"Last Christmas, I believe. When you stopped by with that lovely ham." Stella was glad he couldn't see the expression on her face. Big Daddy's patronage and his lovely hams.

"Has it been so long? Almost a year?"

"Well . . . of course, you're terribly busy now."

"True, true. But there was a time when I believed only Yankees became too busy to find time for their neighbors."

It was obviously one of his pat lines, but she laughed politely.

"I'll bet you called about my note," she prompted, fearing the preliminary small talk would drag on.

"Yes, of course. I want to thank you sincerely for your concern. A concern I happen to share very deeply. I was especially troubled by your report that Chief Archer seemed uncooperative about the incident you witnessed."

This sounded promising.

The senator paused.

She waited to hear more.

"I've spoken with my wife and all of our employees. As you know, airplanes land here quite frequently. My son David often flies in from Houston, and several cane growers I know are pilots."

"The pilot I saw," she felt obliged to comment, "definitely wasn't your son. He was older. Late thirties maybe."

"Did you get a good look at him?"

"Not really. He had dark hair and a solid build. I'm almost sure he's from around here. I mean, I've seen him somewhere, but I can't place him. But the other man was definitely P. G. Toutant."

She almost added that she had confronted Toutant; however, she held the information back. The less she gave out, the more information she might receive.

"I see," Leblanc said. "And you're absolutely convinced it was illegal drugs they were loading?"

"Well . . . I can't say that with total surety, no. But what else would be a white substance wrapped in tight plastic packets and loaded in hurried secrecy?"

"If it quacks like a duck," Leblanc agreed, "it's probably a duck."

Thank God, she thought. Jervis, Aunt Rose, Maman, Toutant—all had pooh-poohed her claim. Leblanc was the first person to take her seriously.

"I talked to Chief Archer," Leblanc added. "And just between me and you, Stella, I don't have much confidence in the man."

More weight seemed to lift from her shoulders.

"I don't mean to imply that I think he's covering anything up," Leblanc clarified. "Frankly, I think he's just a classic example of your small-town sexist. He doesn't take your claims seriously because you're a woman."

Certainly, she believed that too. But some internal alarm sounded. There was an oily smoothness to Leblanc's manner now. Almost as if he knew she wanted to hear something like that, that he knew to cater to her Ph.D. in women's studies.

"So we're going to circumvent Archer completely," Leblanc assured her. "I've spoken with a friend who's with the Special Investigations Division of the Louisiana State Troopers. He's promised to look into the matter for us."

Us. He seemed to hit that word with special, reassuring emphasis, she thought. Or was she, as Rose insisted, just being hypercritical?

"Well, thank you, Senator," she finally replied.

"No, thank *you,* Stella. Too many people today don't want to get involved. We can't win the war on drugs without soldiers willing to fight in the trenches."

Oh, my God, she thought, he's up on the stump now.

"Don't hesitate to call me again," Leblanc added, "if there's any more trouble."

After she hung up, she sat at her desk for a minute, frowning thoughtfully, doodling in the margins of her notes.

What is your problem? she demanded of herself. The man seemed genuinely forthcoming and concerned. Look how quickly he responded. And he promised an investigation into this.

So why, she wondered, did she have this feeling? This uneasy feeling that she had just been handed a phony bill of goods?

Stella descended a curving staircase with a natural sea-grass runner. Downstairs, spun-gold sunlight shimmered off a long dining-room table of polished mahogany set with fine Old Paris china. The wall behind the table featured a varnished eighteenth-century oil painting of an English gentlewoman.

She could hear the monotonous drone of the TV set in the front parlor. Aunt Rose was stretched out in her favorite wicker chaise. Maman occupied a nearby Boston rocker. Both women were sipping anisette and working at their embroidery, ignoring a yammering game show host on TV.

"Who was that on the phone, dear?" Rose asked her.

"Senator Leblanc."

Stella wandered to one of the French doors and gazed out onto the afternoon. White-gauze clouds drifted across a sky of bottomless blue. Watching them, she reported the gist of her conversation with Leblanc.

"See?" Rose demanded, her tone that of a woman

vindicated. "Didn't I tell you he was a gentleman? Despite your melodramatic delusion, he treated you with deference and respect."

Stella fought down a welling of frustration. Aunt Rose was a gentle spirit from a simpler age; her nature was not equipped for suspicion.

"He was quite charming," she agreed. "And seemed quite concerned. Trouble is, he was also quite vague. I just now realized, for example, that he didn't *name* this state trooper friend of his. Which, of course, means I can't contact him."

"Oh, pouf," Rose said. "You're jabbering nonsense."

Maman watched both of them with an expression of bemused martyrdom as she tied a silk French knot.

"The irresistible force," Maman announced, "done met the unmovable object. Boom!"

Stella had to laugh at the truth of that one. Rose was about to say something else. Abruptly, however, Stella was shocked to hear Leblanc's commanding voice fill the parlor. She whirled from the doors and stared at the TV set.

It was one of the new commercial spots soliciting help for the youngest victims of Hurricane Mitch's devastation in Central America. Leblanc spoke in a voice-over as stark images of destruction filled the screen.

"We here in America," he reminded his audience, "have been truly blessed by God. Unemployment is at its lowest point in three decades. Every week, it seems, our stock markets set new records for profits. Yet, only a few hours from our border, innocent children are suffering terribly. Hurricane Mitch spared us here in Louisiana, the state with the highest number of Honduran-born citizens. But Mitch vented his rage on those least able to absorb it. Won't *you* please send whatever you can to the United Southern Children's Charities?"

"There, Stella." Great-aunt Rose pulled her cotton wrapper tighter around her shoulders. "You could learn something from that man's vitality. Can't you just hear it in his voice? We all live by a flame within us. When that flame goes out, *we* go out."

Maman nodded vigorously. "Speak the truth and shame the devil."

"Oh, you two are putty in his hands," Stella scoffed. " 'Vitality,' my butt. That's just the usual line of politician blather. Of course I'm glad he's doing it, he's raising money for a good cause. But concern for 'the little ones' is also an excellent vote-getter."

"Gracious God, that girl cynical," Maman protested. "Stell, you don't even know the man. How can you tell if the wood is bad just from looking at the paint?"

"Maman, I didn't say Leblanc is evil. It's just—'paint' is all politicians are."

Paint, she thought to herself, also covers things up.

"Cynicism's just ashes," Rose said, nodding as she repeated Maman's charge. "That's what left at the burned-out core once the vital flame goes out."

"Cynicism?' Stella retorted. "Just because I don't confuse dung with strawberries? Mattie says *all* governments are run by liars, or else they can't govern."

"Stella's friend Mattie," Rose told Maman, sniffing, "is a big part of her problem. For someone who collects so many men in her bed, Mattie certainly has a low opinion of the masculine sex. But then, what can one expect from a girl raised in New Orleans?"

"That's it," Maman agreed. "Mean ol' city. I won't go there no more 'n I have to."

For a moment Stella was tempted to chide her aunt's hypocrisy. Only four days earlier, Rose had urged her to "intrigue" in New Orleans. Then she noticed that Rose had her slender rattan walking stick beside her today. She used it more and more lately. Stella felt her throat tighten with affection.

Instead of retorting, she laughed in surrender. She crossed the room and stood behind Rose, gently massaging her bony shoulders.

"Mattie does go through men, doesn't she?" she admitted. "She *is* scandalous. But she's not quite the Whore of Babylon, dear. And she does not hate men. She simply doesn't have any illusions whatsoever about them."

"Well, she *should,*" Rose insisted, her tone brooking no defiance. "We all need some illusions. We aren't truly made strong without them."

Stella wanted to tell her how much she agreed with her on that point, but she refrained, remembering the other night when she'd caught Aunt Rose "wandering." The elderly woman was beginning to do it more and more. Stella had thought Rose was asleep in her bed, and then came the crash of an old Newcomb pottery vase. She'd run into the hall and found Rose whimpering about the imperative need to find Myrtle. Stella was helpless to assist her as to Myrtle's whereabouts. Of all of Rose's friends, Stella had never heard of her.

So she'd put her aged aunt back into her bed. The next morning Rose hadn't seemed to recall the incident, and Stella hadn't the heart to tell her about it. There was no need to inform Rose that she was getting old.

We all need some illusions. We aren't truly made strong without them.

Now Maman stopped rocking to look at her friend. Her coffee-colored eyes sparkled for a moment with admiration.

Stella leaned forward and kissed her aunt's stiff-sprayed white hair. "Actually, dear girl, I've told Mattie pretty much the same thing myself."

"Of course you have. That's because you're a St. Vallier. Despite your jaded exterior, romance is in your blood."

"So true," Maman agreed.

Stella recalled the star sapphire pendant her parents gave to her. Indeed, the romantic streak was cast deep down in her bloodline, handed through the generations like a physical trait. *Let this be your lucky star.* That was what she needed too. A lucky star to bring her Mr. Right. So the romantic St. Vallier line could continue unbroken into the next generation.

"Let's only hope in my case the romance is not a recessive gene," she said ruefully.

"The man for you is coming to you soon," Rose assured her. "Myrtle said so just last night. Why, she ran into my room just bursting with the news. And she made my heart glad."

Stella looked at Maman to see if she knew about Myrtle and the midnight wanderings. Maman gave Stella a warning look that said "Don't go there," so Stella closed her mouth.

We all need some illusions. We aren't truly made strong without them.

Stella watched her great-aunt contentedly go back to her embroidery hoop. She wondered what illusions she herself owned that kept her strong. She thought of the all-dressed-up lady. But then she wondered if illusions weren't the heart of the trouble.

CHAPTER

7

"Miss St. Vallier," Garrett Shaw said in a voice just above a whisper. "I'm duly impressed. No wonder you stamp your little foot and pout like Miss Scarlett herself."

He studied the green-glowing letters on the video display terminal. It was midmorning, and he occupied a computer carrel on the second floor of the Lafourche Parish Library. He had the place pretty much to himself except for an elderly gent using the microfilm reader across the wide aisle from him.

Scrolling quickly through the document, a parish history compiled in 1985 by a Cane Town high school history teacher, he was struck by how many times the name St. Vallier was mentioned. Stella de St. Vallier had been a kid when the piece was compiled, maybe just beginning high school. But the author deferred to her as "the most direct living descendant of the first planter family in Louisiana's sugar cane country." She had blue blood in her veins and plenty of it.

So what, he wondered all over again, is her dicker with a shit-heel like Toutant?

His gray eyes lost their focus as he again tried to figure the odd nexus. It had occurred to him, during his drive to New Orleans on Tuesday, that the woman might be the key to putting handles on Toutant. She was certainly pissed at P.G., that much was clear. And it was highly unlikely to be a relationship matter—women like her didn't mix with men like Toutant, not by choice anyway.

So maybe she had a legal gripe with him. Something he could use to leverage Toutant. With the right tiny bit of information, all of Garrett's work could prove golden. The merest incident could play out to produce the Holy Grail.

But without the right piece of the jigsaw puzzle, all of Shaw's plans for exposing the Louisiana Ring were mere brain vapors. He'd learned the hard way the toughest lesson about trying to bust crooked politicians: Indictments far outstripped convictions. Not just because most political types were lawyers wrapped in more lawyers. What made these rings so hard to expose was the fact that they, just like the Mafia, had their code of *omerta*, the mandatory vow of silence.

In fact, the high collective educational and income levels of these men meant nothing. They closed ranks like the toughest street gang in East Los Angeles: Like it or not, you were in for life. New Orleans city councilman Albert Fontainbleau found that out the hard way. He had the misfortune of becoming the target of a casino gambling kickback indictment—the evidence including a clear video of Fontainbleau accepting a cash payment. At the first hint that he might cooperate with federal prosecutors, he made a fatal mistake: He violated the unwritten law.

Then someone close to him—a member of his well-educated and well-heeled circle—had ordered his body put in a cane cutter.

Again Garrett scrolled through the historical database, gleaning a few facts about Shadow Oaks. The St. Vallier plantation house was the oldest continuously occupied family dwelling in Lafourche Parish. But his mind again soon wandered to his latest trip to New Orleans—a "fishing trip," as he called them, though this time he'd caught damn little.

Relying on contacts in the NOPD and FBI, he had thoroughly checked out Barry Woodyard. That was a logical move since he obviously must have something to contribute. Otherwise Leblanc would have no use for the bastard. But Garrett had found nothing one wouldn't find with most pols—just the usual arrangements with the parasites and slugs that cling to the power players in the spoils system of southern politics.

So how, precisely, did Woodyard's little piece fit into the Ring? He wasn't sure yet. But Barry had an older brother who worked in the customhouse for the Port Authority of New Orleans. Garrett had already called Steve Falcone with instructions to shake the lead a little and see what fell out.

But so far Garrett's subjective instincts far outstripped any evidence to back them up. He enjoyed projecting himself into the minds of the men he investigated. Sometimes it was far more fruitful to understand a man's motivations than to judge his actions—though, of course, no one could indict a motive nor extract a DNA sample from it.

Investigating politicians meant you had to know precisely where to look, and the window of opportunity was only briefly opened. Nonetheless, the hard effort was worth it.

"C'mon, lady with the seducing green eyes," Garrett urged the computer screen. "Help me take out some garbage."

* * *

Reverend Billy Baxter was a local celebrity. The preacher broadcasted his own daily radio show and owned the most successful new-car dealership in South Louisiana. He mixed football scores with homey snippets of religious inspiration, making his the number-one radio program in the sugar cane parishes.

"Prayer!" bellowed the voice of this energetic, charismatic preacher. "It's been called the air mail stamp on *your* love letter to Jesus!"

Stella groaned at that one as she switched off the car radio. She wheeled into the cracked-asphalt parking lot of the parish library and parked on the narrowing apron of shade beside the two-story redbrick structure. She had a lot of work to do. Before she wrote her query to Professor Perkins at LSU, she needed to do some additional research. Her particular interest was in recent reports that "bacterial superbugs" were threatening the nation's meat supply, the result of powerful new fertilizers used to grow corn. That corn, in turn, was made into cattle feed. Not just the ground cornmeal itself but much of the plant, too, was prepared as animal food. And evidently, it was the plant itself that harbored most of the dangerous bacteria.

Stella wanted Perkins to realize she was not only motivated to pursue her idea but also informed. She had honed it a bit since mentioning to Autry her idea about finding new markets for bagasse, the waste left behind after sugar cane was pressed dry.

Around front, the late morning sun had begun to heat up the library's flagstone walk. Insects hummed around the azalea hedges and a clump of sweet olive released a heavy perfume. She was about to tug open the glass front door, when a vehicle horn tooted behind her.

She glanced back over her shoulder. A black-and-white prowl car sat waiting for the traffic light at Jackson Boulevard and Second Street. Jervis Archer flashed his disjointed smile at her as he touched his Smokey Bear hat in greeting.

Creep, she said in her mind, you'd better spend a lot on indulgences for your soul.

She realized he was going out of his way to be civil, but she decided to ignore his greeting. There was no point in befriending a rabid dog. She started to turn back toward the door. Then the cop riding with him leaned forward to see around Jervis, and she had a shock of recognition tingle down her nape.

The man checked her out with a gimlet-eyed, bovine gaze that hinted at generations of inbreeding. His nose was humped in the middle from an old break.

She recognized him now in his familiar uniform: Harley Burke, Archer's chief deputy. His eyes met hers, and she felt her heart constrict with fear. Burke was also the pilot who flew that Piper Cub last Saturday. The man who tossed the drugs to Toutant.

She shut her eyes for a brief second, desperate to remain calm.

Don't panic, that's the main thing, she ordered herself. For God's sake, don't let him know that *you* know.

Until that moment, a humid lassitude seemed to hang over the hot and lazy day. Now, however, danger charged the air with a weight and texture she swore she could feel on her skin.

Trying to move at normal speed, she turned away from the car and entered the library. Once inside, she struggled to impose immediate order on her confused thoughts. She recalled Leblanc's phone call yesterday— how he made a point of saying Archer was an incompetent sexist, yes, but not a criminal. But Jervis and Harley Burke had been good buddies since grade school. So how likely was it that the chief of police knew nothing of his deputy's illegal activities?

Not very, was the only answer.

But then—was Leblanc covering for Archer or genuinely fooled by him?

Numb and moving on autopilot, Stella ascended the steps toward the computer room on the second floor. The room was nearly deserted, and she was thankful for that fact. She needed a place to think.

She turned at the first row of partitioned carrels and practically collided with a man seated in front of a VDT.

"I'm so sorry!"

She fell silent, stunned to be looking into the frosty gray eyes of the bouncer from The Scarlet Door.

There was no cocky arrogance in the handsome face. None of what Jervis oozed. Just that closed, shuttered expression that proclaimed him a watcher, like a lion in the Serengeti.

He stood up, his body covering the computer screen.

Instinct made her want to be rid of him fast, but space was tight between the wall and the carrel. She either had to awkwardly back away, or squeeze past his large frame.

"Excuse me." She gave him a derisive glance. There was no point in making small talk when she wanted nothing to do with him. Deciding to brave it out and slide past him, she moved forward, then her eye caught a picture of Shadow Oaks on his computer screen.

"What?" she whispered in a confused voice.

Leaning closer, she realized he'd been looking at the old write-up of the St. Vallier history done years before. Now, along with Cane Town, it had its own Web page for those who were interested. When it was placed online, she was told it would be useful to historians and natives eager to trace ancestors. She never dreamed it might be used by criminals trying to further their drug trade.

"Doing research for your boss?" she spat out, her anger rising.

His eyes filled with unease. He looked around as if to see if anyone was in the computer room. If there had been another researcher there, the person was gone. They were alone, and he seemed disturbingly relieved by that fact.

"I've got my own curiosity. It's a free country." He stared at her, waiting.

She almost snorted. "What? Are you doing your Ph.D. on eighteenth-century privateer economics? You mean you're just working The Scarlet Door to make a few bucks until Wharton accepts you?" She scowled. "Why did Toutant ask you to look up Shadow Oaks?"

"Look, I was bored. There's not much to do in this one-dog town, so I decided to surf. This is all just coincidence," he offered.

"I don't believe in coincidence." She locked gazes with him.

The two lines that framed his mouth deepened. "Coincidence happens."

She nodded to the computer screen. "Coincidence doesn't happen to me. I'm a St. Vallier, remember?"

He studied her. Beneath his scrutiny she wondered if he could see into her very soul. "You've riled a lot of people, Stella de St. Vallier. . . ."

His voice was low and reassuring, yet the use of her full name sent an icicle down her back. He'd not only looked her up and read the piece on her family, he'd paid attention too.

"Maybe I should rile a few more—maybe ask my new friends at the DEA to do a little research on you and Toutant like you were instructed to do on me." She looked at him with glittering eyes.

He seemed to choose his words carefully. "You don't know all that's going on around you, girl. The eye of the hurricane is always peaceful."

Her fear expanded. "Then, tell me what is going on around me," she demanded.

He punched a couple of keys on the computer and cleared the screen. "I know you don't like taking my advice, but first off, I'd hate to see you do any more muckraking. Talking to P.G., for example, would only make matters worse."

"Can they get worse than they are?"

The honesty in his eyes shocked her. He didn't even have to affirm her question.

"What am I supposed to do? Do nothing? Look the other way while you guys turn my land into a drug crossroads? Hope the feds don't take everything my family's worked for for almost three hundred years?"

"There's more at stake here than property," he growled.

"Then, what's at stake?" She stared at him in silence as thick as bayou mud.

Your life. She could see the words on his lips, aching to be said, but they would shatter the quiet. It was clearly more than he could say.

She suddenly realized her head was pounding. Between her fear of Jervis and her worries about Toutant, she felt that a vise was tightening on her brain.

"Stella, if you wait, things might work out."

She was surprised by the gentleness in his words. They were enigmatic but reassuring.

But she didn't possess the luxury of believing them. She was terrified; every paranoid worry seemed to be coming true. And yet, there was nowhere to turn because she couldn't go to the feds with any more evidence until she had some, and by then it might be too late.

She studied him. When she'd first surprised him, she felt it was she who had the upper hand. Somehow, as it had back at The Scarlet Door, the power balance had shifted in his favor.

His eyes fixated on her face. She could almost feel his stare like a caress across her cheek. Without another word she decided it was time to beat a hasty retreat. She tried to step around him, but he easily blocked her path.

"I'm sure your bulldozer methods work at The Scarlet Door," she said, trying to keep her voice down as the Quiet signs requested. "But you can't intimidate me. Feel free to tell your boss the same."

The corner of his handsome mouth twisted in an ironic grin. "By the way, my name's Garrett," he said, moving only when she did, blocking her each time. "Garrett Shaw."

"Pardon me if I don't shake hands with Toutant's Stepin Fetchit." She tried to move past him.

Again he blocked her exit. "Whatever wild hare of an idea you have, I seriously recommend you get over it."

Again she tried to duck around him. "As I said, you can't intimidate me."

"I don't want to see anything bad happen to you."

"Tell me," she tossed at him as she finally backed away. She just wanted to get the hell out of there. "How do you fit into the plan? Do you sell the drugs at the local elementary schools?"

"Be careful, beautiful girl," he whispered, his eyes gleaming with an unnamed fear.

But she was already on the steps, putting the danger behind her.

CHAPTER

8

The story of that past, Lorena, alas, I care not to repeat;
The hopes that could not last, Lorena,
They lived, but only lived to cheat.
      —"Lorena," CONFEDERATE SONG BY
      REVEREND H.D.L. WEBSTER

"Have I ever *not* loved a weekend at Shadow Oaks, Stella? I'm just saying, you know, that your great-aunt Rose will not be a happy camper. The moment I show up, she acts like there's a sewer leaking somewhere."

"Oh, so what? It's a big house," Stella assured Martha "Mattie" Everett over the phone. "We can easily avoid her for a couple days. She's the one who's got the ax to grind. You're always nice to her."

"Hey, at least Rose has a good excuse—she's old. What about these educated butt-clenchers at the university?" Mattie released a long sigh. "But, hey, what do you mean, you need my help?" she pressed. "Doing what? Or is it whom?"

Stella laughed. A conversation with Mattie always had its tonic effect.

"But seriously, base lechery makes us digress," Mattie chided her. "So, c'mon, tell me. What's this favor you want from me?"

"Oh . . . I guess I want you to help me. I don't know. Time-travel a little, I guess. Your specialty."

"Stella. You always do this."

"Do what?"

"Tiptoe all around the edges of whatever's on your mind. Honest to God, it's like solving a Chinese puzzzle to get a straight answer out of you, your mind is so convoluted."

"Grad school ruined you. Absolutely ruined you. You're way too analytical now. Can't I just be devious?"

"Okay. You're devious. Devious as hell."

"That's better. I promise to enlighten you this weekend," Stella assured her.

"It's about the St. Vallier treasure, isn't it? You've been reading Colette's diary again, haven't you?"

"Who paid you to find out?"

"I knew it. You just want to pick my considerable brain again about that damned treasure."

Stella released a wry smile. "I sure wish things were as simple as finding lost treasure, but, unfortunately, there's more going on here than just that. So drive carefully," she said, her tone becoming distant and edged with trouble.

She hung up the receiver and looked down at the leather-bound diary in her hand. Colette's diary. She'd read it a hundred times. Whenever she needed strength, she looked to the familiar words for courage. After the tense conversation with Garrett Shaw at the library, she needed courage enough for ten.

For a long while she stood in the silent hallway, scanning the first entry in neat, mellifluous handwriting. It was dated June 1, 1865—the very first entry the young widow made after the great War of Northern Aggression finally ended.

*God did indeed help Beowulf slay Grendel. But
only after Beowulf stood up on his own two feet.*

Closing the volume, she again felt a fierce pride and
respect for the strong, clear-minded woman whose vo-
cabulary possessed no word for the notion of surrender. What her ancestors had done, she vowed anew,
their living descendant could also do.

It was past five P.M., and Rose was napping in her
room in the west wing. Maman always did the grocery
shopping on Thursday, so Stella had the house to herself. Still carrying Colette's diary, she stepped through
the huge double oak-paneled doors to the east of the
center hallway and entered the ballroom.

It hadn't been used in years. It was an enormous
room that took the entire east wing of the upper story.
It was made for celebration, but none of that had visited
Shadow Oaks in years.

She walked farther into the room. Varied-width cypress floorboards were still varnished to a military gloss.
Along the back wall, a faded tapestry of Prussian red
emblazoned the ancient St. Vallier coat of arms.

The huge, high-ceilinged room made her feel insignificant and vulnerable. Shirred white silk screened
each window, with red-and-cream silk draperies framing
the windows themselves. The silk had "shattered" with
age. Now it hung on the heavy gilt drapery poles in
ghostly shreds. Unsalvageable. Like so much of the
past.

The hall hadn't really been used, she reminded herself with a stab of guilt, since her college graduation
party.

But just then it wasn't the hall she had on her mind.
Again her eyes fell to Colette's beautiful longhand.

*Today I swept out the spider leavings and gave
Jules's secret room a most thorough search.*

She stopped at the tapestry. Behind it was a row of Santo Domingo mahogany panels. A habit she picked up as a little girl whenever she wanted to hide away made her check behind herself to see if the coast was clear. Then she placed her palm on the edge of one panel and braced herself to give it a hard push.

Despite the age of the inner mechanism, a well-greased pulley-and-weight device responded almost silently, rotating a turntable-mounted panel halfway open.

She stepped through after making sure to close the panel behind her.

The tiny, windowless room had never been electrified. She fumbled for the candle and matches, but soon firelight flickered along the old walls that had never known any other kind.

The room had been designed for work as well as seclusion and security. Its furnishings reflected a utilitarian need, nothing more. An early Louisiana armoire stood along one wall, a piece that could have been easily mistaken for country French except that it was made of cypress, not walnut. A bed pressed against the other wall, barely large enough for two. Across the top lay the ornate crewel-work coverlet that had been given to Genevieve upon her marriage to the pirate.

The presence of Jules could still be felt everywhere.

The room was part of the original house that Jules de St. Vallier had built in the eighteenth century. Like many French settlers of his kind, he'd relied on the old methods. A medieval wall construction of bricks between timbers—or, as it was still known in Louisiana, *briquettes entre poteaux*—was how he'd built the smaller West Indian–style plantation house. In the secret room where the plaster cracked and crumbled, the original bricks could be seen sagging, wedged and stacked between enormous cypress beams.

She lowered herself to the only seat, a tufted gentleman's armchair from the Victorian rococo-revival period. The piece was New Orleans made, as evidenced from the Spanish-moss stuffing that peeked out from the frayed horsehair upholstery; it had probably been dragged into the secret room in the 1850s and never left.

Family legend held that Jules slept in his hidden room with his treasure. Clever architecture kept the room hidden. It was the matching cabinet room at the opposite end of the loggia, the one that held no door and possessed no window. All and sundry thought the cabinet room made up the paneled end of the ballroom. But they were wrong. Jules had secreted the room into his very house so that the "privateer" didn't have to constantly sleep with one eye open.

Or so went family lore.

Mattie, one of the few Louisiana historians who knew the room wasn't just pub talk, didn't believe there was a St. Vallier treasure. Not anymore anyway. According to her research, there was a rumor at the time that some valuable Old World jewels were secretly sent to Jules late in the eighteenth century. Mattie believed that Jules returned them after a handsome ransom was paid—in legal tender he quickly spent and invested.

Maybe Mattie was right. And maybe, Stella admitted to herself, the St. Vallier treasure had simply become a siren's song to sap good sense. A foolish dream of a miracle panacea.

She closed her eyes. More than any other room at Shadow Oaks, this one always transported her to the past. As if painted on her mind's eye, she could see her female ancestors in their chemises and lace-trimmed corset covers, their velvet cloaks and fancy carriage dresses. In the timeless silence of the secret room, she could almost hear a fiddle playing, hear voices shouting the lively rhythms of "Old Dan Tucker" and "Jim Crack Corn." Hear, too, the slower, sadder, tearful strains of a harsh voice singing "Lorena," the Civil War ballad blamed for ten thousand Rebel desertions.

She opened her eyes and Colette's diary.

> *I have been contacted by a fine and educated gentleman at the Sorbonne. He assures me that certain letters, once rumored to be in Genevieve's possession, would be worth a fortune in their own right. However, their evil contents might also compromise our family's honor. I'm not sure, just yet, what I would do if I should find such letters. I searched the old armoire thoroughly, but to no avail.*

What letters? Stella had always wondered. There was, of course, a local folk legend that Genevieve was at one time a minor mistress of Louis XV before Jules spotted her and spirited her away to the bayou. Louis's prodigious sexual appetites were renowned.

So, was Colette afraid of the overt and detailed sexual content of the letters, in which, perhaps, a St. Vallier was taking part? Or was she referring to a criminal evil? Something that could rewrite history and yet, in turn, sully the St. Vallier name forever?

Mattie was right—such rumors surrounded many beautiful and wealthy women of that day. The jewels and hidden wealth was probably no more tangible than the shadows of the famed plantation.

Discouraged, she found comfort in actually touching the family possessions that Colette and others had searched before her. Her palm lovingly stroked the detailed needlework of the crewel coverlet; her fingers flitted along the edge of the heavy gold candlestick.

Again her eyes cut to Colette's words.

> *When I write about Genevieve in my diary, I must avoid certain details. For words can claim a terrible authority with Time. They can focus the mind on shadows where, in truth, once was all light.*

Look to the lovers of the past, Rose kept telling her. And it was true the past offered tantalizing clues. But the past was also frustratingly mute. In the workaday world, she had no use for all the memories in this old room, stored like potpourri in a covered jar.

She hugged her knees, recalling something else Rose had told her. How the answers are usually with us all along, just overlooked. She stared hard at everything, trying to see the tiny room with fresh, curious eyes. The key to the treasure *is* the treasure—she may have been looking at the key all her life without realizing it.

Despite her determination, however, it was hard to discipline her thoughts. She stood up and crossed to the wrap-around fireplace mantel. Carefully, she picked up a pretty little witch's ball. The lustrous glass globe was coated with mercury on the inside, so it reflected the room in curving miniature. They had been all the rage late last century, no doubt deposited there by a St. Vallier child who could never locate it again.

She looked at the room in the ball, hoping by magic its secrets would be revealed. However, the image of the room gave way to a dangerous, arrogant face and penetrating gray eyes.

Garrett Shaw was like the secret room, hidden and unexplained. He embraced the seedy lifestyle just fine, but she got the distinct impression there was more to him somehow. A born loser didn't warn women away from danger, and that was exactly what he'd been doing both times she'd laid eyes on him. But was he warning her of the danger? Or was he the danger? She didn't know.

Out of nowhere, chimes sounded, announcing a visitor at the front door. She waited, hoping whoever it was would give up. But a second ring made her frown in annoyance, fearing Rose would wake up and feel compelled to answer. A third ring made her hurry toward the secret room's only door through the paneling.

"I'm coming, dammit," she muttered.

At the fourth insistent ring, however, her irritation turned into vague apprehension. Either there was some emergency, or she had a very rude visitor.

"Evening, Stella," Chief Jervis Archer greeted her when she opened the front door.

For a moment his rough, handsome face jolted her back to earlier that afternoon. Again she recalled the chilling shock of recognition when she saw Deputy Harley Burke in the police car with Jervis.

"Chief," she replied coldly after an awkward pause. She made no move to open the door wider, which would have invited him inside.

Archer's big, hairy hands lifted up to touch his blue blazer. "As you can see, I'm not in uniform. This is a personal call."

"Oh," she replied, holding the door protectively aslant against him.

Jervis had never been invited inside Shadow Oaks. Despite all his years of asking her out, neither she nor her parents ever made him welcome. There were just some kinds of people you didn't want inside your nest, and he had been one of them. Her relationship with Jervis before now had been forged from equal parts distaste and forbearance. Lately, however, the latter feeling had diminished. All that remained was distaste.

"May I come in?" he finally demanded.

He stood there like unwanted furniture, irritating her with the nuisance of his undeniable presence. But those glittering blue eyes of his also conveyed a wordless threat. She felt the hair on her arms stiffen.

"I was just going to take a walk to see Autry," she finally replied. "I've been cooped up inside for too long."

She stepped outside and shut the door behind her, outmaneuvering him. Crossing the wide veranda, she descended the front steps without waiting for him. The officer hurried to catch her.

"I stopped by earlier," he explained when they were on the crushed-shell walk that led around the front corner of the house. "Your colored girl told me you'd be home about this time."

"That 'girl,' " Stella retorted, "is seventy-seven years old. And the word 'colored' was buried with Jim Crow, Chief. Maman doesn't come with the plantation here. We're lucky to have her help."

"That's damn straight," Jervis agreed. "Old Maman's from good people, and she's the best cook in this parish. No offense, Stella. I got no beef with the color— with black people. I had a damn good black deputy once."

Yeah, and I'll bet he quit because he was honest, came her acid thought.

By then they had stepped through the rose-covered trellis that led into the big rear garden. She could see the two wooden cisterns behind the garden that had once supplied drinking water before the well was dug.

She took a deep breath to steel her nerves. Earlier, she had pretended not to recognize Burke. But she had debated things since then and decided nothing encouraged evil like silence. She would tread carefully, yes, because there was real danger here. Garrett Shaw was no kindergartener. But the silence needed to be exorcised with words.

"Speaking of your deputies," she began to say.

"Yeah?"

That single word hung between them like a dare. Suddenly, she found she was looking at the face of a wooden Indian.

"I recognized Harley Burke today," she informed him.

"Whatcha mean, recognized? He's lived here all his life."

"I mean he's the one I saw with Toutant last Saturday. Burke was the pilot."

Archer started to flash his off-kilter smile. But realizing the seriousness in her face, he quickly abandoned the effort.

"This was meant to be a personal call," he objected.

She was determined not to lose control of her temper. Only the blink of her eyes revealed her anger.

"Personal? What, I'm supposed to ignore the fact that your deputy is a drug runner because you're not in the mood to work?"

Her bluntness cracked his veneer of civility. She watched his jaw tighten.

"Nothing ruins truth like stretching it," he informed her in his flat voice. "Sure, Harley's got him a small-plane license. He's a search-and-rescue pilot, if that's okay with you? He's got nothing to do with drug running."

Despite her resolve, the angry words spurted forth before she could check them. "Look, I know you're either covering up for or ignoring these guys, but I'm not going to. I can't give you orders concerning your official capacity as chief of police. But if this is a personal visit, speaking *personally*, I can tell you you're no longer welcome at Shadow Oaks."

She stopped on the crushed-limestone walk and gave him a long, contemptful stare. She then waited, sure he wouldn't continue on with her and take his fight with Autry too. But Jervis stopped with a viselike grip on her wrist.

"Never mind this drug shit and your haughty-bitch act, Stella," he goaded her, his excited breath audible in his nostrils. "You're such a *good* girl, hanh? I'll bet you always sleep with your hands outside the blankets, hanh? Just to resist temptation?"

"Let me *go*." But she felt fear spiking her belly. Archer's face was now a mask of pure hatred. And the strength in him—she felt like she was caught in a steel trap.

"Too good for me in high school, and now, when you haven't got a penny to your name, you're still holding your nose." He got in her face. "Well, I got news for you, Stella *de* St. Vallier, you're looking at a whole new man here. Someday you're not going to be too fine for the likes of me, and I'll be seeing you beg for some of what I got."

"So what have you got, Jervis? What are your assets? I bet one of them's a big fat bank account in the Caymans." She knew it was unwise to taunt him, but she wanted him gone. Now.

A small iron statue of St. Jude stood beside the path. Archer pressed closer to her, pinning her against the statue. His rough breathing frightened her. He forced himself against her harder, so she'd be sure to feel his erection.

"I'll show you what assets I got. Stella, tell me straight, hanh? Everybody knows you ain't gettin' any. Young woman like you has got to have needs. Don't you ever wish it was a man inside you and not some damn batt'ry appliance?"

She gave him a cold-eyed stare that would have frozen Satan. "I'd rather have anything than you, you filthy bastard. You're *hurting* me."

"Yeah, I am. And the question is, do you like the pain, Stella? Hanh? Does it hurt real good? That what gets you wet, Stella? When it's hard and hurting, hanh?"

She was truly frightened. Jervis Archer was a dyed-in-the-wool sociopath and probably had been since he was a boy. By his behavior now, she'd bet all the rumors about him were true even though he'd denied them all.

Last year the corpse of a young woman had been found, headless and her hands cut off, her body floating down the bayou. Some said she was a former dancer at The Scarlet Door who they'd assumed had just taken off for the big city. The girl had been buried in Cane Town Cemetery, the plaque on her vault said only Unknown and the date when she was found. Without hands there were no fingerprints. Without fingerprints there was no looking up the girl who, judging by the nature of her tattoos, probably had several former arrests.

It was very easy to believe Jervis had picked up the

girl one night, used her, then disposed of her. And Stella had to keep that in mind when she dealt with him. His life was beyond the law in Cane Town. He was stupid and excessively powerful. He would make the worst kind of foe.

With sense finally overcoming the instinct for fight, she pleaded with him. "Please, Jervis. Let me go. Autry's going to come looking for me. You don't need to get into it with him. Just leave."

"That's better," he patronized her, though he still hung on. "It's nice to hear a lady say please."

He rocked from his heels to his toes, playing the cop now instead of the red-hot stud.

"You oughtn't've pursued the drug thing so far," he informed her. "You're just going to cause a lot of trouble, and it's going to get you nowhere. You mark my words, Stella. The day is coming, you'll beg for my help. But don't make it too late. Just make sure you don't make it too late."

Right at the split second she feared her legs would buckle under her, he let her go.

Without waiting for an explanation, apologies, or more crude warnings, she took a fleeing-doe glance at him, then ran to Autry and the sugarhouse, her tail up.

CHAPTER
2

They can focus the mind on shadows where, in truth, once was all light.
—COLETTE DE ST. VALLIER

Garrett Shaw pushed the alley door open with one foot and wrestled a mop bucket out through the employees only entrance. He checked his watch as the door swung shut behind him: almost five P.M.

His arm and shoulder muscles bunched tightly, like steel cables, when he picked up the full bucket and started to slosh filthy gray water out into the tall weeds behind The Scarlet Door. But after quick glances up and down the alley, he set the bucket down and pulled a small plastic disk the size of a silver dollar from the front pocket of his jeans.

Two vehicles were parked nearby. Toutant's Jeep Cherokee hugged the back of the building in order to leave the alley clear to traffic. But a black-and-white Cane Town police cruiser blocked the alley—Chief Jervis Archer's favorite illegal parking spot. Archer made a point of always parking the prowl car so he'd inconvenience someone.

By then Garrett had staked out the club and figured out the regular Friday-night routine for Toutant and Archer. The club would close at two A.M. At two forty-five one of Archer's deputies would drop off the chief, in civilian clothes, at the club. Then he and Toutant would leave in Toutant's vehicle. Wherever they went, they always made it back to the club before dawn.

Garrett took one last look in all directions while he moved behind Toutant's Jeep and dropped onto one knee. He peeled a protective paper backing off the adhesive side of the disk, thus automatically activating the Pulse-Air direction-and-distance indicator. Reaching under the vehicle, he felt around for a clean surface, then he pressed the adhesive to a spot onto the gas tank.

He still had part of his arm under the vehicle when the alley door thumped open.

Like a cat he moved, backing away from the Cherokee before Jervis Archer spotted him. But Garrett's mop bucket sat yards away, accusing him of something besides cleaning.

"You hiding back here?" Archer demanded as if he paid the salaries around there.

"Just swabbing out the bar, Chief. It's Dabs's job, but half the time he's too damn lazy to do it."

While he said this, he crossed to the bucket and finished emptying it. A little comber of filthy water swamped over Archer's shiny black uniform shoes.

The chief flinched violently. "Watch what the hell you're doing, asshole!"

"Hey. Sorry."

Jervis stared at him, his mouth set hard like a trap. "Yeah, I see how sorry you look, smartass. You know something, Cowboy? I don't much like your face."

"That works out real nice, then," Garrett pointed out amiably as he began filling the bucket with clean water from an outside spigot. "Seeing how it's not for sale."

Archer was no man to brook defiance, not even the

humorous kind. For a few angry moments a vein in his temple stood out like a fat blue worm.

"Everybody's a funny guy," the chief finally said as he opened the door of his cruiser. "Buncha stand-up comics. Good job for mouthy females."

"You shouldn't park in a delivery alley like this, Chief," Garrett lectured like an offended citizen just before he pushed his bucket of clean water inside the building. "You might block a workingman."

Inside, only the night's first few customers had drifted in. The dancers wouldn't start their pathetic gyrations for a couple more hours. A New Orleans deejay's voice yammered maniacally from the wall speakers, hyping a has-been rocker who would be riding on a Mardi Gras float for the Krewe of Isis.

"'Preciate you doing that," Dabs said when Garrett started sopping up the soapy water behind the bar. The bartender moved around to one of the stools to get out of the way. "I gotta baby this goddamned hernia of mine."

"This keeps me busy till the hell raisers arrive," Garrett assured him. "Where's P.G.?" he added casually.

"Office," Dabs replied. "Feeding his face. You shoulda heard that bullshitter Archer when he was in here. Dropping all kindsa hints how he's trimming that St. Vallier babe. You believe that?"

"Archer?" Garrett snorted, never missing a swab with the mop. "Yeah, right. And I'm doing Madonna."

"I sure wish hot little Stella would come in here again," Dabs announced. His fat, cartoon-character face looked wistful. "If I'm lyin', I'm dyin', Cap. She'd give a *dead* man a woody."

"She's right out of the silk drawer, all right," Garrett agreed as he tossed down the slatted "duckboards" that covered the floor behind the bar.

"You should look into that stuff, Cowboy," Dabs

urged him. "See, I can tell just by the way a woman walks if she's gettin' it steady. That babe ain't been laid since Christ was a corporal."

Garrett's eyes flicked to the office door behind the bar. He needed to see Toutant for a moment, but the bartender's talk had distracted his attention. He bit his lower lip to keep from laughing outright.

"By the way they walk, huh? Sounds like you know women."

Dabs shrugged. "What's to know? A woman's value, if you think about it a minute, is what's between her legs, not a damn thing more. A hole. A frickin' void. The big zero. Nothing. See, that's why they all act like men. Men with a big set on them. Them feminists won't admit it. But a dick is a helluva lot better than nothing, am I right?"

"I'm fond of mine," Garrett agreed, laughing outright. "Christ, Dabs. You put Plato in the shade. Excuse me, big guy."

Garrett rapped three times on the door.

"Yeah?" Toutant's voice called out.

Garrett opened the door. His boss sat at the battered kneehole desk, finishing up one of The Scarlet Door's $6.95 Roughneck Specials. In a state world famous for its cuisine, Toutant ate the same meal every night: beefsteak with onions and french fries, followed by a glass of water and two Alka-Seltzers.

"Cowboy. What's the poop?" Toutant greeted him.

"Place is dead, boss man. I need to wrap my teeth around some decent chow, no offense to your cook. Okay if I walk over to Lafitte's for some gumbo?"

Toutant wiped his mouth on a paper napkin, then pushed his plate away. He nodded as he began counting out the start-up cash for the register.

"Sure. Take your time, Cowboy. It's always quiet around here until eight or nine."

Garrett did walk the two blocks to Lafitte's Café. But he ordered only coffee and pie at the counter before moving to a pay phone beside the cigarette machine in the side hallway.

It was well past six Washington time. Garrett tried Steve Falcone's home phone and got him in two rings.

"This is the meat that feeds the tiger," Shaw greeted his partner.

"Garrett! Glad you called, *paisano*. Line clear?"

"Yeah. The hell's up?"

"Maybe nothing, I'm hoping. I'm not sure of this, okay? But we may have a troubling little pattern here."

"Look, don't be coy," Shaw urged him, his eyes cutting to the door of the café when a customer walked in. "I'm a big boy, spit it out."

"Somebody might be trying to lift your cover. This parish D.A., what's-his-face—"

"Cliff D'Antoni?" Garrett supplied.

"D'Antoni, yeah, my countryman, hah. We've detected secured e-mail traffic between his office and New Orleans. I mean scrambled, bro. We can't break the encryption with our people."

"So what? Nothing sinister there. Plenty of e-mail is encrypted."

"The traffic's been heaviest on the three days you've visited your NOPD contact. Much heavier."

"Shit. Yeah, that's different. We won't even get a case to pretrial if that source at NOPD is compromised."

"Be easier to strangle a jellyfish," Falcone agreed. "This might be a good time for you to skip town."

"Hell with that. Not yet. We've been looking for something we could use to leverage Toutant, right? If we get that little piranha Toutant talking, then we'll be able to make charges stick on the leviathan—the good Senator Leblanc. Well, I think we've finally got it. Stella St. Vallier has accused me of helping my boss hawk drugs."

"See? Didn't I tell you he'd foul his nest? But, hey— Stella St. Vallier? She the one you tossed out of the skin club?"

"The very babe."

"Well, from what you said about her, she wouldn't know a crack pipe from a cracked pipe."

"True, but naive or not, this woman has definitely got her head screwed on straight. She wouldn't make that kind of charge lightly."

Falcone's voice changed slightly. "Hmm . . . coming from you, my man, that almost sounds like a declaration of infatuation. You got a thang for this belle?"

"She's a bit of a ball breaker, but, hey, I've always liked the difficult type. If I was looking, she'd be on the A list."

Garrett's offhand manner wasn't exactly faked, but there was a problem, and it had been nagging at him since running into Stella St. Vallier at the library. Shaw considered himself a jobber, a cool professional. Once he started working a case, it was not his way to worry unduly about collateral damage to others.

So it irritated him that he felt protective of this proud, stubborn, even reckless woman. She would get him in trouble, he sensed that. She put him in mind of a three-year-old Thoroughbred: plenty of strength and good breeding but still not quite enough sense for her own good. The litter of rats she had stirred up would not hesitate to attack and devour her.

"Listen," Falcone said. "I went over everything we have on United Southern Children's Charities, just like you asked. It's so clean, it squeaks. But there might be a good reason for that. You told me to check out Barry Woodyard's brother at U.S. Customs, get a job description. Turns out Doug Woodyard has a very interesting job."

"All this has a nice beat," Garrett assured him. "Don't stop now."

"He's the big pooh-bah who visually verifies the cargo manifest for every shipment that enters or leaves the port of New Orleans."

"What? You mean he certifies what the ships are carrying? Matches the cargo to the cargo list?"

"The way you say. Unless a ship is seized by the coast guard or port authority, nobody else officially eyeballs the cargo. But 'eyeball' is a stretch—it's packed in big metal containers anyhow, and it's a major hassle to open them for any real inspection. Not enough time, given the port traffic. And get this: Even when they do open cargo containers, the seizures are never random. They're worked out between Customs and the coast guard."

"I'll be damned," Garrett said. "So Doug Woodyard would know in advance what ships are . . . Jesus. That would include any ships hauling freight for his brother's organization?"

"Yep. Handy as a pocket in a shirt, huh."

"You *have* been busy, old son. Nice work."

"I'm just another athlete for Christ," Falcone said with mock humility.

"Doug is our favorite boy now. Keep checking that out. By the way, you said you ran the name Jervis Archer?"

"Archer, Archer, oh, yeah, the chief of police down there in Tooter Town, right?"

"Yeah."

"That's affirmative, *paisano*. I ran his name through NCIC, Interpol, the whole deal. He's got a rap sheet but no big surprises for a redneck cop. Couple domestic-abuse charges from his married days. Why?"

"Suddenly, I see him for the mechanic who fixed Al Fontainbleau. He's got dirt worker written all over him. We're pretty sure Leblanc was the man behind the hit; he may have given the order, but somebody had to actually stuff the guy into that cane cutter. I can see Archer enjoying the job."

"One more reason," Steve reminded him, "why you should terminate your fieldwork. If somebody snitches you out, Archer's got plenty of swamp to dump you in. ATF lost a guy down there three years ago, never even found his dental work."

"Cowards to the rear, wus. Not until we pop Toutant," Garrett insisted. "I think I might nail down his drug operation in the next couple days. Toutant only *appears* to be aloof from the Louisiana Ring. He may not actually attend the secret meetings with Leblanc and the others. But Toutant is definitely a player. He knows far more than they think he knows. I *think* he might even have the meeting room bugged. I can't get in there alone to look around. But once I saw a tape recorder in Toutant's desk up in his front office. Plus, there's a PA system with jacks in the wall. He could easily record the meeting directly off a remote mike."

"From where I sit, he's the keys to the mint," Falcone agreed. "The name of this game is cover your ass. Toutant will spill his guts for the right deal. My kingdom for those tapes, bro, if they exist."

A waitress frowned at Garrett and pointed to the sign beside the phone: THREE MINUTES ONLY, PLEASE.

"Miles to go and promises to keep," he told his partner.

"Luck to you, *paisano*. Christ sakes, be careful down there."

Jervis Archer unlocked the door to his house. The 1970s furniture lurked with a decade of dust upon it. Along a path from the front door to his bedroom, the first on the right, the gold nylon carpet had been worn through to the backing.

He used to use the kitchen. After Mama died, he'd make himself a hamburger every now and then and take a beer from the fridge. But now he ate all his meals in his car and drank his beer at The Scarlet Door.

And he sure as hell didn't use the living room. It was a place to walk through, a place to avoid. His mother's worn recliner still sat in the corner, her *TV Guide* still opened to that day in 1988 when she had her aneurism and dropped dead in church.

All his life he'd referred to his mother as a bitch and a nag. He was never good enough, never loved Jesus enough, never picked the right girl to bring home. But that was not the case. He'd joined the police force just to prove to the bitch that he was good enough.

And he did love Jesus. He'd loved Jesus enough to send Reverend Frailey to him. The good rev had gotten all hot and interested in his mom's salvation after she'd confessed to a mispent youth of topless pinups à la Bettie Page. With Reverend Frailey, Mathilda Archer finally found God. And when God's servant began poking her that first night they thought Jervis was at a football game, it was the son who sent him to Jesus with one good hamlike fist to the jaw.

Reverend didn't change his own lightbulbs, but when one of his parishoners found him the next day, dead at the bottom of a stepladder in the rectory, no one questioned the broken skull. It was just an unfortunate fall on a linoleum-topped concrete floor.

But, Jesus, the bitching sure never ended after that. The rage, the curses, the promises of hell, never left his mother's ugly mouth. But neither did a confession. She never told a soul what had really happened to the Reverend Frailey. Instead, she took to drinking.

She died like she lived, in silence.

Some days Jervis even missed her. When he got the house all to himself, he never changed her rooms. He was always trying to make her happy, and he still was. He was a big cop now. And he loved Jesus. And he was going to bring home the right girl. He was going to get Stella de St. Vallier. His mother would have to hold her tongue then.

He trod along the worn path in the carpet to his room. Hanging up his gun, he stripped naked and got into bed.

The familiar white vinyl was delicious on his back. Even in the peak of the summer, when the window air conditioner was unable to keep up with the heat, he would slide against the vinyl-wrapped mattress in his own sweat and revel in the stink. He could get as skanky as he wanted in his little twin bed, because every month or so he'd just rip off the vinyl sheet—marketed to incontinents—and go get himself another.

Stella was just like the white vinyl sheet. Pure and clean. Untainted. All the stink in the world just slid right off her beautiful skin. She was unlike any woman he'd ever known, because only whores were around him. From his mother to his girlfriends, that's all he knew.

But he had his money rolling in pretty good now. And his aim was to get himself a good, clean white-vinyl wife like Stella de St. Vallier.

He turned to look at her picture by his bedside. Her face was all around him in the room. Her beautiful face, laughing at a football game in high school, her pensive expression caught on film while she walked the grounds of the university, deep in thought.

He was no shirker at surveillance. He could get all the pictures of Stella he wanted without her knowing. He'd even tried to get one of her naked once, but then he stopped himself. The naked part was going to have to wait. When he could touch and take and indulge, then he would see her naked.

Until then, his pictures would have to do.

And the whores he found along the way.

He turned the light out and got hard with the feel of his sticky, slick bed.

Yep, he did anything he wanted on that clean white vinyl, and then everything went to the dump, to stay as silent as the old Reverend Frailey.

CHAPTER

10

"I think Jules and his crew of freebooters probably did steal gems intended for the French monarchy," Mattie assured Stella. "And quite possibly they were hidden at Shadow Oaks for at least a brief time."

"But you don't believe they could still be here now?"

Mattie shook her head.

It was Saturday afternoon, and Mattie had arrived almost two hours before. The two friends had spent much of the time since then walking the grounds while Stella plied the history prof with questions about potential hiding places. The old slave quarters, the granaries and other outbuildings, the sugarhouse, all had been scrutinized from without and within.

Mattie spoke about Shadow Oaks with the deep love and respect of a curator at a museum. And she did it so naturally, straight from the heart, that Stella felt self-conscious about her home and family being "public history." Indeed, Mattie's enthusiasm was not favoritism—

she was equally enthusiastic about countless other aspects of the state's history. Inside the self-deprecating wild woman with the kind eyes lurked a dedicated scholar. Her doctoral thesis on the social history of antebellum New Orleans won three major awards and was published by a leading house. Scholars praised it, browsers embraced it. Mattie belonged to that rare intellectual elite who could simultaneously specialize and popularize.

The two friends finished their search as they always did in the secret room off the rear loggia.

"I know you don't want to hear this again. But the best evidence I can find suggests Jules arranged for a ransom," Mattie said. "There's a vague reference to the supposed incident by a nineteenth-century Spanish historian named Miguel Iberrez. He's hardly infallible, but he's generally reliable."

"So you think Jules returned them to France?"

Mattie nodded. "That would neatly explain why he was suddenly able to double his land holdings at a time when his indigo crop had made him barely solvent. Besides, think about it. Even if I'm wrong, there've been several thorough searches since Jules died. It's incredibly unlikely those gems are still around."

Stella sighed so hard, the wind from it fluffed her own bangs. She focused her attention on the topaz shimmer of brandy in the decanter she held in her hand. It was a rare daytime indulgence spurred by Mattie's urging. They had poured two glasses. Candles in brass holders cast bobbing splotches of shadow on the leather spines of classics lining one wall.

"What about those letters Colette mentioned?" Stella persisted. "Genevieve's supposed love letters from Louis Sixteenth?"

"I don't know any more about them—if they ever existed—than you do, Stella. But if they do exist and you could find them, it would be a piece of cake for document experts to authenticate them. A museum or university would pay a small fortune for them."

Stella released an ironic laugh. "Can't you just see it? We've been looking for jewels all along, and it's the letters that are so damned valuable. I suppose this cinches it; Murphy's Law will prevail. I'll discover the letters were burned long ago as fire starter."

The friends shared the edge of Jules's rope bed. A silence wedged between them after Stella's comment, leaving each woman alone with her own thoughts for a time.

It was Mattie who finally broke the silence.

"This thing with the supposed St. Vallier treasure," she began to expound awkwardly. "I've noticed how you tend to get preoccupied with it when there's a lot on your mind."

"Do I?" Stella said more politely than sincerely. She didn't want to confess all her financial troubles even though it was obvious her friend could see them.

" 'Do I?' Does Raggedy Ann have a patched ass? C'mon, Stella, you know you do. Sometimes we get crushed by the flywheel of our own habits. I get into these obsessive little mind-sets—particularly when I'm stressed. You know . . . if I just do such-and-such, then everything will be fine. You do it too."

Mattie's comment made sense. Still, Stella didn't want to lay the depressing facts out. The academic Mattie was so caught up in Shadow Oaks that to tell her the place might have to be razed by an oil company seemed too crushing.

Despite the flattering candlelight, Stella knew strain probably showed around her eyes and mouth. She had always been the serious and reserved counterpart to Mattie's earthy effusiveness, but even she realized the quiet inside her had turned to grimness. The financial problems of maintaining a historical site, along with the family history, and then coupled with discovering drug runners on the property, was amounting to stress over-load. And her childhood chum was no fool. She could see it.

"The fairest flower in all the fields," Mattie admonished her. "But will she go early to frost?"

"Now you sound just like Rose, you know that? Two poets."

"Don't tell her that, she'll feel insulted." Mattie cracked a grin. "But she's right to get on your case. You look like you're ready to split wide open, Stella, and who in your shoes wouldn't be? God, I can barely handle teaching three history courses a week without ending up in the rubber Ramada. And here you are now running an entire sugar operation."

"Running it into the ground," Stella said bitterly.

"You and Autry are going to do fine. I never thought I'd say this to a woman. But you know what you need?"

"Oh, don't be so dramatic. You give me this advice every time we talk. Dr. Mattie's prescription for all female complaints is a good roll in the hay, right?"

"Well, the hay is optional," Mattie qualified with mock pedantry. "Field tests have shown it can chafe a girl's tender skin."

Despite her despondent mood, Stella smiled at her friend's foolishness.

"While we're on the topic of your stress," Mattie added, "I don't blame you for not wanting to swallow all of Leblanc's bunk. Truth is, your family never got along with his. You know, don't you, that your great-great-great-grandfather, Henry, challenged William Leblanc to a duel?"

Stella shook her head, fascinated. "Colette's husband? No, I didn't know that."

"Yup. It's not a fact recorded in the parish register. But I've come across a dozen personal letters and diaries concerning the people around here that record it. Your ancestor Henry found out William was actually—I mean literally—making his slave children eat from a wooden trough like animals."

Stella paled.

"It sure incensed good old Henry," Mattie assured her. "Rather than face a St. Vallier, William Leblanc caved in and stopped the practice. You know, by the way, that Henry freed his own slaves before he joined the Confederate States Army? He fought for the South and states' rights, not for slavery, and he refused to be a hypocrite even if it cost him his entire fortune."

It fascinated Stella how Mattie knew more about her own family than she did.

"The Leblanc family history is full of corruption," Mattie continued as if getting to the nugget of what truly bothered her. "I wouldn't be all that shocked to learn you did witness some kind of drug deal."

Stella grew pensive. "Do you remember how you once told me that family land eventually takes on the status of a family member?"

Mattie nodded.

"It's not just the drugs," Stella said, "but when they did their thing on my land, they forced my *family* into this. Now the St. Valliers are involved against our will."

"In other words," Mattie added, "it's a family honor thing? There's been a stain upon the family escutcheon? And since it happened on your watch, you must set things right?"

Stella laughed. "It sounds so quaint stated that way, but I guess it's something like that."

"You know what?" Mattie said. "I think you're the real goods, Stella de St. Vallier. I'm proud to know you. But I also think you need to lighten up a little, have some fun. But be careful."

Be careful. The image of Burke's sawed-off shotgun clung in Stella's memory like a burr to wool. Yes, be careful.

"Now let's get to the interesting part. Tell me more

about this big, hunky brute of a cowboy named Garrett. Or is he a Garrett named Cowboy? You've thoroughly confused me."

Stella almost needed to shake her head to clear it. "Tell you what. I don't know anything about the guy. I just told you about how he kicked me out of the club."

"So, was he cute?"

" 'Cute'? 'Cute' is not the operative word here. Sleazy, uneducated, and crude is about what one could expect from a bouncer at that dive." Stella paused. "But I suppose in a way he *is* handsome."

"Ah-*hah*. Tell me about him."

"What's to tell that I didn't already mention? I told you about him in the context of this drug thing—I'm not dating him, for God's sake. And I wouldn't. Jervis Archer has more going for him than that guy." She gave a throaty laugh. "And he's got a better job too. At least Jervis is getting kickbacks. Garrett Shaw rakes in minimum wage, no perks."

"Let's go to The Scarlet Door tonight, do a little slumming. I want to see these characters."

"I'll pass on that offer. But I'm not your mother, you're welcome to check it out. But even you, party girl, will regret it if you do."

"Oh, shit! It's a public club. What's to worry about?" Mattie demanded. "When you went there, were you beaten, robbed, sued for snootiness?"

"Of course not—"

"Anybody even grope you?"

"No, but this one guy said—" Stella fell silent, an unexpected grin tugging at her lips.

"Said what?" Mattie demanded.

"This one guy"—she had to laugh outright before she could finish—"this one guy asked me to draw a happy face on his dick."

Mattie howled. She had to roll back on the bed just to catch her breath. "I'd've done it," she boasted, "if he wasn't too dirty."

Then, raising herself to a sitting position and sobering, she said, "Seriously, let me get a gander on these guys. They sound like they're dealing in some heavy doo-doo. If you think the police here are accepting bribes to look the other way, you may end up going to the feds. Having another person back you up might be helpful."

"I appreciate the offer, Mattie, but I've *gone* to the feds. They told me nothing was happening. Leblanc's shiny clean."

"Hey, The Scarlet Door's the only club in town. There's no law we can't go there for a couple of drinks. C'mon. I want to see these skanks. I've always wanted to meet a man named Cowboy. Besides, there are refineries and such all over this part of the Mississippi. We just might meet some chemists or engineers there in the bar who are just as bored and accomplished as we are. Hey, it could happen!"

Stella gave her a wild-eyed glance. "Women dance naked in this place, Mattie. Naked. Skinny crackhead naked. I don't want to meet my destiny there, thank you, no matter how wonderful he is."

"It's Saturday night," Mattie nudged. "I'll protect you."

"You just want to go out drinking."

"Exactly, but we can kill two birds this way. Have a couple of drinks and dumb conversations with some losers *and* get a summation of who you're dealing with at this club."

"It's a porno club, Mattie."

"But we could play Nancy Drew. Didn't you always want to do that when you were a kid?"

Stella groaned. "I'll be recognized there, and I refuse to be seen twice at that place."

Mattie needled. "Just because you're a blueblood doesn't mean you have to be a snob."

"Just how," Stella demanded, "does my refusal to go back to The Scarlet Door—especially after what happened to me there—prove I'm a snob? If I refuse to eat bat guano, does that make me an anorexic?"

Mattie laughed. "Okay. I won't go that far. But, Stella, there's nothing wrong with seeing the darker side of humanity. You know that better than anyone. You're the one obsessed with Bellocq, remember?"

Stella softened a bit. "Those women in his photographs are different, Mattie. You forget that then there wasn't much choice for a woman—she could work in a sweatshop or she could get paid for something she'd probably have to submit to anyway. Don't compare Bellocq's photos to anything you might see at The Scarlet Door."

"Stella, you're a hopeless romantic in a vulgar age. But in the real world, sister, even romantics have to settle for what Nietzsche called 'lies like truth.'"

A skeptical dimple appeared in Stella's chin. "Listen to you. Quoting Nietzsche on love. Who's your expert on longevity—Jack Kevorkian?"

Mattie stood up and sighed dramatically. "Why are we bickering? It's a free country we live in. You stay here tonight with Rose and Maman and I'll go to The Scarlet Door."

"Alone?" Stella gasped.

"Sure. What's going to shock me at some titty bar in little old Cane Town?"

"You can't go alone—you wouldn't!!"

Mattie gave her a sly glance. "Wouldn't I?" She tugged Stella to her feet. "C'mon, sad sack. Come upstairs with me while I unpack my things. I have to decide on what to wear."

"You don't have to bother with a top, that I can tell you," Stella admonished as they both left through the secret panel.

Stella had hoped to get upstairs without running into Aunt Rose, but she was with Maman at the kitchen table, arranging tinted meringues and fondant-frosted petits fours on a clear cut-glass serving plate. Aunt Rose's legs were wrapped in a down comforter.

Maman greeted Mattie with a warm smile and kind words. Rose, however, greeted both of the younger women in her best arch manner. Always one to fulfill the requirements of social etiquette, however, Rose did make an effort to engage their guest in polite chat. Unfortunately, Stella realized with a sinking stomach, she picked the wrong topic.

"Who is that interesting woman pictured on your T-shirt?" Rose asked.

"Well, just ask Stella," Mattie offered, taking an invisible yank at Stella. "She gave me the shirt. It was done to commemorate Women in Business month."

"The woman on it has great character in her face," Rose commented.

Stella cringed, unable to turn the tide of the conversation. She prayed Mattie would quit looking so enthused, but the devil got the best of her friend, and Mattie yakked on.

"She was a character, all right," Mattie offered. "It's 'French Emma' Johnson. She was the most famous madam in Storyville. She built an empire on what she called her 'sixty-second plan.' Any man who could hold off his orgasm for a full minute, once inside her, was excused from payment. Of course, nobody ever could. That's why she got rich."

Mattie had responded with the unflinching candor she might have used to answer a question in class. Stella wanted to die.

"Good heart of God," Maman muttered, turning to the stove to check on a big pot of chicken stock.

Rose, meantime, stared at Mattie in absolute shock. She peered closer and read the words under French Emma's portrait: Hey, fella, got a minute? Rose's mouth dropped open in astonishment, then shut like a drawstring pouch.

"But . . . my lands, Mattie," Rose objected, "what if a man recognizes the allusion?"

"It's a conversation starter," Mattie admitted.

Aunt Rose sniffed, recovering her offended dignity. "Yes, no doubt. So is taking off one's clothes unannounced, I suppose."

"That usually works too, but not in some places," Mattie agreed even though Stella stepped on her toes in warning.

Rose asked in her good-breeding-must-rise-above-all-else voice, "Will the two of you be joining us for dinner, I hope?"

Stella shook her head. "I think we'll probably go out for a bite. It's Saturday night. We might even go for a couple of drinks later."

She knew Mattie stared at her, but the woman could wait for the explanation of her turnaround. Her finally agreeing to go to The Scarlet Door was as simple as just not wanting her friend to venture alone. The woman needed protection as much as a brown recluse spider. Still, Stella couldn't let her go alone. To have a good friend meant to be a good friend.

Rose, however, in her indominable manner, could not let them go without at least a mild admonishment. "In my distant day," she told them, "young ladies did not 'go out.' They remained right at home and let the eligible young men do all the visiting."

The old woman sent a meaningful glance toward Mattie as she added, "As for gathering in taverns to drink liquor, it simply wasn't done by young ladies. There were cider parties, dances, chaperoned excursions to the city to visit the museums, the opera, the theater."

Rose's tone made Stella feel like she and Mattie were errant little girls in starched frocks. They exchanged glances, and Stella rolled her eyes. But Mattie, ever the historian, was far more fascinated by Rose than offended. She was one of the last living witnesses to span what history books now called the American century.

"Things change, Aunt Rose," Stella said. "They always have and they always will."

"More's the pity," Rose said sadly. "Too much change, way too quickly, for no good reason. Myrtle's becoming very sad about it. Very sad indeed. I caught her weeping about it out in the garden just this very afternoon."

"Myrtle?" Mattie whispered to Stella.

Stella looked at Maman.

The older black woman shook her head slightly. "Myrtle got no reason to cry, Rose. None at all."

"But all the beaus are gone. Dead and gone . . ." Rose said, her voice trailing to silence.

"I'm so sorry," Mattie blurted out, clearly moved by Rose's sadness.

Rose sent her a grateful smile.

"Well, on that note, I suppose we need to get Mattie settled," Stella said a bit too brightly. She left the kitchen with her friend on her heels.

"Who the hell's Myrtle? Don't tell me you've got a ghost, because I know the whole family graveyard better than you do, and nobody named Myrtle is buried out there."

Stella shrugged. "I don't know who she is. I've never seen a hair of her. Rose has just started mentioning her. I think the old girl feels more stress than she shows. I've been trying to keep the financial situation away from her, but I think she senses it. And too . . ." Stella's voice trailed away also.

"Too?" Mattie urged.

"Too, I think she's really depressed I haven't married and had children." Stella felt the old sadness hit her. "Rose lost her fiancé when she was young—maybe only sixteen. Angelo was older than her, Italian, everything she was not, but opposites attract. They met and fell in love right here in Cane Town. He'd come from the city to work at The Scarlet Door when it first opened as a gin joint during Prohibition. He was shot dead beneath the neon sign apparently. Somebody didn't like the way the owner was buying the bootleg liquor and took revenge.

"Rose ran to The Scarlet Door that night, and he died right in her arms. They said his blood turned her white dress red. She refused to marry anyone after he went, always said she was ready to join him anytime." Stella's expression darkened. "God, I hate that place. I can't get away from it."

Mattie instinctively hugged her. "It's a bad nexus, I agree. But it's just a place. Just four walls and a sign. It looms large because this is a one-horse town and that's all that's here."

Stella nodded. Turning pensive again, she said, "But, you know, in hindsight, I think Rose would have forced herself to start a family with someone if she thought she'd see the St. Vallier line die out in her lifetime. I think that's part of her trouble."

Mattie made sympathetic moans. Then her face cracked with a huge smile. "Well, Myrtle and Rose can just quit their boo-hooing. I've a feeling we're going to find Miss Stella a Mr. Right in just a few hours."

"Tonight? Then let the St. Valliers die out—" Stella retorted, but Mattie was already up the stairs ahead of her.

Garrett wasn't sure how it would end. With the Pulse-Air, he'd been able to see enough coke hauls that could double the gross national product for an underdeveloped nation. Time and again he watched men with army duffel bags slung over one shoulder like Santa's sack of toys take neat kilos off planes and shrimp boats well hidden in the bayou.

Leblanc was one rich asshole, that was for sure. A filthy-rich asshole, his butt baby-powdered with cocaine.

The need to give the fine senator his payback for all the misery he surely caused was becoming an obsession to Garrett.

But he had other things to attend to. He couldn't miss time at the bar in case it caused suspicion, but that afternoon down in Terrebonne Bay he'd witnessed the arrival of the mother lode of coke. Despite the fact that the drug could be driven to Cane Town in less than one hour, overland transport was too risky. The only highway between Terrebonne Bay and Cane Town was patrolled by state troopers and DEA agents. But private airplanes and boats—mostly used for offshore industry—were virtually off limits to authorities.

With binoculars he was able to get the registration number decaled to the fishing boat's stern, *The Ragin' Cajun*. He'd bet his year's salary that sometime tonight the boat was going to dock in Bayou Lafourche right at Senator Leblanc's landing.

Ducking alongside the stern, he secured the Pulse-Air to a little well in the prow. The signal would be lost if it went too far away, but it should come in again if it harbored in the Cane Town vicinity.

It was warm and humid when Garrett drove north to make his evening shift at The Scarlet Door. The heat always suffocated him, especially on the shore of the Gulf, where it was like breathing molten glass. But he knew that it wasn't just the cloying air that brought on a moment of deep discouragement when he should have felt elated.

The truth was, even with the blatant acts he had just witnessed, the U.S. marshals were far from a guaranteed bust in any of it. "Justice" was as elusive as a bird on the wing, and world events had evolved far beyond murdering marines in their beds. He knew he was trying to be one of the "good guys" in a world where death row inmates now had Web sites for their adoring fans.

As that fiery explosion in Beirut sixteen years earlier proved, there was now a brand-new battlefield where the "front" was everywhere, the "rear" nowhere. His grandpa's GI generation hit Omaha Beach in a clear-cut struggle for freedom. But to be a warrior for the new millennium meant you had to have courage—your ass was on the line all right—however, there would be no parades for the survivors.

But as Garrett had wheeled into the parking lot of The Scarlet Door, his gaze fell upon the lone white crosses that marked the intersection. He thought of Stella St. Vallier. Despite her very feminine form and style, Stella St. Vallier had that tenacious manner and resolve of the warrior elite. He had the distinct impression he would *not* want that green-eyed beauty as his enemy. Again he saw the indignant fury in her eyes when he tossed her from The Scarlet Door.

He'd laughed out loud in the silent car.

"Pretty Stella," he said as if she were there beside him, "fighting all the bad guys. Well, I sure hope we win."

CHAPTER

II

The credit belongs to those people who are actually in the arena . . . who know the great enthusiasms, the great devotions to a worthy cause; who, at best, know the triumph of high achievement; and who, at worst, fail while daring greatly . . . so that their place shall never be with those cold and timid souls who know neither victory or defeat.

— THEODORE ROOSEVELT

Stella and Mattie arrived at The Scarlet Door at eight. The place was packed. A line of people spilled onto Bayou Road to get in. EVERY SATURDAY IS LADIES NIGHT! proclaimed a handwritten banner across the notorious door.

"God, I wish we weren't here," Stella moaned as Mattie parked her Camry.

"I'll protect you," said Mattie matter-of-factly before she gazed into the rearview mirror at her lipstick. "C'mon. See the sign? Ladies drink free till midnight. I'm their girl."

Stella held her breath and got out of the car. It was

going to be bad enough to have to look at her parents' crosses, but what she didn't want to see were the wolf eyes of Garrett Shaw.

They took their place in the rear of the line. Stella had purposefully worn a plain navy blue knit dress and flats in order to look inconspicuous. Mattie, on the other hand, wore a hot-pink silk sheath. The rednecks flocked to her like flies to a pest strip.

"Pinky, that dress makes you look as sweet as cotton candy," said a tall, bearlike man behind them in line.

Mattie turned to him. Doing her best Scarlett O'Hara smile, she instantly made a conquest. "This old dress? Why, I only wear it when I don't care how I look."

Stella inwardly rolled her eyes.

"Sean Daigle. Pleased to meet you, ma'am." He tipped his cowboy hat.

It was the beginning of a beautiful friendship, Stella thought by the time they were next in line to get through the door. Sean Daigle was a commercial diver for the oil patch, Mattie a full professor. They were the yin and yang of the intelligentsia. And if Stella didn't know better, she'd think Mattie was already smitten by the big guy with the bright, easy smile.

The door loomed large and dark when it was Stella's turn to enter. She wished fervently Mattie would quit talking and go first, but the woman just kept yakking, ignoring the Sturm und Drang of her best friend's emotions.

Deciding to be brave, Stella inched her way through the black hole of the door.

But he wasn't there. No bouncer checking IDs tonight. The intense relief that rushed her made her feel almost silly. The Scarlet Door was crawling with criminals, and she was worried about just one of them. If she was lucky, the brute had the night off; she could have her free drink and skedaddle home.

"Let's get a booth. Sean wants to tell me about deep sea diving." Mattie's voice intruded into her thoughts.

"Fine." Stella turned toward the stage, cringing at the idea of a nude dancer, but the sign taped to the barstool on the stage said that the next show wouldn't be for another fifteen minutes.

"So it's how many days in decompression . . . ?" Mattie's voice melded into the drone of the crowd. The place was so packed, it wasn't likely Stella would see anyone she knew. Hugging the shadows of the rear of the booth, she planned on her one drink and her exit.

Then she saw him.

Garrett Shaw leaned against the bar like a gunslinger. He wore a dark blue T-shirt, jeans, and cowboy boots, the ubiquitous uniform, barely visible in a dark club. She prayed he hadn't seen her, but the gray eyes locked on her as if he had night vision. He'd obviously seen her slip into the back of the booth.

"Is that the cowboy?" Mattie asked in a low voice while Sean continued to tell her about his work.

Stella nodded.

"God, what a man. What a fine piece of man." Mattie's gaze slid up and down Shaw, but Garrett's eyes never left Stella.

Forcing herself to tear her gaze away, Stella looked up at the waitress who'd arrived to get their drink order.

"Hey, Stella," the girl said with a furtive smile.

Stella didn't recognize her at first. The last time she'd seen Genny Mulvaney was in high school. She was Greg Mulvaney's little sister. Stella and Greg were on and off all through high school.

"What are you doing here, Genny?" Stella blurted out, still thinking of the girl as a high school sophomore.

"You know," Genny said with a small laugh, "I was about to ask you the same thing." She gave a little helpless shrug. "It's the only work that'll pay my rent and give me time with my kid. After I had Blair, my parents kicked me out. Now I do a little dancing sometimes."

Her last words should have been a bit defensive, but it seemed the defensiveness was beaten out of her. "It's no big deal."

A lump formed in Stella's throat. They were all just surviving, it seemed. But she was educated and unburdened by an out-of-wedlock child. Suddenly her problems seemed much less ferocious.

"So what'll you all have? I play waitress in between shifts onstage." Genny wiped down the tray in her hands.

They gave their drink orders. Stella watched the girl walk away, her thin cotton dress revealing the G-string she wore beneath it.

"You know her?" Mattie asked.

"Sure. She was the sweet kid sister. Everybody adored her. Then, I guess she met Mr. Wrong."

Stella stared at Genny waiting at the bar. The girl turned to their table. She gave a friendly little wave of her hand, then a sheepish smile. It nearly killed Stella.

"Look at her," she said to Mattie. "She's embarrassed and humiliated, clearly downtrodden. And still she's trying to be nice. God, I don't have that much strength."

"That's the fable of womanhood, girl," Mattie offered.

Stella was driven to a bitter response. "The average Storyville prostitute's lifespan in an era of STDs and no penicillin was less than thirty years. Did anybody really care? No. People still portray Storyville as some kind of fun house. They've even trademarked the name and made it into a restaurant chain."

When the drinks arrived, Stella murmured, "But this is no fun house."

"Hey, I'll see you later, maybe, huh?" Genny said.

Sean paid for the drinks, but Stella handed her a twenty-dollar tip. "Sure. I'd love to catch up."

Genny gave a grateful smile. She walked away and Stella said, "I could have married her older brother.

Where the hell is he now that she needs him, I wonder. The piece of crap."

"He's off having a career and a life like most men," Mattie retorted under her breath. Then she turned to Sean and said, "Cheers." She downed her shot glass of whiskey in one gulp.

"Tough crowd," the man said in appreciation.

Mattie just smiled.

Toutant came into the bar from his office. He didn't see them in the booth. Stella nudged Mattie and nodded her head in his direction. Mattie took a long, surreptitious look at him.

"Have you got him in mind now?" Stella asked.

Mattie nodded.

"Great. We can leave, then. You've seen all the characters I know in this place." Stella stood up.

Mattie and Sean gazed at her from the other side of the booth.

"You leavin' so soon?" Sean asked, his arm suddenly going around Mattie.

Stella could see Mattie was actually having a good time. The music started blaring from the stage. She knew she couldn't watch sweet little Genny take her clothes off to make the rent.

"I'm going out for some air. Be right back." She swooped up her drink and went to the door.

It was quiet outside. The highway was pitch dark and Old Bayou Road didn't have a single headlight on it.

Grateful the bouncer hadn't been sitting in the door, watching her leave, she leaned against the black glass walls of the club and stared at the white crosses that seemed to glow in the October moonlight. Alone, she thought about Genny and wondered how things could go so wrong when everything should have gone right.

"Miss them?" came a voice next to her.

Startled, she looked up and found Garrett Shaw next to her, leaning against the same black glass wall.

The last thing she wanted was to get into a conversation with him. So she said nothing and ignored him.

"Yeah, I guess you don't want to talk to a man like me." He released a strangely ironic laugh. "I guess I should like that about you, but frankly, right now I don't." He stared at her, the hard planes of his face almost surreal in the orange neon glow of the damaged sign. "So who's your friend in the shocking-pink dress?"

She couldn't take it anymore. Being the smartass, she said, "Oh, you'd *love* her. Her specialty's lowlifes."

His handsome mouth twisted in a wry smile. "Yeah, but she's already got a guy talking with her—and Sean's okay too. Comes in here a lot. I like him. He's a good guy. Needs a good girl."

She snorted. "You're certainly the right person to judge that."

"Maybe." He didn't seem to take offense. "So you know Genny? You guys go to school together?"

She released a put-upon sigh. "I used to date her brother. She's younger than me." Giving him a covert glance, she added, "I didn't know she worked here. I wish she didn't."

"She needs the money. She's got a kid. Blair's a champ. She brings him in sometimes when she can't get a sitter. He's three."

"She sure as hell needs to stop doing that." She bit her lower lip. "I wish I could help her, but I can't even get rid of the trespassers on my property, let alone hire someone."

"You don't need to worry about Genny." He seemed to release an inward laugh. "You wouldn't know it to look at her, but she's got friends in high places who plan on helping her."

She didn't comment. Getting Genny involved in the drug trade wasn't the salvation she'd hoped for the girl, but there was no need to argue with the man. He was a loser, and to try to get sense out of him would just prolong the conversation.

Dismissing him again, she looked out across Old Bayou Road into the swamp willows that edged the water.

"Why'd you come here tonight?" he asked, unrelenting.

"It's a free country. Where else can one go in Cane Town for a whiskey?" She lifted her still-full glass as if to prove her words.

"Are you leaving the dogs alone, Stella? Or did you come here to rile them?" His words were iron. He wanted an answer; he demanded one. She was shocked by his tone.

"I haven't bothered your master, if that's what you're getting at," she shot back.

"P.G. doesn't even know you're here. I'd have heard about it if he had."

"See? So don't sweat it. You can quit the interrogation and go back to your—your *career,*" she said facetiously.

He laughed out loud. "Lady, you have no idea how true those words are."

She stared at him, surprised. She'd expected irritation. It happened every time a low-status male was reminded of his low status. But Garrett Shaw was different somehow. He didn't seem to mind her cutting remarks or her dismissals. In fact, he seemed to approve.

He was nuts. That's all she could conclude.

"Well, I think I hear the music ending. I have to go get my friend and leave now." She stepped past him. "I'd say I'd talk to you later, but you'll probably be in jail—"

He grabbed her arm and pulled her to him.

"No shit-stirring, okay?" he warned.

She looked down at the hand that was like a velvet-wrapped manacle on her arm. "Gee, I sure wish you'd be my bodyguard. You do way too good a job, Mr. Shaw."

He pulled her close. She was stunned by her reaction. Instead of wanting to break free, she found herself wanting to go closer. As if for a kiss.

"I might take you up on that job offer one day. Just don't make me do it now, 'cause it'll be difficult," he said with emphasis.

She hadn't a clue as to what he meant, but the words seemed to echo with importance.

"Be a good girl. Don't rile Toutant," he whispered harshly.

Uncomfortable with his talk and her attraction to him, she finally pulled her arm free.

He let her go and she walked back into the club to fetch Mattie, determined that she had to find a boyfriend. If she didn't get laid soon, she might eventually find Garrett Shaw's charms seductive.

Garrett pulled his Beretta automatic from the hiding place beneath the console of his car. It was past three in the morning, and Dabs was closing up The Scarlet Door for him again. If Toutant ever got wind of his absence at closing time, his ass, as the phrase went, would be grass.

He was tracking Toutant, the noise from the receiver of the Pulse-Air getting louder and louder. If the drug deal was as big a haul as it looked to be, it could be the way to take Toutant out of the game and make him rat on the fine senator. Garrett didn't know how it would all go down yet. He would just have to play the night out as he saw it.

Toutant's Cherokee swung off the road just past Bayou Lafourche on Myron Leblanc's property. Garrett knew now that Stella de St. Vallier was the senator's neighbor. He sure hoped she was long in bed asleep. If anything went down tonight, he wanted her and her haunting green eyes well out of the picture.

He killed his headlights and slowed way down. The night turned as dark as new tar when a raft of clouds drifted in front of the moon. He spotted the farm lane

Toutant had taken, but it offered little cover. So he backed up, turning instead at another narrow lane on the St. Vallier side of the bayou. Here a line of cypress trees provided cover but gave him a clear view of Leblanc's property.

He unscrewed the inside dome light before he opened the door. Then he took his Beretta automatic and clipped the holster to his waistband.

It had been threatening rain ever since he left The Scarlet Door. As he stepped out into the night, the rain abruptly came slapping down into the surrounding cane fields in huge drops. It lasted only about two minutes, stopping as suddenly as it started. Afterward, it was so quiet, he could hear the sound of water dripping from the green blades.

Wet and shivering, he moved closer to the bayou and followed it for another thirty yards. Now and then a stiff gust wrinkled the black surface of the water. Finally the clouds blew away from the moon, and he spotted the outline of the shrimping boat *The Ragin' Cajun.*

He was in time to watch Toutant heave a duffel into the back of his Cherokee. There was enough light for Garrett to also recognize the other man with Toutant as one of Jervis Archer's deputies, the one who always dropped Archer off behind The Scarlet Door on Friday nights.

Christ, the entire Cane Town Police Department was on the take, he speculated. That only strengthened his theory that Archer—or one of his minions—performed the rubout on Fontainbleau. More back-scratching cousins, all covering for one another.

And best of all, there was this little nocturnal sideline taking place on Senator Myron Leblanc's property. A paragon of moral virtue, savior of the needy kids. True, none of this tonight automatically implicated the senator. But it was one more bullet in the war to take him down.

Teeth chattering from his soaking, Garrett pressed

tighter against a big cypress tree and waited for Toutant to leave.

Stella was still trying to tug herself over the threshold of sleep when she heard it—weeping.

She struggled to sit up, still groggy. The evening as far as she'd been concerned had been a disaster. Bars were always that way, even the upscale ones. The eligible men found there were either mass-tort lawyers with fat diamond pinky rings and a pocket of Antibuse they'd forgotten to swallow that night, or they weren't eligible at all and, yet, invariably failed to mention the fact until one of their chums asked how the wife was. The Scarlet Door wasn't any better. Sean had asked for Mattie's phone number, so maybe the trip had been worth it, but for Stella, she'd had a very difficult time getting to sleep without those familiar gray eyes hunting her down in her imagination.

She looked at the red-glowing numerals of a digital clock on the dresser. Almost twenty after three. The windows were open, and the wind across the thick cane could easily have created the strange sound she thought she heard.

But then she heard it again, this time clearer. It was the sound of weeping all right. Female weeping.

Rising from the bed, she slipped a black cardigan over her black silk nightgown and crept down the hallway to see if it was either Rose or Mattie. But when she peeked through their doors, both women were sound asleep in their rooms.

She returned to the open window in her room. The night was windy and overcast, and she saw cloud shadows move like fast water across the landscape. At first she could see nothing except the dark, solid mass of the cypress brake along the bayou and a lone car parked on her side.

Then a seam opened up in the cloud cover, and silver-white moonlight bathed the garden below. She felt her face flush with surprise when she saw a girl no more than sixteen sitting on a marble bench, her head in her hands.

"Hello? Are you all right?" she called out to her, but the girl didn't move. She continued her plaintive weeping uninterrupted.

"Are you hurt? Are you lost?" Stella tried again, but the girl didn't seem to hear her. With no other choice, Stella clutched the cardigan to her and left for the garden.

"Everything's okay. Come in the house and we'll call someone," she called out when she reached the bench.

But now the bench was empty. The crying silenced.

"What the hell?" she whispered to herself. Convinced now she must be seeing things or sleepwalking, she went to return to the house, but suddenly the moonlight beamed through the clouds again. Dumbfounded, she saw the girl not twenty feet ahead of her.

The girl was walking through a line of gardenia bushes, brushing away tears from her face even though new ones seemed to spring forth relentlessly. Her young woman's figure was barely visible in the waistless, straight-sided white dress she wore. She was certainly young. Again Stella would place her at no more than sixteen. Her dark hair was cut short in a Buster Brown style, making her look even younger, but a sensual, excessively long string of pearls swayed with her every movement, belying her innocence.

"Are you all right?" Stella called out to her, jogging to catch up.

The girl still didn't seem to hear her. She simply picked up her pace until she, too, was nearly running.

Raindrops spattered down. The girl in front of Stella didn't react to the cold shower at all, but Stella was now shivering, drawing her cardigan over her with both hands. They were going in the direction of the car she'd seen from her window. Perhaps the girl just wanted to return to it and go home.

"If you need help, let me help you! Truly, I can if only you tell me what's wrong—"

Stella lost her. The girl disappeared in the cypress as if she were a vapor.

Stopping near the bank of Bayou Lafourche, Stella listened for the faint sound of weeping. Instead, she heard the noise of a motor idling. But it sounded like it was on the other side of the bayou, on Leblanc's property.

She flinched when somebody revved the motor. Across the bayou, on Leblanc's side, she heard the occasional cane stalk being crushed as whoever was driving the second vehicle headed back out toward Parish Road. Probably Toutant, she guessed. His chiseled little head was identifiable in silhouette, for the man was such a weasel.

Watching the car jogged her memory of Leblanc's sanctimonious words: *We can't win the war on drugs without soldiers like you willing to fight in the trenches.* Despite the sharp spike of fear in her stomach, anger ripped inside her. The weeping girl was all but forgotten in her attempt to suppress her rage. Only three days after Leblanc's assurances, and it looked pretty likely the drug runners were back. And not too damned worried about the senator.

She stared at the dark shadow of a shrimp boat across the bayou, desperately trying to calm herself. Anger wouldn't carry her far in the situation. She was one woman against a corrupt police force and drug runners. To unleash her fury could get her killed—could get everyone at Shadow Oaks killed.

Despite her fear and rage, what she had to do was think, calculate a plan of action that would get her the desired result. To begin with, what occurred off her property was not, strictly speaking, her concern. If she was to go to the DEA herself, she needed information. She needed to know the extent of her involvement. The first thing she had to do was to get the license plate number of the car she'd just spotted from upstairs, parked in her field. It could have been parked there by the girl perfectly innocently. But her reason told her it was so much more likely to be involved in the drug dealing. And maybe the weeping girl was too.

Shivering more from fear than the wind that blew right through her damp clothing, she began following the bayou back toward Old Parish Road.

The full moon finally emerged completely from behind a scud of dark clouds. A sixth sense, perhaps just the primeval yearning for cover when predators were near, made her draw up short. Fear made her stomach clench like a fist. Her steel resolve gave way to a numb panic. But like Lot's wife, something compelled her to turn back around for one last look in the generous moonwash.

At that moment she recognized Garrett Shaw.

Her heart skidded to a stop.

With quick athleticism he came at her in a low shooting stance through a thicket of trees, a handgun ready to fire in his grip.

For one bone-freezing moment she was convinced she was an eye blink away from death.

"What the fuck are you doing here?" he rasped. Inexplicably, he holstered the weapon.

She swallowed the lump of fear in her throat. "I followed the girl. The girl in white. She was going to the car, I think."

"What girl?" he demanded.

Then, despite facing death only a moment earlier, her hair-trigger temper went off at once. "I *live* here," she retorted under her breath. "I've a right to be here. The question is, what are *you* doing here—as if I don't know."

"You don't."

"Oh, don't I? Are the drugs in *your* car tonight or in Toutant's?"

"I warned you, but you just don't know when to quit, do you?" Shaw said in his sarcastic drawl.

"I'll quit when you and your cronies stop using my property to stage your operation. And it is going to stop. I'll see to that even if I have to call a press conference to find an honest cop."

He walked up and shook her as if she were a truant child. "Listen, I swear by all things holy, you better be pissed off enough at me to see me killed, because that's exactly what'll happen if you let it be known you caught me here tonight."

She turned on him like a pouncing cat.

"That's *your* problem, isn't it?" she demanded.

"Sure it is. But going to the cops, or anybody else, could also get you killed."

He moved in closer. His handsome face was set granite hard in the moonlight. She realized the gun was superfluous: His physical presence was intimidating enough.

She tried to move back a step, but the vise of his hand on her arm wouldn't let her move. "I—I don't understand you," she stammered. "Are you threatening me or warning me?"

"I am warning you, Miss St. Vallier. There's much more to this situation than you understand. It's noble of you to play the citizen hero. But very, very stupid."

"Look, I know the cops are in on the take. I know I'm up against forces I can't do battle with. But I just want you guys off my property. I don't want any drug running on Shadow Oaks."

"I'm not a drug runner."

"All right. You're all innocent. So is it too much to ask that you contain your innocent midnight dealings to the other side of the bayou? I'll let Senator Leblanc deal with them then."

She stared at him. In the moonglow she saw him

flinch at the senator's name. She was now convinced the senator was up to his neck in it too; it was good information to know.

"I understand why you believe I'm involved in all this. But you're wrong." His grip on her arm was like an eagle's talon. He leaned closer to her until she could feel the heat of his breath on her face. "Before you start blabbing this to *any*body else, you best remember: You will jeopardize the life of anyone you tell. You will also compromise a very important legal investigation that could get all this scum out of your hair for good."

Stella studied him. "Are you telling me," she asked slowly, "that you're some kind of a cop?"

"You're a smart girl, you figure it out."

"I have no reason to believe you're a cop. Tell me why I should."

"Because an honest pagan is better than a bad Catholic, that's why. And this parish is crawling with crooks who go to church. You'd better find somebody you can believe."

"And that's you, right?"

Her tone implied he was claiming to be a Martian. For the first time since he'd caught her, he smiled.

"Baby, it's me," he assured her.

She searched his face in the opalescent moonlight. Some men had no choice but to give you their personalities whole within five minutes of knowing them. However, she suspected someone could know him for years and he'd remain a stranger if he chose to. Which made it impossible to know if he was lying now.

"If you're a cop," she finally said, "let me see some ID."

"ID?" he repeated scornfully. "Christ, lady. I've infiltrated a bunch of low-life slimeballs. You think I'd carry a badge among them?"

"Then—well then, at least give me a name, a number to call. Some law enforcement agency I can contact to verify who you are."

"Not for love or money. I could do that, sure. But the standard operating procedure, once cover is compromised in *any* way, is to yank the undercover operative out of the field immediately. I'm damned if I'm throwing away months of hard work just to satisfy your curiosity. Nothing on God's green earth will stop me now."

A tingle went down her nape. She almost believed him. He sounded sincere. But then, so did Leblanc. At one level Garrett's claim made sense to her, but at the same time it was all so damned convenient and neat for him and his gang, wasn't it, to plead undercover cop.

She was acutely aware of his physical nearness. Again, as she had at the library, she felt her pulse thrumming hard. His gaze dropped to a spot in her throat as if he were searching for her weakness. He seemed transfixed, an erotic arc sparking between them.

With a reluctance that surprised her she forced herself to pry his grip from her arms and step back from him. *Don't* fall for a sincere line of crap, she warned herself. This guy had a certain nice exterior, maybe, but there was that twist to his mouth—maybe Maman was right about meanness showing around the mouth.

"Please just get off my land," she finally whispered harshly to him, her voice lost and desperate.

"You mention a word of this to the wrong person and my body'll be floating in this bayou because you put the bullet in the back of my head. *You,* Stella St. Vallier. Do you understand me?"

"Yes," she retorted, suddenly even more afraid than before.

"I don't want to have to trust you," he bit out.

"I don't want to have to trust you either," she whispered.

"Never enough choices, are there?" He gave a long stare in the moonlight, then he was gone.

CHAPTER

12

On Monday a very tired and harried-looking Myron Leblanc flew back from Washington for a last-minute late-afternoon strategy session in the conference room at the rear of The Scarlet Door. The opportunity to meet somewhere on quick notice, without the threat of media cameras and microphones, was part of the reason Leblanc himself had secretly bankrolled Toutant to cover the purchase of the local club.

This time Leblanc made a point of ordering Toutant to keep the bouncer away from the room. But Cliff D'Antoni, Hiram Steele, and Barry Woodyard were all in attendance. Certain events had reached a critical juncture, so Leblanc also required Toutant and Jervis Archer to be present for part of the meeting.

"Gentlemen," Leblanc announced, "it's no longer hypothetical. Someone is trying to close a net around us. And it's a big net—originates in D.C., matter of fact."

State Representative Steele uncrossed his legs and leaned forward in his seat. "Undercover sting?"

Leblanc nodded from the head of the long Formica table. "I'm convinced of it. Cliff concurs. We aren't just shooting at rovers here. I'd lay odds we have already been infiltrated by the U.S. marshals' special taskforce."

The parish D.A. nodded his agreement.

"Jesus Christ," Woodyard said, paling slightly. "Has this been confirmed?"

"As much as it's going to be until we're arrested," Leblanc replied, snappish from exhaustion.

Woodyard fell silent, duly chastized.

In a milder tone Leblanc added, "There's an administrative assistant who works at NOPD. He . . . well, let's just say he keeps an eye on police business for Cliff and me. He's learned, from office hearsay he trusts, that a U.S. marshal is being 'assisted' by an ace NOPD detective named Justin Breaux."

"All right, but so what?" Steele demanded. "I mean, does your source know for a fact it involves us?"

D'Antoni answered before the senator could.

"Try reading local newspapers once in a while, Hiram. Breaux is a bona fide expert on the late Albert Fontainbleau. Investigated him for years before he bit the—" The D.A.'s expensive retro specs flashed toward Chief Archer.

Archer coolly met the scrutiny, giving the attorney his lopsided smile.

D'Antoni broke eye contact first. "Before his accident," the D.A. resumed. "So read between the lines, Hiram. It's an ugly story unfolding."

"Precisely," Senator Leblanc concurred. He stared at Toutant now. "Which brings us to an interesting puzzle. Who is this U.S. marshal? And is he working from a distance, or is he bearding the lion in its very den?"

Toutant's tight features registered no change. "Senator, surely you're not paranoid enough to hint that it's me?"

"Of course not, don't be ignorant. But I want you to think very carefully. This 'Cowboy' character . . . the name and information off his job application checked out okay. We even confirm a booking sheet on him at the Dallas city jail, something about a brawl and two cops slightly injured in the arrest. But if he's a fed, all that means nothing. Some of the agencies construct very convincing covers for their field guys, especially for deep-penetration ops. Think hard, Percival. Has he given you *any* reason whatsoever to suspect him?"

For just a moment an angry look crossed Toutant's face. But it passed instantly.

"No," he answered. "But I tell you what. I'll watch him close."

"You'd better," Leblanc assured him. "Because if he's a marshal and we miss it, our cake is dough. And speaking of cake—" Leblanc's muddy eyes flicked from one man to the next, moving completely around the table before he spoke. He wanted to make sure he had their attention.

"For the time being I am calling a moratorium on all of our . . . extracurricular activities. Until the danger lifts, United Southern Children's Charities will be run like a tight ship. No cooking the books to cover doctored manifests."

Leblanc's eyes stayed on Toutant and Archer now. "And absolutely no money laundering. Every infusion of cash is no doubt being strictly monitored lately. More so than usual. But that point's academic because there's also a suspension of your landing privilege. My landing strip is completely off limits to deliveries until our status improves."

"Leaving me and P.G. with what?" Archer demanded. "The hind tit? We got customers who depend on us. We pork them, they'll buy elsewhere, and the whole operation'll go down the tubes."

With an effort visible in his face, Leblanc controlled

his temper. He didn't know which he resented more, Archer's effrontery, or his white-trash speech.

"It can't be helped, Chief. Until this code red passes, we're all in serious jeopardy. Now, if you and Percival don't mind, I'd like to speak with the others in private."

"Why, so you can jerk us around some more?" Archer snarled, still angry. "If I'm gettin' fucked, I'd rather know how it was done."

Hearing this, Leblanc's bodyguard rose from his chair by the hallway door. He held the door open and stared at Archer. Dismissed like mere retainers, Toutant and Jervis left.

"This is turning into a goddamn dog-and-pony show," Archer complained as the two men egressed from the narrow hall into The Scarlet Door's sea of tables and chairs. It was five P.M. No customers had shown up yet, and Dabs Boudreaux was cutting lemons and limes into wedges behind the bar.

Toutant ignored Archer. His face was as grim as an inquisitor's.

"The hell's biting you?" Archer demanded.

"I didn't say anything to Leblanc, okay? He would've blown a friggin' gasket. But Saturday night, while I was picking up the shit?"

"Yeah?"

"Cowboy went home early. I found out when I got back. He had Dabs fill in for him. I didn't worry too much about it then. Now it's bugging the hell out of me. Let's see if he's here."

"That might be a fine idea," Archer said sarcastically. "What the hell you saying, you didn't worry? You queer for him or what?"

Both men went out into the drab little foyer where the bouncer usually sat. Cowboy was parked in his tall spring-back chair, leafing through a copy of *Sports Illustrated*. The club was closed on Sundays, so Toutant had not seen his employee since Saturday night.

"Where y'at, boss?" Garrett greeted Toutant. He ignored the stern-faced cop.

"Right on time, as usual," Toutant remarked. "I just pure don't get it, Cowboy. For over a month now you ain't missed a day. Never a minute late, as dependable as the equinox. Then, when you do miss some work, it has to be at closing time, maybe on a Saturday night? And right after I leave, to boot?"

Garrett shrugged, his face a surprised blank. "Well, Christ, P.G. A guy doesn't get the heaves when he chooses to. Did you want me to puke all over your nice clean floor?"

Garrett stared at P.G.

"I had Dabs close up," he reminded Toutant a moment later. "Ain't like I left you in a lurch."

"I don't pay Dabs to do that, I pay you. I don't like this shit, Cowboy. I don't like it at all."

Garrett shrugged again. "Yeah, I see that. Okay. It won't happen again."

"Why did it happen at all?" Archer demanded.

Evidently, however, Cowboy considered the incident closed. Ignoring Jervis, he opened his magazine again.

Archer's normally flat voice rose in anger. "Clean your ears or cut your hair, asshole. I asked you a question."

"It's none of your picnic, Chief. I work for Mr. Toutant."

Most men's eyes telegraphed their intention before they swung, so Garrett knew the punch was coming. Archer threw a roundhouse right at him, which Garrett easily avoided by tipping his head backward a few inches. Never even getting out of his chair, Garrett continued to goad his adversary.

"Police brutality in small-town America. It's a national disgrace," he informed both men in his amiable drawl.

Garrett also knew the cop would lunge at him in

blind fury, for Archer was the raging-bull type. When he did, Garrett made no effort to resist the attack. Instead, he moved with Archer's force, tipping the chair backward and hopping neatly off before it crashed to the floor, letting it tangle Archer's leg. With Archer caught off balance, it was easy to use the rest of his own force against him. Garrett threw him onto his face in the corner behind them.

Before a stunned Archer could recover, Garrett crouched over him and hooked a thumb under one hinge of the lawman's jawbone. He wrenched it outward until the chief yowled like a cat with a torn claw. Instantly, the fight went out of him when he felt his jaw on the painful verge of dislocation.

"Knock the shit off, you two!" Toutant snapped. "This ain't Dodge City!"

"He started it," Garrett insisted like a little kid getting the last word. He wasn't even breathing heavily. He let the chief go and stood up.

"I'll finish it too," Archer promised, his chest heaving as he climbed to his feet and adjusted his hat and heavy leather gun belt.

Toutant and Archer returned to the office.

"His address is on his job application," Toutant said quietly as he led Archer to his cubbyhole behind the bar. "Never mind this macho crap with jumping him in public. Why'n't you toss his place tonight, see what you can find?"

Archer, still massaging his sore jaw, nodded. "I'll comb the place. I already owe that bastard an ass whipping. But if I find out he's our U.S. marshal, he's deader than last Christmas."

Stella dialed half of Myron Leblanc's telephone number before she chickened out—yet again—and hung the handset back in its cradle.

She'd been racked by indecision since the incident

in the cane field two days earlier. She sorely needed a confidante and adviser just then, but these days her world seemed cruelly divided into two groups: those she dare not trust, and those she dare not endanger.

Even asking Leblanc for the name of his state-trooper friend was an act fraught with potential harm. Myron Leblanc, Jervis Archer, and now Garrett Shaw, all fit in the group she dared not trust. She hadn't felt this alone and scared and confused since her parents died. Shaw's warning not to tell anyone what she knew seemed almost absurd given the fact that no one believed her anyway. But nonetheless her forced silence was simply intolerable. It had to be exorcised with words.

Words. As ephemeral as the colored blips on the screen of her computer.

Desperate to take her mind off the events of the night before, she had spent much of the afternoon in her sunny little nook upstairs, composing her query for the approval of Professor Perkins, the LSU agronomist and expert on the sugar cane industry.

She glanced over her letter again. It was to a major cattle feed manufacturer in nearby Meridian, Mississippi. Basically, she was trying to pique their interest in possibly using bagasse in the manufacture of their product. She quoted Perkins's assertions that it was superior to other types of harvest wastage, easier to work with, and friendlier to the environment as well as more nutritious. Now she only hoped Professor Perkins would look over her proposal before she sent it. Perhaps even edit it for technical details.

The little nook where she sat working had taken on an almost ghostly brilliance in the final roseate flush of sunset. She backed up her work on a diskette, then turned off the computer. She returned to the master bedroom suite, still wrestling with the problem of Myron Leblanc.

Again and again she tried to discipline her mind, to

force a decision, some plan of action. The indecision, the fear gnawing at her stomach like invisible incisors, made her wish she could just slough off her ineffective self as completely as a snake sloughs its old skin.

She deliberately avoided looking at the gallery of portraits on the west wall. For lately the St. Vallier women seemed to silently accuse her of some terrible weakness. But her ancestors caught her anyway—the door on the mirrored armoire was slanted open just enough to reflect their accusing eyes.

Genevieve, Colette, Jacqueline, her mother, all the rest. There they were. All urging her to paddle her own canoe, as they had done before her.

"I'm trying, ladies," she said aloud, her voice sounding small and insignificant in the big, silent room. "I really am."

Wandering to the nearest window, she gazed out over the sun-hazed fields of cane. There was still enough light to work, so she wasn't surprised to see Autry. From there he was the size of a bug as he drove the cane cutter through some distant rows, cutting the last of the seed cane for the next harvest.

Her gaze shifted to Bayou Lafourche. She couldn't help but wonder who the strange girl was who she'd found weeping. In hindsight the girl had an unsettling familiarity, and it wasn't hard to go from that notion to the theory of ghosts and hauntings.

To force her thoughts on something more tangible—if unpleasant—her gaze skipped across the bayou to Senator Leblanc's adjacent fields. Again she was seized in a welter of doubts. The veiled hints Garrett Shaw had dropped on Saturday night about being a cop—she did not believe his self-serving claim, of course.

Neither could she slough off the blame should he truly be found floating in Bayou Lafourche. Yet what truly troubled her most was the *need* to believe him. She suspected that was one reason she couldn't complete a call to Leblanc. She didn't want to expose Garrett's lie to herself. She truly wanted to trust and believe someone. She wanted—what did Mattie call it?—lies like truth. So far in Garrett Shaw she had that.

She'd said nothing to anyone. Not even Mattie. There seemed no logical reason for staying silent on his say-so alone. But her reasons were emotional, not logical. Emotional and . . . She put a curtain on her thoughts, refusing to speculate along that dark path.

By then the sun was a bright copper orb balanced on the western horizon. She watched Autry turn the cane cutter toward the sugarhouse, finally knocking off for the day.

Even after the sun finally went down in a brilliant blaze of suffused light, she still stood there in the darkening room. Thinking, worrying, trying with all her might to conquer her growing fear that one of the Four Horsemen of the Apocalypse had returned to Shadow Oaks. And the name that was on him was Death.

CHAPTER

<u>13</u>

Over the years Garrett had developed a useful ability, especially during moments of pressure, to separate himself from the unity of the present moment. In effect, he could become both participant and observer simultaneously. He was still in that divided mind-set now, only minutes after his scuffle with Chief Archer had triggered it.

Obviously, the Ring felt the heat rising. Nothing else could explain Toutant's total one-eighty turn in personality, his extraordinary reaction to Garrett's leaving early on Saturday. But no matter what they suspected, they still couldn't know for sure who or what he was. If they did know, he'd be dead by now.

Garrett knew his room would probably be searched if it hadn't been already. But he was always prepared for that contingency when he went undercover. There was nothing in his room to give him away. Running his name wouldn't help them either. U.S. marshals rou-

tinely operated under their real names, but with a carefully faked paper trail, including a social security number and phony work history, even a fake rap sheet.

Archer left shortly after their encounter. He avoided
Garrett and left by the rear door. The place was still
dead, as usual, this early on a Monday night. Garrett
tucked his mussed-up shirt back into his jeans and went
into the lounge.

"Hey, Dabs, how's the man? Mix me up a Jack and
Coke before the stampede begins, wouldja?"

"Yeah, I guess you could use a drink. What shit went
down out there in the foyer?" Dabs demanded as he
took the Jack Daniel's bottle from the pyramid of glass
behind him. He poured a few fingers over shaved ice in
a pony glass and shot some cola into it. "Sounded like
you and Jerk-us mixed it up a little out there?"

Garrett drank down half his cocktail before he answered. "Ah, it was embarrassing. I've had better fights
on first dates. The hell's Toutant on the warpath
about?"

Dabs shrugged one plump shoulder. "I'm just the
bar dog around here. Personally, I wish you'd whip that
son of a bitch Archer till his hair falls out. If I'm jokin',
I'm chokin'—I hate that bastard. He's one o' them
types with a complex about his little prick."

Dabs was an armchair psychologist with warped per-
spectives. But Garrett figured he might be right this
time. Whatever Archer's personal hang-ups were, Shaw
definitely had not wanted a physical clash with him.
The man was a total write-off as a human being, so his
constant insults meant nothing anyway. But Garrett's
discipline had its limits. All bets were off once a man
took a poke at him.

The problem was Archer's nature. Most men meant
no harm. Garrett never forgot that fact, even in his line
of work. But Jervis was one of the ten-percenters, the
exceptions to the rule. And now that he had a grudge
against Garrett, he'd nurse it until he got revenge.

At least Garrett was warned. He knew what Archer was. However, what about Stella St. Vallier? He no longer worried about her reporting him to anyone. Not because she believed he was a cop, but because she was a class act. And class acts did not risk human life carelessly. Stella St. Vallier, he had already learned, took moral responsibilities very seriously. For the time being she would not mention him to anyone. At least, not until she was pretty damn sure he was lying.

If the truth were known, he was worried about her safety more than his own. He didn't know if common sense would temper her outrage. The squeaky wheel gets the grease, all right. But being "greased" had more than one meaning.

Dabs picked up his empty glass and dunked it in the rinse tank.

"Hit me again."

Dabs whistled. "Goddamn! Cowboy's juicing tonight. You got female troubles?"

"Don't tell anybody, okay?"

Dabs grinned and leaned closer, eager for a juicy tidbit. "Yeah?"

"I think my period's late," Garrett confessed.

Dabs snapped a filthy towel at him, then whooped his appreciation.

But behind Garrett's outwardly clowning facade, the problem of Stella St. Vallier had not once ceased to chafe at him. Dammit all anyway, he had enough problems with this case already, now including a dangerous dent in his cover that might give at any moment. He didn't need this extra complication of a female caught in the middle of the storm. He'd met plenty of women in his life, and now and then even made time for some of them. But Stella was in a category he had never before encountered.

It troubled him that he was so worried about her. He'd be damn lucky to get out of Cane Town in one piece himself—and that was no figure of speech around there, as Al Fontainbleau found out. He needed to watch his own ass. He didn't need an Achilles' heel.

There was still one drastic option: He had enough evidence right now to call in the DEA and bust Archer on a conspiracy to distribute charge. It could be a nice coup with multiple warrants. Steve Falcone had already run the registration numbers Garrett gave him. The shrimp boat down in Terrebonne Bay belonged to Romer Archer, a first cousin to Jervis. As for the Piper Cub, it came back registered to the Lafourche Parish Search and Rescue Squad. The primary pilot, for insurance purposes, was listed as the chief's deputy, Harley Burke.

A drug bust just then might lower the risk for Stella by removing Archer. But button men were plentiful. And a drug bust now would lower, if not destroy, the odds of eventually nailing the real power players, Myron Leblanc included. Busting crooked cops was only swiping at the branches of evil; busting crooked pols meant tearing out the roots.

Again he pictured the pleasant image of Stella de St. Vallier. Those sea-green eyes of hers were so wide and clear, a man could fall into them and fucking drown. But that classy little beauty had a hard lesson to learn. Her own existence was central to her—which was only natural in a human being. But sometimes it was a difficult point to get across to a person of her status that her existence was only peripheral to others. Some personality types wouldn't hesitate to snuff her out if she didn't ease off them.

Maybe, Garrett decided as he finished his second drink, it was time to approach Toutant. Make that famous offer he couldn't refuse, unless he wanted to rot in stir for the next twenty years. But he still didn't know if Toutant knew enough to ensure the prosecutions of the powerful men around him. Questions still went unanswered, the first of which was whether Toutant had tapes or other records, as Garrett suspected he did. It was better to wait, maybe. Better to find out, he decided. In the next few days. Because time was nipping at his ass.

" 'Nuther spot of the giant killer?" Dabs asked, proffering the bottle.

Garrett shook his head and slid off the barstool. "Three drinks and I'll be out on the roof."

Even as he spoke, the door behind the bar opened and Toutant stepped out of his cramped office. His hard, speculative eyes lingered on the bouncer until Garrett turned away.

"You look lovely tonight," Aunt Rose told Stella at dinner on Monday evening.

"Mmm-hmm," Maman agreed. "Pretty as a princess. It's a tonic just to look at her."

It cost Stella considerable effort to acknowledge their compliments with a wan smile. She wore a sleeveless dress of fluid Italian design. Glittering crystal-drop earrings hung from her lobes, and her hair was drawn back tightly in a chignon. The rule about formal dress at dinner had been relaxed at Shadow Oaks over the ages. But Stella often observed it anyway, especially as an antidote when she was dispirited. Tonight, however, it wasn't doing much good.

The three women shared the long oak table in the dining room, under the mysterious smile of the eighteenth-century Madonna hanging on the wall behind them. Stella had been quiet throughout dinner, preoccupied with her thoughts. She met the other women's solicitous glances with distant eyes that proved her thoughts were elsewhere, roaming far afield.

Maman looked at Stella's nearly untouched plate and shook her silver head.

"You *know* this is not a well child," she told Rose. "When's the last time that girl left asparagus on her plate?"

"Stella," Rose said, her voice firm with reproof. "You've been moody and fretful since yesterday. What is it, dear? Is it this business with airplanes and whatnot? Or—if I—that is, if Mattie was offended by anything I—"

"You were fine," Stella assured her. "It's nothing, really."

She no longer wanted to convince her aunt and Maman that something sinister was going on around there. Whether it was true or not, she couldn't shake Garrett's warning that she would jeopardize anyone she told about the drug running.

"Oh, pouf," Rose insisted. "Stella, you're absolutely tormenting yourself about something. I can see it in your eyes. You've always had such expressive eyes. Just like your poor dead mother's."

Maman crossed herself at this reference to the dead.

Aunt Rose raised her voice an octave and recited a little ditty:

> Tender-handed stroke a nettle,
> and it stings you for your pains;
> Grasp it like a gal of mettle,
> and it soft as silk remains.

Stella smiled again, for the wisdom of this advice was not lost on her, even in this mood. But not every problem in the world could be readily grasped. She felt as if she were in a strange land where no one spoke her language. And it wasn't just the trouble with the drugs.

Autry had stopped by to see her this evening before he drove home. They'd accumulated major business expenses, including extensive repairs to the cultivator as well as hiring a labor crew to shore up a flooded section of cane where the levee broke along Bayou Lafourche. The accountant had already warned her the business was now drawing out of her personal account. One more disaster at this time could sink the plantation and force Shadow Oaks onto the real estate market.

She looked at her aunt's small, striking face, the older woman's own expressive eyes undimmed by the years. Rose knew, of course, that profit margins had narrowed lately. But true to most of the women of her generation, she was blithely ignorant of business details. Her faith in the unsinkability of Shadow Oaks no doubt matched what Jacqueline and Edward had for the *Titanic*—and might well meet the same end.

Lost in such thoughts, Stella became aware that Rose was speaking in a wistful tone.

"Myrtle has finally told me all will be well. So we must believe her. She is at rest."

Stella felt a jolt of surprise. If she was seeing a strange girl wandering around the grounds, maybe Rose was seeing her too. Maybe the girl in white had a name and her name was Myrtle.

"What does this Myrtle look like, Rose?" Stella queried. "Because I think Shadow Oaks might have a ghost after all—"

Maman interrupted. "We all live by a flame within us. *Don't* put out that flame, child."

Stella saw the crystal shimmer of tears brighten her aunt's eyes. "Like my flame died out," Rose told her.

Suddenly, Stella couldn't trust her own voice. She stood up and crossed quickly to Rose's chair, giving her a long hug.

Maman dabbed at her cola-brown eyes with the corner of her napkin. "Sakes and saints," she scolded, looking at the tall case clock in the corner. "We'll all cry the night right away! I'll clear the dishes and fix us a toddy."

Stella was devastated. As she looked at her two favorite women in all the world, she knew she could never tell them the only life they knew might soon be over, the victim of negative cash flow and the bottom line. The eventuality would crush Stella, but the blow would be heaviest on these two.

It just can't happen, she resolved, putting ghost stories and drug dealers out of her mind for the present. You can't *let* it happen. Rose and Maman did not deserve such a hard fate in the twilight of their lives.

Her aunt was right. Stella must indeed grasp that nettle. Grasp it so hard that even if she bled, victory would be sweeter than the pain.

Business was slow at The Scarlet Door, so Toutant sent the dancers home and closed at midnight. By one A.M. the place was deserted except for him and Jervis Archer. Both men sat at the S-shaped mahogany bar, shadowy figures in the dim glow of night lights.

"I gave his place a good search," Archer insisted. "Though there's damn little to search. The guy must think he's a fucking Gandhi or somebody. His room is like a monk's cell."

"Skip his personal habits," Toutant said scornfully. "I don't care if the guy flosses. Did you find anything that marks him for our fed?"

"Can't say I did," Archer admitted with evident reluctance. "But our boy was an officer in the marines, you know that? I found a photo. He was a rifle platoon leader."

Toutant was staring into a cup of lukewarm black coffee. His head came up slowly at this intelligence. He looked at Archer.

"An officer? I knew he was in the corps or the Seals or something macho. He put that on his application. That's one reason I hired him." Toutant paused before he added, "But he never mentioned he was an officer."

"Well, if he was, he was also a college boy. How many longshoremen you know with college degrees? And he served in Beirut back in the eighties. That place was a hot zone, good chance he saw combat there. That photo showed a zappo platoon, not a bunch o' clerk-typists."

Toutant seemed interested but not convinced. "So what? Far as college, hell, there's redneck riggers come in here singing 'Bang, Bang Lulu,' and they got master's degrees. And you know, most guys don't talk about combat if they've seen it. He's not covering it up just because he doesn't brag about it."

"Jesus!" Archer exploded. "Do you wipe his ass for him too?"

Jervis was off duty now and had a few too many under his belt. Drunkenness always made his face bloat so much, it reminded Toutant of an image in a chrome door handle.

"I'm telling you," Jervis persisted, "that something stinks. You seen how this Cowboy handles himself in a fight. He's no home-grown street fighter. He's had training in a dojo, lots of it."

"Yeah, that's another reason I hired him. So what? You think I need a sissy for my front-door man? Face it, Jervis. You're just pissed because he handled you. Could be we're all wrong here, Leblanc be damned."

But Archer had slyly led Toutant to the finale. Now he pulled a single three by five-inch sheet of white paper out from his shirt pocket.

"I tore this off the top of a notepad by his bed," Archer explained. "He won't miss it, it's just a blank sheet. But if you turn it just right in the light, it'll show trace indentations. From a note he made on the sheet above this one. Check it out."

Archer pulled a Zippo from his pocket and snapped a flame to life. In its flickering glow Toutant studied the page closely. He could eventually make out the slight outline of the words: *Stella St. Vallier.*

Archer snicked his lighter shut while Toutant pondered this problematic development.

"It could just be," Toutant said slowly, thinking out loud, "a reminder to himself to hit on her. She's a nice little piece, and those two have met."

"When?" Archer demanded. "You never told me that."

"He tossed her outta here—literally. Little over a week ago now. That night I told you about, when she first accused me. After handling her body like he did, it wouldn't be a stretch to think he's got the hots for her."

Archer scowled, not liking anything he was hearing.

"Look, we can sit here all night, making up excuses for the guy," he complained. "You're good at that. But you heard Leblanc. We got no safe landing spot now. Even if we fix that problem like Harley says he can, we got no good cover for the cash deposits. This shit's for the birds. The longer we're shut down, the harder it'll be to get up and running again."

"Granted," Toutant said. "But killing a fed, if he is one, will hardly clear the path for us."

"Maybe not, at first. It could present some hassles, sure. But if he is a fed, tell me this: You think we could afford *not* to kill him? C'mon, I been thinking hard about that problem. You know, this guy's a loner. Cop or not. Lives in a boardinghouse, eats off a hot plate, for Christ sakes. How many losers like that close their own account every year?"

"What, you mean make it look like suicide?" Toutant thought that over. Finally, his thin eyebrows rose a little and he nodded. "That might be a possibility at that. Quite a few cops do that every year. Stress, loneliness, all that. But *only* if we get some solid proof on him. He's a friendless man with mysterious habits. Yet, he's likable and has no ax to grind. To me, that usually means a guy's on the dodge from the law."

"Yeah?" Archer didn't sound convinced.

Toutant ignored this, for something else occurred to him. "Did you have to break into his room?"

"Used a jimmy. It's just an old night latch with a worn tumbler. He won't know I was there." The chief crumpled the sheet of notepaper and flicked it off the bar with his index finger. "Meantime," he said, "for all we know, Cowboy's been grilling Stella St. Vallier. 'Bout time I paid her another visit."

"Never mind any personal grudges," Toutant warned. "This is no time to lick old wounds. Just get any information she's got, but don't piss her off."

Archer snorted. "She's like other high-class bitches I've known. They only get pissed off until they know me better. Then they learn some respect."

CHAPTER

14

Garrett touched base with Steve Falcone on Tuesday morning. He already knew that Mike Hogan, their section chief, was nervous about the Cane Town operation. So was Steve. Accordingly, Garrett didn't mention his dustup with Jervis Archer. Nor did he allude to Archer and Toutant's growing suspicion about his true identity. Garrett's discretion, however, was pointless. Steve dropped a bomb on him anyway.

"It's going to be official tomorrow," he informed his colleague. "When the case-status dailies are issued, Hogan is going to terminate your field assignment and call you back."

Garrett cursed. "I know it's pointless to ask. But why?"

"Don't jump on me, I gave him my best pitch. Basically, I skipped the crusading-lawmen crap. I just told Hogan plain out that termination at this point sucks some major kielbasa."

Despite his crappy mood, Garrett had to laugh. "You used those exact words?"

"Well, not exactly, no. But something close. Problem is, we've got some chancy traffic-analysis reports from the tech boys. The Cane Town P.D. has run your name on the NCIC computers, and so has Cliff D'Antoni's office. D'Antoni is still checking you out on regional crime-info data banks. He's a D.A., he might be savvy enough to expose a canned ID. Anyhow, make a long story short, Hogan's afraid they're about to crack your cover."

Terminate your field assignment. Garrett felt like he'd been hit but not quite dropped. All his hard work and careful planning, all the greasy meals and grueling hours, the risks. One chairborne commando at a desk in D.C., scared that a dead agent might cost him a promotion, could deep-six all of it with a few strokes on a computer keyboard.

"Well, that just flat does it," Garrett decided. "One day is all I have left. All right, then. I'll have to arrest Toutant tonight and talk him into a deal."

"Why not try?" Falcone agreed, although with less assurance in his tone. Both friends were firm believers in the gutsy cavalry charge. But then again, there was always Custer. Steve added, "It'd be better to have even more on him than we do. Like the skinny on his buyers. Better leverage. But we can pile up a pretty nasty stack of charges. Maybe he'll bite, maybe he won't. It's worth a try."

"The way you say. I sure's hell can't take him into custody around here. I'll drive him to New Orleans and book him into central lockup. Let them hold him until we can get an extradition order signed. He's a definite risk for flight, so we can keep him from bonding out."

"Probably. I just hope he knows as much as you think he does. It really would be sweet if he's got tapes of those meetings."

"Even if he hasn't," Garrett said, "Toutant is one to keep accounts. He knows something useful."

"Yeah, well, you listen, hot dog. It just might not be a tragedy even if Toutant stiffs us or jumps bond. We may not need him so much after all."

"How you figure that?" Garrett demanded.

"I mean that was one sweet tip you moled up about Doug Woodyard, Barry's brother, in the New Orleans Port Authority. You were right to call him our favorite boy. I've been working with Applesby at IRS. That dude is a bloodsucker when it comes to cracking into databases. It's creatively hidden, but we've turned up a mega-discrepancy between Doug's income and his annual investment capital."

"Payoffs from the Ring," Garrett speculated.

"Sure, what else? That's why his brother Barry was invited in," Steve supplied. "The Ring needed safe access to Doug. And it all ties up into a neat little bow, because that was Fontainbleau's main function too. See, he was tight as ticks with Johnny Mansetto, the president of the longshoremen's local in New Orleans."

"Oh, yeah. The dude they found floating in the Italian fountain," Garrett said, remembering the sensational case.

"Right, which, of course, made Fontainbleau expendable also. The Ring lost access to the guys who actually load the ships. Now they've got Doug Woodyard. Longshoremen or Customs, either one is good to have in your pocket if you're a crook in the shipping business."

"Ah so. And that's why you're thinking Woodyard might be our ace in the hole?"

"What, has masturbation made you stupid?" Steve demanded. "Toutant can spell out the op at a broad level, sure. But Woodyard can give us the nuts-and-bolts stuff."

"One world at a time, partner," Garrett suggested.

"Toutant has more opportunities to watch and snoop on Leblanc. Let's crack him first."

After he hung up the phone, Garrett pushed open the folding screen that blocked off the room's tiny kitchenette. He put water on to boil while he mulled these troubling new developments.

It was right down to the wire now. He simply couldn't let up, dangerous or no. Not now. He would *have* to convince Toutant—scare the man into cooperating.

Toutant's decision, however, depended on how much he trusted Archer's ability to handle emergencies. Garrett truly regretted yesterday's clash with the chief. Toutant was smart enough to realize the incident left Jervis motivated to kill the bouncer. The club owner might well decide to just let Archer handle the problem of Garrett Shaw rather than risk cooperating with the feds.

Garrett would take that chance. He wasn't playing hero—he simply had too much invested in this case to throw it all down a rat hole now. Not when his eyes were fixed firmly on the real prize: Senator Myron Leblanc.

His main worry was still the lovely Stella. One of the last things Garrett intended to do before he left Cane Town was make a full revelation to her. Give her names, details, badge numbers, Hogan's number in D.C.—anything she required to verify he was not one of the predators currently terrorizing her. It might scare some sense into her. The woman had to be convinced she had stumbled into a minefield.

The real danger, Garrett figured, was Jervis Archer. Shaw knew that Archer—or some minion sent by him—had searched his room the night before. It was an amateur's job. But it didn't require sophistication to pull off a good killing. Just brute cunning. Fontainbleau's gruesome and still unsolved murder proved that. Cane cutters, wood chippers, potter's kilns—certain ways of killing and disposing of corpses left little or no forensic clues behind. It didn't matter how well forensics played on the Discovery Channel, most murders went unsolved—in spite of a mountain of evidence. And even small-town cops like Archer were well aware of that fact. Garrett would lay fifty-to-one odds that Archer fed Fontainbleau into that cane cutter part by part. And what men have done, men still can do.

Stella was perhaps in as much danger as Garrett himself was. Maybe even more since he, at least, was well warned and could at least shoot back.

I'll talk to her before I split, Garrett promised himself again. Meantime, he hoped to God for her sake that she was as smart as she seemed to be.

Before she sent her query for Professor Perkins's scrutiny, Stella needed to ask Autry about something he'd mentioned to her a week before. It was a beautiful day, so bright with sunshine, it made her smile to look up at the sky. She welcomed the excuse to walk out to the sugarhouse through the whispering and wavering of the rapidly maturing sugar cane.

When the wind blew, she could still see above the green sea, though just. The late morning sun momentarily ducked behind a tumble of clouds. Its disappearance turned the surface of Bayou Lafourche into a flat sheet the color of wet slate. The blues and greens of her land were an Impressionist's dream. Giverny couldn't hold a candle to Shadow Oaks on a day like today. It hurt even more to think how weak her grasp was in holding on to it.

She forced her thoughts back to business—her salvation. Autry had said something about drying out the bagasse, once it was squeezed dry of juice, to use as fuel. Something about how the stalks were already partially dried out from the heat of flames that burned off the outer blades. The idea might prove to be another avenue for income, and she was determined to travel every route or die trying.

"Autry?"

The big, pulley-mounted doors of the sugarhouse stood open. Stella stepped inside.

"Autry? Are you here?"

Nothing but stuffy silence greeted her words. Autry's old station wagon was parked outside. And the John Deere was parked in its spot just inside the doors. So the man must be around somewhere.

Maybe he's with the laborers at the broken levee, she thought. She decided to wait awhile in case he returned soon.

It was still early in the day, but her nerves had the stretched, frazzled feel of late night. A pigeon suddenly flitted from a corner of the rafters, wings whipping the air, and she flinched as if she'd been touched.

Glad no one had seen her, she began walking slowly toward the huge iron rollers of the cane press. Her eyes, however, were turned thoughtfully toward the big overhead heat fans used to help crystallize the boiled syrup.

A male voice spoke from the doorway behind her, and this time she was so shocked, she couldn't even flinch. Instead, she felt as if invisible insects were crawling all over her scalp.

"Cotton to the north, sugar to the south. Remember that, Stella?"

The voice was raised, yet stayed equally atonal for each word. She realized who it was and immediately felt trapped. Nonetheless, her features were composed when she turned to face Jervis Archer.

"Pardon me?" she said with bare civility. She was still too confused and scared to feel the anger she had a right to feel at his unwelcome intrusion.

"Don'tcha remember that from grade school?" Archer pestered her, tipping his Smokey Bear hat back as he stepped inside the big, clinker-built structure. "It was Louisiana history. Cotton grows in the north part of the state, sugar cane in the south. We had to draw it on state maps. Everything below the Red River belonged to you God Almighty cane planters. Whoop-dee-fucking-doo, right?"

Even in the subdued light she saw his broad, crudely handsome face twist with insolence. He had slowed his pace, but he was still coming at her.

He's big, she realized, trying to shake the conviction she was on a fast elevator plunging down. He'd never need that gun.

"How did you know I was back here?" she asked, angry at herself. She had vowed never to repeat her mistake of the previous Thursday, when she went into the garden alone with him. This was even worse.

"Saw you walking this way when I went around to the kitchen door," he replied. "So I just sorta invited myself back."

She wanted to back away from his advance, but she feared the consequences of showing she was afraid, of letting him just easily take control of the situation. Not now, not out here. The loudest scream would go unnoticed.

"I see that," she told him, her voice determined and unwavering. "And you did so against my expressed wishes. I told you you're not welcome at Shadow Oaks any longer."

"Spare me the catfight, Stella. This is police business."

Thank God, she thought when he changed direction, veering away from her.

"Yes, well, what is it?" she reminded Archer when he fell silent.

But he ignored her completely. He stared at the side wall covered with cane knives. She felt her skin crawl against her clothing when he slowly reached up and removed one from its hook.

"Damn," he said with husky respect, turning the tool in his big, hairy hands. "The edge is still sharp. These little babies could do a hoo-doo on somebody."

His eyes pinned her across the distance. She suddenly thought of Fontainbleau—of the fact that his remains were so mutilated, only DNA fingerprinting could prove his species, and that just barely, let alone his identity. And his murderer was still at large. She never gave much credence to the whispered rumors about Archer—not until lately.

She looked toward the door and calculated her chances of beating him to it if she ran out. He must have plucked that thought from her mind, for he suddenly emitted a harsh bark of laughter. He hung the cane knife back up. Then he came toward her again.

"Your police business, Chief?" she reminded him yet again.

"Oh, I'm just curious, Stella. Tell me. How well do you know the bouncer at The Scarlet Door? The tall guy they call Cowboy?"

She was grateful for the dim light. Surely his unexpected question made her turn pale. Archer watched her from carefully caged eyes, waiting for an answer.

"I—that is—how is that question germane to police business?"

Jervis stopped only two feet from her. His eyes never seemed to blink as they stared at her.

"I ain't free to divulge details," he told her. "Let's just say I've got an eye on the guy. And you might be smart to remember something. The law holds us accountable when we choose to associate with criminals."

Her insides quivered with indignation. Do you mean criminals like Toutant and Harley Burke? she wanted to demand. But in truth, by then she was too scared. Fear, in turn, engendered guilt. For she had long believed that anyone, just by being brave for even one second, could change the course of history. Certainly, the history of Shadow Oaks had been so altered. Likewise, she believed cowardly silence was what condemned the world to its present woes. Yet, she was willing to be one of the silent cowards if she could just be left alone.

"I *don't* 'associate' with the man," she finally replied. "I don't even know him. I've spoken with him only a couple of times."

That was a lie. It was four times, not a couple. But she saw no reason to include the day in the library and last Saturday night's chance meeting along the bayou.

Archer nodded, his eyes dwelling on the shadow of cleavage exposed by her scoop-necked knit tank. He moved even closer. She imagined she could feel the heat coming off him.

"I hope, for your sake, you're telling the truth," he assured her.

"What—what do you mean? What kind of 'criminal' is he?"

"Either you already know that or you're innocent and don't need to know. I told you I'm not free to divulge details."

She had enough to worry about already. Still— Archer was clearly threatening her. The wrongness of that rankled at her, as did the idea that thugs were trying to intimidate her into silence.

But she also cautioned herself against drawing a dangerously hasty conclusion. Never mind her intense personal dislike for Archer. He could be telling the truth, or something close to it. She mustn't let her physical attraction to Shaw make her forget that he, too, wanted her to just drop the entire matter. He clearly implied he was a cop. But he refused to verify that claim. In truth, she decided, Archer and Garrett could be allies in crime, just faking discord to confuse her. She must not trust *any* of them, no matter what her heart wished were true.

Distracted by this internal debate, she was too slow to react when Archer suddenly grabbed both her arms in a bruising grip.

"You're a hothead, Stella St. Vallier. Let's see if there's any fire behind all your smoke."

Terrified and repulsed, she tried to turn her face

away, but Jervis managed to force his hungry, seeking mouth onto hers. He pressed her back against one giant wheel of the tractor, thrusting his crotch tightly against her so she'd feel his arousal. He smelled like musty leather and cheap mouthwash. Disgust washed over her when she realized he was thrusting over and over with his pelvis, hard, stimulating himself against her like an eager dog.

"Let me *go!*" she managed to get out, fighting to keep him from forcing his tongue into her mouth.

"You want it, you horny little bitch, and you know you do," Jervis said, the words thick and slurred from his urgently building lust. "I'm taking you on the ground like an animal, right here. It won't be rape once you beg for more, will it?"

"*Bonsoir, ma chère!* Am I interrupting?"

Autry Duplantier stood in the open doorway, small and old and stooping forward with age. But right then he was Stella's knight in shining armor.

"Autry! No, no, of course not, come in, please. Chief Archer was just leaving, I believe."

Moving deftly, she ducked around Jervis and freed herself. Autry came inside.

Jervis wiped his mouth with the back of one hand, his breathing still noticeably heavy. His icy blue eyes pierced her like a pair of bullets.

"You think about what I said, Stella," he advised her, flashing his off-kilter smile that failed to include all of his mouth. "I mean, damn. I'd hate to see anything happen to you."

"Good-bye to you, Chief. And I'd sure hate to see anything happen to me too," she nearly whispered as he passed, her voice too constricted with fear to speak up.

CHAPTER

15

On Tuesday, Senator Myron Leblanc attended a political fund-raiser at the downtown Hilton in Washington. He returned to his Georgetown town house late in the afternoon. Still wearing a dinner jacket and carnation boutonniere, he took a carafe of Scotch into the den. He settled into a leather recliner before the TV set and began reviewing proposed thirty-second spots for his next reelection campaign.

At four-thirty the phone on his desk burred. Leblanc hit the pause button on the VCR remote, then answered the phone.

A cultivated southern voice greeted him, so smooth, the words seemed poured rather than spoken.

"Myron, how are you, old son? This is Roland."

Mississippi Congressman Roland Nesbit was a long-time friend and political ally of Leblanc's. He was also currently serving on the Justice Department's Oversight Committee. Both men had been in the same fraternity at Emory University and then roomed together for a time during law school at Georgetown.

"Roland, you incorrigible reprobate, how are *you?* It's been far too long since we chewed the fat." The senator's voice was all charismatic charm with enough warmth to hide the fact he was terrified.

The two men spoke of inconsequential matters for a while, following a well-established protocol between them. Then, when it was clear the ground had been felt out sufficiently, Nesbit ventured to broach the real purpose of his call.

"You know, Myron, our respective states have been competing neck-and-neck for this new NASA fuel-testing facility."

"How could I not know? It's a sweet little plum for whoever can pluck it."

"Six hundred good jobs. Not to mention several major construction contracts. At any rate, scuttlebutt has it the choices are narrowed down to Poplar Bluffs, Mississippi, and Ruston, Louisiana."

"I've heard that," Leblanc affirmed with a practiced plastic grin on his face that no one could see. "And right now the committee is leaning toward Louisiana."

"Thanks to your golden tongue and powers of persuasion, you rascal! You're the only one who whipped me in moot court, remember. But you see, Myron, I'm just wondering lately. Is there any chance the planning committee might lean toward Poplar Bluffs instead?"

Squint lines like spiderwebs appeared at the corners of his eyes when Leblanc smiled. For a few moments he said nothing, only staring through a mullioned window with leaded panes. He watched the neighbor's pair of silky English setters romping in a big side yard dotted with white sycamores.

"I never say never, Roland," he finally replied. "Human beings are deal-making animals. Besides, we Southerners need to stick together."

By protocol, Nesbit knew this was his invitation to make an offer. So far neither man had mentioned United Southern Children's Charities. But five minutes later, when both men hung up, Mississippi had its new NASA facility.

Leblanc checked the ormolu clock on his desk: 4:45. That meant it was 3:45 in Louisiana. He picked up the telephone again and punched in a number.

"Percival? Leblanc here. I was right, my friend. It's just been confirmed by a very reliable source. There's room on Boot Hill for one more cowboy, do you take my meaning? Good. And for Christ sakes, do it ASAP."

Garrett had never been inside Toutant's apartment above The Scarlet Door. But it didn't strike him as particularly ominous, when Garrett called his boss to request a meeting before work, that Toutant asked him to stop by.

Shortly before five P.M., Garrett ascended a steep flight of weatherbeaten wooden steps that led upstairs from the back alley. Toutant answered his knock almost immediately.

"Hey, Cowboy, how they hanging? C'mon in and have a longneck."

Toutant's apartment was spartan and neat. Built in the "shotgun" style, all four rooms lined up in a row. Toutant opened two beers and handed one to Garrett. Then he led the way into the living room.

"So what's on your mind?" Toutant asked, settling in a plaid sofa while Garrett chose a worn armchair across the narrow room. "You want a raise, don'tcha?"

Garrett sure as hell hoped he felt far more nervous than he looked. How he presented all of it to Toutant in the next few minutes would determine the outcome of a lot of hard work. The Cane Town investigation wasn't automatically a total waste if Toutant refused to cooperate. Especially if Steve was right about Doug Woodyard's extensive involvement. But such a refusal would certainly weaken any potential prosecution.

"Pay's fine, Chief, just fine," Garrett finally replied. "I'm the one who's got an offer to make."

Over the next few minutes Garrett laid it all out like a presentation at a sales meeting. Who he really was, why he was in Cane Town, and the fact that Toutant was now, after Garrett read him his Miranda rights, officially under arrest. He also detailed several charges for which Toutant would be indicted, including conspiracy to distribute, which carried a mandatory twenty-year sentence under federal jurisdiction. Finally, Garrett made it abundantly clear that Toutant's full cooperation meant he would see far less prison time.

Toutant's thin, sharp-nosed face remained impassive throughout, as if he were listening to a weather report that didn't affect him. During all this, a game show went forward on the TV set in the corner. Just as Garrett finished speaking, the program cut to a commercial. Myron Leblanc's blunt, leonine head filled the TV screen.

"Pitch in, Louisiana. Every dollar you donate to United Southern Children's Charities buys one week's worth of rice and beans for a hungry child in hurricane-ravaged Central America. Hunger knows no nationality. Won't you do all you can for the children?"

Garrett watched Toutant closely and didn't like what he was seeing. The man did not appear at all surprised or scared. Indeed, Percival surprised him with a sad, almost affectionate smile.

"I'm truly disappointed, Cowboy," he finally responded. "Know that? Disappointed in myself for being such a sap. But I'm also disappointed in you."

"Yeah? Forgive me if I don't feel contrite. Look, how 'bout my offer, P.G.? You don't have to answer this minute, but think about it while I'm taking you to New Orleans. Your cooperation in exchange for a lesser charge. If you're helpful enough, we might even be able to get you less than five years."

"But I take all this *very* personally," Toutant went on as if Garrett hadn't spoken. "There's something particularly treacherous about a narc, Cowboy. That's lower than anything I've ever done. I hire a man off the street, give him a job, trust him, and what happens? He prongs me in the ass."

Alarm bells went off for Garrett. Toutant's responses were all wrong, facial and verbal. His tone implied *he* was the one with arresting power. Garrett took some comfort in the reassuring weight of the Beretta automatic clipped under his shirt. Toutant never carried a weapon that Garrett had noticed. Nonetheless, Shaw shifted slightly in his chair so he could get at his quickly.

"Look, P.G., just skip the outraged-godfather shit. Are you listening to my offer or not?"

"Not," answered a flat masculine voice behind Garrett.

Jervis Archer stood in the doorway that led to the bedroom. The unblinking eye of his Police .38 stared at Garrett. Deputy Harley Burke stood beside his boss, weapon likewise trained on Shaw.

For a moment, caught totally off guard, Garrett was too stunned for any response. Then his face organized itself into a broad smile of false bonhomie.

"Well, well. Cane Town's finest. Shouldn't you boys be out there feeding politicians into Vegematics?"

"Frisk him," Archer ordered his deputy. "Get cute on us, Cowboy, and you'll have a nifty new airshaft in your head."

Toutant gave Garrett a look that knifed him. "You hung around a little bit too long, Cowboy."

Burke, in the meantime, pulled Garrett to his feet and patted him down. He found the Beretta and slid the clip out of it, placing both on a cheap Masonite end table beside the chair.

"You three are just digging yourselves into a deeper

hole," Garrett assured them. "Killing me won't kill the case against you, only strengthen it."

Archer stepped farther into the room. He transferred his gun to his left hand and used the right to unclip the side-handle baton from his utility belt.

"Maybe you're right," the chief told Garrett. "But killing you sure's hell will be fun. Harley, pin his arms for me."

Garrett managed to knock the deputy aside with a fast left elbow to the solar plexus. But thus occupied, he was helpless to fend off the blow when Archer swung the stick with vicious force. Pain grated through Garrett's body. He saw a bright orange starburst inside his ringing skull, then his knees folded.

"That fucker," Burke gasped, down on one knee now as he recovered his breath.

"You can haul him out after dark," Toutant said, staring at the unconscious fed. "If he's still out cold, there's an old rug in the bedroom, you can roll him up in that. Just don't forget. Fontainbleau was eventually identified. We need to avoid that mistake this time."

"Don't sweat it," Archer assured him. "This time there won't be any DNA because nobody is ever going to find his body."

Stella had talked herself out of a bad situation before. But the nervous fear inspired by her encounter earlier that day with Archer only increased as the day waned. The agonizing debate over what to do kept her awake long after she'd gone to bed.

What complicated matters most was her complete and frustrating inability to trust any of the major players in the situation. True, she had no substantial case for suspicion against Senator Leblanc. But his combination of smooth rhetoric and vague details made her totally distrustful of confiding in him again.

Only Toutant and Harley Burke were undisputed

criminals—that is, undisputed in *her* mind. Concerning Garrett Shaw, the jury was still out. Although he certainly had plenty to explain if he wasn't a crook.

As for Archer, in contrast: The man had been on the verge of raping her earlier. Or so he'd threatened. Thank God Autry's arrival had ended the tense situation. Men like Jervis, however, didn't always consider rape a crime. Did his threat prove he was a rapist lawless enough to be involved with Toutant and Burke? Or was it just rough talk inspired by his brand of low-life lust?

Downstairs, the tall case clock in the dining room chimed the quarter hour. Which hour she wasn't sure. She'd gone to bed around eleven, but it seemed like she'd been tossing and turning for hours.

Only ten days had passed since that Saturday when Stella had first spotted Toutant on her land. Yet she felt like she'd been trapped for years in the dilemma eating away at her.

Unable to bear her agonized, silent worrying any longer, she sat up and checked the glowing clock on the dresser: almost one-thirty. An ungodly hour to call anyone. But Mattie always bragged how she was a night owl.

She hadn't forgotten Shaw's dire warning that she might endanger anyone she spoke to about the drugs. But that line perhaps served his interests. Besides, Mattie wasn't a local. At any rate, Stella simply couldn't bear all this alone.

She rose, shrugged into her robe, then went down the short hall into her little reading nook to use the phone.

"Mattie?" she whispered into the receiver.

"Girl? What you doing up this late?" came Mattie's familiar, reassuring voice.

Stella released a silent sigh. Thank God Mattie had answered right away, obviously wide awake and in a mood to listen. Stella apologized profusely for calling so late, then, trying to be coherent and specific, she blurted out the major details. She began with the

Saturday night encounter with Garrett while Mattie was visiting at Shadow Oaks, which Stella had not mentioned yet to her friend, then she described her creepy and frightening run-in with Archer earlier that day at the sugarhouse.

Mattie listened patiently to all of it. Now and then she asked a brief question to clarify this point or that.

"You care to hear what I think?" Mattie demanded when Stella had finished.

"Why do you think I called?"

"Just making sure. 'Cause you won't like it. First of all, Stella, you are far too emotionally complex for your own good. Honest to John, you're going to follow your confused heart into a disaster. Look. This Chief Archer—sure, he is definitely a redneck pig. I wouldn't trust him alone with *my* sheep. But he's probably right about your Cowboy. Cute or no, he sounds like one bad buckaroo to me."

"He's not 'my' Cowboy, I—"

"Oh, Stella, would you cut the crap? Think about it. You catch him red-handed in a big dope deal. And lo and behold. Suddenly, boys and girls, he's a noble G-man, fighting for truth, justice, and the American way. Give me a break! Stella, you'd better take a minute to smell what this dude is shoveling."

Sometimes Mattie could be brutally blunt. But that was precisely what Stella needed. Indeed, Mattie's assurance was downright comforting after Stella's inability to reach any conclusions. Mattie didn't settle anything, of course. Her perspective only confirmed Stella's worst fears. She must trust no one until she knew more. But that, at least, was a firm resolution.

"You're right," she finally conceded. "I'm not thinking clearly. And that could be a very stupid mistake in this situation."

"Atta girl. God knows, he's a certified hunk. This 'Cowboy' is no mere trifle to waste. But men are like a poker game. What you drop in one hand you pick up in the next."

"Ever the idealist." Stella rolled her eyes.

"Idealism," Mattie the historian shot back in parting, "has killed almost as many people as mosquitoes have."

"Yes. Screw saving the family farm, I'd better just save my fanny," she whispered into the receiver.

"Now you're thinking, girl. You've got to tell the authorities what you know, and fast. Promise me?"

"I promise," Stella said. After a few more reassurances that she would go to New Orleans the following day and talk to someone at the DEA in person, she hung up and returned to her bedroom.

But she didn't crawl back into bed. Instead, she stood for a long time in the bay window that faced Leblanc's property. She could make out little in the cloud-obscured moonlight. Just a dark, shadowy mass where cypress trees and a bayou divided the two plantations.

It all seemed quiet, so peaceful. Yet, while she stood there, she abruptly felt her skin prickle. She expected to see the girl with the Buster Brown haircut flit through the garden and into the bayou.

With that thought she returned to bed and covered up for warmth.

She soon fell asleep. But Mattie's warning about Garrett chased her down that long, dark tunnel toward oblivion like taunting children: *You'd better take a minute to smell what this dude is shoveling.*

CHAPTER

<u>16</u>

Day bled into night, but the subtle transition from light to darkness was completely wasted on Garrett. Cuffed and gagged, his ankles restrained, he'd been left on the floor in Toutant's bedroom, still unconscious.

For what seemed a long time he drifted in and out of awareness, as if he were moving through patchy fog. He had no clear idea when he finally came to again. But his throbbing head felt as though the Twentieth Century Limited were using it for a track bed.

At some point he abruptly realized it was nighttime. He knew that from the pulsing light in the room, caused by the old neon sign flashing on and off over the front entrance of The Scarlet Door. He could see the corner of a bed covered with a chintz spread. Behind the bed, a whatnot crowded with terra cotta and majolica ornaments.

Garrett lay on his stomach. A thick, itchy carpet softened the floor beneath him. But his shoulders were an agony of pain as a result of his arms being pinioned behind him for hours.

Not only was it dark outside, he soon realized, but also relatively late. Close to midnight, he guessed, judging from the familiar pattern of sounds below in The Scarlet Door. The jukebox was thumping, not the strippers' taped music. This was Tuesday, meaning the girls had probably knocked off by eleven-thirty or so.

He could also hear voices much closer at hand. Male voices, four of them, he finally determined, emanating from the next room. Even from where he was, without understanding any of the words, he could pick out Toutant's self-satisfied tone. The flat, emotionless drone, of course, would be Archer. The other two voices spoke seldom and were indistinguishable. Garrett assumed one was Harley Burke's.

Carefully, holding in his breath, Garrett moved one of his fingers behind the rear portion of his wide leather cowboy belt. He felt the cool touch of metal, and he expelled his breath in a great welling of relief.

If he had any chance at all of surviving this night, he had just touched it. Anytime Garrett worked a case involving potentially crooked cops, he always kept a universal handcuff key tied to a belt loop with a short piece of dental floss. A handcuff key was smaller than a quarter, and shoved up behind his belt, it was too little to see or feel during even a careful frisk.

Unfortunately, this was not the time or place to employ the key. The room had only one window, and despite the fact that it was the second story, the security-obsessed Toutant had installed wrought-iron burglar bars. They meant that Garrett would have to escape, unarmed and weak as a kitten, through those armed men in the living room. He'd never pull it off.

His tolerance for experiencing danger firsthand, while also observing himself objectively, served him well now. He forced himself to focus down from useless anxiety to calmly work out each step in the probable scenario he was about to face.

They won't kill me here, he reasoned immediately. Way too much risk of leaving hard evidence, especially with forensic tools. And even a two-bit killer knew a living body is infinitely easier to manage and handle than a dead one. Archer knew the bayou better than most men knew their wives' geography. They'll take me to some remote part of the swamps and shoot me there, Garrett decided. Efficient, like Nazis shooting their victims so they fell neatly into the grave.

That meant he had to wait. Be patient and watch for his opportunity. It did not occur to him to wonder if an opportunity would indeed present itself. He already understood it was his job to *make* one happen. That, or his life ended this night.

"This is just to make things interesting," Archer announced.

He tossed a tight, plastic-wrapped bundle of pure cocaine paste onto the Masonite end table. Toutant, Burke, and a rabbit-toothed, vacant-eyed deputy named Jim Bob Larsen, the only one still in uniform, all stared at it. Nobody in the crowd had to ask what it was.

"After we leave tonight to take care of Cowboy," Archer told Larsen, "you're going to plant this in his room. The only dope any cop is authorized to possess for a sting has to come from an evidence locker and be registered by tag number to the cop. So this will definitely be contraband. And we're going to make sure *we* find it before the feds can. Here's the key to his room."

"I like it," Toutant approved. "Agents skip the country all the time with a huge drug payoff."

Jervis flashed strong white teeth behind his disjointed smile. "Drop out of sight. Exactly. Just like he's going to do. The dope won't prove nothing, of course.

But the point is to create doubts about what happened. We can at least plant the idea, in his superiors' minds and in the media, that Cowboy just might have been a rogue agent. A drug dealer who got taken out when a deal went bad, maybe. Or maybe he just absconded."

"Sure," Toutant said. "It gives the TV news and the crap sheets something sensational. And takes the focus off us even if the feds want it there. Spin control."

He looked at Archer and added, "Wouldn't be the first underpaid cop who feathered his nest a little, would he, Chief?"

Archer gave a little snort at the irony of that one. He checked his watch.

"It's five minutes to twelve," he reported. "We'll pull out after the last employees leave downstairs. Harley and me'll take care of it. We'll use P.G.'s car. It's dark and it's got four-wheel drive. You," he told Toutant, "just stay here and supervise the closing like usual. Anybody asks about Cowboy, where he is tonight, you don't know shit."

"I'm cool at this end," Toutant assured him. "You just make sure Cowboy's cop pals don't ever find him. They can suspect all they want against us. But without a body they have no case."

"There'll be no body," Archer stated without equivocation.

Toutant went downstairs to supervise the closing. Jim Bob left with him after first hiding the kilo of cocaine in a folded newspaper. Archer and Burke waited upstairs, sipping beers and watching a porn flick called *Sibling Ribaldry*, taken from a stack of videocassettes Toutant kept by the TV set.

Toutant returned a half hour later and told them the last employee had just left. Archer nodded and glanced at the curtain leading into the bedroom.

"All right," he told Harley. "Let's put our fish on ice."

* * *

His captors removed Garrett's ankle restraints before they led him downstairs and made him lie down flat in the back of the Cherokee. Burke crossed to the prowl car parked in the alley. He returned and tossed a length of tow chain in beside Shaw. Archer untied the rag that covered the prisoner's mouth.

"Relax, Cowboy," Archer taunted him as he slid behind the wheel of Toutant's vehicle and moved the seat back to make room for his legs. "We all gotta die once, you pigheaded son of a bitch. Just couldn't leave things alone, couldja? Now you're about to become worm fodder, hotshot."

Burke took the rear seat so he could keep a close eye on their prisoner. Clearly, he hadn't forgotten the elbow Shaw had jabbed into him earlier. As Archer keyed the starter, Burke threw a short, hard punch to Garrett's mouth. It split both lips open.

"Christ," Garrett goaded him, spitting out blood, "you punch like a little girl."

Before he put the Cherokee in gear, Archer hit the push-to-talk switch on a handheld radio transceiver he'd brought with him from the cruiser. It was used for search-and-rescue work and did not operate on the heavily monitored police band frequency.

"Baker, this is Baker One. Do you read? Over."

"Baker One, this is Baker, over. Go ahead," said Larsen's voice.

"We're taking pretty boy for his manicure now. His car's parked here at the club. I left the keys on the ground behind the front left tire. Search the car good. Then park it back at the Delta Manor. Lock it up and leave the key in his room. Don't let anybody see you. Over."

Driving sedately, Archer pulled out of the parking lot onto State Route 13. The chain slid against Garrett again, a cold, intimate metallic nudge that made him curl his toes in aversion. He knew damn good and well what the chain was intended for.

"Yeah, it's amazing, Harley," Archer commented, obviously speaking for Garrett's ears, "how many half-assed killers plan a good murder, then just panic and leave the body behind like a confession."

"Like you did with Fontainbleau, right, Chief?" Garrett said through swollen lips. There was also a huge goose egg on his right temple where Archer had earlier landed his fist.

Archer laughed. "Yeah, well. That was a fuckup, wasn't it? That's what I get for letting Leblanc play field commander."

Garrett felt the vehicle shudder as it left the paved highway for an unpaved surface. They slowed down and followed a switchback route that repeatedly tossed the chain up against him. The darkness thickened as trees closed in to form a thick canopy. Garrett worked the handcuff key out from behind his belt and held it ready in his cupped hand.

"I'm a good man to let alone, Cowboy," Archer boasted from up front. "You shoulda snapped wise to that fact, might've saved your ass. And you definitely shoulda stayed away from Stella. I don't like it when another man plows with my heifer."

"I didn't think you'd care about a heifer," Garrett replied. "I mean, you being one to prefer the bulls."

Despite his best effort not to, Burke let a laugh explode past his lips.

"The hell's so funny?" Archer demanded.

"Nothing," his lackey hastily assured him. "I just coughed."

The Cherokee lurched to a stop. Archer turned off the motor. For a long while Garrett could hear nothing but the ticking of the hot engine block and the low, eerie rhythm of the swamp breathing all around them.

"End of the line, funny man," Archer announced. "Harley, get the tailgate open."

The moment Burke slid out of the Cherokee, Garrett twisted one wrist to insert the key in the lock of the cuffs. They snapped open, but he kept his arms behind him while Burke tugged him roughly out the rear of the vehicle.

Insects and frogs sent up a competing racket from all sides. Shafts of moonlight showed Garrett a line of grotesquely twisted trees growing beside a wide, dark bayou. The bank had eroded deeply on both sides, leaving the cypress trees to continue on with their exposed stiltlike roots. The place was humid and gave off a dank fetor, the gas released by so much decaying matter.

"This way," Archer ordered, nudging Garrett toward the water with his gun. "Harley, fetch along the chain."

Danger shows in the lower half of a man's face, and that was the part of Archer that Garrett watched constantly in the phosphorescent moonlight. His opportunity would be brief and he'd get only one chance. Measure it twice, he reminded himself, then cut it once.

Both cops had their .38s aimed at Garrett. Clearly, Archer wanted to get some distance away from the lane to make the search harder. Garrett saw Archer's mouth abruptly harden into a grim, determined slit.

Garrett's arms were too stiff for anything complicated or sustained. It was last-ditch commando tricks now.

He let the cuffs drop and jabbed his left thumb hard into one of Burke's eyes, making the man scream at the ripping pain. At the same time, he toppled Archer with a sweeping hook of his long leg.

"My eye!" Burke screamed. "Oh, Jesus Christ, I think he ruint my *eye*, Jervis! He—"

"Fuck your eye, you whining bitch! Bust caps! He's getting away!" Archer hollered, scrambling to his feet.

Garrett willed his stiff muscles into motion and fled like a damned soul escaped from hell. He tried to make out obstacles as he fled over the hostile terrain. Creeper vines tugged at his feet, dead logs tripped him up, pockets of soupy mud sent him skidding and tripping.

Burke continued wailing, overcome by pain. But Garrett heard Archer's .38 suddenly explode behind him, the shots cracking like well-hit billiard balls. Slugs whistled around his ears and sliced through the growth all around him.

The bullet that found him felt like a sledgehammer. It punched into the muscle of his back at the bottom of his right rib cage. White-hot fire seemed to flare in his side. He staggered hard and crashed down into a tangle of brush.

"I dropped him!" Archer shouted in triumph behind him. "C'mon, Harley, hurry! He's down, we've got that bastard now!"

From the depths of a peaceful, dreamless sleep Stella suddenly started awake and sat up in bed.

Her room was dark save for a ghostly glimmer of moonlight. Her stomach felt leaden with apprehension. Had she really heard gunshots out there somewhere in the night? Or was it just part of a dream she didn't even realize she was having?

Slowly, gradually, as the peaceful silence reasserted itself, she grew calm again. She lay back down and burrowed into the cozy nest of her bed.

Downstairs, the case clock chimed reassuringly. Soon she was again wrapped deep in a protective buffer of sleep. But all was not peaceful. For the rest of the night she dreamed strange, disturbing dreams not quite awful enough to label as nightmares, just a fluid montage of odd images and symbols.

One dream in particular was electrically vivid. She was walking through the cane fields by herself. Someone in the invisible background began whistling above the wind, a sad, mournful tune that she eventually recognized from the movie *High Noon,* "Do Not Forsake Me, Oh My Darling."

With the abrupt illogic of dreams, she was suddenly standing in the family cemetery. Aunt Rose stood beside her. "I told you, sweet love," she whispered in Stella's ears. "Look to the lovers of the past."

Stella saw Jules's cracked-marble tomb, only now someone had removed the slab that sealed the entrance. "Go closer," urged a voice, and she knew it was Colette speaking to her across the centuries. "You'll face it like a St. Vallier."

She did move closer and peek inside. But the dead man lying within, wearing the "lucky-in-love" star sapphire pendant her parents gave her, was not Jules.

It was Garrett Shaw.

And as she watched, transfixed but not horrified, his eyelids snapped open and he sat up, reaching out to clutch her hand like a man afraid of drowning.

CHAPTER

17

At first, intent only on escaping, Garrett had no opportunity to inspect his wound or even to stanch the bleeding.

Take the pain, he ordered himself as he struggled to his feet in the tangled undergrowth at the edge of the bayou. He could hear Archer and Burke thrashing through the bushes behind him, drawing closer. He started forward again, following the perverted twists of the water's edge.

He was completely disoriented in the overgrown darkness of the swamp. There were many bayous in the area, but the one in front of him looked pretty big—meaning it might be Bayou Lafourche or Bayou Teche. He decided to stay close to it if he could. Otherwise, he'd end up wandering in circles until he was captured.

He slogged on, branches lashing hard at his face, mosquitoes eating him alive as the smell of his blood drove them to a feeding frenzy. There were other non-human predators to worry about too. The swamp's more dangerous hosts included plenty of alligators, water moccasins, and black bears.

When the pursuit noises finally faded behind him, Garrett paused to inspect his wound.

Probing gingerly, he could feel the ugly, puckered flesh around the edges of the wound. But he thanked God when he realized the round had passed through clean without lodging inside him. If he could just get the wound cleaned out and sterilized in time, he'd be all right. Assuming he didn't lose too much more blood. The wet place on his shirt was getting soggier even as he felt his strength ebbing.

He forged on. His dogged pursuers had not given up. He heard them now and again, sometimes alarmingly close. And they weren't losing blood like he was.

Fortune chose that moment to favor him. Rural Louisianans were in the habit of establishing fishing camps along public stretches of bayous, just crude shacks beside short docks, where a small fishing boat was kept. The camp Garrett happened upon included a lightweight, flat-bottomed pirogue.

Designed for swamp travel, a pirogue's tapered ends and shallow draw allow it to skim over mud banks. It also permitted steady progress with easy paddling—precisely what Garrett's present condition demanded.

He untied the boat, threw the painter into the bow, pushed off from shore, then climbed unsteadily into the small craft. Every exertion sent a hot stab of pain flaring from his wound.

But now, even using only a small wooden paddle, he was able to make better time than he could on land. The slow current was with him. The bayous in the area drained into the Gulf of Mexico; he knew he was probably heading south.

Now and then moonlight leaked through the thick canopy overhead in slanting shafts, stippling the black water with quivering specks of white. At such moments he saw how completely he was surrounded by a seemingly impenetrable forest of cypress, magnolia, tupelo, sweet gum.

With a sudden lurch and shudder the pirogue's forward progress abruptly halted.

Sandbank, he thought, reaching one hand into the water to feel under the hull of the boat. But he had not run aground. Something else had impeded the craft. Even now, as he groped his way to the bow to check it out, he heard pursuing noises behind him again.

His exploring fingers encountered a hard, thin line, and he cursed. He had run into someone's trotline, a strong fishing line suspended overnight above water. Shorter, baited lines hung from it at intervals. He steeled his muscles for the effort to snap it, but it was no use. The line sliced deep into his hand.

He could hear Archer and Burke drawing nearer along the south bank of the bayou.

By lying flat across the pirogue's board seat, Garrett was able to lift up the trotline and let the low-profile boat slide underneath it. Once again he was in motion. But shock, exposure, and exhaustion were taking their collective toll. He realized that getting away wasn't his only problem. He also had to find help before he lost consciousness. Otherwise, there was a good chance he'd never wake up again.

Take the pain, he ordered himself again, wincing each time he pulled the paddle through the water.

His exhaustion reached the point where every breath ended in a slight groan. Again the pursuit noises had ceased, but he had no illusions that Archer had given up the chase.

At least he was finally clear of the swamp. Garrett could see the open fields beyond the tree line. He pulled the pirogue to the banks, got out, and fought for high ground, letting the pirogue—and the evidence he'd been there—float away behind him. It was a relief to finally make the cover of the wind-rustled sugar cane.

Across the distance he could see a house looming into the night sky. He had no idea where he was. There were a dozen plantations still growing cane in Lafourche Parish.

He moved cautiously down the rows of cane, keeping his eyes to all sides. He passed a silent little private cemetery, then a cluster of apparently unused outbuildings. He started to follow a crushed-shell path that led through a garden toward the back of the house.

Then Garrett spotted the silhouette of a uniformed man just ahead of him at the front of the garden. It was obvious he was one of Archer's deputies sent to guard the house from any approach. Garrett realized he was walking into a stacked deck.

His surge of frustration was tempered only by his engulfing weakness. His options seemed to have run out. There was no help to be had in this direction, while escape along the bayou had floated away with the pirogue.

But his life was still held in the violent death-grip of the will to survive. In spite of his pain and fast-approaching weakness, he made a study of his surroundings. He knew he needed medical help, but first he needed cover. If he could find a place to hide, he could rest. Soon he would be too worn down to trust his decisions. Already old superstitions began to gnaw at him. He recognized the rapid clicking sound of wood-burrowing insects called deathwatch beetles. Lore had it that hearing them was an omen of death. And "lore" took on authority as a man lost blood.

Out toward the middle of the field, perhaps a hundred yards from where he stood, he saw what looked like a big barn.

Stumbling weakly, each breath ragged and short now, he headed toward the only shelter he could find, praying that no one saw him. Once inside, he shut out the moonlight and any way for him to scout the geography. Stumbling to his knees more than once, he found what he thought was a stack of unused wooden pallets. He crawled between the stack and the rough wooden wall of the structure, hiding himself like a rat in a crevice. Then the pain overtook him. Everything went black.

CHAPTER

<u>18</u>

"I *never* expected Professor Perkins to respond so quickly," Stella explained at the breakfast table. "Nor to be so enthusiastic. He's very optimistic that my suggestion about bagasse can get some serious attention from the Meridian Feed Company."

She had just finished dressing when Perkins called from Baton Rouge. Now, as she split open a scone and spread orange marmalade on the halves, she quickly summarized their long phone conversation to her aunt.

"And he asked my permission," she concluded triumphantly, "to polish my query a bit before we send it to Meridian. In other words, he'll plug in some specific technical stuff about the advantages of bagasse as a basic ingredient in cattle feed in place of corn stalks. Stuff like the way bagasse is higher in starches and carbohydrates while being lower in tertiary antibiotic residues."

As she nattered on, still excited from Perkins's call,

she wondered if hope had worked into her face. Her good mood seemed to have quickly infected Rose and Maman—neither one of whom looked as if they really followed all the details. It was clear they were just proud of her.

After breakfast Rose and Maman planned to do their needlework in the garden. Rose's favorite old pongee parasol was slanted against her chair. The grande dame had also donned her lavender sateen "modesty dress" for outside wear—its hem was weighted so it couldn't blow upward in the wind.

Stella watched her at the table, thinking about what she'd promised Mattie. She was determined to go to New Orleans, and Garrett Shaw be damned. But doubt still preyed on her mind. She was still unsure. And now that the bagasse idea looked ready to bear fruit, she wished fervently the rest of her problems would just go away.

"Why," she wondered out loud, "does God answer one prayer and not another?"

"I've dog-eared my Bible, Stell," Maman replied, "but I can't tell you the answer to that one."

Maman stood and crossed to the stove, returning with the coffeepot to top off Stella's cup. The woman wore a cotton plaid dress, its high neck pinned at the throat by a brooch.

She has such lovely skin, Stella thought. Despite the years, Maman is still a beauty.

"La!" Maman remarked as she returned to the stove. "Musta been hunters out in the swamps early this morning. Woke me right up shootin' 'em loud ol' guns."

Her innocent remark startled Stella. Her thoughts raced down another track. So the gunshots hadn't been a dream after all. Yet, there definitely *had* been a dream last night. A very bizarre one, featuring Garrett Shaw in Jules's burial chamber. God, let the analysts figure that one out, she thought. It was well beyond her.

"I've got to tell Autry the good news," she announced. She carried her cup and saucer to the sideboard, then crossed to the back door and took her straw hat off its hook beside the door.

"Dear," Aunt Rose called behind her, "what did Chief Archer want?"

Stella, one hand on the porcelain doorknob, turned to look at her aunt. "When?"

"Why, earlier this morning. I glanced out my window while I was dressing, and I spotted him in the garden. He was speaking to someone I couldn't see. I—that is, I assumed it was you, Stella."

"I haven't been outside yet today," Stella replied. Heat rose into her face. But her anger was tempered by a numbing apprehension. She again felt the helpless fear when Jervis had forced himself on her in the sugarhouse. How far would he have gone if Autry hadn't interrupted?

She pushed the shirred curtains aside and glanced out through the door's mullioned panes.

"I don't see him now," she said. "But why would he have been in the garden?"

"That Jervis," Maman said as she cleared the table, "got him a mean ol' mouth. Mean as they come. He ain't no man to mess with, that's it right there. You watch him, Stell. You watch him close."

Not wanting to worry the two older women, Stella released a smile and said, "Don't worry. I've got him all figured out. I'll join you in the garden later." With that, she exited the kitchen.

The smile dropped off her face like a lead weight.

Worry and anger followed her through the gardens. She wanted her energy focused on Professor Perkins's phone call, not on Jervis. The man was definitely becoming a problem. She resolved to drive to New Orleans and talk to someone at the DEA even if she had to go to the newspapers first about drug deals on Senator Leblanc's property.

She forced her thoughts back to the earlier phone conversation with Perkins. At most, she figured the bagasse production would increase plantation revenue only modestly. Still, one success often led to others.

As she emerged from the canopy of the gardens into the brilliant morning sunshine, it seemed only natural to feel joyous. Perkins's hope left her eager to share the potential good news with Autry. In fact, for a few joyous moments she felt like a little girl again, running down to the bayou to catch polliwogs in a jar.

In good moods, optimism guided her hope for Shadow Oaks. However, her optimism was severely tested moments later, when she spotted Chief Jervis Archer.

He was angling toward her through the cane, dressed in civilian clothes but carrying a shotgun in the crook of his arm. Now she spotted two, no, three of his deputies. They were fanning out behind him, all of the men coming from the direction of Bayou Lafourche.

Stella paused in the narrow farm lane, waiting for him. Foreboding mixed with curiosity. Despite her fear, she was determined to take charge before he could.

"Chief," she greeted him coolly, her arms crossed in front of her. "May I ask why the entire Cane Town Police Department is on my property? No one bothered to get my permission."

"We don't need it," he informed her tersely. "This isn't an elective search. We're looking for a criminal, and a warm trail leads to your property."

Again, despite her loathing for Jervis, Stella had to admit he had a strong, masculine, decisive face. But what was that description Rose once quoted about him? *So nearly a gentleman, so fatally not one.*

"A criminal?" she repeated. "Who?"

"Your boyfriend from The Scarlet Door, Stella. Cowboy."

Stella refused to rise to the "boyfriend" bait. "What crime is he wanted for?"

"Several. But I can't divulge specifics on an open case."

Right, Stella thought. Now Jervis is a rule-book commando, but only one day earlier he was ready to rape her.

"You want more information," Archer added, "watch the news in the next couple days. Maybe you'll learn something. For now, let's just say we're talking major drug felonies."

"That's been my contention all along," she informed him, holding her fear in check. "The question is, exactly *who* are the felons?"

As she said this, her mind raced with questions. If the law was looking for Garrett Shaw, she had come to the fork in the road. Either he was telling her the truth about being a fed—in which case Archer was definitely out for blood—or he was the drug runner she thought he was, and now he'd finally been caught in the act.

She watched the deputies conduct their search of the grounds while she struggled with indecision.

"Know what, muffin?" Archer replied. "You got more cheek than is good for you."

His words might have angered her had his tone not been so dangerous.

"You should understand something, Stella. If Garrett Shaw's on your property and you're helping him, this could be very costly for you. New federal laws allow for the seizure of any property owned by drug felons. You assist him, you become a drug felon too. Shadow Oaks could end up being sold for trailer park lots."

The enormity and unfairness of his words left her stunned. One moment she was enjoying a rare good mood; the next, she was being threatened with utter destitution.

When she recovered, she said with icy precision, "Obviously, I can't stop you from getting a warrant to search my house too. So, go ahead and search it now. I won't even require a warrant. Garrett Shaw is a virtual stranger to me. And I swear I don't know where he is."

Archer's glittering blue gaze roamed over her like unwelcome hands.

"I believe you," he finally informed her. "And I hate to go riling that old bat of an aunt you have with a search of the big house. But understand me, Stella, this is a dangerous fugitive. And very intelligent. He'll lay down a convincing story about being a fed. But don't fall for it. He'll drag you down with him."

With that, Archer abruptly turned away and headed toward the row of old slave quarters at the edge of the cane, where his men had begun their search. However, he thought of something else and turned around again.

"Where were you going now?" he demanded.

"To the sugarhouse. *Autry's* expecting me," Stella added with pointed emphasis. She certainly didn't want Jervis following her, especially if she had trouble finding Autry. The last thing she wanted was another encounter with him alone.

Archer looked past her, toward the sagging structure. "We searched in there just after sunup, but we'll probably search it again before we leave."

"I can't stop you," she murmured unhappily.

He nodded. "Later," he told her, making that single word a multilayered threat that tingled her scalp.

Even before Stella stepped through the big pulley-mounted doors, she realized Autry wasn't inside. Down in the southwest corner of the cane field, a chugging roar sprang to life. Autry must have started the pump that brought down the water level where the levee had recently been repaired.

She had no intention of returning to the house—not until Jervis was farther away. So she went inside.

Pigeons watched her from the rafters. Almost immediately, her gaze focused on the wall full of cane knives. She shivered at the memory of Jervis Archer turning one of the knives in his big, hairy hands—just before he attacked her.

Frightened, she returned to the open doorway and

peeked down the lane. Thank God Archer's broad back was still retreating.

A sound that might have been wind groaning in the eaves made her turn back to the semidark interior.

She stood there listening for perhaps a full minute. Then she heard it again: a low moaning noise that seemed distinct from the wind.

"Autry?" she called out, uncertain. "Autry, is that you?"

In the big building her words were instantly swallowed up like stones tossed down a well. Only deep silence answered.

Then, faint as a retreating echo, she heard it again. It seemed to come from the shadowy corner behind the huge iron cylinders of the cane press. Cautiously, she moved around the press to investigate.

At first she saw nothing unusual. Just several empty wooden pallets stacked atop one another. Then her eyes adjusted to the dimness. A moment later her breath snagged in her throat when she spotted a muddy cowboy boot. It protruded from behind the pallets. Then she saw part of a blue-jean-clad leg.

Even in those first confused moments she never once doubted it was Garrett Shaw lying there. Somehow, evidently trying to hide, he had wedged himself into the narrow space between the pallets and the wall behind them.

Clearly, he was still alive. But just as clearly, judging from his pitiful moans, he was badly hurt.

Doubt quickly plagued her, but her immediate response, however, was not one bred of "law and order"— it was pity for a fellow human being who was suffering.

She crept over to the pallets and shoved them aside. If the man knew someone stood over him, he didn't show it. His shoulders were rock-tight in his unconscious attempt at fighting off pain, his body curled almost in the fetal position. The copper smell of blood, warm and fresh, hovered over him like the Grim Reaper.

First she had to get him out of where he was. The wedge of space behind the rollers was not enough room for his huge frame, let alone another person. She cleared away the pallets altogether. Gripping the big man by his ankles, she summoned strength she didn't realize she possessed. Slowly, she tugged his long body out into better view.

His moan was dark and low. She knew the movement caused him pain.

Kneeling down to him, she had to bite her lower lip hard to keep from crying out in horrified shock. His lower right back was maroon with warm, sticky blood. He'd lost a lot of it.

Which was why his face, even in the stingy light, looked as pale as moonstone. His eyes were closed but his lips moved, muttering something incoherent. Through the jolt of pain she had given him, he was trying to regain consciousness.

Cold panic filled her, and she raced back to the doors. But Jervis was nowhere in sight now. Before she returned to the unconscious man, she stopped at a grimy metal sink where workers used to wash up when the harvest was done manually. She found an old Coke bottle and filled it with water. Kneeling down to him, she cupped his head while she let the water trickle into his mouth. After a moment or two she realized he was drinking it.

"You're badly hurt," she whispered, not sure if he could hear her. "I'll call the ambulance as soon as I—"

"No!"

His eyes flew open. He stared at her with the piercing silver gaze of a wounded wolf.

"That's crazy, you're badly—"

"Listen. You don't—"

A harsh spasm of pain interrupted him, and he sucked in a hissing breath, gritting his teeth against it.

"You don't understand," he resumed when he got his breathing under control again. "By law, hospitals have to report any gunshot wounds immediately to local police. That's Archer and his goons. Then they'll get me in custody and kill me."

Clearly, he wanted to tell her more. But even that sustained effort at speaking had exhausted him. She knew it was pointless to press him with questions now.

"Call," he muttered to her. "Call . . . Steve, he'll . . . tell you."

"Who's Steve?" she demanded. But he'd blacked out again as soon as she said it.

Looking up to the rafters as if for help, she understood with agonizing clarity what it meant to be stuck between a rock and a hard place. She was caught between two men, neither of whom she had any reason to believe. Help Garrett, and she might risk everything she owned—everything she *was*. But help Jervis Archer, and she just might be killing an innocent man.

Many thoughts vied for prominence in her mind at that critical moment. But one dominated all others, from a cross-stitch sampler Maman had made for the kitchen: *The quality of mercy is not strained, it droppeth as the gentle rain from heaven.*

She looked down at the helpless man and realized he was trembling despite the day's warmth. The strange dream image returned to her: Garrett Shaw lying in Jules's tomb. The big, strong man desperate for someone to cling to.

In that moment she made up her mind. Despite her questions and misgivings, priority number one was to keep the man alive. If calling an ambulance was tantamount to an execution, she couldn't call one; it was as simple as that. But no way could she move him from the sugarhouse while Archer and his men were crawling all over the place.

Archer had said they'd searched there already. They must have missed him in the faint dawn light. But he'd said they would search it again. She would have to hide Garrett until she could move him. Fate would have to govern the rest, including keeping him alive until she could give him medical attention.

Again she ran to the doors, making sure the coast was still clear. Then she rummaged through an old gear locker and found a filthy fleece-lined jacket. She tucked it around Garrett like a blanket. At least he stopped shaking so violently.

Then, pulling him inch by inch by his arms, she got the injured fugitive hidden again in the wedge behind the cane rollers. She filled the old Coke bottle with water again and dribbled it slowly into his mouth.

It was hardly adequate first aid. He might die. There was no getting around it. But she was doing everything she could think of. He claimed Archer would kill him, and knowing Archer, she had to respect that claim until she knew otherwise. It was better to be duped by a felon than to destroy an innocent man forever.

But even if it costs you Shadow Oaks, a sinister voice whispered inside her skull. She wanted to clamp her hands over her ears and keep it out, but there was no silencing it. Yet, her mind was made up, and she had not descended from a line of wafflers.

Standing, she cast only one glance behind her from the doorway, making sure he was hidden from view. Then she took a deep breath to steady her nerves and headed back toward the house.

The most dangerous part now lay ahead of her.

CHAPTER

19

"**M**oney in my pockets," Senator Leblanc repeated, his normally suave tone now sharp with sarcasm. "*That's* what you kept calling this idiotic drug arrangement of yours. Now you see what it's gotten all of us."

Toutant, his hands occupied in addressing a padded mailer, held the phone wedged between his shoulder and his ear by cocking his head.

"What's the point of getting your blood in a boil, Myron? After all, you originally set all this in motion when you gave the order to off Fontainbleau. Cowboy wasn't sent down here to sniff out drug lords. That's just for leverage in court. It's politicians he's after."

All this was true, and both men knew it. But Leblanc only said, "Whoever told you *I* ordered Fontainbleau killed?"

Toutant looked at the tape recorder on the desk in front of him. Life's little ironies were delicious—even as the phone rang, he had been making a backup copy of all three master tapes. His thin, tight face showed a little seam of a smile.

"Logical inference," he replied.

"Really? Well, never mind playing detective," Leblanc snapped. "There's plenty of trouble for all of us if Cowboy surfaces alive. I can't believe Jervis botched such a simple assignment."

"It's always easier to give the orders, Myron, than to carry them out. This guy is good. We *all* got sucked in by him."

"You especially," LeBlanc added with deadly resentment in his voice. "Now, look, this agent must be taken out. But the public relations game is also very important. Apropos that, I do give Jervis credit for the touch with planting dope in Cowboy's room. Now the feds will have to go slow while they figure out if they've been had by a rogue—their own P.R. disaster. Have the media been alerted?"

"Jervis and Cliff D'Antoni held a press conference at noon today," Toutant affirmed. "Should hit the network news this evening."

"That press conference may be the key to our salvation. You just remind Jervis how to keep spinning this. Cane Town is a conservative community where church membership determines one's friendships. They don't trust outsiders, and they hate drugs. So have him pound away at those two themes: outsiders and drugs. That way there'll be relief when Cowboy turns up dead. The feds, meantime, will be so mortified, they'll quietly cover it up. They're obsessed with keeping a squeaky-clean image."

While Leblanc said all this, Toutant finished addressing the padded envelope to the law firm of Jones Walker in New Orleans. Copies of every audiotaped meeting in the "conference room" would be sent for safekeeping to Percival's attorney. Toutant had mentioned nothing to Senator Leblanc about Shaw's offer yesterday of "a deal" if Toutant turned state's evidence.

Because Toutant liked to keep an ace up his sleeve—no telling yet how all this might turn out.

"P.G.?"

"Yeah?"

"What's your best hunch? Where do you think our boy is holed up?"

Toutant had just been thoroughly briefed by Jervis Archer. He also recalled that name Jervis found in Cowboy's room: *Stella St. Vallier.* He had no proof, but it was quite possible those two noble crusaders had joined forces. If they had, God help the bitch.

"He probably bled to death in the swamps by now," Toutant replied. "Jervis says he plugged him pretty good. He's bringing in a team of dogs from Donaldsonville, won't take long to locate a dead body in this humidity. If he's still alive, my best guess would be that Stella St. Vallier is hiding him."

"Her again?"

"She likes to play the buttinsky."

"Too bad for her if she is," Leblanc assured the other man. "She'll have to go with him."

"Like you said."

By the middle of the afternoon Stella's nerves felt like they were stretched taut on tenterhooks. Jervis and his deputies combed the grounds at Shadow Oaks, searching every building except the house itself. Finally, in frustration, Jervis demanded an entrance to the house. Stella, Rose, and Maman stood by while deputies walked with muddy boots through their bedrooms, cast aside their dresses in an attempt to check out the armoires, and demanded entrance to Maman's pantry, where Rose kept a private stash of absinthe. In the meantime Jervis left and returned several times.

But, to Stella's unspeakable relief, no one had yet discovered Garrett. At four P.M. Jervis decided the plantation was secured. However, before he and his men left for a badly needed rest, Jervis warned Stella he'd be returning with bloodhounds and their handler early the next morning.

After Archer left, Stella went outside briefly to make sure no one was standing guard on her property. As she rounded a front corner of the house, she saw a section of latticework lying on the lawn. She realized how thorough Jervis had been, searching even the open spaces under the veranda.

Now, as she waited impatiently for darkness—and the chance to return to the sugarhouse unseen to check if Garrett was still alive—she worked efficiently. Her plan meant that both her car and Jules's secret room had to be prepared.

First of all, she went into the storeroom off the kitchen and retrieved a heavy sheet of clear plastic that had once wrapped a new mattress. She took it to the porte cochere and spread it so it completely covered the back of the French sedan. It wasn't neatness she had in mind but potential scents for a bloodhound—not to mention forensic evidence should the man go and die on them.

With her car thus prepared, she turned to the secret room. Jervis and his deputies had no idea it existed. Garrett could stay there until he was better, which she hoped would be soon. The quicker he was standing and walking away, the better off she and her family's property would be.

She changed the musty sheets on the bed, then stocked the night table with clean towels, medical supplies, and bottled water. She finished by five. It was getting dark; she could go to the sugarhouse soon. But one huge logistical problem still loomed. She couldn't move Garrett by herself. Nor could she hope to conceal his presence from Aunt Rose and Maman. That left her only one unpalatable alternative: She had to enlist the older women to her cause.

Ironically, the problem was partly solved by the five

o'clock TV news broadcast out of New Orleans. Maman and Rose had come in from their needlework session in the garden to catch their afternoon soaps. They were already watching TV in the front parlor when Stella joined them. She had not really expected anything yet on the news, but Jervis had told her to watch. What she saw, however, left her with a hard, cankering doubt at her core. She watched the television in stunned silence.

A very accurate police sketch of Garrett Shaw abruptly filled the TV screen.

"—*rogue federal agent terrorizing Cane Town?*" speculated a porcelain-smiled, silver-haired news anchor who looked like the trusted doctor from an aspirin commercial.

"My stars!" Aunt Rose exclaimed from her wicker chaise. "Look! There's Chief Archer."

"—*Cane Town Police Department have been watching this man for some time,*" Chief Archer assured the camera. "*We have no confirmation at this time that he is in fact a federal agent. However, he evidently used this cover to conduct his drug-dealing activities.*"

Stella sat on the edge of the chair cushion, still immobilized. Again the camera switched to a new graphic: Lafourche Parish D.A. Cliff D'Antoni displaying the kilo of cocaine found in Shaw's room.

"*The fugitive reportedly injured one deputy and has fired at others,*" the news anchor concluded. "*He was shot during his escape, and he is considered armed and dangerous.*"

She knew she had no logical reason to believe Archer's account of events. Nonetheless, the persuasive power of the TV images was undeniable. Even if it was all a lie, it was a very convincing lie. If Archer could pull it off, that meant Stella was harboring a fugitive. In fact, Archer and Shaw could both be criminals for all she knew.

"Lord have mercy," Maman said as the broadcast moved on to national news. "Drug runners right here in Cane Town. Just like Stell tried to warn us before. That must be why the police was here all day."

Aunt Rose paled. "He's still at large. Why, we could be murdered in our beds!"

Well, at least now they know about it, Stella reasoned. The TV took care of one big problem, broaching the subject in the first place.

"I think we'll survive the night," Stella assured her aunt. But she glanced out the windows as she spoke, gauging the darkness. The sun would set within the half hour. Then they would have to work quickly and efficiently.

"Will you two take a ride with me?" Stella asked, looking from Rose to Maman.

"A ride, dear?" Rose repeated. "To where?"

"Just out back to the sugarhouse."

"Whatever for, child?" Maman queried.

"You'll see," Stella promised grimly.

Aunt Rose's curiosity was piqued. Stella could see that. The two older women exchanged a long look.

"But, Stella," Rose protested. "It will be dark soon. Should we be traipsing around in the cane with a dangerous criminal hiding in this area?"

"We'll be safe," Stella promised, hoping to God she was right.

Don't hit the brakes or the lights will go on, Stella reminded herself later as she guided her Peugeot along the narrow, rutted farm lane in the darkness. Although she had seen no one watching, she couldn't be sure Archer or a deputy weren't keeping an eye on Shadow Oaks.

Maman and Aunt Rose, completely mystified, shared the front seat with her.

"Hon," Maman said, "how's come you got that plastic spread all over the backseat?"

"So we don't get nothing on the seat."

"What might we get on the seat?" Rose inquired, her eyes as big as buttons in her pale, lined face.

"Blood," Stella whispered, sure her face was as lined from worry as Rose's.

"Blood?" Rose repeated. The old woman pronounced the word as if not quite sure of its meaning.

Stella parked in front of the big, shadowy mass of the sugarhouse and turned off the engine. The ensuing silence that surrounded them was as strained as the quiet in a courtroom before a verdict.

"Call the police," Maman insisted while Stella, holding her breath, led them behind the cane press to the stack of empty pallets.

"He's still here," she whispered, kneeling by the pallets. "And still breathing. But he's unconscious and his pulse feels weak."

Carefully, she tugged him out into the open.

Maman muttered, crossing herself when Stella's flashlight beam revealed the wounded man's back. "Lookit all that blood!"

Rose, studying the man's features, said nothing.

"You mean to tell us," Maman said incredulously, "that man we just saw on TV is inside the sugarhouse right now?"

Taking a deep breath, Stella launched into a tightly compressed explanation. First she reminded both women about the drug deal she had witnessed involving Toutant and Deputy Harley Burke. She then explained her chance encounter with Garrett, his implied claim to be a cop. She also made it clear that she considered Jervis Archer a potential criminal himself. And finally, she stressed the key point: Garrett's claim that he would be murdered by Archer if she went to a doctor or the authorities now.

"Honey," Maman said, shaking her head in the yellow glow of the tiny flashlight, "this is all wrong, and that's it, y'unnerstan'? Now, I don't trust the likes of Jervis Archer, I'll go that far with you. But, sweetheart, this man is wanted by the law. We help him, *we* become criminals."

At this reminder, guilt lanced through Stella. It was true that Rose and Maman were now involved willy-nilly. And it wasn't just the legal implications of abetting a fugitive—they were also being placed in danger since Stella had no idea yet who could be trusted and who could not.

"I—I'm sorry. I had no choice but to involve you," Stella said in a small, apologetic voice. "I can't help him alone."

"We need to go back to the house right now," Maman insisted. "Call the police."

"Oh, pouf," Rose finally spoke up, surprising both of her companions. "It's all frightfully romantic and dangerous," she added. "Let's do what Stella says."

Stella glanced at her aunt's face, which seemed completely transformed in that meager light.

You live as long as Rose has, Stella realized, and even your most vivid memories can become dead scabs. But the deep feeling in Rose's eyes now—Stella could not remember seeing her aunt so alive and full of purpose.

Even Maman's harshly disapproving features softened as she studied Garrett's face.

"Good-looking man," she pronounced. "Got him a honest face."

"How will we move him?" Stella wondered out loud, flashing her beam around them.

"Move him to where?" Maman demanded.

"Jules's secret room."

"Gracious God," Maman said. "We gonna hide him in the *house?*"

"It's perfectly bold and daring," Rose approved. "What better use for a secret room?"

"Perfectly *insane,*" Maman muttered. But like Stella, she was glancing about for something to help them. The light passed over a spot where one wall had been reinforced with tin from old flattened-out fruit and vegetable cans.

"Hold it," Maman told Stella, spotting something in

the light. "If he's heavy as cargo, might's well move him like cargo."

Maman crossed to the wall and returned wheeling a little handcart.

It was still quite a piece of work. But the three of them managed to get the unconscious man loaded onto the cart, then into the back of the sedan. Then Stella wrestled the cart into the trunk, although she couldn't close the lid.

She had not forgotten that Archer was due to return with tracking dogs. So she did not return directly to the house. Instead, she followed the connecting maze of farm lanes away from the sugarhouse. Near Bayou Lafourche, at least two miles west of the house, she stopped. She removed the scent-laden jacket she'd wrapped around Garrett. Dragging it across the ground, she left it in the tangled undergrowth beside the water.

She took a different route back to the house. With the cart to assist them, the determined trio of women got Garrett across the vast ballroom and into the secret room with no major difficulties.

"I think we three make quite a team," Rose boasted when their unconscious patient was finally stretched out on the bed.

"Hunh. Maybe we all get the same prison cell," Maman grumped. "Be a team behind bars."

Still scowling and shaking her head, Maman returned to the kitchen to put on water for tea.

"I hope this isn't a mistake," Stella said softly.

Rose stood there silently at her side, gazing at the mysterious fugitive. She took Stella's hand and gave it a firm squeeze. "Right or wrong, dear," she said softly, "have you ever felt more *alive* than you do right now?"

Startled by the question, Stella stared wordlessly at the older woman.

"We all live by a flame within us," Rose reminded her. "And yours is finally burning, Stella. Burning bright and strong. Legal trouble or not, that *can't* be a mistake."

PART TWO

THE PRINCE

CHAPTER

<u>20</u>

Death tiptoes politely with rude surprises in its hands.

—SOUTH AFRICAN PROVERB

After dark Steve Falcone loved the view from his section chief's office on the twentieth floor of Washington, D.C.'s massive Federal Law Enforcement Center on D Street. At night, lights blazed a soft halo over the city, and the Potomac reflected colors like a new marble floor.

But now, in the stark and pitiless morning glare, the view lost its romantic glow. Most of the trees were already winter bare. Even the stately obelisk of the Washington Monument was currently receiving a face-lift, and a silly, flapping skirt of blue mesh disguised the vast scaffolding.

"Look, Steve," said Mike Hogan, head of the Special Warrants Division of the U.S. marshals. "I know Shaw's your partner and a good buddy. But right now I can't put your personal feelings before the good of the bureau. A mop-up raid is out of the question until we have better intel on Shaw."

"Can't I at least make a few calls? This St. Vallier woman might—"

Hogan lifted a peremptory hand from his side of a wide glass-topped desk, silencing his subordinate.

"Honest to God, I'd solve all the world's problems today if someone would hire me to do it. But lacking that mandate, my hands are tied. You know the protocol when a field op drops out under suspicious circumstances. We back up, regroup, and wait."

Falcone sat back in the chair and squared his shoulders, trying not to push any of Hogan's buttons. His boss was middling honest and plenty smart. Unfortunately, Hogan also lived by the motto Never Make Waves. This still-confusing situation with Garrett Shaw was highly threatening to the image-obsessed agents in administration.

"Hell, Garrett's no rogue," Falcone insisted. "That dope in his room—it's amateur stuff. He was set up by the Cane Town P.D."

"That's a distinct possibility, and I believe it too. But as honcho here, I have to play Thomas the Doubter. I'm the skeptic who has to stick his finger in the nail holes before I'll believe."

"Garrett wouldn't," Falcone persisted. "Shaw is the most committed cop I've ever known."

"Yeah, well, what about Aldrich Ames? That dude had six letters of merit in his file, but he still screwed Uncle Sam and his own buddies. Even got a few of them killed. Look, Steve, what if Shaw *did* put the shaft to us? It's possible. Last year alone, a dozen federal cops took the money and booked. Do you realize where we'd stand if we tried to bring down a senator as connected as Leblanc with a case built by a rogue? Our credibility would be less than zero, and heads would roll within the ranks. Right now we've got no choice but to hold off, see if Shaw surfaces and what the hell's going on."

" 'Surfaces' is the word," Falcone said bitterly. "Our only function will be to recover his body from a bayou."

"Steve, get real. If they did put a hit on Shaw, it's done. He'll be just as dead in a few days as he is now."

"If it's done, sure. But what if he's being hunted right now?"

Hogan shrugged. "Tough break, sure. But Shaw's won the Purple Heart and survived some nasty urban warfare in Lebanon. He didn't request a field assignment down south because longevity was his chief concern. This is what Shaw trained for, this is what he wanted."

Steve couldn't gainsay the truth of this. Nor was it his way to buck the chain of command. Falcone was a simple, unpretentious man who liked war flicks, drank a little too much beer, and sang Sinatra songs in the shower. He considered himself an average man with no outstanding qualities. He had no authority—or inclination—to challenge his superiors. But he was also honest and possessed a strong sense of loyalty. Dammit, this was just *wrong*.

"I'll do what I'm told," he assured Hogan. "And I know it's not your fault, Mike. But I think it's just shit-ass rotten to leave Garrett swinging in the wind like this."

Steve stood up to return to his own office on the eleventh floor.

"Listen, Steve," Hogan added. "He won't exactly be left swinging, okay? The fee-bees are already making discreet inquiries from the New Orleans regional bureau. It's just, right now, we can take very little action. The public affairs flacks are handling any press queries with the usual 'we can neither confirm nor deny' doodah. But once we get a solid fix on Shaw, we'll go in like gangbusters, I promise."

Steve nodded, knowing at least that he could trust Hogan's promise. But on the elevator ride down to his office, he was in a despondent mood. He couldn't help recalling the Eastern wise man who summed up all of human history in a pithy sentence: *They were born, they were wretched, they died.*

But along the way, Steve reminded himself, many of those humans also found moments of joy, fell in love, made babies, occasionally even glimpsed a moment of beauty or truth. What about the lonely men like Garrett Shaw, who fight all their lives to make sure the center holds for others? Weren't they, too, entitled to their brief moment in the sun before eternal darkness claimed them?

"Hang on, *paisano*," Falcone whispered in the solitude of the elevator. "You just hang on, buddy."

Jervis Archer glanced up at the westering sun. Reaching upward, he could fit four fingers between the horizon and the sun. That meant there was only about a half hour of daylight left.

"All right," he called to the dog handler out ahead of him. "Let's call it a day, Baylis."

Jervis removed his hat to whack at pesky flies with it. His face was red and sweaty, his hip boots heavy with muck. His nerves were on edge from all this goddamn yapping of dogs. Fat lot of good they did.

Whatever trail the dogs were following had taken enough turns to make a cow cross-eyed. Jervis had stumbled along behind the clamorous pack through swamps and cane fields, woods and bayous. Early on, the dogs had picked up a strong scent trail that led from the St. Vallier sugarhouse to Bayou Lafourche. After discovering a jacket Cowboy must have worn, they eventually lost the trail near water. Since then, the confused dogs had signaled several more scent trails. But each one simply petered out.

Jervis returned to the cruiser he'd parked at the edge of Bayou Lafourche. He peeled off his filthy waders and tossed them into the trunk. His private mobile phone rang as he slid in behind the wheel.

"Yeah?"

"Any luck?" Toutant's anxious voice inquired.

"Didn't find squat. But something don't tally here. The dogs didn't mark any scent trail leading to the house. Yet there's no clear escape trail anyplace beyond the perimeter we've already secured. The dogs're saying he ain't here, but he ain't left neither. It's like that fucker just vanished in thin air."

"Try telling that to Leblanc. He called again," Toutant informed him.

"Pissed, huh?"

"Pissed? Christ, he's screaming blue murder."

"Tough tit," Archer said. "He can swagger it around all he wants to. He ain't the one with his ass in the mud."

"He insists you search the house again. He's convinced Stella St. Vallier could be harboring our boy. And I think so too."

"You can both pitch that theory straight to hell," Archer said as he started the cruiser's engine. "I told you there's no scent trails leading to the house. Besides, if Cowboy was in her house, would Stella have invited me to search it without a warrant?"

"Yeah, but when did she make that offer?" Toutant reminded him. "Today?"

"No," Jervis admitted. "That was yesterday."

"Right, and things can change quick. As for the scent trails, I did some hunting in my day. I know that dogs do better in the open country. They can get confused and lose a trail where a lot of other scents compete. Like in the yard of a house."

"Yeah, Baylis mentioned that too."

"So search the house again."

Jervis hated to be ordered around. But Toutant's suggestion did make sense. Those dogs were well trained. Yet, they had definitely failed to find any escape route Shaw might have used. And no corpse had turned up. That suggested Cowboy was holed up somewhere. Wounded as he was, he'd surely have to have help if he were to stay alive.

"All right," he finally told Toutant. "I don't think he's in her house. But I'll stop by there before I return to town."

After getting Garrett safely into the secret room Wednesday night, Stella removed his boots, cleaned out his wound with hydrogen peroxide, and let him rest till the following morning. By then he regained enough awareness to swallow a few mouthfuls of broth Maman had prepared, after which he slipped back into a fever-ish delirium.

Stella knew infection remained a very real danger, especially in his weakened condition. So besides regularly cleansing the wound, she started Garrett on some prescription antibiotics she had leftover in her medicine cabinet, mixing them in the salty broth he swallowed a few sips at a time.

By that afternoon Stella faced the somewhat awkward task of more thoroughly cleaning up Garrett. His ordeal in the swamps had left him and his clothing filthy. She had simply covered the bed with an old sheet and placed him on it. But he had to be more adequately bathed, then made more comfortable.

For a minute or two before she began, she studied the unconscious man. His face, though pale, seemed calm and at rest now.

God, please tell me I made the right decision, she prayed.

Grimacing at the contact with his filthy clothing, she gently scissored his shirt and worked it off him, careful of the back wound just above his right hip. Even relaxed in sleep, his chest and shoulders were corded with muscles. He was athletic and fit: She'd expected it. What she did not expect were the scars that ragtagged their way down his chest. They were the thick red scars of burns, and all she could think was that he must have been in an auto accident at one time.

Trying to be "professional" about it, yet feeling the vague excitement of a voyeur, she unbuckled his jeans and worked them down over his hips. A minute later he lay naked on the bed. Despite her determination to "just be a nurse," she could not deny the erotic thrill of looking at him. He was a beautiful man. Watching him as he lay sleeping naked on the white sheet, she felt like he was her own piece of sculpture, only it breathed and moaned, and—hopefully—would wake up and leave.

She bathed him carefully but thoroughly, using warm water, soap, and a sponge.

You're not supposed to be enjoying this so much, she admonished herself, but she undeniably was. She moved the damp sponge over his athletic body with the caressing touch of a lover.

It *has* to be done, she kept reminding herself to assuage her guilt at the pleasure.

However, her "lover's caress" soon created an unexpected dilemma.

It happened quickly. She drew the wet, warm sponge in circles across his lower stomach, inching into the thatch of pubic hair. At one moment his penis lay against his thigh, long, pliant, and unthreatening. The next, he had swollen so erect that his shaft pulsed with every heartbeat.

The unexpected sight immediately made her warm. Her breathing quickened. For a long while torrid images filled the screen of her inner eye. She had to admit it to herself: she was hungry. She could barely remember the last time she'd gotten laid; she just recalled that the last experience had left her empty and unsatisfied. The lawyer she'd dated on and off again for years, Henry Osborne, had not been the one to keep up with either her mind or her appetites.

But Garrett Shaw—even unconscious Shaw looked as if he could keep up with both.

Then doubt set in.

She couldn't have fantasies about this man. For one

thing, she knew next to nothing about him—who or what he was. She reminded herself of the huge story in that day's edition of the local newspaper, *The Parish Register.* True or not, it reinforced the TV news claim that Garrett Shaw was a major criminal.

Besides all that, he was an injured man, not her private sex toy. Her physical attraction to this handsome man was, of course, understandable given her state of deprivation. But she couldn't get attached. He could die; he could send them all to prison. So what if he was handsome. Jervis Archer was handsome. He was still bad news.

She drew the sheet over her patient. Nonetheless, she couldn't suppress a brief smile. After all, she should take heart that at least one of his "vital signs" seemed healthy—very healthy indeed, thank you. Would irrepressible Mattie have left the poor guy alive if the opportunity had been hers? But what a way for him to go.

She leaned down to his unconscious face and whispered, "Behave." With a smile she added, "If I might remind you, sir, there are ladies around here."

A heartbeat later she flinched when she heard the chimes sound within the main house.

CHAPTER

21

If you want a thing well done, get a couple of old broads to do it.

—BETTE DAVIS

Stella had a sinking feeling she knew who the visitor was. Her hunch was confirmed when she reached the huge double parlor at the front of the house. Maman had already admitted Chief Jervis Archer. She and Aunt Rose were both hovering solicitously over his chair by the time Stella arrived. They were treating him like a celebrity, and he was eating it up.

"Naturally, we are all frightened half out of our wits, Chief," Rose was assuring him when Stella walked in. "Three women alone in the country, and a desperate criminal on the loose. It's positively terrifying! Thank God for our stalwart lawmen."

"We do our best, Miss Rose," Jervis assured her humbly. As he said this, his glittering blue eyes were trained on Stella.

She entered, praying she looked fresh and unharried in a cool sleeveless dress of creme-de-menthe silk she had just changed into.

"Good evening, Stella," he greeted her. "I hope all you ladies are doing well?"

Men like Jervis considered politeness a sign of weakness. The one exception, however, was dealing with old ladies. He was actually being civil, even charming, in the presence of Rose and Maman. His hypocrisy galled Stella.

"Shoo," Maman said, "you look like you must be starved, poor thing. You had your supper, Mr. Jervis? Or even your lunch?"

"Actually, no. I've been out in the swamps all day, and I—"

"La, your backbone must be rubbin' 'gainst your ribs by now!" Maman exclaimed. "You come out to the kitchen this very minute, Mr. Jervis. I just made a big ol' batch of jambalaya."

Step into my parlor, said the spider to the fly . . . Stella thought as she watched Rose and Maman scurry for Jervis. The scene around her recalled the movie *Arsenic and Old Lace,* except those two old ladies didn't have malice toward their victims. Maman and Rose seemed positively devilish in their solicitations of the chief's "well-being."

"Well, seeing how you're the best cook in the parish, Maman, looks like I'm under citizen's arrest. Maybe just a quick bite."

Stella, amused by the older women, followed everybody into the kitchen. So far she'd had it easy. Maman and Rose would be adept at keeping Archer too distracted to focus on her.

"You gonn have a quick bite? Of my cookin'?" Maman scoffed. "And you call yourself a southern boy? La, I only like big eaters. You show me a man with a hollow leg, and I'll fill it up."

Archer parked himself at the gateleg table in the kitchen while the two women continued to fuss over him. If Jervis had expected a chilly welcome, he was pleasantly surprised. Even Stella kept her face neutral and forced herself to sit at the table with him.

But she picked the chair farthest from his.

Jervis sipped a glass of lemonade while Maman fixed him a heaping plate of jambalaya and corn bread and poked it into the microwave.

"I 'member Mr. Jervis when he's just a little shaver," Maman reminisced while Jervis divided his attention between his plate and Stella. "Lord, he's man-grown now, ain't he, Rose?"

"Handsome devil too," Rose added, flirting shamelessly.

Jervis swallowed all this flattery as easily as he swallowed Maman's superb cooking.

"No wife to cook for you," Rose clucked. "Poor thing. Leora, make him a big plate to take home too."

"'Preciate it," Jervis said, still watching Stella as he ate.

"This fugitive you're after," Rose said, "is he as dangerous as the news stories claim?"

"Even worse," Jervis assured her between chews. "That dope found in his room was just the tip of the iceberg. Turns out this guy is the U.S. linchpin in a drug cartel that originates in Bogotá and terminates in Texas."

Although Jervis said this for all three women to hear, he was really talking only to Stella.

"He's also been linked to four murders," Archer added.

Stella saw Maman and Rose exchange a shocked glance. "Two of the victims were females," Jervis tacked on as he wiped his mouth on a linen napkin. "He . . . ahhm, violated both of them before he killed them."

Maman's long, aristocratic face registered shock. "Saints preserve us," she muttered, making the sign of the cross.

"You seem to know a lot more than has been reported," Stella pointed out.

"It's always that way, Stella," he replied condescendingly. "The media fear lawsuits more than anything else. That's why everything is always 'alleged.' "

Damn his lying bones, Stella fumed. Acting so polite and gentlemanly to impress Maman and Rose—it made Stella look like a lying bitch for complaining about him so much. Even worse, his lies about Garrett were scaring the older women. At least, Stella *prayed* they were lies. In truth, however, she certainly couldn't prove otherwise.

"Reason I stopped by, Stella," Jervis said when he had emptied his plate, "I want to search the house again. Seems the dogs couldn't get a good nose on our boy. Just want to make sure your place is safe. You understand?"

Stella stared at him with a wooden face. "If you really think it's necessary," she replied calmly.

"I really think it's necessary," Jervis assured her a bit too enthusiastically. "The higher-ups have taken this one over, and they want the place searched. I'm just a small-town flatfoot. I do the donkey work and ask no questions."

So modest all of a sudden, Stella thought. If feds or whoever wanted a search, she figured they'd be here doing it themselves. But again she realized she had no proof she was harboring a "good guy." The fact that she hated Archer didn't automatically mean Garrett was trustworthy. This was real life, not some fairy tale where there was one hero for every villain.

"Guess I should get started," Jervis told her. He scraped his chair back and stood up. "By law, someone has to be present with me. If one of you lovely ladies will be so kind as to accompany me . . . ?"

As much as she hated to volunteer, Stella knew she had to. She feared Archer might weasel something out of Maman or Rose. Best to have just one liar in charge, she thought wryly.

"I'll do it," she spoke up.

Archer's eyes moved over Stella with almost tactile force, making her nape tingle in revulsion as if she'd touched a dead thing. He could not suppress a glint of triumphant gloating in those eyes. After all, it was exactly one week ago today when she had denied him entry to her home.

"That'll be real pleasant," Jervis replied with an ambiguity that was menacing. "After you, Stella."

Despite his assurance that the search of the house was "ridiculous," Jervis went at his work with a methodical thoroughness that intimidated Stella.

First he checked every room downstairs, including every bathroom, every storeroom, the furnace room, the laundry room, even the tiny shed that held the water heaters. He peeked into armoires, poked into every dark corner of every cabinet. It was the same systematic precision upstairs. He squatted to search under every bed, even stepped outside to check the iron lacework between columns. Every room but one—the secret room off the loggia—came under his intense scrutiny.

As Stella had feared, Archer's manners underwent a sea change once he had her alone. Her fear spiked on two counts: Garrett being found, and her being trapped alone again with Archer. The house was huge, and a cry might not be heard downstairs. So she stayed vigilant, making sure she did not let Jervis come between her and an open escape route.

Finally, they ended up in the doorway of the master bedroom suite. Jervis flicked his eyes toward a sheer negligee visible past the partially opened door of the satinwood armoire.

"I like where the haughty mistress sleeps," Jervis remarked. "Mighty fancy bed. Plenty of room," he added with crude innuendo. "Don't you ever feel lonely in all that bed?"

"Is sexual harassment part of the search?" she derided coolly.

Archer's lips twitched into his odd, asymmetrical smile. "To protect and serve, Stella. That's my job. To protect and serve."

"Yes, but you confuse protecting with hazing."

"Opinions vary. Some women like my style just fine."

"Bully for them."

They were still standing in the doorway, looking into the bedroom. Jervis touched her arm, and his hand felt gummy and warm. She instantly recoiled from his touch.

"Please finish your search, Chief."

Jervis laughed, shaking his head. "Some people never learn, Stella. You oughta be nice to me. Like I said, the day might be coming, and soon, when you'll beg for my help."

"You've made that clear," she told him, treading carefully between her anger and her terror. "Now, please finish your search."

He laughed again and stepped into her bedroom. She waited in the hall. Jervis quickly searched the big walk-in closet and looked under the bed.

"Would you step in here a minute," he said casually, "and open this door up the rest of the way?"

He nodded at the armoire. She studied Archer's calculating, predatory face and hated him all over again. She had read somewhere that even primitive men have God's laws written on their hearts. But did Jervis Archer? All she felt, watching him, was the insidious, haunting presence of evil.

"You have my permission to open it yourself," she told him. Obviously, Archer was trying to lure her in. She was damned if he'd succeed. Why should she help him rape her in her own bed?

Jervis confirmed her suspicion when he simply laughed again and didn't even bother to search the armoire. She felt a huge weight lift from her shoulders when he returned downstairs with her.

But the ordeal was not yet over.

Early on during the search downstairs, there had been a tense moment in the loggia. Archer had glanced speculatively at the row of mahogany panels in the rear wall. Standing directly in front of the turntable-mounted panel that provided entry to the secret room, he had asked her, "What's on the other side of this wall?"

"The ballroom," she had answered, her heart lurching.

All Jervis did to confer his confusion of the floor plan was to remark "big house," and they had moved on upstairs. She figured the danger was past.

Now, however, downstairs in the ballroom again, Jervis paused in the center of the room. His handsome face looked somewhat confused. She felt her blood chill when she guessed he was taking a mental measure of the room—and perhaps realizing there was too much distance between this room and the supposedly "adjacent" loggia.

"I heard a rumor once," he said, vocalizing his thoughts more than speaking, "that one of the old-time St. Valliers built a secret room at Shadow Oaks."

Her mouth went dry as cotton with sudden nervousness.

Maman and Rose had joined them again by then. Maman spoke up, her voice earnest.

"Secret room? Never been no secret room. But we got us a ghost at Shadow Oaks, Mr. Jervis."

"A ghost?"

Maman nodded vigorously. "A slave ghost," she confided. "Mmm-hmm. Sometimes he gets to hollering and thumping like one them hell-and-damnation preachers. But mostly he sings to us."

Archer's strong jaw dropped open. Stella could tell he didn't know whether to laugh or call a shrink.

"Sings," he repeated woodenly. "Hunh. I'll be jig-gered."

"That's it," Maman confirmed. "You can hear him. Singing spiritual songs and old field hollers. Been with us since ever I can remember. Mr. Jervis, sometimes when he sings "My hand to Jesus," put tears in your eyes."

"He'll sometimes sing for visitors, Chief," Aunt Rose chimed in.

"Mmm-hmm, that's it right there," Maman agreed. "Friendly ghost, just loves company."

"The best place to hear him," Rose explained, "is in my room. Won't you come listen?"

Despite the danger Jervis represented, Stella had to bite one corner of her lower lip to keep from laughing out loud. Rose had placed a sly hand on Archer's arm as she made the invitation. She had at least fifty years on the lawman, but Rose's offer obviously nonplussed him. By then he'd done precisely what these two wily old dames intended him to do: forgotten whatever he meant to ask about a secret room.

"Miss Rose, I truly would like to stay and hear that ghost sing," Jervis assured Aunt Rose. "But duty calls. You ladies be careful now."

Maman pressed a foil-wrapped plate into his hands. Moments later Jervis beat a hasty retreat.

Stella turned to her two companions. "'Slave ghost?' You two are something, you know that?"

Impulsively, Stella pulled both of them into a hug. "Thank you, both of you."

Their clever deception, however, had not left either Rose or Maman in a gloating mood.

"Hon," Maman told Stella, "that Jervis has always been meaner than Satan with a sunburn. I just pray to God he's a liar about . . . our guest."

Rose, too, had obviously been sobered by Archer's claims, claims bolstered by the media slant on recent events. She took Stella's hand and squeezed it hard.

"Sweet love, the man probably isn't half the monster Jervis is . . . but do you remember those old slave irons rusting away in the sugarhouse?"

"What? You want me to shackle him to the bed?" Stella asked half in jest.

Both women nodded.

Stella stared at them for a long, long while. "It won't be too comfortable for him."

Rose was the first to speak up. She quoted herself. "'Survival is a decision between the unpalatable and the disastrous.' If he truly is a man of the law, he knows it better than we do."

Maman nodded in agreement.

Stella nodded in resignation and did as she was asked.

CHAPTER

22

After Archer left, Stella escaped to her bedroom for some badly needed solitude. For a long time she stood in the bay of the biggest window and turned everything over in her mind.

A ragged parcel of cloud drifted over the moon, making shadows shift in the yard below.

That's the future around here, she thought darkly, a shape-changing shadow.

Just when her hopes started to build concerning the sugar cane operation, the emergency with Garrett cropped up. Now, right or wrong, she was in too deep to do anything except see it through. God alone knew what it might cost her. Or what it might cost Rose and Maman if she lost Shadow Oaks.

It had been almost two weeks since she'd witnessed the first drug deal. Since then, late October had given way to early November, adding only a light snap to the early morning air. Yet, so much now seemed on the verge of change: radical, traumatic change.

As if she were a marionette being tugged from above, she crossed to the west wall of the room. The gallery of St. Vallier women seemed to be expecting her. She silently greeted each one of them by name down through the generations, from Genevieve to Patricia.

For some reason, it was the eighteenth-century silhouette of Genevieve and Jules that again held her attention. She reached up and carefully took the rosewood-and-glass frame down from the wall to study it closer.

Like wind whispering in a dream, she again heard Aunt Rose's enigmatic advice: *Look to the lovers of the past.*

The phone in the nearby alcove burred. Still holding the portrait, she stepped around the corner into her reading nook and answered it.

"My God, girl," Mattie's excited voice greeted her. "I just read the *Times-Picayune*. Cane Town has turned into China Town! Are you all right?"

"I'm fine," Stella assured her, although the conviction was in her voice, not her heart.

"Hey, this Cowboy guy *is* a bad boy, isn't he?" Mattie nattered on, bubbling over like shaken champagne in her excitement. "Woo-*woo!* I didn't peg you for a gangsta's old lady, Stella."

"Mattie, take all of it with a grain of salt. He might be perfectly innocent of what people are claiming. You of all people should know how much you can trust the newspapers."

"Today's headlines wrap tomorrow's garbage, sure. So what are you saying here? You don't think Garrett Shaw is guilty?"

"Now, how would I know that? I'm just saying you shouldn't believe the 'official' version either. Remember who the officials are."

Mattie paused for a moment after this, and Stella inwardly cringed. She should have known better than to say even that much. Scholar Mattie excelled at rooting out the "subtext," whether in a Russian novel or a gab session. When Mattie spoke again, her voice had altered.

"Well, well. Wha'd'you know? Our conservative, circumspect, oh-so-proper Miss Stella believes Garrett Shaw is innocent."

"*Could* be innocent."

"Right. Stella believes he *could* be innocent. And lo and behold! Garrett Shaw has completely disappeared. No body, no trail, no *nada.* Hunh. Does any of this signify? I wonder."

"Don't be an idiot," Stella scoffed. "That creep Archer searched my house today. From top to bottom."

"Oh, did he? Tell me, what'd he say when you showed him Jules's treasure chamber?"

"I—that is, he didn't see it."

"Oh?" Mattie's single word spoke volumes.

"Knock it off, Everett. What's the point of a 'secret' room," Stella asked reasonably, "if you're going to show it to everybody?"

"Exactly," Mattie agreed. "Especially if it's occupied, right?"

Stella was angry at herself, not at Mattie. Look how quickly her indiscreet remarks had led Mattie to suspect the truth. True, Mattie was brighter by far than plodding cops like Jervis Archer. Still, the breech of security did not bode well.

"Mattie, you're turning a molehill into a mountain. All I did was remind you you're getting only one version of the facts."

"All right," Mattie agreed. Her voice sounded diplomatic now. "You're right. It takes two sides to make a war, and each side usually has the blessing of the church. But don't forget, Stella. History shows that one side is almost always more wrong than another. Try to be on the least-wrong side."

Mattie was a good friend who'd do anything for her. But Stella always had to endure these little lectures from her. Still, she realized she had just been let off the hook—for now.

"So what else is new in Cane Town?" Mattie inquired. "Besides handsome escapees from the law?"

It was a lame effort to turn Mattie's interrogation back into a mere chat.

"Mmm...well, I had another message from Professor Perkins today," Stella reported. "He wished me luck. My query about bagasse is now winging its way to the Meridian Feed Company."

"You go, girl," Mattie approved. "I wish you luck too."

Mattie sounded sincere, but something awkward had become wedged between the two women. Stella was not about to confirm anything, but she knew Mattie had guessed something was very wrong at Shadow Oaks.

"You okay?" Mattie asked. "You seem distracted."

"I'm fine," Stella assured her. "Maybe a little preoccupied with business stuff, is all."

"You know, last time you sounded so tense, you were preoccupied with the idea of finding the St. Vallier treasure. Tonight, nary a peep about it. What's the new thing that's replaced the old preoccupation?"

"Believe me, I still want to find the St. Vallier treasure. But, c'mon. It's a delusion. A beautiful one, perhaps—one that Rose certainly clings to—but she clings to the delusion of unfounded love and destiny too. And what's that gotten me?"

Indeed, Stella thought wryly. If her destiny was taking her to her great love, so far it had only bagged a drug-dealing rogue cop who might be turning cold in her secret room as they spoke.

"Stella, honest to John. I'm cynical like everyone else. There's lots of things I secretly think but haven't got the courage to say. But may I be eternally damned if

I ever tell you anything I don't sincerely believe. That's why I pooh-pooh the treasure. I won't lead you on. But you know what?"

"What?"

"Sheesh! I feel like the grinch who stole Christmas. At least the treasure gave you a dream. I'm not so sure I *want* you to give up the search."

Yes, thought Stella as she studied the black-velvet silhouette she still held in one hand. *An eager expectation,* Aunt Rose called it. And Rose was right. What good was any life without it?

"I've always had this itch to find it," Stella admitted. "But I'm completely mystified how to translate that ambition into effective action."

"You're sort of like a horny eunuch, huh?"

Stella laughed, enjoying the feeling of it after all that had happened lately.

"Leave it to our Miss Mattie to come up with that comparison."

Another awkward silence stretched out between them, and Stella feared Mattie was going to ask her again about Garrett. Instead, Mattie wrapped up her call.

"Well, back to the salt mines," she told her friend. "I've got midterm exams to grade. Hey? Do you know how I want to see you end up, Stella St. Vallier?"

"How?"

"Glutted with happiness, that's how," Mattie replied. "You deserve it. Please be careful."

Stella replaced the cordless phone on the holder. With Mattie's phone call still playing in her mind, she decided to check on Garrett.

Downstairs, she found Maman setting the dining room table for dinner. Aunt Rose, exhausted from her Oscar-quality performance to fool Archer, was napping in her room.

"What you doing with that, hon?" Maman asked.

Only then did the preoccupied Stella realize she was

still carrying the framed silhouette of Jules and Genevieve.

"I don't know—I guess I'm feeling superstitious. I thought I'd put them both back in their room," she answered haltingly. "Just for luck. After all, Jules built the room. I guess he's sort of the patron saint."

Maman set a lovely *famille rose* plate down on the linen tablecloth. "We need saints, all right. A doctor wouldn't hurt none neither."

Maman spoke with quiet reproof. Her tone let Stella know she would support her, but with serious misgivings. Stella headed toward the kitchen and the back door.

"Stell?"

She turned around. "What, Maman?"

"Honey, Maman ain't no calamity howler. But . . . child, what if the worst happens? What if that young man . . . well, what if he dies here?"

Stella's face drained at this suggestion while Maman crossed herself for speaking such things. But Maman was right. It would present a nightmare. Yet, what was the alternative? Garrett was convinced that seeking medical help would be even more dangerous than going without it.

Without answering, for she had no answer, Stella went around to the rear loggia and entered the secret room.

Garrett still lay motionless like a sullen animal, unconscious, his handsome face pale as fresh linen. Wrapped around his ankle was a leg brace. The old rusty chain was covered in towels to protect the bedpost from scratches.

She placed the framed silhouette of Jules and Genevieve on the old nightstand. Then she carefully inserted a thermometer under Garrett's tongue and checked his temperature: 101 degrees. That wasn't a serious fever. But she was worried. His temperature had been up and down all day, fluctuating between 100 and

103 degrees. That was a sure sign his body was trying to fight off an infection. His wound was still clean. She only hoped the antibiotics she was giving him would be enough.

His unconscious state posed another serious problem: the danger of choking as she tried to get some badly needed fluids inside him. All the blood loss, plus this chronic fever, had left him seriously dehydrated.

The only solution she could prescribe was patience. Over and over she dribbled cool water into his mouth. Fortunately, basic reflexes took over. He took the moisture, automatically swallowing small amounts that couldn't choke him.

It was slow and painstaking, but she stayed at it well into the night, determined to keep moisture in him. At one point, wiping perspiration from his face with a washcloth, she recalled Maman's haunting words.

Child, what if the worst happens?

Her fears affected her with the force of a slap to the face. What in God's name am I doing here? she wondered. She had already gone through Garrett's pockets in a useless attempt to establish his identity. She must, she reminded herself, find out who—and what—he was as quickly as possible.

That name he had mentioned before he passed out in the sugarhouse, this Steve. The moment he came to his senses, she resolved to press him for more information about the guy.

Face it, she thought, trying to harden herself to the wisdom of Mattie's advice. You're dangerously vulnerable, Stella St. Vallier. For years now you've been plodding along in a state of unutterable loneliness. Solitude has warped your better judgment.

Still . . . She studied his wan face in the lamplight and her fears seemed to dissipate. Yes, there were certainly handsome criminals in the world. There were handsome chiefs of police too. But she wondered if beyond the pleasing lines in his face lay a depth of character too.

She desperately wanted to read it there.

So it's come down to this, has it? she thought with a little smile. That famous delusion known as "woman's intuition"? What was it he told her that night she caught him lurking in the cane field? *An honest pagan is better than a bad Catholic.*

His eyes flickered open for a second.

Startled, she placed the cup of water back on the nightstand and leaned over him.

He groaned and tried to turn, but the clamp on his leg didn't give him the expected freedom of movement. As if furious—or delirious—he tossed back and forth on the mattress, unconsciously trying to unshackle his leg.

"Hush," she soothed, placing her hands on his shoulders. "Don't waste your energy. You haven't got it."

He groaned. Again and again he murmured, "Welcome to sunny Beirut . . . sunny Beirut . . . the gateway . . ." He tossed and twisted, seemingly in agony.

"Shhh," she whispered, massaging his thickly muscled shoulders with her hands. "It's all right."

". . . the gateway to hell."

She knew he had to be remembering something, but what, she didn't know. The only Americans she'd ever heard of being in Beirut were either in the military or were there illegally to run guns or drugs. With Garrett Shaw, all she had to do was spin the wheel. Any answer might fit.

". . . . gateway to hell . . ."

She looked down. His eyes were open; he stared at her with unnerving focus.

"Are you awake finally?" she whispered, her words anxious, her voice gentle.

He lifted his hand. Slowly, painfully, he touched her cheek, caressing her jawline with his thumb.

"Rare angel . . . saved me," he murmured as if the words calmed his very core. He lowered his hand, but his feverish gaze stayed trained on her face.

"I—I think you'll be okay," she stammered, trying to think of things to comfort him. "You're—you're not in Beirut, by the way."

"I know . . . I've found my way to heaven," he whispered before his eyes closed once more and he fell into a deep, near-comatose sleep.

CHAPTER

23

On Friday afternoon, three days after Garrett Shaw apparently fell off the face of the earth, Senator Myron Leblanc flew back home to Louisiana. He arranged a hasty emergency meeting with Toutant and Archer. Because he feared the media spotlight was still shining too brightly on Cane Town, Leblanc insisted on meeting in New Orleans.

To further avoid publicity, the prominent politician chose the small, venerable Hotel de Fôret along St. Charles Avenue. It was ideal for discreet meetings; indeed, more than one coup d'état or daring espionage mission had been planned there over the centuries. Opening off three sides of the huge central ballroom, with its magnificent circular stairway and crystal gasoliers, was a series of private meeting rooms.

"This situation is rapidly getting out of hand," Leblanc told his companions in his powerful voice that could fill a canyon. "We have *got* to locate Shaw before he can contact anyone. Otherwise, he'll sink us fast."

The three men sat in comfortable wing chairs. Antique blue-and-white porcelain lamps cast a ruddy glow. The French doors had been thrown open to the inner courtyard, for it was a beautiful fall evening, the sweet, olive-scented air soft as the breath of a young girl.

"Aren't you being just a bit pessimistic?" Toutant suggested. "I mean, he might very well be dead. Besides, Cowboy is cooked even if he does surface. Don't forget we set him up good with that coke in his room."

"The ass waggeth his ears," Leblanc retorted caustically, for he was in a foul mood. "The setup is fine *if* he's dead, sure. But it will never hold if he surfaces alive."

"Never," Jervis affirmed in a rare show of support for Leblanc. The cop elaborated. "Internal Affairs will make him take repeated lie detector tests and he'll pass them. They'll even shoot him full of sodium pentothal."

"The hell's that?" Toutant asked.

"So-called truth serum," Leblanc took over. "Makes it virtually impossible to lie convincingly once you're hypnotized or drugged into a light trance. His superiors will eventually determine Shaw's telling the truth. We might still survive, sure. But from now on, we'll be like parolees with ankle-bracelet alarms. We won't be able to make one wrong move without being monitored."

The implications of Leblanc's comment were clear: Not only would United Southern Children's Charities be forced to go legit from then on, but no more drug profits either.

While all three men mulled this over, the St. Charles Avenue streetcar clattered past out front. A hubbub of noises reached them, for a wedding reception was being held on the front veranda. Now and then white-jacketed waiters glided past their door, huge trays balanced on their fingertips.

Leblanc drained a tumbler of Scotch—his second in

only ten minutes—and shifted in his chair to stare at Jervis. "Any progress at all, Chief?"

"Right now," Archer admitted, "we're just washing bricks. But there is one possibility."

Jervis paused even though the other two men were waiting for more. He had not forgotten those rumors about a secret room at Shadow Oaks. In fact, since yesterday it had been rankling at him, in retrospect, how all that "ghost story" crap by those two old bags had got him off the subject pronto. Jervis knew a diversion when he saw it, even if it was after the fact.

"There's talk around Cane Town about a secret room at Shadow Oaks," Jervis told his companions. "I can't confirm it. But it would sure's hell explain why we can't find Cowboy, dead or alive."

Leblanc was instantly intrigued. "A secret room? I never heard about it, but then, I'm not around home all that much. Can anybody verify this? Are there blueprints or whatever?"

"I been wrasslin' with that one," Archer said. "Stella's got this historian friend who teaches at Southern Louisiana College in Thibodaux. This chick's an expert on Shadow Oaks. She writes articles about the place for state newspapers. If anybody knows, she would."

Leblanc removed a pen and the flip-back pad he always carried in his inside breast pocket. "What's her name?" he demanded.

"Hell if I know. I don't hang with academic doubledomes."

Leblanc scrawled a quick note. "Won't be hard to find out her name," he told the other two. "We can go to her with some 'convincing proof.' You know, assure her Cowboy is a puppy killer and a baby raper, all that, get her to cooperate for Stella's sake."

Leblanc looked at the chief again. "But time is of the essence here. So get back to Shadow Oaks too. Try the same strategy on Stella herself."

"She won't believe Jervis," Toutant objected. "She hates his frigging guts."

"She won't trust his mere word, no. But perhaps some kind of . . . supporting documents might sway her."

"Like what?" Jervis demanded.

"I'll work on it," the senator assured him. "I'll contact Cliff D'Antoni. He has access to excellent desktop printing capabilities."

"Might work at that," Jervis agreed. "Stella's pissed at me, but she's also mighty damned law abiding. Some kind of 'proof' might make her feel guilty if she really is harboring a fugitive."

"But we'll have to move fast," Leblanc reminded his co-conspirators. "The longer those two are together, if they are, the more she'll start to believe him."

All day Friday Stella was in and out of the secret room, tending to her patient.

Her careful ministrations had begun to yield hopeful results. Though still slightly feverish, Garrett's temperature now peaked at only 100 degrees. And though he remained unconscious all day, he changed his position several times instead of lying motionless, like a man in a deep coma.

Because she had also tended to him during the night, she was exhausted by the middle of the afternoon. Maman fixed her a light lunch, then she retired to her own room for a nap.

She woke up at that odd time of day Autry called "between dog and wolf"—no longer daylight but not yet dark either. She quickly showered and donned a simple rose damask dress. Then she returned to the master bedroom suite; in her bathroom she found lavender shaving foam, a disposable razor, and towels. She stuffed everything into a woven raffia tote and went to shave off her patient's sandpaper-rough beard.

Garrett was still unconscious but resting comfortably, his color better. She laid out her tools and covered Garrett's face with the foamy soap. Carefully, she began shaving him. She moved the razor across his cheeks in short strokes, scraping off the tough bristles.

My God, but he's a handsome man, she thought as she studied the planes and angles of his face. There was a pleasing evenness and symmetry to his features that she associated with the Greco-Roman idea that beauty was a function of perfect balance and harmony.

She reached the tricky part, the sharp angle of his chin. Busy concentrating on her task, she hadn't noticed yet that his eyes had been open for some time.

"Please keep that damn thing away from my neck."

His sudden words, in a weak but clear voice, made her cry out and reflexively jerk her hand.

"Now you've made me cut you!" she scolded, hurrying to apply a damp towel to his bleeding chin.

"It's not like I can spare the blood," he quipped. Then, just as unexpectedly, he said, "Christ, I gotta take a piss."

Her eyes widened. Fumbling in the nightstand, she removed an old covered chamberpot. She helped him right himself and did her best to give him some privacy.

She had intended to ply him with questions the moment he regained awareness. Instead, she cleaned out the chamberpot, then sat next to him to continue to shave him while she answered his questions. She explained briefly where he was and how he had gotten there.

He was lucid but obviously weak and tired. She finished filling him in, then said, "Now it's *your* turn to do some explaining. For starters, who's this guy Steve you told me to call?"

"I promise you'll get a full disclosure," he assured her. He tried to sit upright in the bed, but she still had to help him. Once settled, he irreverently pulled the covers from his shackled leg. A derisive raised eyebrow served as his only question.

"It seemed prudent," she said hastily, nervous beneath his predator's stare.

"Prudent?" He studied it. "I take it you put it on me, then; it doesn't look like police issue."

"It's not. It's a good hundred and fifty years old. Supposedly, it was kept here for runaways, but we never ever used it."

He looked around the ancient bedroom. "I take it you had a big problem with that?" He was clearly being sarcastic.

Her jaw set. "There's no making slavery pretty. But the St. Valliers set our slaves free before we had to, and very few of them left. Maman's family on this plantation goes back as far as ours. And we're both still here, looking after each other." She looked away. "I guess I'm proud of that fact."

"Unusual family, unusual woman," he stated, his gaze holding hers.

She looked away. "But enough of this. I need to know how to contact Steve."

"Listen to me," he said grimly, "I know damn well that two sleazeballs like Toutant and Archer would not miss the chance to set me up somehow for a fall. Before I tell you anything, I've got to know my status with the law."

"Well, it's not good. I can tell you that much," she said as she finished wiping his smooth-shaven face clean of leftover soap.

The effort at concentrating and speaking was obviously taxing his strength. He leaned his head back against the pillows. "So they set me up."

She didn't know what to say to him. To give words of comfort and support his innocence would make her into too much of a hypocrite, given the iron around his ankle. And now that he was awake and gaining strength, she was sure as hell not going to unlock him.

He spoke aloud, as if going through the surmise in

his head. "If the setup was convincing enough, that means I'm probably a wanted man. My agency can't clear me unless I can *prove* I was set up. But once you contact them, and I'm remanded into custody, there goes my best chance. That means Leblanc, Archer, Toutant—they all go free. Still your friendly neighbors."

That reminder made the blood leave her face. "Leblanc?" she interjected. "You're saying he's definitely implicated too?"

"Implicated? That's drawing it mild, pretty girl. He's the whole point of this investigation. Toutant and Archer are dangerous all right. But they're only small potatoes. Leblanc's sick little toadies."

"What do you want Leblanc for? Drug dealing?"

"He ordered the execution of Albert Fontainbleau, for one thing. Among other things, he's using his children's charity as a front to pack the political coffers of himself and a few of his cronies. They're also using it to launder drug money."

"Toutant and Archer's drug money," she finished for him, wanting to believe him more and more as the pieces of the puzzle fell into place. Indeed, his welcome words fell on her ears like rain to dry earth. It all simply made too much sense to be a criminal's cover story. Perhaps she could sleep finally without guilt. Perhaps after all, she had done the right thing.

She rose from the bedside and brought him newspapers from the last few days. He scanned them, then tiredly laid his head back on the pillows. He was pale from the effort.

"The situation's tenuous," he told her. "If I tell you who to contact, they'll have to bring me in. It's their only choice with open warrants out for my arrest." He paused. His words came dark and heavy. "But either way, if I don't wrap this case up on my own, I'm dead."

Tiring rapidly now, he seemed on the verge of passing out again. She declined to press him. They still had more time. Besides, he was not yet the picture of health. It would take a few more days for him to leave Shadow Oaks on his own two feet.

"Why are you doing all this for me?" he asked her as his eyelids grew heavy.

"I've been wondering that myself."

The corner of his mouth tugged with a wry smile. "So are you sorry?"

"No," she replied honestly. "I'm scared."

With his last bit of strength he put his hand on her nape and pulled her to him. He kissed her full and deep on the mouth, the gesture filled more with promise than gratitude.

She could barely hear his final words before he slipped again into unconsciousness.

"Next time 'round, I'll save you," he whispered softly. "Angel of mercy."

His words made her eyes shimmer with feeling for a moment. She was so glad he had come around, but their conversation had been frustratingly brief. Far too much had been left unresolved, including some kind of plan of action.

Jervis Archer, she realized full well, had not given up. Aunt Rose and Maman had sidetracked him all right. But they hadn't derailed the badge-toting bully. He'd be back.

She looked down at the man beside her. Her lips burned with his kiss. With his eyes closed he looked handsome and serene: Michelangelo's rendition of a fallen Greek god. He didn't look dangerous at all if one didn't think about the rusting thick iron band holding him to the bed, nor the idea that had just occurred to her that when she was ready to release him, she'd do well to have a gun trained on him until he was good and well off her property.

CHAPTER

24

Myron Leblanc and Lafourche Parish D.A. Cliff D'Antoni worked with amazing speed and efficiency.

They were assisted by the behind-the-scenes efforts of Mississippi congressman Roland Nesbit, who originally tipped off Leblanc about the federal sting. Using his leverage as a member of the Justice Department's Oversight Committee, Nesbit was able to tap into a federal law enforcement computer—databank not accessible to the general public.

Thus, he was also able to circumvent the "canned IDs"—fake identities routinely established for the real names of undercover agents—and download reliable documents on the U.S. marshals. These documents included the ID card photo of U.S. marshal Garrett Shaw. That photo was electronically transmitted to D'Antoni's office with the press of a key.

Only twenty-four hours after the meeting in New

Orleans, Chief Jervis Archer returned to Shadow Oaks. It was Stella herself who answered the doorbell.

"Chief," she greeted him noncommittally. She held the door aslant rather than open it wide to invite him in.

But clearly Archer was not eager to be double-teamed again by Rose and Maman.

"Could you step outside for a minute, Stella?"

She noticed the flyer in his hand. She came out onto the veranda and closed the massive oak door behind her.

"Something I need to show you," he told her. "Just came in today from the National Crime Information Center. It's an FBI wanted poster."

She took the flyer from his hairy fist. The first thing she spotted below the words WANTED BY THE FEDERAL BUREAU OF INVESTIGATION was a mug shot of Garrett Shaw. For a moment her stomach felt as if it had just been pumped.

She refused, however, to show any outward reaction.

Keeping her face impassive, she read the brief summary of charges against Shaw—identified on the flyer as Duane Leroy Johnson of Odessa, Texas. Charges included bank robbery, drug running, attempted murder, and interstate flight to avoid arrest.

"He ain't one of their ten most wanted," Archer remarked in his toneless voice. "But he's not exactly a scrubbed angel either."

The flyer described Johnson as a brilliant con man who used aliases and sometimes hid his criminal activities behind the guise of a "federal agent." For a moment, after reading that, she felt as if she were trying to stand up in a canoe on a turbulent river.

Her gaze shifted to the bottom of the page. A small line in one corner read: U.S. Government Printing Office, Washington, D.C.

"Sounds like a dangerous man," she finally commented, handing the flyer back to Jervis. "I'm surprised the media haven't mentioned any of this."

"They will. Nobody but me's made the connection yet."

For a few moments Stella glanced through Archer, not at him, as her thoughts wandered elsewhere. The flyer was damning, all right, and she felt a hard little nubbin of doubt work its way inside her. But one fact stood out in her mind: Garrett had named Senator Myron Leblanc as the target of his supposed investigation. Why, if he was a con man? What could be the point of such a lie, and why that name unless he *knew* Leblanc was up to something?

Archer said something Stella missed.

"I beg your pardon?"

"I said, did you fall, Stella, or were you pushed?"

She stared at the cop's ice-chip eyes, uncomprehending. "I don't understand."

Archer flashed his bent-wire smile. "What I mean, girl, is that it's not too late for me to help you get off scot-free. If you *choose* to hide a criminal, well, it's your tough luck. But if this dangerous guy *forced* you—you know, threatened Rose or whatever, why, hell, no one will charge a leading citizen like you with anything. Of course you'd protect your family. That's no crime."

She did a slow boil as Archer's point came clear.

"Straight-arrow now, Stella. Are you hiding him here?"

Her wide, angry eyes confronted Archer with fearless scorn. "I don't believe you have one good reason to ask me that question. You've searched my house twice now." She gave him a dismissive glance. "I've always admired strong men, Chief Archer," she informed him in her crisp, precise enunciation. "But knowing you reminds me just how much I despise bullies."

She started to turn away, but Archer seized her arm in his steel-trap grip.

"Somebody has to take charge in bed," he goaded her.

By then she could practically whiff the anger coming off him. But she had to say it. "You know what, Jervis Archer? You are the biggest asshole I have ever had the misfortune to know."

She summoned strength she didn't know she possessed and wrenched her arm free. As she turned to the door, he taunted from behind her, "Yeah, I'm not *sensitive* like your wounded pretty-boy in the secret room, anh? Does he treat you sweet in the sack, Stella? Who gets on top? Or do you two *discuss* that?"

"Go to hell," she fumed, slamming the door and locking it.

It felt good, at least momentarily, to tell the overbearing bastard off to his face. But even as Archer's cruiser roared down the drive, she had fresh doubts assail her. For the same old truism still held: Her hatred for Archer did not mean Garrett was innocent. And obviously, Archer had been nurturing his suspicion about Jules's secret room. If he got a warrant, he'd find Garrett next time unless she could get Garrett good and gone by that time.

As for that wanted poster . . . She closed her eyes, weary from the tension. True, it looked convincing; yet, the cowl does not make the monk. It could have been printed by anybody.

Still, doubts piled up again in her mind like clouds on the horizon. Determined to clarify this situation once and for all, she headed toward the rear loggia and the entrance to the secret room.

"Archer's word isn't worth a rap. You know that."

Garrett had been asleep when Stella entered the room. But he was better now, and "sleep" no longer meant unconsciousness. It required only a light touch to his face to waken him. She quickly summed up her clash just now with Jervis.

She looked into those nimbus-gray eyes and forced herself to remember again: Never mind her strong conviction, yesterday, that Garrett was not a criminal. In truth, what she *hoped* was reality must still be somehow proven. The heart was indeed a lonely hunter. She could accept a risk for her own sake, but Maman and Rose were also involved. For their sake she *must* be a doubter.

Garrett managed a smile. "He's got you worried, doesn't he?"

"It's only rational to be worried when a cop comes knocking on your door with a wanted poster for the man who's lying in your house," she said more testily than she wanted to.

"I'm willing to go if you let me." His gaze lowered to his still-clamped ankle. "I'm weak, but I have a feeling I'll be my usual insulting self in no time flat."

She almost smiled at his comment, but the smile was ousted by a worried frown. His words about his real self goaded at her now: What, she wondered, was his real name?

"I'm not saying I believe Archer," she told him matter-of-factly.

"Christ, I hope not. Archer would have no problem putting either one of us down like a foundered horse. I can't prove it from this bed, but I'm convinced it was Archer who fed Albert Fontainbleau into that cane cutter. On Leblanc's orders."

Her stomach lurched at the thought. "I'm sure he's capable," she said quietly, "but his character isn't the only one in question here. Do you accept people's word in your line of work? Or do you verify the supposed facts?"

He studied her face. Her determination seemed to move him.

"Gentle in manner, resolute in action. I admire that. No wonder your family has endured," he said.

"Flattery helps, but it won't get you off the hook."

He sighed. "All right. Since I can't charm you, let's negotiate. State your terms."

"I need *some* assurance, is all. I understand why you can't just tell me everything and simply let me confirm it. But isn't there some middle ground? Some way I can at least confirm your identity as a cop? I mean, without revealing where you are?"

For a full minute he closed his eyes and mulled her words over.

"I think we can do that," he finally said. "This fellow Steve that I mentioned? He's my control base. He's my partner who works behind the scenes to support an undercover operative in the field."

"May I call him?"

"Yes, but it's not quite that simple," he cautioned. "It's got to be done just right. He's my partner, sure. But he also took an oath, and Steve is a rulebook commando. Some agents will break the rules, but Steve won't even bend them. And don't forget, Stella, right now I'm a fugitive from the law—and Steve is the law."

She nodded.

"If we force his hand, he's obligated to apprehend me. So we have to be very careful that we don't make him an accessory."

"Obviously, you know the law better than I. How do we do that?"

"First of all, mention *no* names when you call. Not mine, not yours, not even his. See, technically speaking, so long as Steve is not actually told anything specific, he's not compromised. The law can't nail a person for reading between the lines. He's smart enough to catch on quick, and he'll play along."

She nodded. "All right, no names."

"And call from a pay phone," he added. "He's got caller ID, so he'll know you're in area code 504—which, of course, will also tell him it's southeast Louisiana. And he'll soon track the number to Cane Town. But we can't help that."

Again she nodded. "But then, what *can* I actually say?"

Despite the exhaustion evident in his face, he smiled. "Now, that, Miss St. Vallier, is going to seem like the strange part."

By the time Stella reached Cane Town, the streets had begun to fill and thicken with the usual Saturday night activity. She pulled into the parking lot of a Quik Serve mart and parked in front of the pay phones.

One last time she rehearsed what she was going to say. Then she fed a handful of quarters into one of the phones and punched in the Washington, D.C. number Garrett had given her.

"Garrett?" a tense male voice answered on the second ring. She was taken aback for a moment. Then she realized: With his caller ID, Steve obviously assumed it was his partner on the line. Who else would be calling him from Louisiana?

"Please listen to me carefully," she said without any introduction or preamble.

After a brief hesitation, "I'm all ears."

"Please do *not* ask me any questions, I can't answer them. But I do have a question to ask you. First, however, I also have a message for you from someone you know very well. Your correct answer to the question he sends in the message is intended to verify that I have permission to ask my question. Do you understand?"

"I think I do. Go ahead."

"Tell me: How's your sex life up there?" She closed her eyes and gave a silent prayer.

The man immediately laughed. Then, his voice both curious and relieved, he replied, "Well, you can tell your friend I'm holding my own, mystery lady. So what's your question?"

"The man who sends you this message: What is his profession?"

"Ma'am, Garrett Shaw's the best damned U.S. marshal I've ever had the privilege to work with. You have my cast-iron guarantee on that."

Only now, as tears of relief and joy blurred her view of the night, did she finally realize how important these words were to her.

"Thank you," she told him. "Thank you so much."

"Wait, please! Umm, I mean—well, can I tell you something else?"

"Yes?"

"Tell him to give himself up. They tell me he's gone bad, but I don't want to believe it."

Her heart lurched.

"Call me if you can work some sense into him. I'm here any time you need me, all right?"

"Yes," she said in a trembling voice. "Thank you."

The call did little to get either of them out of danger. Garrett was still being pursued by Archer, and she was still not sure whether Garrett Shaw was a rogue cop. Nonetheless, she felt almost light-headed with elation as she drove back to Shadow Oaks.

She ran to the secret room.

"It's okay," she told him the moment his eyelids eased open. "Steve was there. I know who you are now. Good cop, bad cop, at least I know you were a cop."

He nodded, mustering a wan smile. Instead of returning to sleep immediately, however, he reached out and took her chin in his grasp.

Her brow furrowed with curiosity.

"Come closer," he whispered.

She did. A moment later she felt his lips lightly brush hers. It ignited pyrotechnics within her.

"I've been wanting to do that all day," he said simply.

She laid one cool hand on his cheek. " 'This is the man, all tattered and torn, that kissed the maiden all forlorn.' "

He took another kiss, then another one, a deeper one. His tongue dove into the recess of her mouth, eliciting pent-up sexual desire. She moaned as his hand slid down her cheek, her throat, her collarbone, to seek the generous swell of her breast.

"Can you finish this?" she asked, wanting yet unsure.

He took a deep, long breath. With tired, worn-out eyes, he leaned back against the pillows and dropped his hand.

She stared at him for a long time.

He stared back, his face hungry and hard.

Unspoken paragraphs were exchanged.

She knew then that her needs were eventually going to get the best of her with this man. Their carnal union was now no longer an if. It was when.

CHAPTER
25

*The prince, being thus obliged to know well how
to act as a beast, must imitate the fox and the
lion, for the lion cannot protect himself from
traps, and the fox cannot defend himself from
wolves. One must therefore be a fox to recognize
the traps, and a lion to frighten the wolves.*
—NICCOLÒ MACHIAVELLI

"He ate every bite of your gumbo filé, Maman,"
Stella reported as she returned to the kitchen.
She stopped at the sink to rinse out the bowl Garrett
had just emptied. "He sends his compliments to the
chef."

Maman and Rose sat at the kitchen table, sipping hot
toddies over their mah-jongg game.

"Now he got his appetite back," Maman said, her
tone heavy with innuendo, "maybe he'll be leaving soon?"

"Leora," Rose admonished quietly, "where's your
Christian charity?"

"I prayed for his recovery," Maman retorted. "And I
cooked for him. I got no more Christian charity in me."

"Believe me," Stella assured her, "he's got no desire to hang around here any longer than he needs to, but he still needs a little more time."

"Stell, don't you be so sure you know what he 'desires.' We got no window on that man's thoughts."

Stella crossed to the table and took a seat.

"Maman, you have every right to be suspicious. But I made a very important phone call earlier today. I verified that our guest is indeed a law officer."

Maman slapped a tile onto the table, her mouth turning down at the corners in a frown. "Hon, Jervis Archer's a cop too, so what's that prove? 'Sides, I don't care if he's Prince Charles. That man trouble for all of us. This is your house, and you can do what you will. I just wish he was gone."

"Oh, pouf," Aunt Rose scoffed. Rose had noticed Stella's chipper mood, and she seemed to rejoice in it. "A little danger is like good poetry, Leora. It provides a sense of the enchantment of life."

"Humph! Strong coffee will do that. Everybody around here's a philosopher, but good poetry don't kill you in your bed."

"*I've* been sleeping just fine, thank you," Rose countered.

Despite everything that still troubled her, Stella had to laugh outright at these two. Actually, she appreciated Maman's skeptical attitude—she was the voice of reason under the circumstances. It was Aunt Rose who was being reckless. She was treating all this as if it were a mere lark. Perhaps, at her age, life itself had become her favorite soap opera. But this was not TV melodrama. Jervis Archer could return at any time. They were just waiting for the guillotine blade to fall.

"Both you two done lost your buttons," Maman muttered. "Saints preserve us."

Aunt Rose, wrapped in a comfortable, loose-fitting cotton dressing gown, only smiled mysteriously.

Perhaps she simply does not realize our danger,

Stella mused. The fact that Garrett was a cop didn't change his rogue/fugitive status—nor the motivations of those who wanted to kill him. And all three women were still aiding and abetting a felon, cop or no. Even if Rose grasped that fact, however, she couldn't possibly know just how dangerous Jervis Archer really was. Losing Shadow Oaks wasn't the only risk the three women faced.

"I have to drive into town and buy a few things," Stella announced, standing up. "If Archer returns . . ."

Her voice trailed off. Rose and Maman glanced up at her, waiting for Stella to finish. But the younger woman had suddenly recalled how these two crafty old gals had duped Chief Archer on Thursday. They didn't need any advice from her.

"If he returns," Stella repeated, "God help him when you two get done with him."

Garrett was awake and sitting up in bed when Stella returned from Cane Town.

"I picked these up for you in town," she explained. "For when you're ready."

She pulled new blue jeans, navy cotton knit boxers, socks, and a short-sleeve knit shirt from a plastic shopping bag. She set them on a chair at the foot of the bed.

"Your boots were fine after I cleaned them up," she said. "But the rest of your stuff was either torn or too bloody. These things should fit. I got your sizes from the other clothes before I threw them out."

"Thank you." He watched her for a few moments with a sarcastic smile touching his lips.

"What?" she demanded.

"Oh, nothing. It's just . . . you have me at a slight disadvantage."

"How so?"

He threw off the sheet covering his leg. "How am I

supposed to get those clothes on when you still have me in chains?"

"Oh, I have that all figured out." She dug through her purse and drew out the old rusty skeleton key.

Then she dove through the purse again and pulled out a small but loaded automatic.

She shrugged. "What can I tell you? We're three women living alone."

"I see." His eyes never left the automatic. "I guess the call wasn't enough."

"It made me feel a helluva lot better about my decisions, but it didn't clear up all my worries. You're still being sought as a rogue cop. I don't want to take any chances." She waved the gun at the boxers. "You want to put those on?" She threw him the key.

With a teasing smile she added, "I'll try not to look."

Stiffly, he placed the key in the lock, his gaze freezing her every time he looked at her. Unshackled, he rubbed his ankle to get the circulation going again, then threw the sheet away and stood.

She suddenly realized it was hard to hold a man at gunpoint without looking at him. Embarrassed by his total unabashed nudity, she wanted to turn her head, but there was no way to do it.

"Allow me to introduce myself, Miss St. Vallier," he began acidly, his stare never wavering from her own. "If you look down, you can see I happened to be a male of the species—and yes, the equipment seems to still be in good working order, for I was shot here." He placed his hand gingerly on the bandages wrapped around his lower torso. He slowly nodded his head only once. "And the burn scars come from the fact that I have ghosts pushing on me." The mirth departed his eyes like a fading afterimage. For just a moment, a bitter hardness shaped his mouth. It passed quickly.

He added in a matter-of-fact tone, "I was in Beirut in 'eighty-three when the marine barracks near the airport was blown up. But I got lucky. I was in the B.O.Q.—the bachelor officer's quarters—next door and caught only the periphery of the explosion. There were two hundred forty-four enlisted men who weren't so lucky."

Unbidden, she felt tears sting her eyes. "Believe me, I—I didn't mean to—"

He smiled. His gaze dropped to the automatic. "Just make sure you keep the barrel up, darling. It's sinking on you, and I'd hate to lose the family jewels after all I've already been through."

She glanced down and raised the barrel. Her nerves were stretched taut. "Okay. Then—ah—please proceed."

He was wobbly. No doubt light-headed from all the loss of blood and from lying down for so many days. The nurse in her wanted to steady him and help him put on some underwear. But the survivor in her kept her away with the automatic trained on him.

He gave her one baleful glance, then held on to the bedpost and stepped into the navy knit boxers. Without protest he lay back in the bed, clearly exhausted by the ordeal.

She stepped to the bedpost and with one hand slipped the iron around his ankle, locking him in once more. With that, she put the gun back in her purse and placed it far from his reach.

"If the truth be known, I bought the gun as much for protection from Archer as from you," she admitted softly.

"I feel much better, then," he retorted. "You know," he said, watching her with cold, assessing eyes, "if I ever get out of all this crap I'm in, I sure as hell hope you leave this chain here to remember me by. I figure I might come back and do the same for you sometime."

She shivered. The sexual innuendo was certainly in his word, but the notion of payback unsettled her more. Especially coming from him. She feared it would be all pleasure spiked with pain.

"What do you plan to do?" she interjected, changing the subject. "I mean, when you get enough strength back?"

"Is that a hint that I've overstayed my welcome?"

"Absolutely not. I won't *let* you go until you're ready. Not after all my good nursing. I'm just curious, is all."

"Well, it's best if you don't know the fine details. But first of all, I mean to somehow get Toutant alone again. I'll take one more stab at turning him."

"'Turning' him?"

"You know—try to convince him to cut a deal with the prosecutor. His testimony against the others in exchange for a lighter sentence."

"You told me he refused your first offer."

He nodded. "Sure did. Laughed in my face, matter of fact. But that was before their plan to kill me fell through. And before the subsequent media blow-up. He's got to be sweating good by now. His safety hangs by a thread, and old Percival might be eager to cooperate now."

"What if he isn't?"

"If not, my hands are pretty much tied. Then I go with option number two. I'll turn myself in to my own people and take my chances."

"Are you . . . I mean, will there be legal trouble for you?" *Or me,* she might have added but didn't.

"Maybe. But it's damned hard to frame somebody. Their setup will never hold water; it probably won't get past the pretrial phase. It would have been good enough, maybe, if they had succeeded in killing me. Good enough, anyway, to cast serious doubts on me. But option number two is still unacceptable to me."

"Why?"

"For one thing, while I'm flapping my way through the legal system, they'll have a good amount of time to take another swing at me. Don't forget that option number two also leaves the bad guys unscathed. And for another, it leaves *you* vulnerable. To Archer especially."

"He scares me," she admitted. "He always has."

"He should. He's one sick little fuck."

"Right now he's fixated on the idea of finding this room."

His jaw turned hard. "The snake won't bite you," he said, refusing to elaborate.

She released a soft smile. "I can't tell you how many times I've wished I had enough money to wield some influence around here. I'd get Archer kicked off the police force, and I'd shut down that damned Scarlet Door."

She crossed to the night table and picked up the pair of silhouettes she'd left there.

"What've you got there?" he inquired.

"Lovers of the past," she replied enigmatically. "According to my aunt Rose, they are the key to everyone's survival at Shadow Oaks."

"Is this the skeleton in your closet?" he inquired, a smile in his voice.

She laughed. "You know, there were a couple of days there when Maman thought *you* were going to be a skeleton in the closet." She sat back down on the edge of the bed next to him. "I have to admit, there were a few moments there when you didn't look so good, and I sure wondered how we were going to bury you."

Hitting the main points, she explained the old mystery about Jules, Genevieve, and the famed St. Vallier treasure. While she talked, he took the framed silhouettes from her and studied the lovers. She also reported Mattie Everett's take on the story—how the gems were finally delivered to the French monarchy after a huge ransom was paid.

"It's a romantic tale," he agreed when she finished. "Intriguing. But frankly, I think your friend Mattie is probably right. She sounds not only well informed, but a little more objective than you can be."

"Oh, I know." She sighed. "I mean, after all, my only ally in all this is Aunt Rose. And she's the epitome of an incurable romantic. She's convinced there's a St. Vallier treasure." She released a sheepish grin. "And, too, she speaks to people who aren't there—at least, I thought they weren't there. Now I don't know what to think."

"There's at least one real St. Vallier treasure," he said, suddenly very sober.

He looked at her, and his stare seemed to pass through her very soul.

"You know what, Agent Shaw?" she said, desperate to break the moment and find cover for her vulnerable emotions. "I'd say, judging from that light in your eyes, that you're getting better. Much better."

"Sometimes we both talk too much, Miss St. Vallier."

"And just how else can two people learn about each other?"

He grinned, and this time the light of sheer deviltry in his eyes was proof to her that he was on the mend. "Like this," he whispered before taking her lips in a deep kiss.

She closed her eyes and savored him. His tongue was hard and thorough as it penetrated her mouth; it promised that he was capable of the ultimate sexual fulfillment if only she would let down her guard. When he broke from her mouth, he ran his hot mouth down her throat, then across her chest as he grazed her nipples through the fabric of her shirt.

Expertly, his hand rode up on her waist, pulling up her knit shirt. She almost lay on the bed now. Almost drugged with the effects of his lovemaking, she didn't realize her shirt had uncovered her bra. Gazing down at the pink confection of lace, the reality of what they were doing hit her like an ice storm.

She stood up, pulling the shirt over her breasts. As breathless as if she'd just had a hard run, she said, "Since you're still an injured man, I suggest you get more rest. You really need to conserve your strength."

"For you?" he demanded, his eyes glittering like a deprived carnivore.

She didn't answer. But with a strange hunger she'd never felt before, she forced herself to leave the shelter of the inner sanctum to return to the dangerous world outside.

CHAPTER

<u>26</u>

Southern Louisiana College was a sleepy redbrick campus located just outside Thibodaux, a sugar-processing center situated on Bayou Lafourche about thirty miles northwest of Cane Town.

Jervis Archer called the college first thing Monday morning to find out Professor Mattie Everett's office hours. Turned out she was available on campus ten A.M. until noon. Wearing civilian clothes and using his own vehicle, Jervis left Deputy Harley Burke in charge and drove to Thibodaux.

The campus was a postcard-perfect cliché exuding southern charm: white-blossomed dogwood groves alternated with stately live oaks dripping Spanish moss. With the help of a campus locator map at the student union, Jervis tracked down the history department on the third floor of the Liberal Arts Building. He got Professor Everett's office number from the department secretary. A minute later he was smiling at the woman in her open doorway.

Mattie, busy calculating midterm grades, glanced up from her desk to see a big, handsome, dark-haired man watching her from sexy blue eyes that rivaled Paul Newman's.

"Well, hell-*oh* there," she greeted him, closing her grade book. "May I help you?"

"Professor Everett?"

"All the way down to the ground," she assured him with an inviting smile.

He slid a wallet from his hip pocket and flipped it open. A badge flashed at Mattie. Her smile faded.

"I'm Jervis Archer, the chief of police in Cane Town. May I speak with you for a few minutes?"

Mattie's expression shadowed with premonition. "Cane Town? Oh, my God. Something's happened to Stella."

Archer's eyes narrowed a little. "She's fine, far as I know. Why do you think she isn't?"

"It's just—I've read the newspapers, I know there's trouble down your way, is all. Guess I overreacted. Please come in, Chief Archer. Have a seat."

Jervis seemed a bit intimidated by her office. Mattie had never relegated her first love—history—to the dusty vaults of the past. Instead of the usual sterile academic decor, her office looked more like the parlor of a luxurious nineteenth-century bordello. Reproductions of paintings by Degas and Fragonard covered the walls and sheer apricot-colored curtains billowed at the open window. Two shell-covered hutches replaced the usual filing cabinet; lamps with milky glass shades had been substituted for the glaring overhead fluorescents Mattie refused to use.

Jervis settled into a cane-bottomed armchair in front of the desk.

"How may I help you, Chief?"

"I understand, Professor Everett, that you are an expert on the Shadow Oaks plantation?"

"An expert?" Mattie repeated cautiously. "Well, I do have an interest in the place, yes. It's quite charming. That's how I met Stella, you know, doing a story on it."

"But you've written articles about Shadow Oaks?"

"Popular articles," she qualified. "Newspapers, Sunday-supplement stuff. One needn't be much of an expert to write fluff pieces for the public. Ah, may I ask why you want to know?"

Jervis seemed to sense that she was trying to wrest control of the conversation from him. And clearly, he didn't like that. He was definitely not the type to appreciate a woman he classified as a ball breaker.

"I only ask," he assured her, "because I think your friend Stella might be in grave danger."

"Danger?" Mattie heard alarm bells going off all over the place now. Her initial tendency to flirt with this strong-jawed hunk had given way to fear. Especially in light of last Thursday's phone conversation with Stella. Her friend had obviously been keeping some kind of secret.

"I confess I'm utterly mystified, Chief Archer. What do you mean, Stella's in danger?"

"Yeah, guess I should explain instead of being so mysterious."

Archer methodically laid out the folded flyer like a police Identikit. "This man, as you can see, is wanted by the FBI. I believe she might be harboring him at Shadow Oaks." He leaned back in his chair and watched her. "Garrett Shaw was wounded in a police chase. If he is hiding in that house, he's probably forcing Stella, under threat of harm to Rose or Maman, to care for him." He paused. "It's also possible," he added, "that he's . . . manipulating her emotionally. Using her. The guy's a brilliant con man. He's seduced more than one woman into helping him."

At this juncture in Archer's account of events, Mattie found the chief's evidence and his speculations quite convincing. It hardly mattered that Stella was smart. When it came to the opposite sex, plenty of smart women made dumb decisions. I.Q. did not control one's heart. How many of Mattie's most promising female students had scuttled brilliant careers to become breeders for illiterate jerks who slapped them around like punching bags?

This Garrett Shaw, Mattie thought as she studied the photo on the poster—he was quite the looker. If he was even half the con man that Archer implied, Stella could be in some deep yogurt.

"I've heard tell there's a secret room in the old house. You know anything about that?"

Mattie heard his question. She really started to worry about Stella now.

Thursday night's phone call came rushing back to echo in Mattie's memory, Stella's awkward denial foremost:

That creep Archer searched my house today. From top to bottom.

Oh, did he? Tell me, what'd he say when you showed him Jules's treasure chamber?

I—that is, he didn't see it.

"Professor Everett?"

"I'm sorry, Chief Archer. Excuse me for spacing out. I was just trying to recall if I've heard or read anything about a secret room."

"Have you?"

Despite her very real fear for Stella's safety, Mattie still held back from telling Archer the truth. For one thing, she had heard the troubling rumors—from Stella—about Archer and New Orleans councilman Albert Fontainbleau.

Mattie didn't attach much credence to wild rumors. Especially those that sprang up in the rural South. But like many professional women who were trapped under the glass ceiling in a male-dominated world, Mattie had learned an important rule about survival: Never surrender all your options, never give up control of a situation. Yes, Archer's story was credible and frighteningly convincing. However, rather than acquiesce right away, telling him about the secret room, she wanted to buy some time. She wanted, at the very least, to talk to Stella one more time before she cooperated.

"I don't recall anything reliable about a secret room, at least not from memory," Mattie finally responded.

"Stella never mentioned it or showed it to you?"

"But I have plenty of notes on Shadow Oaks. Do you want me to take a look at them? If anything turns up, I'll give you a call."

Disappointment moved across Archer's face like a cloud shadow. It was followed, in rapid succession, by suspicion, then irritation.

He's not the brightest light on the porch, Mattie told herself, but he senses I'm evading.

"You're sure you don't remember anything about a secret room?" he pressed her, those icy blue eyes boring holes into her conscience.

"As sure as I can be right now."

Archer finally nodded and stood up. The polite veneer had cracked, revealing an angry, resentful man who obviously felt duped by a feminist conspiracy. Archer seemed to know damn good and well that Mattie already knew all about the secret room.

"Well, maybe after you review your notes," he told her in his atonal voice, "you'll remember something."

As Archer was about to egress into the hallway, an old sepia-tone photo hanging near the door caught his eye. It was an odd portrait featuring a corseted, black-stockinged woman in her cotton shift, sitting on a chair. The woman's face was obliterated by a mess of scratches.

"That's a Bellocq photograph. He's Stella's specialty," Mattie informed him. "Bellocq took a lot of pictures of Storyville prostitutes. He was a strange little man—a dwarf really. One of the explanations of why he scratched out the faces on some of his negatives was that he fell in love with the girl and was rejected. Had some kind of Madonna/whore syndrome."

"But she was a hooker, right?" Archer said, pointing at the photo.

Mattie nodded.

"Then, who gives a damn why he did it." He shrugged and left her office.

"Then, I guess you get my point," she facetiously told the remaining silence.

"I'll be out of here by tonight," Garrett announced to Stella.

He was dressed in the clothes she had brought him, though he still lay chained.

"Are you sure?" she asked. "You've improved dramatically over this past weekend. But you're still looking pale. You lost a lot of blood, you know."

"Lady, it's been six days now that you've risked keeping me here. Thanks to you, I'm still alive. But we can't keep pushing our luck. It's been days now since Archer made any kind of play. By now Leblanc and the rest must be desperate to locate me or my body. I've *got* to get out of here and confront Toutant. Then, when Archer comes sniffing around, you can show him the room and get rid of him. He won't just let it go."

She sat on the edge of the bed. She knew he was right. But by then, her fear for Maman, Rose, and Shadow Oaks was balanced by her fear for him. Yes, it was risky for him here. However, he would face new dangers when he left. It was a case of preferring the devil she knew to the devil she didn't know.

"I know you have to go," she conceded slowly. "But I still don't think you're ready to walk out of here. You get light-headed." She remembered all the times he needed to go to the can. He wobbled the whole way at gunpoint, her at his back.

His strong white teeth flashed in a smile. He placed a hand on her bare arm and gently rubbed the smooth skin.

"Believe me," he assured her, "if I was ever tempted to stay . . ."

Tempted. She'd been wrestling with temptation herself. The question wasn't one of desire—his touch on her arm just then was all it took to quicken her heartbeat. Nor was his health any longer the impediment. He was still weak but certainly vital.

No. The real dissuasion was him. Her attraction to him was motive enough, but it didn't absolve him of the need to prove his character. Their situation was opportune on the face of it—a secret room with a big bed. But opportunity and motive was good enough to prove homicide, not enough to prove love.

He ruminated out loud as he made his plans. "It's best if I leave after dark. I'll just have to take my chances with those sentries you mentioned."

"We can get you past them," she promised. "C'mon, I've something to show you."

He was still chained. She unlocked him, the automatic held firmly in her hand.

She led him to the large colonial armoire against one wall. "I didn't bother to show you this before," she explained, "but it will get you past the sentry."

Just inside the door she knelt and inserted a finger in what appeared to be a knothole in one of the lower planks. She lifted a small trapdoor. The top rungs of a wooden ladder were visible.

"When Jules built this house, there was still some threat from local Indian tribes. Most homes built before 1830 or so around here included 'Indian tunnels.' This ladder goes down to the original wine cellar, which is now sealed off from outside the house. But the actual tunnel starts in the wine cellar and comes up in one of the slave shanties out back of the garden. That will put you practically in the cane fields."

He grinned. "I'll be damned. This Jules was quite the character, wasn't he? I like him already."

"A man of action," she agreed.

"What's in the wine cellar?" he asked, curious and fascinated all at once. "Okay if we go down there?"

"You sure you feel strong enough?"

"I'll have to do it tonight anyway. Might as well make a practice run."

"Take this," she said. "There's no light down there." She reached into the raffia bag on the floor and handed him a flashlight.

He flicked it on to make sure the batteries were good. Then he tucked it into his waistband. Moving slowly to conserve his strength, he led the way down into the cool, damp darkness beneath the house.

At the bottom he thumbed on the flashlight and waited for her. The space was a small room lined with a rough x-shaped wine rack. Rammed earth served as the floor.

"Shine the light over there," she told him, guiding his hand. "See, there's the tunnel entrance, over in the corner. It's cramped—you'll have a fairly long crawl."

"Sure beats trying to dodge bullets," he assured her, flashing the beam all around them. "Look at that," he marveled.

The flashlight beam revealed a beautifully detailed painted mural on the rear of one wine rack. Time and weather had dulled the pigment somewhat, but it was still impressive.

In bold, striking colors it depicted the figure of Jesus Christ. The supplicants gathered at his feet, each holding on to his robe with one hand and looking at him with exultant expressions, were blacks dressed in slave brogans and field clothes. Broken chains lay all around them, and all were bathed in the radiance of a rising sun. The mural was dated 1859 and titled, in the lower left corner, NEW DAWN BREAKING.

"Who did it?" he asked in a low voice.

"We'll never know the name. But it was one of the . . . *our* slaves," she forced herself to reply. "Since it's titled, it almost had to be one of the house servants, because they were far more likely to be literate. According to Colette St. Vallier's diary, it was done without my great-great-grandfather Henry's permission. But no one was ever punished. In fact, Henry requested in his will that it never be covered over. It wasn't too long after discovering it that he freed all his slaves. Colette thinks this mural was the main reason he did."

"What abolitionist rhetoric couldn't accomplish, the power of art could," he said pensively.

They stood in silence for some time, both admiring the faded testament to human yearning. Then he went to a wine rack and pulled out a green hand-blown bottle. "Look at that. Still full."

She smiled and shrugged. "Probably vinegar. I had a wine expert come out to see if I could get anything for them. He told me to pour out the wine and sell the blown-glass bottles for five bucks apiece—hardly worth the effort."

"Let's try some." He stared at her.

She waved him back up the ladder with the automatic. "Sure. You first."

"Am I your guinea pig?" He lifted one dark eyebrow.

"I can assure you, after drinking Rose's home brew, if the wine doesn't kill you, it sure won't kill me."

"You know, we have a ghost here," Stella mentioned with a giggle. The bottle of wine was almost empty, and it wasn't vinegar after all. Some kind of merlot, she figured, reasonably smooth. In any case, both she and Garrett had enjoyed it immensely, and they stayed in the secret room, comforted by the one lone candle that puppeted shadows along the walls.

"A ghost, huh?" He leaned back against the head-board, the beaker of red wine relaxed in his hand. She'd relocked the shackle on him, then, feeling strange about joining him on the bed now that they were drinking wine together and making merry, she made a big point of bringing in a light fancy chair from the ballroom. The gold-and-velvet piece looked as out of place in the rough, unfinished room as she did sit-ting on it, drinking with a man who was chained to a bed.

"Is it the ghost of Jules?" he asked, looking at her with lowered lids.

The corner of her mouth tipped in a smile. "I don't think so. Her name's Myrtle. My great-aunt Rose seems to see and talk to her all the time. But the first time I saw her was the night I discovered you by Bayou Lafourche."

"That's right. You were following a girl, you said. She was crying, wasn't she?"

She gave a little nod. "I never found her again. But Rose said Myrtle had been sad." She grew pensive, a thought suddenly coming to her. "Now, inexplicably, Rose says Myrtle's content."

"What do you think it means?" His own harsh mouth twisted in a smile. "I mean, I'm with the marshals, not with the *X-Files.* I feel obliged to tell you outright I don't believe in ghosts."

"I don't believe in them either." She frowned. "But I can't help feeling the girl was familiar somehow. That the incident had some kind of meaning or message." She shook herself. "Maybe it's just the wine that's get-ting to me. I don't know."

He studied her as she sat across from him in the chair. "This place has got a lot of past. Maybe it just rears up sometimes. I suppose things like that could happen."

She studied him back, taking in his broad chest, his handsome face cast in flickering candlelight, his well-muscled but entrapped leg. It was difficult, but she masked her emotions well when she asked, "So what's your past, Marshal Shaw? Have you been kissing me with a wife and four kids waiting for you to get back home to Texas?"

He laughed. "No wife. No kids. I'm a career fed, and I work undercover. Doesn't give me much time to date girls."

"Was there ever anyone special?"

Shrugging, he said, "Maybe there was one. Right after I joined the Corps, I got engaged to the Cattle Queen of Rosenberg, Texas. Man, were we a sight. I was all of twenty, and she was seventeen. We were young and beautiful—and stupid." His expression darkened. "After the barracks were bombed, I came home damaged, with more scars than were just apparent on my body. The Cattle Queen couldn't handle it." He released a harsh laugh. "She married an orthopedic surgeon. I hear he cheats on her all the time, but she's got her charities and her Lexus, so she just keeps handing out that beauty-queen smile and looks the other way." He shrugged again. "I mean, what else can she do? She's forged her own trap."

"Did—" Her voice wavered. "I guess you must have really loved her."

He shook his head. "I was a kid. I didn't know anything about love. And all I learned out of the whole thing was hurt." He glanced at her. "What about you, Miss de St. Vallier? Why haven't you hooked up with Mr. Right?"

She smiled wanly. "I've met only Mr. Right Now. I always discuss my dates with my friend Mattie, and before I'm even through the analysis, she's screaming, 'Next!'" She laughed. "I don't make such hot choices. I mean, you're a good example. This is the first glass of wine I've enjoyed in a man's company since I don't know when, and I have to hold a gun to you half the time."

He released an ironic grin, then his expression turned brooding. "You know it's best I leave tonight. I don't know when or if I'll see you again. Depends on how all this plays out."

Something strange burned in her eyes, almost as if they were tears. "I—I hope when I see you again, it's under better circumstances."

He stared at her for a moment. Finally, he whispered, "I always wanted to meet a girl who knew what loneliness was. But I always pick the beauty-queen type, and if they know what it is, they sure as hell never mention it."

"I know exactly what loneliness is," she told him, emotion quavering in her voice. "It's having to survive because the whole damned world depends on you, and not wanting to survive because you don't have the luxury of depending on anyone."

Her words seemed to move him. The muscle in his jaw bunched; his eyes gleamed.

She stood and filled her glass with the remains in the bottle. "Should I go get us another bottle?" she asked, turning to him.

He placed his beaker on the nightstand. "I don't think we need another bottle of wine."

"Then, what do we need?" she asked in self-derision.

"I think I want to be that person you can depend on."

She looked away, not wanting him to see her eyes. "You're leaving, and in all probability you've been lying to me. You may either go to jail or get killed. Pardon me if I say so, but I don't think you're a good candidate to lean on."

"I may not be the best candidate, but I'm not a fucking politician, Stella. And this isn't a runoff."

"No, it isn't," she answered, wiping the moisture from her eyes.

He reached up and took her hand and pulled her to the bed. "Look, I don't know what tomorrow's going to bring." His eyes grew steely. "I went into the marines and into the U.S. marshals knowing full well I could get killed at my occupation, and truly, it never bothered me all that much. Not even Beirut. It never bothered me— until now."

She gazed at him, her breath quickening by his proximity.

"Why does it bother me now, Stella de St. Vallier?" He shook her lightly. "Why now?"

"Because . . ." She didn't finish. There was no point.

He let her go. Reaching for his wine instead, he said, "Shit, maybe you ought to just go get that other bottle."

She shook her head. Slowly, shocking even herself with her deliberateness, she took the glass from his hand and replaced it on the nightstand.

He didn't move. He looked up at her with the wary gaze of a trained killer.

Leaning on the edge of the bed, she bent down and placed her lips against his. The muscles in his chest tightened as if her action had caught him by surprise. She kissed him with tenderness, then with something stronger, her mouth taking his with a hunger long buried.

"Girl, I don't want you to regret this." He caressed her cheek, his eyes seeking.

"Tell me you're one of the good guys. Just promise me," she asked, yearning etched on her face, the loneliness in her soul finally catching up with her and overcoming her.

He stared at her. Solemnly, he said, "I promise you. No matter what's been said, I'm the good guy."

She nodded her head. Gently, hesitantly, she unlocked the shackle around his leg. He pulled her on top of him and took her in a hot kiss. Briefly, she wondered if she was losing all sense. The gun still lay across the room in the raffia bag. If he wanted to take her hostage or kill her outright, he could do it. He might be lying about the marines and Beirut, but one thing he was not lying about was his physique. He had all the hard muscle of a marine recruit fresh off Parris Island.

But the moment had lost all sanity, all caution. Passion and destiny seemed to pull stronger now. As she kissed him and let him tug on her shirt, she wondered if the girl she saw was truly there for a purpose. "Myrtle," or whoever the girl or figment was, had brought her to Garrett that night. He'd been forced to confess to her. And now, if his answers were merely lies like truth, then she would take the lies for the night. For a few small hours she would banish the loneliness that eroded her soul like an unstoppable tide. For a brief moment in time she like her ancestors before her, would know the total fulfillment of mind, body, and soul.

He slipped off her top and allowed his knuckles to caress her breasts through the lace of her bra. She could feel him harden beneath her, especially when her pale pink bra strap fell to one shoulder, tempting him to rid her of it entirely.

He pulled off his own shirt, and she put her hands on the chest she knew so well from caring for him. When he unbuttoned his jeans and slid them off too, his boxers proved his readiness. He slid those off too, and he rolled on top of her, trapping her.

He was a Ph.D. at bra removal, and vaguely she wondered if that was some kind of class they took when they learned "Semper Fi." His mouth tugged on her large, soft nipple, and despite herself she closed her eyes, savoring the exquisite torture. Her breast filled his hands, and he took it greedily, like a sailor who'd finally made port.

Kissing it, he finally moved up to her mouth, filling her with his tongue as he pulled down her panties.

"Garrett, it's been a while," she confessed, her breath coming hard and fast with her arousal.

His hand stroked the sensitive triangle between her legs. He smiled, his face lean and handsome in the flickering candlelight. "It's just like riding a bike, sweetheart. Don't worry, I won't hurt you."

"But—but what if—" she stammered, "what if I don't please you?" she confessed in a tense whisper.

"Not possible," he groaned when he parted her damp thighs and entered her, filling her to overflowing.

She lay her head back, holding on to the spindles of the headboard as if to steady her reeling emotions. He moved on top of her with a heathen rhythm, kissing her, caressing her, whispering into her ear things she didn't hear but fully understood. The pressure built within her, heavy in her loins until she cried out his name. Her orgasm came hard and almost painful, it had been so long.

But his was long and brutal and wealthy. And when it ended, he buried his head in her hair as if to find solace.

They slept entwined in each other's embrace for only moments before he awoke her and proved that he ached for her again.

CHAPTER

<u>27</u>

How can love survive in such a graceless age?
                                    —DON HENLEY

"Gentlemen," Senator Myron Leblanc said, "we're down to bedrock and showing damn little color. The only good news I can report is that it doesn't seem likely Garrett Shaw has made it back to Washington yet. Unfortunately, Roland Nesbit has detected possible signs that Shaw may not be dead after all. Signs, by the way, that definitely bode ill for our little operation."

"What signs?" D'Antoni demanded.

He, Leblanc, state rep Hiram Steele, and New Orleans city councilman Barry Woodyard had met in emergency session at D'Antoni's hunting lodge in the pine woods east of Cane Town. The four members of the Louisiana Ring were gathered at a big redwood picnic table on a bench of grass beside Tupelo Creek.

"For one thing," Leblanc replied, "if the U.S. marshals thought Shaw was dead or possibly discredited, they would stand down their operation until they knew more. Instead, they are all of a sudden trying to subpoena the records of the shipping company that handles freight for United Southern Children's Charities."

This announcement landed with the impact of a Cruise missile. D'Antoni went pale around the mouth. "Are you sure?" he demanded.

As usual, Leblanc was controlling the meeting as if he had a God-ordained right to do so. He had remained in Louisiana since flying back last Friday, ostensibly to host a town meeting in nearby Morgan City. His real reason for staying, however, was to keep tabs on the manhunt for Marshal Garrett Shaw.

"Absolutely," he replied. "Nesbit has intercepted e-mail to the Justice Department, requesting permission to serve the subpoenas. That tells me the U.S. marshals are confident not only that Shaw is alive, but that he's still dependable."

Hiram Steele frowned, not fully understanding. He had small, dull eyes, like a turtle's.

"Why sweat the records?" he asked. "Didn't Barry's brother make sure they'll pass muster?"

"I'll *tell* you why," Leblanc snapped. "They aren't interested in studying just the cargo manifests. They're going to match those cargo lists with the embarkation records of the various organizations that supposedly received the aid."

"Oh, shit," cursed D'Antoni. "I see Myron's point. It's basically like an extensive income tax audit. Eventually, they'll realize there's been some phantom shipments that exist only on paper."

"Exactly," Leblanc affirmed. "And they'll conclude we banked the money."

"Then, what's the big deal," Steele persisted, "if we kill Shaw or not? I mean, sounds like our ass is grass anyway, if records are all they need."

"Hiram," Leblanc admonished the other man impatiently, "why don't you get your head screwed on straight? They can't pop us on the basis of records alone—not easily, at any rate. It's going to be an uphill fight for them, thanks to the widespread corruption and graft in Central America. Foreign aid has a way of disappearing in Third World nations before anyone ever sees it."

"Which makes Garrett Shaw the man of the hour," D'Antoni chimed in. "We don't know how much *he* knows. For example, what if that fucker was wearing a wire when Barry made that *stupid* remark about how we only take 'a small percentage of the gate'?"

"So we stand a good chance of weathering this," Woodyard asked, "so long as there's no smoking gun? We don't know that Shaw has tapes or records, right?"

Leblanc shook his crew-cut head. "It's not that simple. Outright conviction isn't our only risk. In our business, you don't have to be convicted to be ruined. Even his simple testimony, coupled with those incriminating records, could sink us. A strong circumstantial case against us will sic the media bozos on us. Politics is a game of perceptions. If it's even *perceived* that we screwed over little kids and duped churches to feather our own nests? Why, Christ Almighty. Jimmy Swaggart will be a folk hero compared to us."

All four men fell into a gloomy silence while the horrible truth of all this sank in.

"So the conclusion is inevitable," Leblanc reiterated. "It's even more imperative than ever that we take out Shaw. Immediately. Every minute we delay now is just another nail in our coffins. We've got to play this game through, boys."

As if precisely timed to underscore the senator's point, a Cane Town police cruiser turned off the gravel road out front and parked among the vehicles clustered in the side yard. Leblanc had arranged to have Jervis Archer present for the latter part of this meeting.

Archer's face radiated contempt for the politicos as he ambled across the grass to join them, thumbs hooked in his leather gunbelt. His Smokey Bear hat was tilted low in front, leaving half his face in shadow.

"Chief," Leblanc greeted him. "How's it going?"

"Same shit, different day," Jervis replied tonelessly. "What'd you call me out here for, Senator?"

"Any change in the situation at Shadow Oaks?"

"If there is, you'll hear about it."

Leblanc's mud-colored eyes narrowed in anger. "Why don't you unpucker your asshole, Chief? We're all on the same team here."

Archer baited him with his bent-wire smile. "That's mighty white of you, Senator. Is that why I'm the last one to arrive?"

"Keep a civil tongue in your head," Leblanc snapped.

But Archer was in an especially foul mood lately. The day had begun with his wasted trip to Thibodaux, and all he'd had to eat all day was coffee and doughnuts. Even worse, Toutant had just informed him they'd lost their valuable drug contact in Austin. This was the first weekend in several months that Percival and Jervis had been unable to deliver the dope. Their contact had left in a rage, taking huge profits with him.

"Rot in hell, Leblanc," Archer snarled. "You ain't got the stones to fight me, old man. So don't talk the talk. Alla you," he added, taking in the rest of the group with a sneer, "buncha glad-handing baby-kissing, whip-dick politicians. I'm saying it one more time, and then I'm outta here: What did y'all call me out here for?"

A long silence greeted this scathing outburst. But if Jervis thought he could intimidate Myron Leblanc, he had underestimated the man's iron will.

"You're just whistling past the graveyard, Chief," he replied with quiet control. "But all your macho bluster and tough talk mean nothing. I summoned you out here to tell you it *must* be done tonight. Whatever it takes, Jervis, I want Shaw located and killed *tonight.* Do you understand?"

"Loud and clear. But why should I? There's nothing in it for me, now you've queered my drug op. It's you politicians who stand to burn, not me and Toutant."

Leblanc smiled. He slid his thumb and forefinger into his shirt pocket. "I figured you'd take that view of things. So let me give you some incentive."

He removed a folded sheet of paper and opened it up before he handed it to Archer. It was a copy of a computer transmission record originating from the National Crime Information Center at the request of the Special Warrants Division, U.S. marshals. It listed both the Piper Cub's and Romer Archer's boat registration numbers.

"Obviously, Shaw staked you, Percival, and Harley Burke out, perhaps with the help of Stella St. Vallier," Leblanc said.

Archer stared at the sheet. It didn't directly incriminate him. But Toutant's words now snapped in his memory like burning twigs: *Cowboy went home early.*

"Under the new federal sentencing guidelines for distribution of Category One controlled substances," the D.A. put in, "it's a mandatory twenty-year sentence with no possibility of parole."

"You'd be older than I am now by the time you got out, Chief," Leblanc reminded him. "Assuming you survived in prison, that is. Which isn't likely, given what cons do to former cops who get locked down."

For once Jervis was speechless, the bluster gone out of him.

"Chief, you're the one who put the councilman in the cane cutter. You're also the one who fixed the brakes on St. Vallier's car when you knew he talked to that paranoid Fountainbleau about all his worries."

"Upon your orders, Senator. Upon your orders," Archer hissed.

"So we're in it together, then, aren't we? Why play hardball?" Leblanc continued in a more reasonable tone, "I suggest we all cooperate for our mutual benefit. I can have my friend Roland use his influence to make sure DEA does not move on the new information. Deal?"

In fact, despite his bullheaded talk, Jervis had planned all along to do what Leblanc wanted. Stella St. Vallier had pushed him as far as she was going to. But this was indeed the ultimate incentive.

"Deal," Archer agreed. "But I'm convinced the St. Vallier broad has Shaw hidden at her place. It could get ugly. Real ugly."

"Whatever it takes," Leblanc repeated without hesitation. "If there's any mess, we'll clean it up afterward. But it *must* be done tonight."

It was well into the evening before Stella came out onto the loggia and around to the kitchen. She'd left Garrett asleep in the bed, his muscular legs entwined in the sheets, the scent of their lovemaking perfuming the room. It wasn't like her to be so reckless. Logically, she knew she should be filled with regret over her weakness with him, but she wasn't. Instead, a new warmth filled her soul. She couldn't wait to fix them a tray of food and nestle back into their hideaway for a few more precious hours.

The TV droned in the front parlor—the two older women were imbibing their evening fix.

She crossed to the window over the sink and glanced outside into the darkness. After a moment she spotted a small dot of red light.

Jim Bob Larsen, Archer's rabbit-toothed deputy, was in the garden, leaning against an oak tree, smoking a cigarette. It angered her, his uninvited presence. He had no legal right to simply camp out like this, but she knew at present she couldn't make an official complaint. For as Garrett had pointed out, their continual presence here was probably why Archer had refrained from any further, more drastic actions. She would rather endure them at a distance than Archer in her face again.

She was slicing cold turkey for a sandwich when she

heard the phone ring. "I'll get it," she called out to the older women in the adjacent parlor.

"Hello?"

"Stella, it's Mattie. You okay?"

Something in her friend's tone instantly alerted Stella. "Sure I'm okay, silly. Are *you* okay?"

"I've had better days," Mattie admitted. "A benighted savage visited me this morning."

Stella understood immediately. Her stomach suddenly felt as if she were plummeting in a fast elevator.

"Archer," she said woodenly.

"Yes, that disgusting lout of a 'cop.' I was all set for some uncomplicated lust when I first saw him. But then he opened his mouth. What a reptile!"

"What . . . what did he want?"

"Oh, Stella, for cripesakes, stop playing your coy little games with me. This is Mattie. You *know* what he wanted. He asked me if there's a secret room at Shadow Oaks."

Stella's calves went weak as water. "Did you tell him?"

"Girl, I told him nothing about it. I could tell, one minute after I met him, this was the kind of low-life creep who would stoop to robbing poorboxes."

She felt a warm flood of relief. "Thank you, Mattie."

"Thank a cat's tail. You listen to me, Stella de St. Vallier. I know what's going on there, and so does Archer. I didn't lie to him because I believe all the things you're foolish enough to believe, understand? Archer may be the son of Godzilla, but that doesn't mean you're providing sanctuary for Prince Valiant."

This was Mattie's first overt reference to the fact that Stella was hiding Garrett Shaw. Stella didn't bother to confirm or deny—Mattie clearly knew the situation.

"Did he believe you?" Stella pressed.

"I couldn't tell. I mean, how does one read the body language of a snake? I put him off with some crapola about going over my notes and maybe calling him later. Stella, for God's sake, what are you *doing*? Did you drop acid? This is insane! You've always been the sensible one in this friendship. Have you just lost it completely?"

"Mattie, you don't understand the situation."

"No, but neither do you. You just *think* you do. Stella, forgive me for waxing academic. But I'll tell you what I tell all my students: The process of observation defines one reality. But the places where you're *not* looking are just as real. Do you understand? You're seeing only what you want to see. Trouble is, you're completely tuning out some terrible dangers."

"No," Stella insisted. "*You* don't understand. Mattie, I made a very important phone call on Saturday. To Washington, understand? I confirmed some facts. A certain person is exactly who and what he claims to be. In fact, he comes with the highest recommendations."

There was a considerable pause while Mattie digested this. During the silence Stella noticed that Maman had set a vase of fresh cream-colored carnations on the dining room table. Carnations—funeral flowers, she couldn't help thinking with a little shudder.

"Okay, let's say you're right," Mattie finally replied. "Whoever you called told you the truth. Fine. That means there's this huge conspiracy involving Leblanc, Chief Archer, hell, toss in Muammar Qadhafi for all we know. Do you realize what that means? Don't you see where that leaves *you*? They must want this guy worse than souls in hell want ice water. So what if you're technically in the right? Being on the moral high ground only means you stick out even more. You are still in the house of cards."

"You're right," Stella concurred. "And even if *I* could continue to accept a risk, I can't keep endangering Aunt Rose and Maman. So let me just assure you without providing details: The situation here is about to ease. As of tomorrow I will have nothing to hide from anyone."

"Promise?"

"Cross my heart. I'll give you the all-clear as soon as it

happens. Then you can call Jervis and act like you're cooperating. Tell him, yes, you've found notes or whatever that confirm a secret room. I'll let the creep check it out, and hopefully that'll be that."

Mattie seemed somewhat reassured by this suggestion. "I s'pose I can live with that arrangement. Tomorrow, huh?"

"Tomorrow night, actually. And meantime you'll promise not to help Jervis?"

"Help *him*? Stella, I wouldn't pee in his ear if his brains were on fire. But I'm also not going to leave you in serious danger indefinitely. I'll be waiting for your call. Don't stiff me."

"No way. Thank you, Mattie."

"Meantime, you be careful, hear me?"

"I promise. You'll see. This will work out."

But even as she hung up the phone, Stella felt that premonitory tickle of doom. Under the present circumstances, tomorrow was still a long, long time away.

CHAPTER
<u>28</u>

"I don't know how Toutant's going to react," Garrett admitted to Stella. "But I've got to get to him. First thing, I've got to go back to The Scarlet Door and confront him. As it stands now, the charges against him include attempted murder of a federal agent, which ups the ante a little. He might agree to a deal if he sees me alive. If he does agree, I promise you I'll have Archer and his flunky deputies locked down tight within forty-eight hours."

"And if Toutant refuses?" she asked.

"Then, unfortunately, things are going to move a little slower. We still might be able to nail at least Archer, Burke, and Archer's cousin down in Terrebonne Parish for the drug scam. But not immediately. Which leaves one big problem I don't like at all, Stella."

The two of them lay in the bed. They'd eaten from the tray she'd brought, then Garrett had undressed her. They'd made love, this time slowly, exploring each other's body with their hands and their mouths. Sated finally, they lay in each other's arms, talking of the future.

He rose up on one elbow. His fingertips lightly traced the fine structure of her cheekbones.

"Jervis will still have ample opportunity to harass *you,*" he continued. "I agree with the plan you and your friend Mattie have cooked up to show Archer this room after I leave. But that's not going to allay his suspicions that you hid me. And I'm worried he might conclude you're the one he has to squeeze to learn my new whereabouts."

"So am I," she admitted without hesitation. "But that's just a chance I'll have to take. You didn't strap me with this mess. I got into it in the first place because I took a stand. I decided it was unacceptable to let drug runners do their thing on my family's property. I'm scared, sure, and a couple of times I wanted to back off. But looking back now, I see that Archer has to be stopped."

He studied her for a long while, then he lowered his mouth to hers. For a moment the urgent need for him surged inside her, and she pressed her body tightly against him. Her pulse grew so loud in her ears, it sounded like surf noise.

A moment later, however, it was she who pulled back. Cold tentacles of fear had gripped her heart as she recalled her earlier phone conversation with Mattie.

She really didn't know who Garrett was. Her heart told her he was worthy, her head told her to at least keep her emotional distance if she hadn't kept her physical distance. Too, Archer was obviously getting more desperate—this was no time to risk four human lives just so she could make him linger and sate what was becoming a bottomless desire for him.

"My fuse is *very* short tonight," she apologized as she sat up, then took the extra precaution of getting out of the bed.

He had to wait a few moments until his own breathing evened out and he could trust his voice.

"I'd call you a tease," he complained, sitting up himself, "but I know time is running short."

She smoothed the wrinkles out of her olive-green slip dress. Then she crossed to the fancy chair and plopped down into it.

"There hasn't been one thing normal about this relationship," she pointed out with an unhappy smile. But Aunt Rose's question resonated in her mind: *Have you ever felt more alive?* She never had.

"I guess," she added ruefully, "we should consider this sort of like a wartime romance. You know, desperate kisses while the Nazis advance on Paris. Danger has accelerated everything."

"Accelerated, yes," he agreed uneasily.

"Look, if there's really anything between us," she said with more emotion in her voice than she wanted, "besides mutual lust, I mean—well then, there's always the future, isn't there? Not that I'm knocking lust."

"Always? Don't take the future for granted," he advised her coldly.

In the days that she had nursed him back to health, she had radically revised her initial impression of him. He was not the man she first met at The Scarlet Door. He was a dedicated, driven man whose profession forced him to spend much time alone. And loners simply did not think, or act, like the majority. Since he did not have to please others, he was free to ignore herd instincts and be his own man. That was both exciting and disconcerting to her. The Great American Loner might be a hero to Hollywood, but in the real world he could sure bring out a woman's insecurities.

She looked around the room that Jules had built, supposedly to protect his treasure. The things within it were not just the detritus of the dead—they were the concrete reminders that the past could not be neatly separated from the present moment. And that each present moment was destined to pass. She blinked away the moisture that suddenly sprang to her eyes.

He watched her for a minute in silence, then he crossed to where she sat in the center of the room.

"If this really is just a 'wartime romance,' " he said, "there's a good chance we won't be seeing each other again. You know, I don't know what's going to happen. But I don't want this to be the end of it."

"I don't want to see you ride off into the sunset like the end of a western. But . . . but we'll have to wait and see. Right now you're very grateful to me, I realize that. I helped you when you were in terrible trouble, and that's its own kind of bond, isn't it?"

"Yes," he agreed.

She looked at the silhouettes of the lovers Jules and Genevieve. In a low tone she said, "I know what I *want* to be true." She glanced away, her thoughts painful. "My father," she said with her head turned from him, "used to like rowing on the bayou, and I'd go with him lots. I loved those times. I remember him telling me how no bayou, river, or stream is ever really straight, even when they look to be. They turn, they cross themselves, they even go backward so that sometimes you can't tell the bow of the boat from the stern."

She looked at him. "I was too little then to understand his real point. But I think I do now. It's the same way with the stream of life. We *think* we're charging straight ahead, always making steady progress. But in fact we have to follow the meanders, wherever they take us."

He nodded. "I would have liked your dad. He must have been quite a man."

"He was all St. Vallier."

"Just like his daughter," he added, his eyes gleaming with some unnamed emotion. He went to kiss her, but a woman's muffled scream suddenly shot out from somewhere in the house.

Stella's blood seemed to stop and flow backward in her veins.

A numbing panic filled her. Whoever was inside the house—for she didn't doubt an intruder was the cause of that scream—had not requested entry. Rose and Maman were alone and vulnerable.

All this looped through her confused thoughts as she raced to the mahogany turn-panel. Her only need, in those first frightening moments, was to help Great-Aunt Rose and Maman. Desperate, she threw open the double doors of the ballroom, then raced through the darkness of the hall and into the kitchen.

The moment she opened the kitchen door, she heard a male voice raised in anger: Jervis Archer's. There was a resounding crash, as of glass shattering, and another feminine scream.

She spotted Deputy Ira Pitts the moment she ran into the dining room. He was halfway up the curving staircase—no doubt heading upstairs to search for her, judging from the way he rushed back down upon seeing her. Someone had already wrought destruction on the dining room: The ivory lace tablecloth had been roughly pulled off the long table. Fragments of broken china littered the floor.

The nightmare was happening too fast for her to assemble all the horrifying images. In the front parlor she found Jervis and Harley Burke. Aunt Rose and Maman, obviously terrified but apparently unharmed, were huddled together in front of the French doors. The Boston rocker, Maman's favorite chair, lay tipped on its side, several of the spindles in the back broken. She had been sewing the rickrack braid on a dress as the two friends watched television—now the dress lay puddled on the floor among the scattered contents of Maman's sewing basket.

"Archer!" Stella shouted, unbelieving anger overwhelming her fear. "What in God's name do you think you're doing?"

"Well, well," he said. "Here's the mistress of the

manor now. Done screwing your stud, are you? Glad you could make it to the party."

Even as she watched, Burke smashed the TV screen with his police baton.

"Stop it!" she screamed.

"Fuck you, you blueblooded bitch," Archer said with a cold calmness more chilling than rage. "I'm giving the orders around here now."

"The downstairs bedrooms are clear," announced Jim Bob Larsen, emerging from the hallway that led to the west wing.

"Get back upstairs," Archer snapped at Pitts. "Check it out good. Jim Bob, go outside behind the house and watch for him to escape into the fields."

"What are you doing?" she demanded again.

"Like you don't know," Jervis goaded her. "Is your stud boy so hot in the sack, he's worth Shadow Oaks?"

"My God, you're insane! Jervis, *stop* this, please!"

"That's more like it. I like it when you beg, Stella. You keep that up, we'll get along."

In fact, she did alter her manner from anger to pleading. One good look at Aunt Rose had frightened her into a more submissive mood. Although evidently unharmed physically, Rose had to cling to Maman to support herself. And poor Maman—her eyes were red and swollen from weeping. How long had the two women been terrorized while she had been with Garrett?

While Burke and Pitts swarmed over the place like warrior ants, Jervis advanced toward Stella. He slid his police .38 from its holster and leveled it at her. She stared at it as if mesmerized by its single unblinking eye.

"Where's your boyfriend, Stella?"

For a moment she tasted the coppery bile of fear. Her own automatic had been left behind in the raffia bag in her panic to find out what was wrong. But then a cold, determined anger settled into her bones.

"I don't have a boyfriend, Chief. And there's no one hidden in this house. It's some ridiculous obsession of yours. You scoured the place once before, didn't you? Search it again."

Rose, she noticed, had nearly fainted when Archer leveled the .38 on Stella. But the old woman held her silence. Surprisingly, so did Maman. Despite Maman's reluctance to shelter Garrett in the first place, she seemed determined to back Stella now. Perhaps, Stella realized, because she now understood the true depths of Archer's criminal depravity. The look on her aristocratic face now clearly implied she was determined to make Satan get behind her.

Stella's calm determination had clearly frustrated Archer. For a moment his anger was so intense, he looked as if he were suffering from facial neuralgia.

Desperate now, he turned the weapon toward the two older women. "Where is he, ladies?" the chief demanded.

"Shoot me if you must, Jervis," Rose replied bravely. "I've had my life, and I'm not afraid to die."

"Shame on you, Mr. Jervis," Maman scolded. "Last time you's here, we fed you and treated you kind."

Surprisingly, Archer must have had some fragment of conscience left, Stella realized—Rose's and Maman's responses did in fact shame him, at least a little. He holstered his weapon.

"I don't want to hurt any of you," Jervis told them. "But I'll tell you right now, and by God I mean it—I know Garrett Shaw is hiding here. You've got a secret room somewhere, and he's hiding in it."

He can't really know that, Stella told herself. If he knew it for a fact, got it from Mattie or wherever, then he'd also know where it is. So he's bluffing. But how far would he carry his bluff?

"I'll give you one last chance, ladies," Archer said, his tone more reasonable now. "You show me that room, and all of you are safe. Any damage we've done here will be paid for, I promise. We're not after you, we want Shaw."

"Who's we?" she retorted. "You and Senator Le-blanc?"

Jervis stared at her. "You think I'm such a bad guy, hanh? But I'm not so bad. It wasn't me who gave the order to fix the brakes on your daddy's car. Not me at all."

Body-paralyzing shock hit her like a locomotive. Rose's cry seemed to come from somewhere beyond the horizon, not in the room where Stella stood herself. What Archer was saying didn't seem possible. It didn't. And she would not accept it.

"You're lying. My parents died of an accident. It was an *accident!*" she screamed at him.

He laughed in her face. "Yep, I guess you want to be-lieve that. That it was an act of God and not some pre-meditated preventable murder. But who the hell do you think took your daddy aside at that fund-raiser and gave him an earful of woe? Al Fountainbleau. The very same. Leblanc didn't like how that played out at all. So he had your daddy taken care of. I know it. And your good Senator Myron Leblanc knows it."

The horror of what he said was like he'd slammed his fist into her gut. Doubling over, she swore she would be sick. Tears burned in her eyes, but somehow she didn't let them fall. She'd rather die than let him see her bro-ken.

"Now, don't get any fancy ideas about having your parents exhumed, little girl. Their bodies'll only show they died in a car crash like they was supposed to."

Maman went to her, but nothing could comfort the grief in her soul. She didn't have a chance at justice. Jervis himself wrote the report on the condition of her parents' car. If the brakes had been tampered with, it was his word against theirs. And they'd have no proof without the car that had been taken to the dump and scrapped.

"You're an evil man, Mr. Jervis. A right evil man. And God has a plan for you," Maman told him.

"God may have a plan, but right now I'm the one in charge, and now you know it too, just in case you didn't before." His face turned rock-hard. "I want to know where that secret room is and now."

Stella knew she faced a desperate man; further belligerence was foolish. But she'd never turn an innocent man over to be slaughtered like a sacrificial animal. Even if she weren't in love with Garrett, she couldn't do it. Archer'd looked the other way while Leblanc had ordered her parents killed. Clearly, he was here to kill Garrett.

"There is no secret room," she answered defiantly.

"If you think I'm doing all this based on air pudding, you'd better think again. And understand this: I don't have any choice in the matter. Even if I wanted to let this go right now, I couldn't. There's a chain of command, you understand? So I'm asking you one last time. Where is that secret room?"

This was the end. Stella knew it. By the look on their faces, Rose and Maman knew it too. Archer's tone, manner, and words made everything clear. He was a puppet being controlled by a higher master, and *he* was pulling the strings.

Stella looked at Rose and Maman. After all, this was their home too and they had a say in this. But both women gave no sign of backing down. Indeed, their eyes told her they were with her in this come hell or high water. Even as fear struck the power from her limbs, Stella felt a fierce pride in both of them. Their strength reinforced her own.

She took a deep breath. "If you refuse to believe me, I have nothing more to say, Chief Archer."

Archer cursed.

"Harley! Ira!" he shouted, for both men were in earshot at the moment, searching rooms at the head of the stairs. "C'mere!"

When they had retreated downstairs, Jervis nodded at Rose and Maman.

"Harley, take them two outside in the yard and keep an eye on them. Don't hurt them, just watch 'em close. Ira?"

"Yo!"

"Since Stella won't help us locate Shaw, we'll make sure he doesn't survive the night. Run out to the cruiser and get the gas can out of the trunk. We're going to torch this fucking place."

CHAPTER

29

Stella's soul was too small to contain the grief and rage inside her. Fury gripped her. She lunged at Archer like a madwoman, mimicking his own insane rampage.

His strength was formidable. In seconds he had her arms in a painful lock behind her back. She struggled and cried out, but to no avail. The determination in those ice-chip eyes told her he meant to see this through to the end.

Garrett, she thought with a welter of renewed panic. Only now, in her dazed confusion, did she realize that if Archer actually did this, Garrett would be killed in the blaze.

Harley Burke had already herded Aunt Rose and Maman onto the crushed-limestone path that led into the big rear garden. Ira Pitts came huffing around the corner of the house, lugging a five-gallon gasoline can, its contents sloshing.

"We'll start it back here," Archer told him. "That way it'll get a good start before anyone can report it. Splash gas all over them wisteria trellises, that's it."

"Jervis!" Stella could feel herself breaking. "No, please! You can't do this!"

"I can't, huh?" he taunted her. "You just watch me, sugar britches. I'll burn this whole bitch of a plantation into a pile of ashes, I swear it. And your stud along with it."

Ira finished soaking the wisteria trellis and the wall behind it. The pungent odor of gasoline stained the humid night air. He backed off and screwed the cap back on the can. Archer pulled a book of matches from his pocket and struck one to life. It described a glowing arc when he flipped it toward the gas-soaked section of wall.

The wisteria trellis flared up with an airy *whumpf* sound like a gas oven igniting.

He's doing it, she told herself, numb to the pain of her shoulders as he twisted her arms to her back. He's going to burn Shadow Oaks to the ground.

For just a moment she saw Maman and Rose in the ghostly moonlight. There was enough of a fire now to bathe their shocked, frozen faces in an orange glow. Both women stared at the flames as if viewing the furnace of hell itself. Even now, however, as Archer passed the point of bluffing, they bravely held their silence. Stella was the mistress of Shadow Oaks, the last St. Vallier. They had pooled their fate with hers, and she had endangered them and failed them.

Greedy tongues of flame literally devoured the fragile, dry wood of the wisteria trellis, licking their way up the side of the house in a noisy blaze like cellophane crackling. And in that awful, critical moment of decision, she realized the full meaning of the old saying, Choices are the hinges of destiny.

But "choice" was now a mockery. Whatever she did now, either Garrett would die or she would lose her home. If he was astute, he was long gone through the tunnel anyway.

The barest possibility of a plan occurred to her in that desperate moment. A far from perfect plan, yes. One fraught with risks to herself. But it might at least spare Garrett's life and stop this terrible act of destruction.

"Please!" she begged above the crackling of the flames. "Put it out, Jervis! I'll show you the secret room."

"Now you're whistling," Archer said triumphantly. "Ira! Harley! Stella's finally wised up. C'mon, grab hold of the trellis with me."

Within seconds the three men had snapped the latticework trellis loose from the face of the house and dropped it, still burning, into the lush Bermuda grass of the yard. The wall of the house behind it was barely scorched.

"Harley, have your gun ready," Archer ordered. "You come inside with me. Ira, stay here and keep an eye on the old gals. Jim Bob!" he added, raising his voice so the deputy farther back in the garden could hear him. "Stay right there and keep a weather eye out. Our boy might make a break for it."

Jervis gripped Stella's arm above the elbow and squeezed it with intimidating strength. "Lead on, girl," he told her in his flat, toneless voice. "And I'm warning you: You've had your last chance. Any parlor tricks now, and I'll order Ira to shoot Rose."

Stella closed her eyes, choking down the panic. Her guardian angel had better be with her now.

"There *is* a secret room," she admitted as she led Archer and Burke through the double doors of the ballroom. "But there's nobody inside it. In fact, none of us has even been in there for years."

Archer snorted in scorn. "That's bullshit, Stella. If it's empty, why'd you let me torch the house 'steada just showing it to me?"

"I—that is, I was convinced you were bluffing, is all," she said, knowing how lame that sounded.

"You're a piss-poor liar," Archer assured her as they crossed the shiny floor toward the rear of the ballroom.

"Yes, well, I haven't had your vast years of practice."

"Quit batting your gums, Miss Goody Two-shoes," Archer growled, "and show us this room."

"It's behind one of these mahogany panels," she explained. "But I forget exactly which one. The mechanism is old and it sticks," she added, giving one of the panels a few good thumps with the side of her balled fist.

"Knock that shit off!" Archer said roughly, slapping her face. "You're signaling to Shaw!"

Precisely what she hoped she was doing.

"That's ridiculous," she insisted. "I'm just trying to activate the turntable. But there's so many panels, I've forgotten which is which."

She managed to rap a couple more times on another panel before Jervis, cursing a blue streak, threw her roughly aside.

"Stella, goddammit! I'm warning you for the last time. I'll shoot you to doll rags right here if you do that again! Harley, push on these damn things, see if—"

Jervis abruptly fell silent, for he had just discovered the right panel. It turned easily and silently.

"It sticks, hanh?" he muttered, keeping his voice down. "You lying bitch. Harley, get ready, bud. This time we don't bother hauling Shaw anywhere before we off him. We'll air him out on first sight."

Roughly, Jervis pulled Stella in front of him, using her as a shield in case Shaw had a weapon.

"No more of your cute little games, Stella, or I swear it, I'll kill you right here and now."

Archer edged into the room, Burke right behind them. The chief was quiet and cautious as he glanced at the empty bed, then toward the armoire. He nudged Burke, signaling that he should check under the bed.

Jervis, meantime, maintained his grip on Stella's arm while he sneaked up to the armoire and flung the doors open. But there was no one there. Just an empty armoire.

"Nothing," Burke announced as he straightened up.

Stella, trying to put a brave face on it, nonetheless felt her legs trembling as Jervis spotted the serving tray and beakers on the nightstand beside the bed. Dragging her across the room, he stuck his finger into the wine remaining in one of the glasses.

"You lying *bitch!*" he exploded, backhanding her face so hard that the force of it made her skull ring. "Nobody's been in here for months, huh?"

Jervis threw her with all his considerable power halfway across the room. She collided hard with the wall, then collapsed, a crushing, numbing pain in her chest.

Archer was over her in a minute, the muzzle of his Police .38 crammed hard into her windpipe.

"You lissen up, and you lissen up good. I'll play *no more* fucking games with you. No more, you understand me? Tell me one more lie, and I'll blow your stinking cunt head off right here and now. My hand to God, I will. *Where—is—Shaw?*"

It was a struggle to force a breath past the brutal presence of the gun. She wondered if she'd broken a rib. "I saw you coming, and I warned him. He ... sneaked out through the back of the house."

Jervis, his face bloated with rage, demanded, "What's his plan now? How's he gettin' around, where's he going to from here?"

"I don't know. If he has that worked out, he didn't tell me."

Archer brutally increased his pressure on the weapon. Her head was pinned to the wall behind her. All she could do was endure it until he finally backed off.

"I said no games, Stella. Don't push your luck."

Again she opted for the truth. "I swear to you, he told me nothing. I assumed he didn't want me to know, I—I didn't ask."

"We screwed up," Harley told his boss. "We shoulda posted Jim Bob out there the second we drove up, shoulda—"

"Shut up," Jervis snapped. "Don't matter now what we should've done."

Despite the considerable anger Archer clearly still wanted to vent on Stella, his urgency to capture Shaw appeared even greater. He stood back up, holstering his weapon.

Stella took her chance. Grabbing for the raffia bag that was next to her, she shoved her hand inside and felt for the automatic. But her hand found nothing. Garrett must have taken the weapon with him in the tunnel.

Her hope was lost.

Archer's booted foot crashed down on her hand. She cried out with pain.

"What the fuck's in there?" He stooped down and slid the bag away, his boot still on her hand. Turning the bag upside down, he threw it across the room and chuckled. "What, you have a nail file in there, girlie? You gonna kill me with some toe polish?" He forced her to her feet.

"No point standing around here with our thumbs up our ass," he told Harley. "Get outside quick and tell Jim Bob and Ira what's happening. First priority is to get the keys out of the cruiser and make sure there's no other vehicles he can take. Without wheels, he can't get that far. Not way the hell out here. We'll sweep this area. The cowboy took this trick, but we'll cold-deck him yet. *Move*, dammit!"

Burke hustled out of the room to carry out his orders. Jervis, however, stood right where he was, watching Stella as if she were a bug under a lens.

This is it, she realized despite the terror of facing it. He's going to rape me or kill me, or both.

"You know what this is, Stella?" He took a bottle of pills out of his pants pocket. Depositing several in his hand, he put the bottle back and held out the dark green ovals. "It's called *rohypnol.*" He smiled. "It's illegal."

The terror and strain was visible in her drawn face, and it seemed to soothe him. His tone was much softer now. "You know I've aluss loved you, Stella. I don't want to kill you. I just want you to forget about this stuff. Rose and Miss Leora are too old to go causin' me trouble, but you, you might really be taking this personally."

She glanced down at the green ovals. There had to be five of them there. Probably enough to kill her. Or fry her brain but good.

"If you're going to kill me, just shoot me. Why make me take poison?" she hissed.

He reached up and touched her face.

She tore away from his hand as if it burned her.

"All you had to do," he told her, "was cooperate with me. You brought all this on yourself, Stella. Bullheaded pride. You'll be lucky if you don't die 'fore the night is through, and for what? For a man who don't care 'bout you and never could."

Tears abruptly spilled over her eyelids—the reality of all she had just gone through, and the pain throbbing in her chest, were just too much to bear on top of his ignorant lecturing. A sob hitched in her throat, and she buried her face in her hands, just wanting Archer gone like a bad dream.

"I don't want to kill you. I want you to forget. Forget everything. This is a heavy-duty sedative. It'll make you do it." He went to the nightstand and crushed the pills with his knuckles. Sweeping the powder into the remaining beaker of wine, he swirled it in the glass, then put the .38 to her head.

"Drink it, darlin'."

She gave him a deadly stare. Slowly, she brought the liquid to her lips. He adjusted his crotch, and it was clear her helplessness excited him. He was going to rape her when she had enough of the drug in her system and could no longer fight back. He might hold her somewhere for days and just play with her. Then, if he decided she was too much trouble, he might just kill her anyway and dare Rose and Maman to complain.

She took a sip of the wine. It tasted bitter, like old burned coffee. Holding it in her mouth, she tried not to swallow it. Instead, she placed it against her gums and took another, this time bigger, draft of the wine.

"That's it, Stella. This'll wipe everything out. I gave you enough to dull you forever, for sure. You'll never be the feisty bitch you once were," he cooed.

She lifted her head and sprayed him with the mouthful of wine. His hand flew to his burning eyes, and she shoved the gun from her face.

"Fuck you! Fuck you!" he screamed, clawing at his eyes.

She didn't wait to retort. Pain spiking from her injured ribs, she slipped out of the secret room and ran. It was time to get help.

CHAPTER
<u>30</u>

Garrett soon settled his apprehension on one point, at least—the old St. Vallier "Indian tunnel" hadn't caved in anywhere along its route. Despite its age, it had been well constructed. Like the stopes of a gold mine, it had been timbered periodically to stave off collapsing dirt. The timbers were partially rotted by now but still served their purpose.

Nonetheless, his escape was grueling in his present condition. The tunnel had not been made to accommodate his six-foot-two-inch frame. The angle at which he was forced to crouch put excruciating pressure on his still-knitting back wound.

The distance seemed interminable. All the flashlight beam revealed was the unending walls of the tunnel, still pocked with the marks of picks and shovels. Finally, however, he glimpsed more wooden rungs and realized he'd reached the terminus.

Slowly and cautiously, he ascended the ladder and

shoved the trap upward. Its rusted hinges groaned loudly in the musty stillness. With his flashlight turned off now, he waited a few minutes for his eyes to adjust to the near total darkness above. Gradually, the dim outlines of two small windows appeared, moonlight seeping through the narrow cracks of their closed batten shutters.

Stella had told him the tunnel ended in an old slave quarter. Wincing at the flaring spikes of pain in his back, he emerged in the middle room of a three-room shotgun shanty. The unplaned planks of the floor felt dangerously spongy under his weight as he moved cautiously toward the small building's only door.

He cracked the door a few inches and eased out into the moonlit night. His night vision was good now after the darkness of the tunnel and the shanty.

Immediately to his left he could see the rear of the big garden and the looming mass of the plantation house beyond it. Straight ahead, perhaps one hundred yards or so, lay the same fenced-in cemetery he had passed last Wednesday, the night he was shot. To his right, the vast cane fields started, now more audible than visible as vagrant breezes rustled the blades with a sound like dead leaves skittering across pavement.

Suddenly, a man shouted in the distance, and he flinched. Another man answered the first. Neither voice sounded dangerously close to his position. But he realized Harley and his men must be starting a sweep of the grounds.

Holing up where he was was tantamount to suicide. They would surely check the outbuildings. The cane fields were vast, and he could surely hole up in them for a time with some security. But every instinct told him to run, to put as much distance as he could between himself and these butchers.

However, that was impossible. He couldn't leave Stella. But he wasn't in the best shape to commando back into the house. His exertions in the tunnel proved it; he was weaker than he had realized. His muscles were trembling as if he'd just completed a twenty-mile forced march.

He shut the door behind him and edged along the front of the shanty to the nearest corner. Glancing around it, he spotted the dark mass of the big sugarhouse rising out of the cane like a ship on a wide sargasso-filled sea.

The sugarhouse.

He thought back to last Wednesday, when he had taken shelter there. That big John Deere tractor that had been parked just inside the doors. Chances were good the key was in it. It could get him through the fields, take him where police cars would quickly bog down.

Then he could circle back.

True, starting the engine would announce his whereabouts. But with all the adjoining fields, the tractor paths must stretch on for miles. He would have them all on a wild-goose chase before they knew what hit them.

He moved quickly out into the sugar cane. It took him ten minutes to reach the wide doorway of the sugarhouse. He glanced inside and saw the tractor parked where it had been last time. He crossed to it and, wincing at the twinges of pain, hoisted himself up into the well-padded seat of the partially enclosed cab.

He had to feel around in the darkness until his fingers brushed the ignition key. He released the tense breath he'd been holding. But even as he stabbed the clutch in and bumped the gearshift into what felt like neutral, he worried about getting the damn machine started and in motion quickly enough. He hadn't driven a tractor since his summer job harvesting alfalfa in West Texas as a teen.

The John Deere's engine fired up almost the moment he keyed the starter. But then it sputtered and stalled out. Cursing, he felt for what he hoped was the hand choke. He tugged it out halfway and started the engine again.

This time it kept running. Even as he double-clutched and crammed the gearshift into what he hoped was reverse, he heard the first shouts from outside. And at least one of the voices sounded dangerously close.

He released the clutch, but the tractor shot forward, not backward. Rather than waste time trying to find reverse, he gave up on the idea of backing to the doors. Instead, he fought the tractor around in a fast, hard right turn, and barely missed colliding with the huge iron rollers of the press. Wood splintered under one of the giant rear tires when he rolled over the same pallets he had crawled behind just days before.

The big John Deere roared through the pulley-mounted doors into the narrow lane that led to the sugarhouse. Now he faced another problem: He had jammed the transmission into "creeper" gear, the lowest speed used for heavy pulling. No matter how much throttle he gave the engine, he couldn't get beyond walking speed.

Guns opened up behind him, one especially close. The men ran for their cruisers, as he'd hoped for. Cursing again, he double-clutched and crammed the gearshift—with a fierce grinding noise—into another gear. The John Deere picked up a little more speed, but he was still in one of the lower field gears. He knew there had to be a set of road gears somewhere in the pattern, capable of at least thirty mph.

"C'mon, sweetheart," he coaxed the tractor, "let's make tracks."

He finally found a road gear with his next shift. Behind him, the glassed-in cab shattered as a bullet caught it.

"Stop his ass, Jim Bob!" he heard Harley shout from the distance as their car engines accelerated. "Stop that son of a bitch!"

Harley was still out of effective handgun range, but

Larsen was dangerously close now, judging from the number of slugs that whanged into the big metal fenders and punched into the cab. At least one bullet struck one of the big tires too—Garrett could hear the slow leaking of air.

Larsen must have speed loaders on him, Garrett decided, because bullets were fairly raining in on him now. One struck the seat right behind him with the force of a hammer blow, but the well-cushioned seat stopped it. Another slug whipped past his ear so close, he heard its blowfly drone.

By then he was on the verge of leaping off the tractor and taking his chances in the cane. That's when he got a better look at the bulky equipment bolted to the right fender.

So far, intent on getting the tractor started and in motion, he had paid little attention to the odd twin-tanked apparatus, which resembled a set of scuba tanks. But now, in the moonlight, he noticed the bright yellow letters and numerals stenciled on them: M2A1. He also saw the big gunlike device connected to the tanks by a rubber hose. Now he realized it was a military surplus flamethrower. They could be legally sold because they were not classified as firearms or explosives.

He had never specialized in the weapon. But a flamethrower specialist had been assigned to his Zappo platoon in Lebanon. Because of the weapon's potential usefulness, he made the trooper show him how to use it in case of an emergency.

He sure as hell hoped he still remembered enough about it to activate it.

Even as more glass shattered over his head, he jammed on the tractor's brakes. Then he grabbed the flamethrower's pressure-tank valve and twisted it.

A satisfying hiss told him he had released the compressed air that propelled the thickened fuel mixture of gasoline and napalm. He unhooked the gun unit and leapt down beside the tractor, more bullets screaming in all around him.

Now he saw the squad car of Jim Bob Larsen, perhaps thirty yards away and drawing closer. Garrett squeezed the fat trigger, and thickened fuel came jetting out the gun's nozzle, failing to ignite.

Garrett forgot at first that the trigger had to be depressed rapidly two or three times to ignite the incendiary charge of the ignition cylinder in the gun's muzzle. As a result, Larsen and his car were soaked in the gasoline-napalm mixture before Garrett remembered how to ignite the fuel.

A whipping stream of fire arced through the darkness, and abruptly more flames shot at least thirty feet vertically into the air when Jim Bob realized what was about to happen. He squealed the brakes, leapt out of the car, and ran for cover in the cane. A hideous boom lit the night as Larsen's squad car ignited.

"Jesus Christ!" Garrett heard one of the frightened lawmen cry out. The horrible sight shocked them into inaction as Shaw jumped back into the tractor's seat and got the John Deere rolling again.

After a brief delay Harley and his minions opened fire again. But the flamethrower had an effective range of at least forty yards. As he figured out where the high-speed gears were, Garrett continually sent a sweeping wall of flames behind him to keep the crooked cops respectful.

Then he finally found a road gear, and the big John Deere lunged forward, quickly putting the Cane Town lawmen out of bullet range. Despite the elation he felt at his immediate getaway, however, he knew the critical part still lay ahead of him.

He sent back a long stream of flames, then, jumping and rolling to the ground, he ran for cover in the cane and headed back to Shadow Oaks, and the woman he realized he cared for more than his own life.

CHAPTER

<u>31</u>

Monday nights were usually slow at The Scarlet Door, and this one was no exception. Toutant sent the strip dancers home and turned the outside light off at eleven P.M. By midnight Dabs Boudreaux and the rest of the help had finished their cleanups and clocked out.

Toutant emptied the cash register into a canvas money pouch and locked it inside the safe in his office. As usual, he turned out most of the lights and then proceeded to leave by the employees' door at the rear of the building. The moment he opened the door, however, a shadowy figure waiting in the alley collared him by the front of his shirt. Before he could react, Toutant was slammed hard into the wall behind him.

A second figure moved inside and shut the door. A hand slapped at the light switch, and Toutant realized the man holding him pinned was Myron Leblanc's bodyguard. Leblanc himself stood nearby, studying Toutant from his muddy eyes.

"Senator! The hell's this all about?" Toutant demanded.

"Pat him down, Jimmy," Leblanc ordered, and the young bodyguard quickly frisked their prisoner.

"I never carry, Senator," Toutant protested. "You know I ain't into the macho tough-guy crap."

"Evidently, Percival, there's plenty I *don't* know about you."

"He's clean," Jimmy confirmed.

"Senator, what's this all about?" Toutant demanded again.

Leblanc indicated the door beside them with a tilt of his massive crew-cut head. "Got the key to the conference room with you?"

Toutant ignored, or pretended to ignore, the sarcastic tone of this request.

"Sure. Always got it on me."

"Yes, I've noticed that. So we'll talk in there. Your favorite room."

Toutant, hands trembling only slightly, unlocked the door and turned on the overhead fluorescent light.

"Have a seat," Leblanc invited him, though his voice removed any element of choice. Toutant started to say something, then shrugged a shoulder. He scraped back one of the chairs at the long, burn-scarred table and planted himself in it stiff-spined. Leblanc and his bodyguard remained standing. Now Toutant saw that Jimmy held a white takeout sack in his left hand.

"Senator, would you please—"

"Shut up," Leblanc ordered, his powerful, field-commander's voice adding extra authority to his orders. "I'll direct the conversation, and you'll answer what you're told to, understand?"

Toutant nodded. A slick sheen of sweat covered his skullish features.

"I heard some amusing things earlier tonight,

Percival. I had a little chat with Cliff D'Antoni. Seems he's been doing a bit of background checking on his own initiative. He turned up some fascinating information about an incident that took place in Memphis in 'eighty-eight."

Leblanc paused, studying Percival as if he were a substance undergoing transformation in a test tube.

"Cliff tells me," the senator resumed, "that you cleverly plea-bargained your way out of a serious racketeering charge. Even sent a D.A. to prison, matter of fact. It's all malicious rumor, right?"

By then, despite his efforts to stay calm, Toutant was trembling as if with ague. His body had guessed what his cowardly mind could not yet face.

"Why . . . something like all that happened, Senator, sure. I had a sweet little piece of some racetrack action. Trouble was, my bagman turned out to be an undercover cop. A . . . good lawyer got me off."

"No, we both know it wasn't the lawyer, Percival. A first-year law student could have done it for you. Because it was the *tapes* that mattered, wasn't it? You had that crooked D.A. on tape, many times. Had him by the short and curlies, eh? A little insurance policy when it all came crashing down?"

Sweat beaded at Toutant's receding hairline, then rolled, zigzagging, across his forehead. His jaw fell open, but he said nothing.

"Are we being taped right now, Percival?"

"Senator, don't be ridiculous. That was more than ten years ago, I—"

"Where's the microphone hidden, Percival?"

"Senator, there is no microphone! I—"

"Maybe you've even embedded one of those fiber optics in the wall or ceiling so you can view the room?"

"I swear there's no—"

"Shut up," Leblanc snarled. He turned to his bodyguard.

"Tie him good," Leblanc ordered. "The squeamish

little insect pisses me off enough to kill him right now. But the evidence isn't in yet. Gag him good too, Jimmy. He gives you any trouble whatsoever, kill the insectile fuck."

The young black with the shaved head pulled a new rope and a roll of duct tape from the sack. When Toutant started to object again, Jimmy smacked him so hard, he almost fell off the chair. A minute later Toutant was securely bound, his mouth sealed shut with tape.

"There's not too many places to hide a mic in here," Leblanc told Jimmy. "If it's still here, won't take long to find it."

While Toutant watched, face pouring sweat, the bodyguard dropped onto his knees and searched the underside of the tabletop. Next he examined the bottom of each chair. Then he stood on a chair to search the overhead egg-crate light fixtures.

"Unscrew the wall plate on the light switch too," Leblanc suggested.

Jimmy used the point of a penknife to remove the tiny screws in the plastic plate.

"Bingo," he announced a few moments later. He stepped back and pointed to a tiny "condensed mic" about the size of an electrical fuse. It was connected to a green wire that disappeared into the wall.

Leblanc stared at the device to better determine where the wire led. Then he tore the mic loose and dropped it into his pocket. He turned to look at Toutant.

"All's grist that comes to your mill, eh, Percival?"

Leblanc turned to Jimmy again. "Screw the plate back on. Ten to one we'll find the recorder up in his office. With any luck the tapes will be there too. This guy is strictly small town. Get his keys and let's go."

Both men moved up front to the little cubbyhole office behind the bar. The tape recorder sat on the battered kneehole desk, now innocently holding a Patsy

Cline tape. But this building had a P.A. system, and the convenient microphone jack on the wall over the desk, though logical, also further damned Toutant.

It took only five minutes to locate the three tape cassettes. They were concealed under masking tape on the underside of the desk's single drawer. Leblanc, using fast forward to save time, listened to all three and confirmed that they covered every major meeting in the conference room. Even as warm relief flooded over him, Leblanc briefly considered the possibility that backup copies existed. It had never occurred to him they would be anywhere but upstairs, not with a congenital loser like Toutant involved.

"Take any cash in the safe for yourself," Leblanc told his hireling, handing him the keys. "Leave the door open so robbery is at least suggested. Won't sidetrack the feds, but it helps with the media situation and our defense later, if it comes to that."

Leblanc and Jimmy returned to the conference room. Toutant's face turned a sickly ashen gray when Leblanc held up the trio of cassettes. For a moment Leblanc debated whether he should rip off the gag and ask where the copies were. But then the senator remembered that he needed to search the apartment anyway, for evidence besides tapes. This would be his last chance before the place was put under federal seal.

"Sin, Percival, is the general state of things. No man can avoid it, and I don't expect them to. However, transgression is very personal and involves a conscious choice to sin. Each transgression must be judged on its merits. And your particular transgression is unforgivable."

He nodded at Jimmy, who pulled out a vintage Walther P-38 Luger from the body holster under his left arm. The man then took a long, modified Maxim silencer from the pocket of his corduroy jacket and screwed it into the muzzle of the pistol.

Toutant, meantime, went from frozen stillness to a

berserk flailing and whimpering. He tried desperately to say something through the thick duct tape.

"I'm sorry, Percival," Leblanc said almost soothingly. "I like you personally. But no one asked you to put your oar in my boat. The fault is all yours."

Leblanc crossed to the hallway door and started to let himself out.

"Hurry up," he told Jimmy. "Get the upstairs key so we can search his apartment. I'll wait in the hallway for you."

It was the drug that was making her crazy. It was the drug that made her forget and turned her time and again back to the house.

Scrambling through the cane fields she knew like the back of her hand, Stella still couldn't find her way out to the road and town. The dark blades cut at her, the pain in her chest was fire inside her, but worse was the forgetting. The confusion. The uncertainty.

She hadn't had much of the drug, but the concoction had been lethal. Just the powder that had soaked into her gums was making it difficult for her to walk, let alone battle the cane stalks that were higher than she was.

"Girlie!"

She startled and turned around in her saw-bladed prison. There, this time she was sure she heard it. He was calling her. But she couldn't be sure she could trust her judgment, or the voice.

A light passed within twenty yards of her right. She hunkered down and closed her eyes, hoping the darkness would enhance her other senses and help her think.

"Come on, girlie. Just come on out. I want to talk to you."

A whoosh, then a crack came after the words. For the life of her, the sounds were familiar, but she couldn't place them. And for some reason she wanted to go home, but she didn't know why. Something at the house beckoned her, but she didn't know anyone there. Suddenly, she wasn't even sure of her own name.

"Aw, it's all right. Come on out. Game's over," came the voice.

She wobbled to her feet and went to call out. But then a strange spike of fear shot through her. Her tongue grew thick, and she hunkered down again.

Why was she afraid?

She opened and shut her eyes several times. The ground was swaying. The light was moving away.

She lit in the other direction, slipping her slender form quietly through the rows of cane. The road to town had to be somewhere. If she found it, she was going on it. To The Scarlet Door. That's where she needed to go. To The Scarlet Door. He would be there, and he would help her.

If only she could remember his name.

"Girl, I'm gonna hack your pretty ass to pieces if you don't show yourself," the voice called out, now not ten yards away.

She had a flash in her mind of a badge, a police cruiser, and ice-blue eyes.

The *whoosh* and *crack* sounds came more violently now. So close, the cane swayed against her shoulder.

Cane knives.

But it couldn't be. The cane knives she remembered were strapped to the wall of the sugarhouse. They didn't use them anymore. *They didn't use them anymore.*

Despite her logic, she slid farther down the row.

"C'mon, girl. Unless you're passed out on your ass, you'd better come here now or there'll be hell to pay."

She closed her eyes. The fleeting ghost images of a gun held to her head played in the tangled beam of a flashlight. The voice was finally getting near. Too near.

She duckwalked down the row, falling twice with her vertigo.

Suddenly, the flashlight went out.

All was dark.

"I'm telling you, girl," came the voice, soft and low to her right.

She bit the scream from her mouth until she tasted blood. On her hands and knees, she went down the next row, then the next. Behind her, the cracking and whooshing got louder and louder. Finally, when she could feel the air pass from the swing taken at her head, she stumbled out of the cane onto an old macadam road. Old Bayou Road.

"Girlie, girl," came the voice behind her, still cracking and whooshing.

She ran, and she didn't look back. Tripping and weaving along the old road, she knew she had to get to The Scarlet Door. The neon blazed in her delirious mind, chasing her. She had to get there. If the end was near, she had to meet it there. Fate called her, as it had called her parents there; as it had called Rose there. She could feel it. Her epiphany was near. She would go to The Scarlet Door, crawling if she must. Because the red entrance was the womb where she wanted to return. It was the hell that took Rose's flame and her parents' lives. And it was now her turn.

CHAPTER
<u>32</u>

Garrett was able to put plenty of distance between himself and his pursuers. He had to move slowly, though, to conserve his strength, but the house lights in the distance encouraged him.

Then he saw the flashlight beam, and heard Archer's voice, cursing in the sea of cane to the right. Archer was after someone, and it could only be Stella.

Stealth was an ally. Garrett had learned that from Beirut.

Quietly, he crept up to the whacking cyclone of light where Archer stood. He waited seconds, then stepped into the row where the chief stood at the end, his back to him, a long cane knife in one hand, a flashlight in the other.

"Lost something?" Garrett asked coolly.

Archer turned his head.

Garrett raised the automatic he'd taken from the raffia bag.

"Stella's gone. Help me find her, fool, before somethin' happens to her. She's not feeling well," Archer mewled.

Shaw just grinned. "You always go looking for a girl with a knife in one hand? Dickless, no wonder you got women problems."

"Fuck you, dead man."

"Drop the weapon, Archer. Drop it, then turn around, and I might not shoot your red neck."

Archer dropped the cane knife. It lay like a long, straight snake against the flattened cane blades.

"Where is she—" Garrett didn't have the words out before Archer beamed the flashlight in his eyes, then switched it off.

The chief grabbed the knife while Garrett was temporarily blinded.

Marine instinct took over. Garrett dove into the thick row of cane to his left just as the knife cleared his nape. He sprinted into the needle-edged cane blades with Archer fast and furious at his back.

It couldn't last. Archer was in damn good physical shape for a redneck cop, and Garrett could already feel the warm blood seeping through his shirt. His old wound had opened in all the activity. He might not bleed to death, but he wouldn't have to with psychocop at his rear.

"Shaw, I'm gonna put you away for good this time, you prick," came Archer's angry voice.

Garrett gripped the automatic. Then he whipped around and made a kamikaze run at Archer.

The chief didn't have time to lift the cane knife. Garrett rammed him from the side. For a few brief moments the two men struggled for the gun, but when Archer's steely hand pulled on the automatic, Garrett knew he didn't have the strength for a prolonged fight. So he pulled the trigger and shot Archer at point-blank range.

* * *

After what seemed hours of excruciatingly slow progress, he reached the paved highway. Garrett drove the Peugeot to Cane Town, but he was forced to rest several times in the pitch darkness.

When he'd gotten to the big house, Stella wasn't there. She was gone. If she went to look for him, he reasoned, to get them help, he could think of only one place she'd go.

Reaching the town limits, Garrett parked on the side of the Great Bayou Road. Limping, he still ran. A woman lay at the entrance of The Scarlet Door, her pale gold-red hair almost surreal in the neon glow.

"Girl, you've got to be all right. You've got to be," he whispered, taking her gently into his arms.

For a brief moment she struggled with him, his words seeming to frighten her. He tried to calm her as he bled all over her olive-green silk slip dress. But then she stared up at him with those beautiful, haunting sea-green eyes. She didn't seem able to even right herself, let alone walk, but she never looked away, not once, even though tears spilled from her eyes and mingled with his blood. And all she could say, over and over again, was "You came."

THE STAR

She was a Phantom of delight
When first she gleamed upon my sight;
A lovely Apparition, sent
To be a moment's ornament;
Her eyes as stars of Twilight fair;
Like Twilight's, too, her dusky hair;
But all things else about her drawn
From May-time and the cheerful Dawn;
A dancing Shape, and Image gay,
To haunt, to startle, and way-lay.
—WILLIAM WORDSWORTH

CHAPTER

33

Three days after the night of terror at Shadow Oaks, a trio of women gathered in a semicircle around Stella's bed: Aunt Rose, Maman, and Mattie Everett.

Mattie, her face glowing with gathering excitement, read aloud from a letter that had just arrived for Stella that morning. Stella had already read it, but Rose and Maman were just now learning the contents, as was Mattie.

"'I am pleased to inform you,'" Mattie read, "'that our initial analysis of the bagasse sample supplied by Professor Perkins confirms your general observations about its nutrient content. Furthermore, we are quite impressed by its potential handling and storage capabilities as well as its relative lack of chemical additives.

"'Our research and development department is very interested in setting up a pilot program to produce an experimental batch of cattle feed that substitutes bagasse for the corn by-products we currently use. If a national field test produces positive results, we will apply for a patent. However, we will first negotiate with you to determine a fair price for the patent rights, based on our projected earnings.

"'In the meantime, and if your are interested, we would very much like to purchase a significant quantity of bagasse from your operation as soon as the upcoming sugar cane harvest makes it available. This would be used in our trial program. If this initial trial eventually produces a commercially viable cattle feed, we would then hope to contract with your operation (and others in your local cooperative, as demand requires) for long-term supplying of bagasse.

"'Again, sincere thanks for your excellent and insightful proposal. We here at Meridian hope it marks the beginning of a long, lucrative, and mutually beneficial business relationship. I look forward to hearing from you at your earliest convenience. Yours truly, Sebastian J. Martin, President, Meridian Feed Company.'"

Mattie's voice fell silent. For a moment, stunned by the wonderful news, none of them uttered a word.

"Well, merciful God," Maman exclaimed, finally breaking the silence.

Aunt Rose was seated in a straight-back chair near the bed. Like Stella, she had been forced to take to her bed following the ordeal. But she was fully recovered now and beaming with pride for Stella.

"Our girl grasped the nettle all right," she announced triumphantly. "But I'm not really surprised at this. She's a St. Vallier, isn't she?" Rose glanced toward the gallery of portraits and photos on the bedroom wall. "Character *will* out after all," she added.

"That's it right there," Maman agreed, fluffing up Stella's pillow for her. "Then again, they say every family tree's got a few nuts."

Stella accepted this reproof with a rueful grin. She had suffered three badly broken ribs when Archer threw her against the wall. The emergency room had wrapped her up and just that day she was sent home from the hospital. Maman and Rose had been hovering over her ever since, treating her like a wounded war hero.

Mattie bent over the bed and gave Stella the best hug she could at the awkward angle. "I'm not surprised either. I knew Stella's idea was a winner the moment she first told me about it. Look at you, girl! Turning into an industrial kingpin right before our eyes."

"This 'kingpin' had a lot of help from Professor Perkins," Stella deprecated.

"Sure," said Mattie, "but weren't you smart enough to know exactly whose brains to pick? That's how winners get ahead—they know just which gravel makes the best launchpad."

Despite the ebullient mood in her room, Stella felt a curious detachment and a poignant sadness that baffled her. Nor did it help to remind herself this mood wasn't justified, given recent events.

The news today from Meridian was certainly welcome. Even more welcome was the message from Steve Falcone, left yesterday afternoon on the answering machine, telling her that Garrett was in Bethesda Naval Hospital doing well after his surgery. She herself had little memory of their last moments together. She got them in flashes—of an ambulance, the state trooper cars screeching to a stop around them, and finally a kiss that was achingly sweet and much too quick.

Falcone had told her that in a few short weeks they expected Garrett would be well enough to testify against Senator Leblanc. Until he was put away, all three women at Shadow Oaks breathed easier with Louisiana state troopers keeping a close eye on the place around the clock.

Despite all these good tidings, Stella still felt as if she had lost something precious that she'd never find again. Already the memory of the hours she'd spent with Garrett in the secret room seemed like a long-ago dream—or perhaps the beginning of a beautiful painting that would never be finished.

She could not, *would* not, blame Garrett. The danger they shared and his dependence on her had made both of them vulnerable. At least now she knew he'd never deceived her.

"I read about that Chief Archer," Mattie said, making conversation in the face of Stella's silence. "He was a bad one. I knew it the minute he walked into my office."

"Humpf," said Maman, showing no pity. "He deserved whatever he got. He held a candle for the devil, didn't he? All 'em deputies, buncha criminal bullies."

"Who would believe," Rose added, trying to perk up Stella, "that three quiet, peaceful women could get involved in such derring-do?"

Stella flashed a wan smile that didn't fool her aunt.

"Let's go downstairs, Leora," Rose told Maman. "Our shows have already begun. We'll leave the younger generation to hatch their own schemes."

Mattie moved quickly to help Rose up from her chair. Rose came closer to the bed and leaned over Stella.

"True love is never smooth sailing, dear heart," she said quietly. "We must pass through the bitter water before we reach the sweet. Keep the faith, Stella, just as the lovers of the past have done, and you'll be rewarded."

Stella tried to school herself in that belief as she watched Maman take the older woman's arm and help her out of the room.

"Speaking of hatching schemes," Mattie said, digging into her big leather tote, "I looked up this translation and made a copy for you. You know, just in case you catch the bug to go treasure hunting again."

Stella glanced at the title of the photocopied article: "Pirates, Ransom, and Rare Jewels in New Spain" by Miguel Iberrez.

"It mentions Jules St. Vallier and the Louisiana connection," Mattie added.

"Thank you, Mattie," Stella replied listlessly. She placed the article on a nightstand without looking at it.

"Well," Mattie commented with ironic good humor, "that little suggestion went over like a lead balloon, didn't it?"

Stella tried to stay focused on their conversation. But there were still too many loose ends concerning Garrett's fate. Yes, thank God he was physically safe. But she had read about the murder of Toutant, and, as in the death of Archer, Leblanc was on his soapbox tirading that Garrett was the murderer.

Again Steve Falcone's disappointingly prosaic message, taken by the answering machine, played in Stella's memory: *You won't be hearing from Garrett for some time. That's standard procedure in cases like this. Garrett sends his apologies for taking the John Deere without permission, and he trusts the vehicle has been returned. You will be compensated by the U.S. government for the costs of any damage.*

To hell with the tractor, Stella had told herself. Who would compensate for the "damages" that couldn't be itemized—or repaired?

"Hey, girl," Mattie complained. "Is it just me, or is this conversation really a monologue?"

Stella mustered a contrite smile. "Sorry, Professor. Just building castles, I guess. I'm worried about Garrett. I just found out I won't be seeing him until all the mess gets cleaned up. With so many politicians involved, and so many murders, I'm afraid it'll be quite a while."

"Garrett? Un-hunh. Well, listen," Mattie advised, her tone kinder now. "Just remember that your tall, handsome stranger has ridden off into the sunset. I wouldn't be dwelling on him too much if I were you. I've got experience with his type. He'll be on to the next shag as soon as he can."

Mattie waved the letter from Meridian, which she

still held. "You've got more productive things to focus on right now."

Stella took no offense because Mattie was right. And she *had* tried to put Garrett out of her thoughts. But she might as well have tried holding the ocean back with a broom. Even the thought of returning to Jules's secret room to clean up the mess Archer had made was more than she could bear—she had spent all of her time with Garrett there.

The bitter water, Aunt Rose called all this. And the sweet was still nowhere in sight.

Mike Hogan's eyes puckered with satisfaction as he turned off the tape recorder. It contained one of the three tape cassettes Toutant's lawyer in New Orleans had Fed-Exed to the U.S. marshals immediately after his client's death, as per Toutant's own instructions.

"High-fives all around, gentlemen. Doug Woodyard listened only to a few minutes of this before he agreed to cut a deal with us. We've got him in the witness protection program to make sure he doesn't meet Toutant's fate."

Hogan, Garrett Shaw, and Steve Falcone shared Garrett's small but adequate quarters in an unmarked federal safe house on Constitution Avenue. By then no one believed Garrett was guilty of the serious charges against him. But until conspiracy could be proved against the Cane Town Police Department, Garrett was still officially in federal custody. And as a federal agent under investigation, he was automatically denied bond. He had his own room, decent meals, even cable TV, but he could not leave the guarded compound. He was also denied phone calls and mail privileges while he was being investigated, so he couldn't contact anyone on his own.

"This was some smooth operation Leblanc headed up," Hogan, the head of the Special Warrants Division, conceded. "Every now and then Woodyard certified a phantom cargo that existed only on paper. The invoices were billed to United Southern Children's Charities, every dollar tax exempt. The money was actually transferred to several numbered Swiss accounts."

"Well, good-bye to all that," Falcone announced. "I'm celebrating by getting drunk as Davy's saw tonight."

"Look," Garrett warned, "let's not spend it till it's ours. Leblanc is one infinitely resourceful bastard."

"If we want your opinion, *paisano*," Falcone scoffed, "we'll beat it out of you. Between these tapes and Woodyard's confession, Leblanc and the rest of the Ring are dog meat."

"Steve's right," Hogan agreed. "Audiotapes alone are powerful circumstantial evidence. But Doug Woodyard is the rock they'll split on. And he's being deposed"— Hogan tugged one sleeve back to consult his watch— "even as we speak."

Despite his genuine elation, Garrett couldn't fully join in the celebratory mood. Again and again he conjured an image of wide green eyes and flawless mother-of-pearl skin. He didn't know when he would get back to Stella, and it was driving him crazy.

"Planet Earth calling the *paisano*," Steve cut into his reverie. "You with us here? This is gonna be the biggest goddamn bust of your storied career. So why you looking like somebody just kicked your dog?"

Garrett leaned forward in his chair, resting his elbows on his knees. He said nothing to this. Falcone winked at Hogan.

"Would your blue funk," Steve added, "have anything to do with a Southern belle named Stella? Because, man, I fell in love with her over the phone. If her body's half as sexy as her accent, I can sympathize with you."

Hogan met Falcone's eyes and raised his brows speculatively. Garrett Shaw had long held a reputation as a workaholic and a lone wolf. Seeing him preoccupied by something besides work was a genuine novelty.

"You won't be rotting in here forever," Hogan reminded Shaw.

"Great."

"You're due some time off. Maybe, when they spring you out of here, you'll just have to take a little vacation."

"Maybe I will at that," Garrett agreed.

Stella had put it off long enough, waiting, at first, for her broken ribs to heal. Then the harvest geared up and took all her time and energy. Then it was Christmas and then came a lonely New Year's Eve. She'd endured and prevailed through all of it. But now it was a whole new year, and the ghosts of the past had to be cast out. Nonetheless, her heart and limbs felt heavy when she turned the mahogany panel to the secret room.

She stood at the entrance, surveying the room. It was a time capsule. Everything was exactly in place: The bed still lay twisted with the sheets that had been warm when she last left them, and the night table still held the beaker of wine ripe with crushed rohypnol.

The truth of the room spoke to her. Garrett Shaw had come into her life, and then he had left. And the emptiness within her made her wonder if it wouldn't have been better never to have had him. His absence left an ache in her that hadn't been there before, far more acute than the mere ache of loneliness. Unlike Great-aunt Rose, she did not yet possess the luxury of long years to buffer the immediate physical hurt of painful yearning, of unfulfilled love.

The objects in the room suddenly bent and blurred when tears filled her eyes. Embarrassed and angry at her own self-pitying behavior, she resolutely went to the bed and began stripping it of the sheets. Then she noticed it: the shattered glass plate of the frame encasing the silhouettes of Jules and Genevieve.

It lay faceup on the floor beside the bed. In her scuffle with Archer, it must have crashed from the table.

She bent down and examined it. The silhouettes themselves appeared to be undamaged. She had forgotten she'd left them in there, and she'd done it for luck—another sad irony, she thought as she knelt to pick up the broken frame.

As she picked the bigger fragments of broken glass from the frame, she noticed the backing had come loose—that, in fact, it had popped up slightly from the bulk of a cache of letters pressed in behind it.

Carefully, she pulled them out to inspect them. There were no envelopes or internal addresses that she noticed during her initial perusal. But the old French hand—at once ornate in its flourishes and loops yet neat and disciplined in its uniformity and spacing—made her heart quicken. So far as she knew, French ceased to be in common use around Shadow Oaks before the Civil War.

She removed and very carefully unfolded several sheets of vellum. The same writing covered other pages of less expensive stationery too, as if the writer had used whatever came to hand when the impulse to communicate had struck.

Her eyes widened when she read the date written at the head of one letter: May 1781. The mystery deepened when she realized the writer had omitted any names in the greeting or signature—an unusual discretion hinting that one or both in this dyad were of high position.

She could read French much better than she could speak it. In the first letter the writer fondly recounted his former infatuation for a certain "difficult but charming lady," expressing his limitless pleasure at receiving her tokens of affection. He also assured her, however, with diplomatic assertion, that "even though you say you have found the love of your life, I beg you, do not abandon me. I need you so. I live for little but the thought of you and your return to me."

The letter, like the others, was unsigned. The mood

and tone fluctuated wildly between letters, perhaps reflecting both the social status and the tempestuous nature of the author himself.

Heat filled her face as the probable truth sank in. She couldn't prove it right then and there, of course. But these must be some of those rumored letters Mattie had mentioned—billets-doux exchanged between Genevieve and her lover, Louis XVI. Mattie's remarks about the letters were still fresh in memory: how it would be a simple task for document experts to authenticate letters. A museum or university would pay handsomely to acquire such missives.

She warned herself to calm down. Again and again she reread the letters, missing the more poetic conceits when her translation skills failed her. But one simple, expressive line leapt out at her, perhaps because it spoke her need also:

> *I have heard that, sometimes, a broken bone heals stronger. May God also let that be true for the heart.*

She found not even the slightest mention or clue, however, about Jules's hidden treasure, but she couldn't help thinking it again: The key to the treasure *is* the treasure. Now she, too, sensed the truth of what Aunt Rose had insisted.

Like God in the universe, Rose had also insisted, the St. Vallier treasure is everywhere felt but nowhere seen. Real, yet ethereal; the substance behind hopes; the waking dream.

Stella grasped the letters in her hand, eager to show them to Rose. But even as she headed back toward the main part of the house, the ache for Garrett returned, subduing her momentary elation at this discovery.

Yes, she now had more St. Vallier history to draw upon for comfort and strength. But it was the past, and she had to live in the present. History seemed a cold comfort indeed when she longed most to be held, to be loved.

"Aunt Rose! Maman! You won't believe what I found," she said as she burst into the parlor. She expected Maman's reproof at the racket, but the parlor was as quiet as a church on Saturday.

But not totally silent. The sound of weeping came from the corner where the women watched television. Stella turned to the sound, lead in her heart.

"She said she wanted to sit down for a while. I'm so sorry, child." Maman wept as she lay her head in Rose's lap.

Stella stepped toward her great-aunt. Rose was still in the chair, prim and proper even in death. But her face was filled with peace. Her youth had returned at last.

Tears streamed down Stella's cheeks as she, too, knelt by Rose.

The only other St. Vallier had waltzed herself to sleep.

Now Stella was the last one. The last one.

CHAPTER
<u>34</u>

The spider, dropping down from a twig,
Unwinds a thread of her devising;
A thin, premeditated rig
To use in rising.

And all the journey down through space,
In cool descent, and loyal-hearted,
She builds a ladder to the place
From which she started.

Thus I, gone forth, as spiders do,
In spider's web a truth discerning,
Attach one silken strand to you
For my returning.
—E. B. WHITE

Rose's funeral took place the coldest day in January. Everyone from the parish was there except Stella's neighbor, Senator Myron Leblanc. He was being held without bail.

The other absence was taken note of, and then Stella

made a determined effort not to think of him again. It would do no good in any case. It only hurt more.

"I'll take the tray in, Maman. You rest. You look worn out." Stella cleared the long dining table that had been set with trays of food. Everyone had gone now. Shadow Oaks was empty save for the two women.

Maman wiped her nose with a damp handkerchief. Her companion was gone; Stella knew the hollow that must have left in her.

"You know what I'd like to do," Stella announced brightly when the table had been cleared. "I'd like to find the best picture of Rose and put it in the master bedroom. The gallery holds all the portraits of the St. Vallier women but her."

Maman sniffled. "That's a mighty fine idea, child. Rose would like that for sure."

Stella went to the walnut secretary and pulled out boxes of old family photos. "What's the best picture of her, Maman? You would know that better than anyone."

"Why, that'd be her engagement photograph."

Stella paused, then shook her head. "I don't know if we should use a sad photo."

"Sad? There was no sadness that day. Rose was as happy as I'd ever seen her. She was full of love and brightness. See?" Maman dug through one box and pulled out the old photograph.

Stella looked down at the image. The hairs prickled on the back of her neck as if a ghost hand had caressed her there.

"This is Rose?" she gasped.

"'Course it is. And wasn't she a beauty?"

Her breath quickening, Stella sputtered, "But how could this be? This is the girl in the white dress. The one I saw weeping in the garden. I thought maybe we had some ghost named Myrtle and—"

"Child, this is Myrtle," Maman explained patiently. "Your great-aunt Rose's full name was Myrtle Rose de St. Vallier. After the tragedy of her engagement, she refused to use the name Myrtle again because that's what he called her, so she became Rose." Maman put an arm over Stella's shaking shoulders. "It was only lately she started having conversations with Myrtle. I knew it'd upset her to have to explain who Myrtle was. I always guessed you knew about it."

Stella shook her head as if trying to shake sense into it. "How can this be explained? I didn't see a ghost. So what did I see?"

"Maybe you saw her spirit, child. You saw the youth inside her. Myrtle was her name when her flame was brightest—just before it went out."

Tears began running anew down Stella's cheeks. Suddenly needing to be alone, she grabbed her jacket and decided to walk down to the cemetery and visit with Rose one last time.

It was gray and blustery outside. The perfect day for a burial. Stella stopped by Rose's tomb, and for a long time she stood motionless, saying nothing, just content to be there.

When she finally moved, it was to raise one hand and tug the star sapphire pendant out from under her blouse. She gazed at the words inscribed on its back: *Let this be your lucky star.*

A large, heavy teardrop fell onto the stone. She understood what Rose had been trying to tell her. Rose hadn't wanted the St. Valliers to die out. So she had somehow led Stella to love. But unfortunately, it hadn't worked.

Pain twisted inside her. She was still trying to let him go. To heal the hurt within her, the ache deep inside that only got worse with time. With the discovery of Myrtle Rose, Stella felt she was on the threshold of some essential truth. But truth, like love itself, eluded her. She wondered if with his absence her flame had gone out. She was just one more fool who forgot: When it came to "romance," cynical Mattie was right. It was just a made-up notion, an invention of poets and singers to perpetuate their jobs. Or, worse, an illusion invented by the devil to drive humans mad.

The hurting place within her could never heal until she stopped thinking about Garrett Shaw. She had to get on with her life. She'd saved Shadow Oaks, and no matter how deep the hurt, there had to be someone out there she had saved it for.

Heart aching, hand trembling, she pulled the necklace over her head. She dropped the star sapphire pendant onto Rose's tomb.

"He's gone too," she told her aunt softly, fighting her tears. "But thank you. Thank you," she whispered.

She stood motionless until she was sure the tears were in check. Then she turned to leave.

And saw him.

He stood at the entrance, an additional presence among the moss-covered cherubs and crumbling tombs. He waited on the other side of the carved iron gate, his eyes never leaving her.

There was no mistaking the wide shoulders or the long, muscular arms entwined through the fence. It was Garrett Shaw. He was thinner, even older-looking than when she last saw him. Stress had taken a toll on him, but it made him more mortal and therefore more handsome, if that was possible.

For a moment her legs simply refused to move, as if they no longer belonged to her. So many emotions competed within her at once that none won out, and all she felt at first was a hot rush of adrenaline. Her self-control finally worked. She managed to walk toward him.

The corner of his mouth lifted in a hesitant grin. "There's a rumor going around that you're looking for some extra help around this place."

For a long while the day seemed to be stopped on freeze-frame. She even suspected her heart forgot to beat. The chilly numbness she'd felt earlier seemed to be melting.

"You don't owe me anything, Marshal," she confessed, wanting that to be clear from the start.

"You saved my life. And then you made me fall in love with you. Of course I owe you," he answered gravely.

Without realizing it, she ran to him. His arms wrapped around her, and he picked her up a few inches off the ground. She locked her fingers in his hair and turned his head so she could taste his lips again. She clung to his strength. Over his shoulder she could see the cemetery behind him.

"You came," she whispered for the second time, giving silent thanks to Rose.

He kissed her deeply, passionately, soulfully. "I'll never leave again," he said before taking her hand and walking her back to Shadow Oaks.